WICKED BLOOD

A VAMPIRES of OXFORD NOVEL

Margot de Klerk

COPYRIGHT

Copyright © 2022 Margot de Klerk

This is a work of fiction. Names, characters, business, events, and incidents are the products of the author's imagination. Any resemblance to actual persons, living or dead, or actual events is purely coincidental.

All rights reserved.

No part of this publication may be reproduced, stored in a retrieval system, or transmitted in any form or by any means (electronic, mechanical, photocopying, recording or otherwise) without the prior permission in writing of the author, nor be otherwise circulated in any form of binding or cover other than that in which it is published and without a similar condition including this condition being imposed on the subsequent purchaser.

The right of Margot de Klerk to be identified as the author of this work has been asserted by her in accordance with the Copyright, Designs and Patents Act 1988.

First paperback edition 2022

ISBN
978-1-9196213-3-3 (paperback)
978-1-9196213-2-6 (ebook)

Book Cover Design by www.ebooklaunch.com

BOOKS BY MARGOT DE KLERK

VAMPIRES OF OXFORD SERIES

Wicked Magic
Wicked Blood

PRAISE FOR THE VAMPIRES OF OXFORD SERIES

WICKED MAGIC

Filled with action, drama, romance, and political intrigue, Margot de Klerk's intricately woven young adult adventure tale is bound to entertain lovers of the supernatural genre.

Pikasho Deka, *Readers' Favorite*

The plot moves quickly, and the creative details bring this entertaining world to life, making this witty and weird novel full of potential for a new series.

Self-Publishing Review

WICKED BLOOD

A hugely original work of YA fantasy. Chock full of exceptional world-building, unique characters, and jaw-dropping secret identity twists, *Wicked Blood* is more inventive than many works of paranormal fantasy, all set against the bewitching background of contemporary Germany.

Self-Publishing Review

In this tale of abandoned buildings and misplaced trust, Cynthia finds Berlin's history entangled with ancient magical theories and creatures. *Wicked Blood* is easy to sink your teeth into and such a sweet thrill to read. [...] *Wicked Blood* is a book I'd read again with pleasure.

Independent Book Review

GUIDE TO BERLIN

Brandenburg: Brandenburg is the state surrounding Berlin. It is well-known for its large forests and lakes, as well as the old Prussian palaces in the west of the state. The capital of Brandenburg is Potsdam. It takes circa 30 mins by regional train or 45 mins by S-Bahn to get from central Berlin to Potsdam.

Grünewald: A forested area in the west of Berlin. The Grünewald is also home to a number of lakes.

Hackescher Markt: Hackescher Markt is a square in Berlin Mitte. It is a popular nightlife destination.

Hauptbahnhof: Berlin's main train station.

Kreuzberg: A district of Berlin known for its arts scene and alternative subcultures. One of the most culturally diverse areas of Berlin.

Mitte: The central district of Berlin, it is home to Hauptbahnhof, the Brandenburg Gate, and a number of other historic sites. It's also a popular location for bars, restaurants, and museums.

S-Bahn/U-Bahn: Berlin operates two intercity train systems. The S-Bahn is an overground train, with lines reaching all the way out into the further suburbs. The U-Bahn is the underground, which serves the inner city.

CHAPTER ONE

MONICA: I AM MELTING

Monica: No joke

Monica: Why am I the only one stuck in bloody England with no bloody air con in the middle of a bloody heatwave

Monica: But enough about me. How's Berlin?

Cynthia brushed her sweaty hair off her forehead, smiling as she scanned her friend's messages.

Cynthia: 38 degrees C

Cynthia: Not a supernatural in sight

Tucking her phone back in her pocket, Cynthia approached the counter of the ice cream shop she was sheltering in. An array of brightly-coloured flavours promised relief from the unrelenting heat. The waitress was flicking through Instagram on her phone, whilst above her, a TV was showing an interview with a tearful woman. Cynthia couldn't understand the German, but she'd seen this same story all over the city in the week since she'd been here. A busload of tourists had died mysteriously last year, and the families of the victims were pleading for justice. Lola, Cynthia's childhood friend and host, had explained the story a few days ago, a pinched expression on her face the whole while.

The waitress looked up expectantly. 'Kann ich Ihnen helfen?'

Stumbling over the words, Cynthia managed to ask, 'Vanille, bitte?'

'One scoop or two?' The waitress switched to English without missing a beat.

'One, please.'

German was not her forte, and that hadn't been the only obstacle in coming to Berlin for three weeks. Cynthia's mother had fought tooth and nail to get her to stay home. Arguments had been almost nightly at one stage. Spurious excuses had been invented, only to vanish the very next day. Plan after plan had been vetoed. Cynthia had been at the point of just boarding a plane and ghosting her mum for the summer, when a compromise had finally been reached: She would stay with a host family for the duration of the trip.

It was an unideal solution.

The problem wasn't money—although Cynthia was hardly swimming in it—or maturity—she considered herself more mature than most of her peers—or that she'd never travelled before—she'd lived in seven countries and counting. The problem was a question of species. Cynthia and her family were shapeshifters, people with the ability to shift into the form of any animal. And shapeshifters had been hunted for their magical blood for millennia.

Blowing her hair out of her face with a sigh, Cynthia passed over a handful of euros in exchange for her ice cream. 'Danke.'

'Bitte sehr.'

That pretty much exhausted the small amount of German she knew. It hadn't helped her case with her mother that she'd insisted on visiting a country they'd never been to before.

If Cynthia was being fair, it wasn't Cathy Rymes's fault that she was over-protective. She had a pretty good reason to be: She'd had a complex relationship with Cynthia's father. Her second relationship, with Cynthia's stepfather Daniel, had ended in tragedy. For most of Cynthia's life, they'd moved from place to place, living with shifter communities and moving on before they drew the attention of the local witches.

It had been a lonely existence, but they'd enjoyed relative security for the last two years in Oxford, the home of the Supernatural Council.

In Cathy's eyes, Cynthia was flouting that.

She licked her ice cream and checked her phone once more. But yet… she was eighteen and finally done with school. It was time to branch out on her own.

Her phone buzzed.

> **Monica:** Only you'd think that was a good thing
> **Cynthia:** What, being safe?
> **Monica:** Being bored
> **Cynthia:** Humans aren't boring
> **Monica:** So are, though. No blood. No death
> **Monica:** Been to any good clubs?

Cynthia: Nope

Monica: … why do I bother?

Her phone vibrated again, and Cynthia switched chats.

Lola: I'll be at my parents for dinner tonight. You free tomorrow?

Cynthia: No plans yet

Lola: Cool, my friends are doing a BBQ

Cynthia: Sounds fun!

In the end, her mum needn't have worried. There hadn't been any supernatural sightings—not witches, the natural enemy of shapeshifters, nor vampires looking for a late-night snack. Cynthia was probably safer here than she'd ever been back in Oxford, surrounded by all manner of supernatural miscreants. Mum needed to relax and stop seeing enemies on every street corner.

After finishing her ice cream, Cynthia braved the heat again. Berlin was sweltering; even worse than England had been. Europe was in the middle of a relentless heatwave.

Checking her phone once more, this time for a map, she began navigating towards the nearest S-Bahn station. It was almost five, and Brigitte Decker would be prompt about dinner—and even prompter about alerting Cynthia's mother if she was home late.

It was still light, but the late-afternoon sun was starting to cast shadows between the buildings. Cynthia dodged around women with buggies and businessmen making their way home.

It was kind of odd, though, wasn't it? That she hadn't seen a single supernatural?

Oxford had a population of a hundred-something thousand, a small city by anyone's standards, but you could hardly walk down the High Street without crossing paths with at least one witch or vampire. The city was swimming with them. Cynthia had lived in tonnes of places, from Athens to Malmo to New Orleans, and cities always attracted supernaturals. Berlin was young, trendy, and chock-full of tourists. It ought to have been a haven for thirsty vampires.

Yet, Cynthia hadn't seen a single witch or vampire. No werewolves. Not a warlock in sight. The only other supernaturals she'd seen were her host family, who were also shapeshifters.

Where were all the monsters?

It wasn't even as if they only came out at night. That was pure myth, but Cynthia had been out after dark plenty. She should have at least run across a vampire or two.

Thankfully, it wasn't her problem. She was here for two more weeks. She'd explore the city, enjoy the lack of parental authority, and hopefully start figuring out who she was and what she wanted to do with her life. She'd leave Berlin's supernatural problems to Berlin. She wasn't curious. She—

A man stepped in front of her suddenly, and Cynthia crashed into his side.

'Sorry!' She jumped back. 'Ah, um, entschuldige. Sorry, I—you're—Justin?'

The man froze, his mouth open to speak. He was tall and blond, with tanned skin and a distinctive scar on his face. For several heartbeats, they stared at each other. He'd emerged from the S-Bahn stairs. He was wearing a white polo shirt and jeans, clean and neat. Cynthia scrambled for words.

'Justin Gastrell?'

Abruptly, he turned on his heel and broke into a sprint.

'WAIT!'

Cynthia dashed after him. She was a good runner, but he was better. He cut through the crowds with ease, as Cynthia stumbled and bumped into people. Within moments, she lost sight of him. Still, she jogged until the crowds cleared a little. She peered into side streets and examined a little park. Finally, she leant against a wall, panting furiously.

He was gone.

But she was sure, absolutely sure, that she had recognised him.

That had been Justin Gastrell.

Her father.

CHAPTER TWO

'ARE YOU SURE?'

'Absolutely and utterly.' Cynthia adjusted the phone against her ear, pouring over a selection of peaches. Lola wanted fruit for a salad. 'It was definitely him.'

'I thought you didn't know what he looked like.' Monica's frown was audible in her voice. 'You only saw him that one time.'

'Nathan found me a photo of him, uh…' Cynthia hesitated, 'before we broke up, I mean.'

Nathan was Cynthia's ex, as well as a vampire hunter. It was a prickly subject.

Monica brushed right over it. 'Seeing a photo isn't the same as seeing him in real life.'

'Monica, I'm sure.' Cynthia chose a few peaches and took them for weighing. 'It was him. He recognised me, too.'

'Okay, okay. I'm just making sure. I'd hate for you to set yourself up for disappointment.'

Cynthia scowled. 'Thanks.'

'I mean, I know that's why you wanted to go to Germany…'

This was a secret that Cynthia had kept close to her heart for the last year and a half. She'd seen her father once before, in a very brief encounter in Oxford, where he'd saved her life. A few months after that, the postcards had started arriving. He'd written to her more than half a dozen times, each time from a different city. Sometimes, he'd tucked a few euro notes, or a small souvenir into the envelope, and each time, he'd ended by requesting that she didn't reply or try to look for him.

Monica had been the one to pry the secret out of Cynthia. She'd also been the one who encouraged Cynthia to do the opposite.

'Why would he write you if he didn't want you to look for him?'

she'd asked.

The most recent postcard was from Berlin, so Berlin was where Cynthia was starting.

'It's so weird. A week and not one witch, then suddenly he's right there.'

'Where's there?' Monica asked. 'For research purposes.'

'Hackescher Markt—hold on.' Cynthia lowered the phone, smiling carefully at the lady behind the counter. Mum had always insisted on being polite when they travelled.

Don't pick fights with the locals unless you can shout at them in their own language.

Weird advice, but Cynthia was quite happy to follow it. She didn't really like confrontation.

'Guten Abend.'

'Abend,' the woman replied, ringing up the purchases.

Through the phone, Monica said, 'I'll check with Nathan and see if he knows of anything in that area. And I'll speak to Jeremiah again for you.'

'Don't bother Jeremiah. I'm sure he's much too busy.' Jeremiah was the head of the Vampire Council. Monica treated him like her personal gopher, a relationship that had always made Cynthia a little uncomfortable.

'Chill, he won't mind.'

Cynthia was pretty sure he would mind, but she bit her tongue. Arguing with Monica was pointless. Monica was incredibly intelligent, ruthlessly bitchy, and had almost no filter. Great when you needed support, but terrible as an enemy.

'Thanks,' she said instead.

'You're welcome. Listen, I have to go. I'll text you as soon as I hear something, alright?'

'Sure. Bye… and thanks.'

'Bye.'

Cynthia hung up and pulled out a twenty euro note to pay.

The supermarket was a way away from the Deckers' apartment, but Cynthia was borrowing Lola's bike, so she made quick work of the cycle through the Grünewald. The western outskirts of Berlin were green and littered with lakes, perfect shifter territory. Finally, she locked the bike outside a three-story faux-Tudor house on a cobblestoned street, where the Deckers occupied the top floor apartment.

'I'm back,' Cynthia called out as she let herself in. 'Brigitte?'

The skittering of claws over the ground alerted her to the impending arrival of the family dog, Gracie. A moment later, the large German shepherd slid around the corner and leapt up to lick Cynthia's face. Laughing, Cynthia pushed the dog down.

'Gracie, nein!'

It was always strange to lay eyes on a new animal. Cynthia's shifter nature allowed her to pick up the form of the most recent animal she'd seen. Just that day, she'd seen a smattering of pigeons, four different dogs, a stray cat, and a squirrel. Now, her last form was edged out by Gracie. Cynthia had a sudden, intense desire to run through the forest, sniff things, and chase squirrels. For a few seconds, she could imagine exactly how it would feel to be a dog, and she was seized by the urge to transform.

Brigitte interrupted the moment.

'Cynthia! How was your day out?'

Cynthia nudged Gracie back down to the ground, breathing in the reassuring smell of polish and slightly stuffy air. Human. Right.

'Great, thanks.' She waved her shopping bag at Brigitte. 'Can I put this in the fridge? It's for Lola.'

'Of course.'

Brigitte followed Cynthia into the kitchen. As Cynthia put the groceries away, she asked, 'Did you go anywhere interesting?'

'I saw the Otto Weidt Museum—that was my last stop. This morning, I just walked around Mitte. And I had döner at that place Lola suggested for lunch.'

'Brilliant, lovely.' Brigitte leaned past her and pulled out a bottle of sparkling water, pouring them both a glass. As she passed one to Cynthia, she awkwardly asked, 'Did you… see any…'

'Not a single vampire, nor witch,' Cynthia assured her. 'I've been careful. Like I promised.'

'Good, good. I know you're careful.' Brigitte smiled. She was in her fifties, with bottle-blond hair and crow's feet around her eyes. As usual, she was immaculately made up.

Cynthia didn't mind staying with the Deckers, per se. Brigitte was nice enough, although Wilhelm was a little intimidating. It definitely saved her money, not having to pay for a hostel. But all shifters were a bit over-protective—Monica called it Mama Shifter Syndrome—and it was a little grating. The point of this trip had been to stand on her own two feet, which was kind of difficult when someone was peering over her shoulder all the time.

Cynthia forced a smile. 'I might take a quick shower before dinner.'

'Go ahead. Wilhelm will be back from work shortly. Oh, and Lola will be here, too.'

'Yeah, she said.'

'Great.' Brigitte shooed her out. Cynthia crossed the open plan living and dining room and took the little corner staircase up to the attic. There was only one room upstairs, Lola's childhood room. The walls were covered in old sketches and paintings, and a standing fan kept the heat at bay. Cynthia pulled out clean clothes and checked her phone once more. She'd found that sending an update to her mum every so often kept the oppressive parental worrying at bay.

Lola arrived just as Cynthia was coming out of the bathroom. Her entrance was heralded by excited barking from Gracie. When Cynthia entered the hall, Lola was laughing.

'Gracie, stop!'

Cynthia had first known Lola as a pigtail-wearing nine-year-old with an aversion to boys. That had been eleven years ago. Now, Lola was a buff twenty-year-old who served with the Berlin police force. She wore her blonde hair in a pixie cut, and was diminutive in height but incredibly strong. When she saw Cynthia, she smiled.

'Hey, you're looking tanned.'

'Finally!' Cynthia returned the grin. 'How was your week?'

'Eventful! I'm so glad it's weekend.' Lola turned to her mother. 'How long until dinner?'

'We're just waiting for your father.'

Dinner was ham sandwiches, eaten on the balcony. Lola told them what she could of her work, which ranged from tracking down stolen bicycles to helping out lost tourists. After that, she asked Cynthia about her plans for the next week.

'I have a few days off coming up, so if you want, I could get a group of friends together and we could go out.'

Mindful of Monica's chiding about being boring, Cynthia said, 'Sure, sounds fun.'

'We'll show you Kreuzberg by night.'

'Lola,' Wilhelm said sternly.

'Relax, Papa, nothing's going to happen.'

'That's no reason to invite trouble.'

Lola rolled her eyes and mouthed, 'Later,' at Cynthia.

After dinner, they clambered up to Lola's old bedroom and cracked the skylights open. This was the most pleasant time of the day, by a long way. The heat had turned down a notch, and there was a light breeze. Lola stood beneath the window and lit a cigarette.

'I hope Dad's not getting you down too much.'

'He's been fine,' Cynthia said, rummaging through her suitcase for clothes to wear the next day.

'You don't have to lie. I know he's strict. If he had his way, I'd never go to Kreuzberg or Friedrichshain, or Prenzlauer Berg. All the fun places. All the places where witches hang out.' Lola rolled her eyes and took a drag of her cigarette.

'He doesn't say much to me,' Cynthia admitted. 'But I don't really want to run into witches or vampires.'

'Eh, you'll be fine. Mostly, Berlin's supes are a cool lot. Anyway, not a lot of them around at the moment.'

Cynthia sat on the edge of the bed. Seizing the opportunity, she asked, 'Is it usually like this?'

'Couple of months, now.' Lola shrugged. 'I'm not complaining. No draining victims, no weird stuff to explain away. Berlin's safer than ever.'

'How come?'

'Hmm…' Lola blew a smoke ring, which dissipated into the night air. 'No one really knows. Vamps blame the witches, witches blame the vamps… The usual. Who cares? They leave us alone.'

She was right. Vampires and witches were always at odds. And yet… not. Vampires needed fresh blood to survive. They had to be getting it from somewhere.

'Do they steal blood from the hospitals?'

'Huh?'

'The vampires,' Cynthia elaborated.

'No idea.' They heard footsteps on the stairs. Lola hastily stubbed out her cigarette, putting a finger to her lips. Cynthia nodded.

'So, tomorrow,' Lola said, 'the barbeque will be at twelve. There's a bunch of my school friends coming.'

'Lola?' Brigitte asked, knocking lightly on the stair railing as she stuck her head through the floor. 'Papa is looking for you. He wants to ask you something.'

'Coming.' Lola shot Cynthia a significant look, though what it meant, Cynthia wasn't sure. The older girl followed her mother back downstairs. Cynthia grabbed her pyjamas, her mind still on the vampires. It wasn't that she wanted to see conspiracies everywhere, but her mother had taught her to be suspicious of everything. When everything was a potential threat, you got a bit edgy if someone suddenly told you there was no danger.

No vampire or witch activity?

Too weird.

Later, lying in bed and trying to find a cool spot, Cynthia still couldn't get it out of her head. Where were the vampires feeding? Witches didn't need a food source; they were mortal and ate human food. But vampires needed blood. Even so, the lack of witch activity was just as strange. About one percent of the global population were witches, and large amounts of magic left traces in urban areas, especially dark magic. And it was unthinkable that there were no dark mages around, doing wicked things. Cynthia could name at least one.

Strange.

But so not her problem.

Cynthia forced the thoughts from her head and closed her eyes. The heat gave her enough trouble sleeping; she didn't need to make it any worse.

Lola woke Cynthia at the crack of dawn the next morning.

'I'm going running, if you want to come.'

'Whuh?' Cynthia croaked, still half-asleep. 'Running?'

'Shifting, I mean.'

'Oh! Sure… give me five minutes to get changed.'

Ten minutes later, they locked their bikes against a tree and began trudging through the underbrush of the Grünewald. It was just starting to get light, the sun casting gentle rays between the thick foliage, and making the whole world glow green. The air was still cool, and there wasn't a soul around. It was perfect.

Cynthia loved the outdoors, the smells, the wind in her hair… This was paradise.

Eventually, Lola paused next to a massive tree and indicated a little hollow in the trunk, about a metre from the ground. 'We can leave our things here.'

'Will they be okay here?'

'Sure, I always do that.'

With impunity, Lola yanked off her T-shirt and bra. Cynthia looked away awkwardly, toeing off her flip-flops. Okay, getting naked in a forest. It wasn't the worst thing she'd ever done. Shifting always caused clothing-related issues. She'd gotten eyefuls of both her mother and sister, and had definitely flashed Monica a few times by accident. She could do this.

After a deep breath, she pulled her top and shorts off.

Once she was naked, Cynthia reached inside herself for the knowledge of the dog. She pictured walking on all fours, having a long tongue and a snout. The dog awoke inside her, excited to have a form. The change rushed over her, and she was being pushed, pulled, and squeezed, uncomfortably but not painfully. Finally, her human-self slipped into the background, and the dog took over.

Cynthia stretched, testing out her new paws. The world had become very simple, reduced to scents, sounds, and a sense of excitement.

Beside her, a second dog yipped. *Lola*, Cynthia's human brain supplied.

Dog-Lola barked again. It wasn't a language Cynthia could put into words, but she understood on a primal level: Dog-Lola wanted to run. Cynthia barked in reply, nosing her way through the brush. Dog-Lola trotted away, and Cynthia chased after her.

For the next hour, they ran. Cynthia's human worries slipped away as she enjoyed the feeling of the breeze in her fur and the smells of summer. She chased squirrels and batted at butterflies. She picked up sticks and sniffed at flowers. She rolled in the dirt and play-fought with Lola.

Finally, her spine began to itch with the effort of holding back her human form. She signalled Lola with several urgent barks, and they ran back to where they'd left their clothes. Moments later, Cynthia was being poked and prodded back into her human body. When her vision settled, she was crouched on all fours in the grass, her chest heaving.

Lola scrambled up beside her and passed her a T-shirt.

'Have fun?'

'That was great!' Cynthia used the outside of her T-shirt to brush dirt away. She was caked in it. *Yuck.*

'Mum and I used to do that every weekend.' Lola slipped her flip-flops on. Cynthia clambered unsteadily to her feet, her body relearning how to walk upright.

'You don't anymore?'

'Now I live in the city. Sometimes I become a bird and go flying. It's not the same though.' Lola smiled fondly. 'Mum doesn't really like it. She says shifting gets boring as you get older.'

'I don't think I'd ever get bored of this,' Cynthia said enviously. Back in Oxford, they were in the city. The most she got to do was curl up in the sun in her garden as a cat. This was completely different. 'A bird could be fun. I'd want it to be a big bird, though.'

The smaller the form, the harder it was to maintain.

'Owls are the best.' Lola dropped Cynthia's flip-flops in front of her. 'Come on, I'm dying for breakfast.'

'I'm dying for a shower!'

Lola laughed.

They passed a few early-morning dog walkers and cyclists on the way back, but the paths were mostly still empty, so no one saw two rather dirty young women meandering back, still exhilarated from their run. Wilhelm was up already when they entered the apartment, talking on the phone in terse German. He nodded sharply at them and retreated to his study. Lola made a face.

'You want to shower first?'

'Thank you,' Cynthia said in relief. She loved shifting whilst she was doing it, but it was always an adventure to return to human form. You never quite knew what you'd get—strange tastes, mud in weird spots… Animal brains and human brains just didn't have compatible priorities.

At lunchtime, they headed out again, this time loaded up with fruit salad and bags of crisps. Cynthia had donned a bikini under her shorts and T-shirt, which Lola assured her was appropriate. 'Don't expect to swim, though. The others are lazy.'

The pleasant morning had developed into sweltering, sticky heat. The twenty-minute walk down to the lakeside left Cynthia with rivulets of sweat on her face and back. She dried herself self-consciously with her T-shirt as they climbed onto a grassy bank where people were scattered about, sunbathing and picnicking.

'LOLA!'

Lola glanced around and broke into a grin. Up the hill were a group of young adults, standing around a portable barbeque. Everyone had their shirts off. A pretty girl who had to be over six feet tall was waving.

'Come on.' Lola dragged her up the hill, and they were immediately engulfed in a wave of chattering and excited hugs. Eventually, Lola pulled back to invite Cynthia into the circle.

'Guys—guys, English,' she interrupted. 'This is Cynthia. I've known her since I was nine. Cynthia, this is Fritz, Luisa, Klara…' She pointed to each person in turn. Fritz had very curly blond hair and a nice smile, Klara was the tall girl, and Luisa had dark skin and very even teeth.

'Hi!' Fritz greeted in a thick German accent. 'New to Berlin?'

'Yeah… I'm staying with Lola's parents.' Did that sound lame? That sounded lame. 'I just finished school, so I decided to travel.'

'Cool,' Luisa said brightly, linking arms with Cynthia. 'Has Lola taken you to Kreuzberg yet? Lola!'

Lola had drifted off a few feet and was talking to a tall man with several tattoos. She waved a beer at Cynthia.

'You want?'

'Sure.'

'Lola, we have to take Cynthia out to Kreuzberg!' Luisa called.

'Next weekend!' Lola re-joined them, passing Cynthia a bottle. 'Kreuzberg has great bars and clubs. You'll love it.'

'Okay.'

Lola's friends were a pretty easy-going group. There were about twenty-five people there in total; Lola didn't know all of them, and Cynthia only remembered the names of about half of the people she was introduced to, but no one seemed to mind. Lola got sucked into an intense debate with Fritz, and Cynthia ended up by the barbeque watching a handsome blond man cook the meat. His name was Jesse, and he was half-American and quite happy to chat to her in English.

After lunch, another group joined them. Cynthia and Jesse found a spot to sit out of the way.

'You thinking of travelling anywhere else?' Jesse asked, waving to a few girls who were unpacking more beer.

'I'm not sure yet.' Cynthia hugged her legs. 'I'd love to go to Amsterdam, maybe Brussels and Paris. A friend of mine is also travelling around the US at the moment. It'd be kind of cool to meet up with her.'

'Where is she?'

'Uh…' Cynthia had to think back to the extensive itinerary Lily had produced. 'Either San Francisco or Los Angeles. I've been to Los Angeles, though. I'd like to see New York or Chicago.'

'I could give you some tips.'

The sun highlighted the outline of Jesse's chiselled muscles. Was he flirting with her intentionally, Cynthia wondered, or did he speak to all girls like this?

'I'd like that.' She smiled.

At that moment, Lola squeezed out of the crowd.

'Hey, there you are.' For a second, she seemed worried, but it was gone too quickly for Cynthia to be sure. 'I think maybe we should head back. I'm just going to the toilet, okay?'

'Sure,' Cynthia said. 'I'll wait here, alright?'

'Okay.' Lola darted a glance at her friends. 'Be right back.' She hurried off.

'You known her a long time?' Jesse asked.

'Yeah, since I was seven.' Cynthia fiddled with a strand of grass. 'You?'

'We met at school.' Jesse shrugged. 'She's kind of… weird, no? Secretive.'

'You think?' All supernaturals came across as secretive, by the very nature of hiding what they were. Still, Lola struck Cynthia as pretty straightforward.

'I don't know. Sometimes it just seems that way.' Jesse shrugged again. 'How long are you still in Berlin for?'

'Two weeks.'

They chatted for a few more minutes, before Jesse was summoned away by a few of his friends. Cynthia watched him lope off, frowning. It was always worrying when people got suspicious of supernaturals. Bad things happened if you got found out, and shifters often copped the worst of it. She'd have to warn Lola.

'You keep dangerous friends, Dog-Girl.'

Cynthia jumped. Twisting around, she came face-to-face with a short girl with long brown hair. She was about Lola's age, and her eyes were narrowed in anger. Cynthia had never seen her before in her life.

'Can I help you?'

The girl tilted her chin up haughtily. 'Not if you're friends with Lola, you can't.'

'Um, okay.' Cynthia stood, brushing grass off her legs. 'Well, I didn't come over and insult you or your friends—'

'You think she's really your friend? I suppose one snake likes another—'

'Oi!' To Cynthia's relief, Lola had returned. She jogged over to them. 'Get the fuck out of here.'

The brown-haired girl's expression turned deadly. 'You.'

'You have no business harassing my friend.' Lola crossed her arms. 'Keep it up and I'll book you.'

'I'd like to see you try.' The girl shot an angry look at Cynthia, then snapped at Lola, 'Wonder if this one will go the same way as the last one.'

'Fuck off!'

The girl stomped off. Lola watched after her, arms still crossed, expression furious.

'Who was that?' Cynthia asked in confusion.

'No one important. I used to know her.'

'Jilted lover?'

'No, nothing like that. Her name's Renata. We were at school together.' Lola shook her head. 'Look, just forget about her. She's a sour, jealous bitch. Let's go.'

'Alright,' Cynthia said, grabbing her bag. Lola was already marching towards the footpath. Cynthia waved to Jesse and chased after her, putting the altercation out of her mind.

She had no right to pry into Lola's old friendships.

Even if Renata had a light blue aura.

She was a witch.

CHAPTER THREE

THE INCIDENT AT THE LAKE bothered Cynthia for the rest of the weekend despite her efforts to put it out of her mind. Lola seemed to have moved on from it, throwing herself into playing tour guide, but Cynthia kept thinking about it.

Lola knew a witch. The implications of that were huge.

Cynthia only knew one witch personally, and that was Monica. They'd met two years ago. Before that, she had only had negative experiences with witches. She'd certainly never sat in a classroom at school with one—her mother would have pulled her out of school post-haste if that had ever happened.

Generally, at least as far as Cynthia was aware, witches were home-schooled—although maybe that was only true for England. At least, Monica had always made it seem as though witches didn't attend normal school. So, yeah, it was weird that Lola knew a witch. It wasn't strange that they hated one another, but the altercation had been teeming with unresolved tension, like they knew each other better than they let on.

It really bothered Cynthia.

On Sunday, when they stopped for lunch out near the East Side Gallery, Cynthia chanced texting Monica. She always felt guilty doing that in front of Lola—it was the same at home with her Mum—as though Lola might be able to read from her face that she was texting a witch. The shifter-witch prejudices ran deep, and Cynthia didn't want to give Lola a reason not to trust her.

She was just curious.

> **Cynthia:** You once mentioned to me that most witches are home-schooled
>
> **Cynthia:** Would a witch ever go to normal school?

Monica was probably at work, because no reply was forthcoming.

Cynthia forced the matter out of her mind, focusing on sightseeing. There was really no reason to pry into Lola's business; Lola was her friend, and she'd been nice. She was cool. Cynthia wanted to rekindle their relationship, keep the opportunity to visit Berlin again open, and start building a network that wasn't dependent on her ex-boyfriend. Those were all good things.

Getting nosy would jeopardise that.

After dinner that evening, Lola bade Cynthia goodbye. She was working again on Monday and would be returning to her apartment for the week.

'I'll text you about drinks,' Lola promised. 'Probably Thursday, so keep that night open.'

'I will. Have fun at work.'

Lola made a face. 'Maybe we can get lunch together one day. When I'm in the office, and not out telling tourists to mind their wallets better.'

Cynthia laughed.

Once Lola was gone, Cynthia joined Brigitte and Wilhelm in the lounge. It felt rude not to, although it also felt rude to intrude. Brigitte had the TV on mute and was doing her nails.

'It's the problem with shifting, isn't it?' she asked as Cynthia sat down. 'Ruins your nails.'

'Uh…' Cynthia looked down at her own nails, trimmed short. 'Maybe? Lola told me you don't shift too often these days.'

'Not really.' Brigitte smiled. 'I suppose it's lost its appeal a bit. These things were more fun when I was young.'

'I can't imagine.'

'Well, you're young still.'

Cynthia smiled awkwardly. 'Yeah… I might turn in early.'

'Sure, go ahead.'

She said her goodnights and ascended the stairs. As she emerged into the sweltering attic, her phone vibrated.

> **Monica:** I was home-schooled until I came to Oxford. It depends on the witch. Some covens run classes, mine did, but I was always ahead of the other kids. It was a big coven though. Small ones wouldn't do that
>
> **Monica:** In Oxford I wasn't in a coven, so Jeremiah sent me to normal school

> **Monica:** Why?

Cynthia skimmed the messages twice over, thinking. Finally, she tapped out a reply.

> **Cynthia:** Just wondering. Met a witch yesterday. Lola said they went to school together
> **Monica:** Interesting. Friends?
> **Cynthia:** The opposite
> **Monica:** Double interesting
> **Monica:** Oh, hey, Nathan wants to Skype tomorrow AM. You up for it?
> **Cynthia:** Why?
> **Monica:** Just a sec

Chewing her lip, Cynthia tossed her phone on the bed and started getting ready to sleep. Maybe this was about her father. That would make sense, right? Monica had said she'd mention it to Nathan. It wasn't that her ex-boyfriend, who was older, more attractive, and scarily perfect, still wanted to speak to her. That would be awkward.

You're in a different country, she thought irritably. *Get over it, already.*

But getting over Nathan wasn't that simple. He'd been brilliant. A hunter, he'd been employed by the Vampire Council straight out of school. He made everything look effortless, from fighting to politics to relationships, and Cynthia had just felt… small. She'd never been able to step out of his shadow. She didn't want that shadow following her here.

Her phone buzzed again.

> **Nathan:** Hey, how's it going?
> **Nathan:** I know you don't want any supernatural drama, but
> **Nathan:** I need a tiny favour. Skype in the morning?
> **Cynthia:** Sure

She just couldn't help herself.

The next day dawned warmer than ever. It was the hottest day they'd had so far, and the attic was like a sauna. Cynthia had the windows open, the fan on max, and was wearing as little clothing as possible. She lay on her bed with her laptop propped up in front of her.

At exactly eleven, her Skype began to ring. She answered, hastily putting on her headphones. 'Hey,' she greeted when Nathan and Monica appeared on the screen. 'Um, how are you?'

'Cynthia, hey.' Nathan grinned. Brown-haired, freckly, and

handsome, Nathan was the sort of guy who made you want to smile. 'Sorry to disturb your holiday. How are you?'

'Alright. Hot.' Cynthia grimaced. 'How's Oxford?'

'More or less the same. Vampires are vampires, witches are witches. They never get along, and as long as they don't, I have a job.' Nathan gave her a thumbs up. 'Monica, you on?'

'I'm listening,' Monica said. 'You're not saying anything interesting.'

'Monica's been in a bad mood all month. She hates summer,' Nathan confided.

'You try being a redhead in summer, alright, some of us don't tan!'

Cynthia giggled. Monica stuck her tongue out. She was obviously suffering from the heat. She was wearing a tiny tank top and pair of shorts. Cynthia had never seen her looking so underdressed before.

'How's Berlin?' Nathan asked once Monica's complaining had ebbed.

'Fine, thanks.' Shuffling back so she was more in the path of her fan, Cynthia added, 'I'm having fun. It's nice to be on my own. Lola's been really sweet. And there haven't been any supernatural shenanigans.'

'Except your dad,' Monica said.

'Except that.'

'You're sure it was him?' Nathan asked.

'I'm sure. He recognised me, too.'

'Weird coincidence.'

'Yeah.' Cynthia paused. 'No, well, not really. I knew he might be in Berlin.'

'For real?' Nathan asked.

'He, um, he sends me postcards sometimes. The last one was from Berlin. I wasn't exactly looking for him—I know Mum would disapprove—'

'Relax, we're not going to tell on you.' Monica snorted.

'I was just curious!'

'Alright, alright.' Nathan chuckled. 'So you want me to look into that for you? I can pull the hunter file on him, see if they know anything new.'

'If it's not too much trouble.'

'No trouble. Consider it payment for the favour I'm going to ask.'

'Right.' Cynthia straightened up a little. 'What is it?'

Nathan's expression turned a little sheepish. 'I wouldn't ask this of you normally,' he started, 'but it's actually pretty easy. It shouldn't take more than an hour or two, and it's really not worth us sending someone over.'

'Go ahead.'

'We need someone to check in on the Hunter Council in Berlin. They haven't sent us a report in ages, which is just weird. They're usually full of complaints. I can text you all the authorisations and everything. Just go in, ask them if anything is going on, and let me know what they say.'

'Okay, yeah, I don't mind,' Cynthia said. 'Where's their office?'

'I'll check and get an address to you.' Nathan tapped a few keys on his laptop. 'Just so you know, they might try to mess you about. Just tell them you're there on behalf of the Council. Feel free to throw your weight around a bit.'

'Why?' Cynthia asked, unable to help worrying.

'German supernaturals fall under the remit of the KUA—the Kommission für übermenschliche Angelegenheiten—and they're headquartered in Bonn, not Berlin, because Bonn used to be the capital. So, I'm not sure how much authority the KUA in Berlin has, and whether they're going to use that to fob you off. That's what they did to me when I tried to call them.' Nathan shrugged. 'Hunters will be hunters. Share information? They'd rather drink hot oil.'

'Yuck!'

'Tasty.' Monica leered at her computer. 'I could think of at least three dozen spells that ask you to do that, and half of them are sex spells.'

'Okay, thanks, I think that's need-to-know only, M,' Nathan cut in.

'Your loss.'

'That depends on your perspective.'

Monica waggled her brows. Cynthia interrupted before they could get too far off track.

'I don't mind popping by, but I can't promise it'll be today. I can't really lie to Brigitte and Wilhelm about where I am, that's not fair, so it'll have to be when I'm in the area.'

'Too bloody ethical,' Monica said.

'That's fine. Leave her, Monica. As long as it's in the next day or two,' Nathan said. 'And thanks. It saves me from finding someone on the ground.'

'Good luck with that. I've been here over a week and all I've seen is my dad and one other witch.'

'Yeah, that is strange.' Nathan frowned.

'Maybe they hibernate,' Monica suggested.

'I wouldn't blame them,' Cynthia said. 'I could hibernate.'

'At least you tan.'

'I burn too, trust me.'

'I'll laugh,' Monica said cheerfully, 'if after all your mum's freaking out, you don't see a single vampire and drop dead of heatstroke, instead. That'd be hilarious.'

'Thanks, Monica.' Cynthia rolled her eyes. 'Anyway, if that's all, I might head out now.'

'Sure,' Nathan said. 'Thanks for making time.'

'No problem. Speak to you soon.'

They rang off, and Cynthia fetched her shoes. Downstairs, Brigitte was working on her laptop at the dining room table.

'Heading out?' she asked.

'I was thinking of going to the museums today.'

'Museumsinsel? That will be fun. We used to take Lola there all the time, back when she was still planning on studying art. She loved it. Hang on.' Brigitte fumbled through her papers. She worked for a company that ran tours, and always seemed to have colourful flyers and excel spreadsheets lying around. 'Here, I knew I had this somewhere. Discount vouchers.'

'Thanks.' Cynthia took the booklet. 'I think I'll be out until dinner time, if that's okay.'

'Of course. Enjoy it! Watch out for vampires and witches.'

Cynthia resisted the urge to roll her eyes. 'I will, I promise.'

Gracie trotted up to the door hopefully when she heard Cynthia leaving, staring mournfully at her leash hanging from a hook on the wall. Laughing, Cynthia scratched her behind the ears.

'Maybe later, if your papa doesn't take you.'

Her phone buzzed on the stairs.

> **Nathan:** Just emailed you the details. Have fun
>
> **Cynthia:** Thanks

She read the email on the train on her way into the city centre.

Hey Cynthia,

Hunter HQ is just east of Alexanderplatz, address below. The head honcho seems to be Herman Ditka. Let me know when you're heading over, and I'll make an appointment with him.

I've checked with the KUA in Bonn via both hunter and vampire channels. There hasn't been an update to the Berlin branch's logbooks since December. Would be great if you could find out why/ask them to send the updated logbooks.

There are a couple of security flags from the last quarter of last year that I don't have information on (hunters put everything behind security walls so that I have to request clearance, don't ask). It shouldn't matter, just so you're aware if they mention it.

Also check if Ditka is the best person to speak to, or if there's someone in admin.

Thanks for your help.

Nathan x

PS: The attachment is a map of supernatural hotspots in Berlin using data from the last ten years. Might help you in looking for your dad. In my experience, witches always go where there are other witches. Good luck!

The tone of the email made Cynthia smile. It was just so… Nathan. After checking the address, she let him know she'd head out there the next morning.

Nathan: Great, I'll give them a call

The heat was still turned up to max the next day, and Alexanderplatz was teeming with sweaty tourists. The hunter offices were a couple of streets back, in a building which was uninspiring from the outside but appointed with reasonably modern furniture within. Cynthia climbed to the third floor, traversed a hallway lined with generic landscape photos in blocky black frames, and passed through a door with a plaque reading, *KUA—nur nach Voranmeldung/only by appointment.* The reception area was sparsely furnished, with air-conditioning on full blast, lending a gentle hum to the atmosphere. A woman with perfectly coiffed blond hair was reading a magazine behind the reception desk. On the wall behind her, a TV screen was playing the local news.

'Hello?' Cynthia asked tentatively.

The woman glanced up. 'Wir sind geschlossen.'

'Um, hi… Sorry, do you speak English?'

That netted her another dismissive glance. 'We're closed.'

'Oh, but...' Cynthia checked her phone. 'I have an appointment with... Herman Ditka.'

The receptionist appraised her disinterestedly. 'He's on vacation.'

'He is? But I thought...' Cynthia consulted Nathan's email again. 'Shouldn't he have notified the Council that he was going on holiday?'

'He files his vacation time with KUA, not that it's any of your business.' The woman frowned. 'If you'd like to speak to a hunter, you'll need to make an appointment.'

'I did make an appointment.'

'There's nothing on the system.' The woman didn't even glance at her computer. 'There's no one in to see you. You can't have made an appointment.'

Cynthia swallowed her frustration. 'Excuse me a moment.'

The woman gestured dismissively. Cynthia stepped into the hallway to call Nathan. He picked up after several rings.

'Hey, what's up?'

'I'm at the hunter offices. The receptionist says there's no appointment.'

Nathan hummed. 'That's weird. I definitely made an appointment for you with Herman Ditka.'

'He's on holiday apparently.'

She could hear the frown in Nathan's voice. 'Okay, that is strange. Are you still there? Can I speak to the receptionist?'

'Sure.'

Cynthia slipped back in. The receptionist had gone back to her magazine. The screen behind her was showing an error message, but she was too absorbed to have noticed. Cynthia cleared her throat.

No response.

'Um, excuse me?'

The woman looked up. 'You're still here?'

'My contact at the Council in Oxford wants to speak to you.'

The woman sighed. 'He has to call the office PA for appointments.'

'Just speak to him and explain, please.'

Cynthia pushed the phone in her direction. She accepted it with visible reluctance and began her spiel again, this time in German. Whatever Nathan said in return brought her up short. Finally, she barked sharply, 'Das ist das Gebiet des KUAs—nein, nein. Bitte sehr. Auf Wiedersehen. Bitte.'

Angrily, she thrust the phone back at Cynthia. 'You tell me what you need, and I will call Mr Ditka.'

'The logbooks for the last few months,' Cynthia said.

'Very good.' The receptionist gestured towards an armchair. It smelt vaguely dusty when Cynthia sat down.

'Still there?' she asked down the phone.

'Still here,' Nathan replied. 'Rude woman.'

It took quite a lot of doing for Nathan to call someone rude.

'Not sure what that's about. This place is sleepier than Sleeping Beauty's castle.'

Nathan snickered. 'You're probably right. Look, see what they dredge up, but don't sweat it. I'm going to try and get hold of the Vampire Council contacts on the ground.'

'Wouldn't that have been easier than going through the Hunter Council?' Cynthia asked.

'It should have been. The Vamp Council has been weirdly quiet lately, too.' Nathan thought for a moment. 'I might have you nose around them, see if you can wake them up—pun intended, please don't actually feed them—'

Cynthia snorted. 'No thanks!'

'It should be on your to-visit list, anyway. They're out in Potsdam. It's gorgeous. Well worth a trip. Plus, Jeremiah will pay for your travel and food if you go.'

'I don't mind. He doesn't have to pay me,' Cynthia said uncomfortably. 'I... I want to be able to help out.' *Like you do.*

'You're a big help, don't worry. Call me back later? I'm about to go into a call with some guy from Spain—the witches there are protesting again—but once I'm done I should be free for the rest of the day.'

''Kay. Later, then.'

'Bye.'

Cynthia tucked her phone back in her bag and glanced around. She was alone. The receptionist had vanished through a doorway into the back. The TV was still showing an error message, over footage of the parliament. A moment later, the door swung open again and the receptionist emerged with an overweight, balding man, and a teenage boy about Cynthia's age. The receptionist gestured to Cynthia, and the man eyed her critically, before they both went behind the desk.

The boy wandered over. At a second glance, maybe he was a little younger than Cynthia: sixteen or seventeen. He didn't shave yet, at any rate. His light brown hair was long enough to cover his ears, and he had the sort of rangy build of someone who had grown up faster than out.

'Wer bist du?'

'Do you speak English?' Cynthia asked.

'Sorry. Who are you? We never get visitors.'

'Cynthia,' Cynthia replied uncomfortably. 'I'm from, uh, the British Council for Supernatural Affairs. In Oxford.'

The boy's eyes went wide. 'Really?' He sat down beside her. 'I'm Gunther Ditka.' He stretched his legs out. 'Hunter, well, hunter-in-training.'

'How long do you have to go?'

'Five months.'

So, he was seventeen. Hunters usually graduated training just after their eighteenth birthdays. Cynthia fiddled with her bag strap awkwardly.

'Uh, that's nice. Are you excited?'

'Of course.' Gunther grinned. 'How did you get to work for the Council? Are you a witch?'

'What? No!'

'What then?' He studied her as though he was trying to read her DNA. 'You're not a vampire.'

'You can't see my aura?' Cynthia darted a glance at the reception desk, from which furious whispers were emanating.

'Nooo, course not. I'm a normal, boring human.' Gunther rolled his eyes. 'Are you a hunter, then?'

'No, no, nothing like that. I'm just… friends with a hunter. He asked me for a favour.' Cynthia shrugged uncomfortably. 'I don't, I mean… I'm only eighteen. I'm on holiday.'

'Oh.' Gunther deflated visibly. 'Well, you came to Berlin at a good time.'

'How come?'

'We haven't had an incident in months. I'm meant to be doing training hunts and stuff, but—'

'Gunther,' the man said sharply, 'let's go.'

Gunther sighed. 'I have to get back to training.' He started to get up.

'Wait, what were you about to say?' Cynthia asked, but the trainer was tapping his foot impatiently.

'Don't worry about it. Nice to meet you,' Gunther said.

'Can I get your phone number?'

Gunther hesitated, but a terse word in German had him turning away again. 'Sorry,' he called to Cynthia, 'maybe next time.'

He vanished through the swinging door. Cynthia huffed. Damnit, and he'd been just about to say something interesting, as well.

Five minutes later, the receptionist waved her over again.

'I will email the file to Mr Delacroix,' she said. 'You can go.'

'Alright, thanks,' Cynthia said. 'Bye. Um, thank you for your help.'

'You are welcome,' the woman replied, but she didn't sound happy in the slightest.

CHAPTER FOUR

'OKAY, THAT IS WEIRD,' Monica said. Nathan was still on his call to Spain, so Cynthia had got hold of Monica instead. Monica also worked for the Council; she'd be able to pass on the message.

'She was really rude,' Cynthia complained. 'I don't know what her problem was.'

'You're young and pretty and she didn't feel like doing her job,' Monica said cynically.

Cynthia paused at a traffic light. 'Nathan never has that problem.'

'No, but he's Nathan. Shit glides over him like water off a duck's back.'

'Language.'

'Yes, Mum.' Monica snorted. 'Anyway, don't let it get to you. People are rude. Ignore them.'

Cynthia huffed. The light went green, and she started to cross the street. The air had turned muggy, and dark clouds were gathering. Cynthia could feel the oncoming storm, like a tension in her belly and at the back of her neck. Shifters had a sort of sixth sense for changes in the weather. She always knew when it was going to snow, too.

'Anyway, I got what Nathan needed, I guess,' Cynthia said. 'Tell him to ring me tonight? And if he wants me to go to Potsdam, I'll plan it for tomorrow.'

'Okay. I'll do that,' Monica said. 'In the meantime, don't let it distract you from your holiday.'

'Alright.' Cynthia chewed a loose piece of skin on the inside of her lip. 'Hey, when you speak to Nathan, will you…'

'Ask him about your dad? Don't worry, we haven't forgotten.'

'I know, I know. It's just… I have under two weeks left, and Berlin's a big city.'

'You could extend your stay,' Monica said. 'Lily has a place in

Berlin. I'm sure she'd let you crash there.'

'I couldn't ask her that!' Cynthia protested.

'Sure you could,' Monica said dismissively. 'Lily won't mind. Besides, Damien's here and she's in San Francisco. The place is standing empty.'

'Still!'

'I bet it's really nice,' Monica wheedled. 'Just think about it. I mean, you're right. This is too good a chance to pass up.'

'I'll think about it. Let's see what Jeremiah and Nathan dig up.'

'You can nose around on your end, too.'

'I wouldn't even know where to start. You guys are the ones who are good at that sort of thing.'

'Come on,' Monica said. 'You've hung around Nathan for long enough to pick up a few tricks. Just ask around.'

'Ask who? I can hardly ask the Deckers. You know how shifters get.'

'What about the witch girl you mentioned?'

'Who? Oh, you mean Renata? I don't have a contact number for her,' Cynthia pointed out.

'I bet Lola does. Try and get it out of her.'

'I don't want to pry, Monica.'

'It's not prying. You're not asking questions about their history. You're not hurting Lola. All you want is a phone number.'

It wasn't that simple, though. Lola would want to know why she needed the number, and there'd be all the usual warnings about witches and danger.

'I'll see. But I'm not pushing her.'

'Hmm,' Monica said sceptically, 'well, it's your life. Anyway, I've got to go.'

'Don't do that!' Cynthia snapped.

'What, go? I'm working the afternoon shift today. Let me know how it goes with Lola.'

'Monica! Look, come on, just because it's not that easy for me—'

Monica clucked her tongue. 'You're holding yourself back. All I'm saying is the option exists. If you want to take it, take it. If you don't, don't get mad at me.'

'I'm not mad, I just—' Cynthia shook her head. 'I don't want to fight. Sorry. Have a good time at work.'

'Will do. I'll speak to you tomorrow.'

'Bye.'

Monica hung up. Cynthia stared at her phone for a few moments, irritation roiling in her belly. The worst thing was that Monica was probably right. If she were here, she'd have just asked Lola. Monica specialised in cold hard truth, no matter how much it hurt. She'd have steamrolled right over Lola's feelings to get what she wanted. That was just the way she was.

Cynthia couldn't be like that. Sometimes it seemed like she felt too acutely. She was overwhelmed with guilt just thinking about the idea of prying into Lola's business.

Then again, she did want to find her father. She had so many questions and so few answers.

Her mother hadn't breathed a word about her father for sixteen and a half years. It hadn't been until Cynthia was kidnapped by dark mages, who wanted to sacrifice her for her magical blood, that her mother had finally fessed up. Her father wasn't just some random mistake. He was one of the dark mages. The same day she'd found that out, Cynthia had met the man in question. For ten brief seconds, so fleeting they seemed like a dream, he'd stood in front of her. With a single spell, he'd felled two men. Then he'd vanished, just like that.

In the aftermath, she and Nathan had gone digging through the Hunter and Vampire Council records. She'd asked her mother question after question. But her mother had returned to her usual reticence, and the Councils seemed to always be a step behind her father. She had a name and a photo, but that was it. Justin Gastrell was a mystery.

Cynthia was dying to figure him out.

And Monica might just be right. When you needed to find a supernatural, you had to ask a supernatural. Witches, like shifters, tended to build communities, covens. Apart from the rare exception, like Monica, all witches had a coven, so Renata probably did too. That meant she had access to the knowledge of the coven, as well as who sat on the KUA for the witches. Whoever that was, they ought to know if there was a dark mage in the city. It seemed like a mountain to climb, but Cynthia had climbed mountains before. It all started with a single step.

Like speaking to Lola.

And maybe apologising to Monica, too.

Following Monica's advice was easier said than done, though. The next day, Cynthia took the train into the city to meet Lola for lunch.

Lola was based out of a police station near the Zoological Garden. Cynthia met her in the reception area, which had a counter down one side and a dozen plastic waiting room chairs.

'I can't be long,' Lola said as they descended the stairs to the street. 'I have to do security for a press conference this afternoon. They're expecting trouble.'

'How come?' Cynthia had never really had a lot of dealings with the police; her mother had tended to avoid them. She found herself pretty curious about the inner workings of Lola's job, especially as Lola was fairly tight-lipped about a lot of what she did. 'If you can tell me, I mean.'

'This isn't a secret. They're doing a press conference about that bus accident last year. It keeps coming up again. Last time, someone threw tomatoes at the chancellor. The families are really upset.'

'I suppose I would be, too.'

'Well, yeah.' Lola trailed off, her lips twisting. 'Anyway, let's talk about something happier. What did you do this morning?'

'You can't tell?' Cynthia asked slyly.

'No. How could I?'

'My aura?'

Lola stopped walking, studying her for a few seconds. 'Oh! An otter? The zoo?'

'Yep.' Cynthia grinned. 'I was so tempted to shift when no one was watching.'

'Cynthia! You didn't!'

'Of course not! But I was tempted.' Cynthia rolled her eyes. 'Come on, don't you want to see what it's like to be… a tiger? I've never been a tiger before.'

Lola laughed. 'Once, Santi and I went there and managed to get the forms of the pandas and keep them 'til we got back home. We transformed into pandas whilst we were in the Grünewald. It was hilarious. Dad was furious.'

'Santi?'

Lola tensed, her expression turning alarmed. She looked away hastily. 'No one, just another old friend.'

'A shifter friend? I didn't know there were other shifters in the city.'

'Of course there are,' Lola snapped. 'There's about twenty of us in total. Look, just leave it, okay? I shouldn't have said that.'

Her voice was brimming with pain.

'Okay,' Cynthia said. 'I'm sorry.'

'It's fine. Let's go to REWE and get sandwiches.'

They crossed the road to the supermarket, Cynthia trailing after Lola as her mind raced. There were other shifters in the city? It had somehow never occurred to her that there might be. Of course, Berlin was a big city, with over a million people. There could easily be other shifters around.

As they were standing in the queue to pay, a man came up behind them.

'Lola?'

'Hmm?' She turned. 'Oh hey, Anton.'

Cynthia glanced up at the man. He was around thirty, with darkly tanned skin, brown hair and eyes, and a rugged look, as though he wasn't afraid of hard work. Unlike Lola, he wasn't in uniform; instead, he wore a suit without the jacket. When he caught Cynthia's eye, he held out a hand.

'Anton Matussek,' he said.

'Anton's my boss, sort of,' Lola explained. 'Well, I work with him on some things, anyway.'

'Nice to meet you.' Cynthia shook his hand and gasped as static electricity shocked her.

'Sorry. It's an effect of the magic.' Anton gave her a politician's smile. Cynthia stared at him, blindsided that he'd just mentioned magic so casually. Belatedly, she focused her second sight and checked his aura. It was electric blue mixed with neon green, so bright it hurt her eyes. She blinked furiously, letting the second sight slip away again.

Another mage.

'That's okay.' Cynthia cast her mind back to think if Monica had ever mentioned bright blue auras. She really needed to start keeping a list of what the different auras meant.

Anton gestured for them to precede him in the queue.

'No, you go ahead,' Lola insisted.

'Thanks.'

When they left, Anton was waiting for them at the door. 'Walking back to the station?'

'No, I thought we could sit on a bench and eat.' Lola's tone was edgy, and she kept glancing between Cynthia and Anton.

'Do you mind if I join you?'

'That's fine,' Lola said unhappily.

That scuppered any chance Cynthia had of mentioning her father. They sat together on benches in a nearby park, eating their sandwiches and making polite conversation.

'Ready for the conference this afternoon?' Anton asked suddenly.

'Of course.' Lola tore a piece of bread off her sandwich and tossed it to a pigeon. 'You?'

'Seems like it should go smoothly. The boys in Mitte said they're not expecting any trouble.'

'Depends on what questions come up, I guess.' Lola shrugged. 'Let's not discuss this. Cynthia probably finds police stuff boring.'

'Oh, come on. Everyone loves a good murder mystery.' Anton caught Cynthia's eye. 'Did you hear about this back in England?'

'Hear what?'

'About the bus accident.'

She had, of course. It had been one of those news stories that everyone obsessed about for a few weeks, and then it seemed to come around again every so often. Like plane crashes and other tragedies. Things people couldn't let go of.

'I heard a bit about it.'

'Really?' Anton leaned forwards. 'Not the full story, I bet.'

'Anton, don't. She's only eighteen. You'll scare her,' Lola protested.

'I don't scare that easily!' Cynthia said indignantly.

'See?' Anton said. 'Stories can't hurt you. So, last October, a bus full of tourists hits a guy in the middle of Invalidenstraße. Bus brakes suddenly, doors open, no one gets out. Cars start queuing up behind it. When the police get there, everyone on the bus is dead. No explanation.'

'From the crash?' Cynthia asked.

'Hitting a person doesn't crash a bus. They died after the bus stopped.' Anton's smile grew broad and smug. 'Every last one of them, drained of blood.'

Cynthia felt a sudden chill down her arms, despite the hot weather. 'You mean—'

'It's a cold case,' Lola cut in. 'The only reason they're still talking about it is because of the families. People want closure. Anton, we're not supposed to discuss this stuff.'

Anton leaned back, shrugging, and some of the tension ebbed out of the air. 'It's not hurting anything. We're not telling her anything the newspapers haven't reported.'

'Conjecture,' Lola said. 'Let's go back, we have work to do. Cynthia, I'll see you in a few days, alright?'

'Okay,' Cynthia said reluctantly. She lifted her sandwich. 'You go. I'll stay here and finish eating.'

'Right,' Lola said. She and Anton stood.

'Bye, Cynthia,' Anton called. 'Nice to meet you.'

'And you.'

Lola dragged her feet a little, letting Anton move ahead. 'Look,' she mumbled to Cynthia, 'just ignore him. He thinks he's cool.'

'I will.'

'Okay. Will you find your way back alright?'

Cynthia nodded.

'See you soon, then.'

'Bye.'

Cynthia sat there for a long time after they were gone, eating slowly, lost in thought. That had been a strange encounter all around. Was Lola hiding something? Or was she just uncomfortable talking about her work? And what was up with Anton's aura? Cynthia had found him a bit disconcerting in general. Did he just like spooky stories?

Maybe.

But one thing was for sure: He was wrong. Unintentionally or on purpose, he had let something slip that hadn't been in the papers. The bus crash victims had been drained of blood.

And there was only one creature that could do that.

CHAPTER FIVE

THAT AFTERNOON, CYNTHIA HEADED TO KREUZBERG.

Nathan had been too busy to speak to Cynthia, or maybe the logbook had checked out, and he'd just forgotten to let her know. It brought back a familiar old hurt. This was how it had always been when they were dating: Nathan would disappear for a while, caught up in work. The trouble with working for the Council was that the work could come any time. He could get called out at five AM, five PM, lunchtime, or midnight. It hadn't bothered Cynthia in the beginning, but then they'd had to cancel a lot of dates, and… these things just added up.

In Nathan's absence, she decided to do something for herself. Kreuzberg was an area which Lily von Klichtzner—a mutual friend of Cynthia, Nathan, and Monica's—had ardently recommended, and the Deckers had just as fiercely warned her away from, because it was witch territory. Nathan's map of supernatural hotspots concurred.

When you needed to find a witch, you had to ask a witch. If there were witches to be found, they'd be here, and the paranoia and general reticence of her friends wasn't going to stop Cynthia from finding one.

It had rained the previous night, cutting the temperature to a comfortable twenty-seven degrees, perfect for a hike. The area was named for a cross-shaped memorial atop a hill. According to the guidebook Brigitte had foisted on Cynthia when she arrived, it would provide excellent views across Berlin. It also seemed like the sort of place that would attract supernaturals: old and historically significant. Cynthia decided to start there.

The steep climb through the trees did her good. Cynthia had always felt more at peace in nature, and the freshness of the air and the smell of the trees eased some of her stress.

By the time she reached the summit, she was breathing hard and sweating lightly. The trees stopped suddenly, giving way to a grassy slope, in the middle of which was the memorial. A short flight of stairs climbed up to the podium. The memorial itself resembled a church steeple, with statues of Prussian kings and princes set about a third of the way up. On the stairs, Cynthia passed a girl who was graffitiing the anarchists' A on the wall; she skittered off when Cynthia reached her.

The podium was full of people. Four teenagers were passing a beer between them and talking in staccato bursts. A group of tourists were taking photos. Cynthia meandered around, looking out at Berlin. It was a big city, and so spread out. Somewhere here... somewhere amongst all these people... was her father. But how to find him?

She settled on the eastern side, pulling her phone out to check Nathan's map. It didn't give any details, that was the trouble. Kreuzberg wasn't small. What were the chances that she'd bump into a coven setting up some obvious ritual in the middle of the park? Slim to none.

'Du störst mein Gemälde.'

'Huh?' Cynthia turned, recognising the speaker at the same time as the girl recognised her.

'Oh, it's you,' Renata said grouchily. Her hair was pulled back into a bun, and she was carrying an A3 sketchbook. 'Go away, Dog-Girl,' she added.

'What have I ever done to you?' Cynthia asked.

'I mean, apart from right now you are preventing me from finishing a painting that is actually part of my university grades, so please fuck off?' Renata asked.

'I'm just sitting here. If you want me to move, just ask nicely.'

'Please take your stupid shifter magic and put it somewhere else,' Renata said.

'Why?'

Renata sighed exaggeratedly. 'You're making the memorial transform.' She gestured irritably with her stick of charcoal. Cynthia turned and regarded the face of the memorial in surprise. Where previously there had been a statue of a king with a fancy shield behind her, now there was a niche. A cast iron wreath of poppies rested at the bottom, and words were carved into the back:

Denkmal für die in den Hexenkriegen verlorenen Vorfahren 749 – 1179 AD

Beneath that was a list of names, similar to what Cynthia had seen on memorials for soldiers lost during World War One. She scanned the list with interest. There were no birth or death dates, and most of the names didn't have surnames attached.

Adalhard

Helga

Leonhard

Theobald

Towards the bottom, there were a few names with surnames, and sometimes even multiple people sharing the same surname. Four names from the bottom, Cynthia froze in shock.

Gerhard von Klichtzner

Amelina von Klichtzner

Siegfried von Klichtzner

Magdalena von Klichtzner

Von Klichtzner was Lily's surname. Of course, it could be a common surname—Cynthia had no way of knowing, really. But the memorial was made with magic, and Lily was a half-vampire… She pulled her phone out to snap a photo.

'Yeah, that's not going to work, Dog-Girl. Your phone can't see magic.'

'I have a name, you know.'

'Do I look like I care?'

Cynthia turned. Renata had her arms crossed and was scowling. 'No, not really.'

'Then move.'

Cynthia edged away, studying the memorial. Once she was about a metre away it flickered, and the list of names vanished. She moved over to Renata, who sat down and turned her attention back to her sketchbook.

'What are you doing?'

'Homework,' Renata said. 'Please leave.'

'Why do you hate me so much?'

'Do you always ask this many questions?'

Cynthia shrugged. 'Pretty much.'

'If I answer, will you go away?'

It hurt, being hated by someone she didn't know. 'If you want me to.'

'I do.'

'Okay, but first tell me why you hate me.'

Renata huffed and lowered the sketchbook again. 'I don't hate you. You're annoying. And you stay with Lola, who is a liar.'

'Lola's never lied to me,' Cynthia replied, easing down to sit beside Renata, her back against the railing.

Renata laughed. 'You're joking.'

'I'm not! I like Lola. She's down-to-earth, friendly—'

'A liar? She works for the police so she can cover up her family's crimes. And a hypocrite. 'I hate witches,' she says, but she'll do deals with them, won't she?'

Renata's anger was a living thing; Cynthia could feel her magic like electricity over her skin.

'I don't know what you're talking about!'

Renata snorted derisively.

'I don't!' Cynthia protested.

'You're really that naïve? What the fuck are you doing here, then?'

'Visiting?' Cynthia asked. 'I'm on holiday, that's it.'

Renata regarded her disbelievingly.

'I am! I just came to Berlin for a few weeks for holiday.'

'I know your people, you don't just do things,' Renata said. 'Too scared of witches and vampires. All shifters are good for is hiding in the woods.'

'We're not all that bad.' Cynthia hugged her knees. 'Fine, I'm looking for someone, okay? My father. And before you say, he's not a shifter, he's a—a mage, like you, so don't be nasty.'

'Pfft, what, and you thought you'd rock up in Berlin and just ask KUA for his address?'

'It's none of your business!'

'I bet he's not even here. He doesn't want to see you. If he did, he'd pick up the phone and call. He's probably off fucking some other woman—'

'SHUT UP!'

Cynthia's voice came out too loud, too harsh, and the words lingered between them oddly. She never usually got angry, was always too scared of upsetting people to say how she really felt. But now it was out.

'Shut up,' Cynthia repeated in a quieter voice. 'You don't know what you're talking about, okay? And yes, I could just walk up and ask KUA, because actually, I know people who work for the Council in Oxford. And I do know he's here. I've seen him.'

'So go speak to him, then.' Renata made a shooing noise. 'Quickly. And then get out of town, before you go the way Santiago did.'

Her rudeness grated on Cynthia. She took a calming breath, before asking, 'Who is Santiago?'

'Lola didn't tell you about him?'

'I don't like to pry into Lola's private life.'

Renata snorted, but with less hostility this time. 'Santiago was a shifter, like you. He died four years ago.'

'Oh.' Cynthia picked at a loose thread on her shorts. 'You were friends?'

'Something like that.' Renata shrugged, turning back to her sketch. 'I don't want to talk about it.'

'Okay.'

They were silent for a few moments, during which Cynthia tried to puzzle out all the connections. Lots of things could kill shifters; they healed fast, but they weren't immortal. The number one cause of death was usually witches.

'You should get out of town,' Renata said. 'It's not safe for your kind here.'

'Lola's family is safe here,' Cynthia said.

'That's different.'

'How?'

'I don't know.' Renata stared at the memorial, as though it might tell her the answer. 'I wouldn't trust them if I were you.'

Cynthia had never had a reason not to trust shifters before. Witches, vampires, humans… they were all the enemy. But shifters were her people. They didn't turn on each other.

'I'm not leaving until I find my father.'

'Then you're stupid,' Renata said in a condescending tone, 'and naïve. And don't come crying to me if something tries to eat you.'

'Getting eaten is the last thing I'm scared of,' Cynthia replied. 'And I'd never cry to you. Witches can use tears for dark magic.'

Renata laughed, a humourless, angry laugh. 'Stupid dog. Get out of here.'

Cynthia was tired of trying to win Renata over. She clambered to her feet. 'You know what, Renata? All supernaturals lie. It's what we have to do to keep our secret. So Lola might be a liar, but at least she's kind.'

'Better to lie kindly than to be unkind and honest?' Renata asked. 'You are such a child.'

She made a shooing gesture. Cynthia picked her bag up and left. Only at the bottom of the stairs did she look back. She could just see the top of Renata's head, her bun wobbling as she worked on her sketch.

What was wrong with being kind?

Renata reminded her of Monica. Monica was also unkind and honest. And Monica would have said the same thing.

And Monica was usually right.

But not this time. Cynthia had no reason to distrust the Deckers. They'd been kind, generous, even. She'd speak to Lola next time she saw her, clear everything up, and be done with it. It was just a misunderstanding. Renata was just a witch.

And witches couldn't be trusted.

Nodding to herself, Cynthia set off down the hill. A little while later, she pulled her phone out. Unfortunately, Renata had been right about one thing: her phone couldn't see magic. The photo of the memorial showed the bearded Prussian king. That was a shame.

Impulsively, Cynthia tapped out a message to Lily.

Cynthia: Hey, how's the US?

Cynthia: Would love to talk sometime, if you're free x

The chat remained disappointingly silent. Belatedly, Cynthia checked the time. It was seven AM in San Francisco. Lily was probably still asleep.

Sighing, Cynthia set off again. She'd walk around Kreuzberg and see what she found. There had to be a friendly witch somewhere in this city, right?

CHAPTER SIX

NO MORE WITCHES MADE themselves known, friendly or otherwise. Instead, as Cynthia eventually called it a day and headed to the U-Bahn, her phone rang.

'Hi, Nathan,' she greeted.

'Cynthia, I am so sorry.' Nathan groaned theatrically. 'I told you I'd call you, but I literally haven't even been home since yesterday. Monica just updated me. I'm sorry!'

'It's okay.'

'It's not, don't lie.'

Maybe if Cynthia had been in a better mood, she would have.

'No, you're right, it's not. If I do you a favour, it'd be nice if you get back to me. Even just a text message would have been fine.'

'I know.' Nathan sounded really unhappy, and that made Cynthia feel instantly guilty.

'Sorry, it's not you I'm mad at.'

'Did something else happen?'

'Just a weird encounter with this witch that Lola knows. Don't worry about it.'

'I do, you know,' Nathan said. 'If you need help, you can always ask.'

'Thanks,' Cynthia said. She paused awkwardly. 'Um, did you need something?'

'Right. Is this a good time?' Nathan asked.

'It's fine.'

'Alright, well… the hunters got the logbooks to me, but they didn't tell me anything I don't already know. We've tracked the few incidents there have been, and they're all concentrated around central Berlin.'

'Makes sense.'

'Well, not entirely, because the vampire branch of KUA always used to be based out of one of the palaces in Potsdam—it's the area where the Prussian emperors used to live—so there should be incidents happening there. As best I can tell, there isn't even a hunter stationed out there anymore.'

'And you want me to go take a look?'

'If you don't mind,' Nathan said. 'Like I said before, Jeremiah will pay expenses—train, lunch. You're welcome to tour the other palaces whilst you're out there. Actually, you should. You'll attract less attention if you act like a tourist, and Jeremiah wants to keep this a bit under the radar for now.'

That was interesting.

'Does he think something weird is going on?' Cynthia stepped around a group of teens who were blocking the entrance to the underground.

'We're honestly not sure what's happening,' Nathan said. 'I might have to travel out there.'

'Oh.' Cynthia tried not to wear her distaste for that idea too openly. 'That'd be, uh, cool.'

'Don't want your ex overshadowing your holiday?'

'No, it's not that.' It was exactly that. 'I just, uh, you might scare my father off before I can find him.'

'Oh, about that,' Nathan said, 'I have some info. I'll email it to you as soon as I get home. It's not much, but it might help.'

'That'd be great.'

'You're welcome. I hope you find him.' Nathan paused. 'Let me know if there's anything I can do to help. I know I can be… slow to reply… but… I've always got your back. And if you're in trouble, I will always help out.'

'I know,' Cynthia said, and she did know. She did. 'But maybe this is something I have to do on my own. For me.'

'Maybe,' Nathan said, 'but don't forget that we're there for you if you need us.'

'I won't.'

'Cool. Let me know about Potsdam.'

'Yeah, I'll go tomorrow,' Cynthia promised. 'Talk tomorrow evening? Put it in your calendar!'

'I will, I promise.'

They said their goodbyes and hung up, just in time for Cynthia's train to pull in. As she boarded it and found a spot amidst the rush hour commuters, she tried to sort through her feelings. Renata had been weird. Nathan was frustrating, as always, and immune to her complaints. He'd make a joke about it, and then carry on doing exactly what he always did. That was Nathan. There was no point in getting mad.

And Renata, well, she'd need to speak to Lola about that.

That evening, curled up in bed with the windows open, she checked her emails. Nathan had indeed sent her information, and it was as sparse as he'd intimated it would be.

Hi Cynthia,

I took a photo of Jeremiah's notes for you (good luck!). I've also included the info from the hunter database.

Nate x

She opened the photo first. Jeremiah's handwriting was loopy and old-fashioned, and it took Cynthia a few minutes to decipher it.

Justin Emmanuel Gastrell

Born 4th April 1969, Chicago, Illinois

The rest of the notes mapped out his last known movements. He had left Oxford on the edict of the Council in February 2016. He had definitely resided with the London Coven for at least three months, after which he had travelled to Egypt—*believed headquarters of the Sahir in Cairo, unconfirmed,* Jeremiah had noted—and then he had flown first to New York, and six months later to Frankfurt. There, the trail went dead. There was also a list of dark mages registered with the KUA in Bonn who fit his profile, more or less: *Frank Emmerich, Gideon Hüber, Lukas Meier.*

Nathan's notes from the hunter database confirmed the same travel details. The trouble was, they didn't match the postcards. Monica had theorised that he was buying postcards and sending them from random places. Cynthia wondered if he was travelling on a fake passport.

None of the information brought her any closer to an answer, though. Sighing, Cynthia buried her face in her pillow. It wasn't fair. The world was such an easy place for people to hide. And once she'd thought that was a good thing.

Her phone buzzed insistently in her hand, and she lifted her head. It was home.

'Hello?'

'Cynthia!' a familiar voice wailed. It was her sister, Emma.

'Hey, Em. What's up?'

'I. *Hate.* Mum!' And the nine-year-old burst into tears. Cynthia had to suppress a laugh.

'Oh dear… what happened?'

'She's just being awful, she won't let me go to Alex's birthday party and she's so… ughhhh… Cindy, stop laughing at me!'

'I'm not laughing.' Cynthia forced the smile off her lips. 'I'm taking you seriously. I know what Mum's like. Want me to talk to her?'

'When are you coming home? Mum's talking about leaving again!'

'Why? Has something happened?'

Emma sniffled. 'I don't know. But Mum never tells me stuff.'

'I'll speak to her,' Cynthia promised. 'Aren't you up kind of late?'

'I snuck into Mum's room to get the phone. She's downstairs.'

Cynthia had to smile. She could picture her little sister, sneaking all stealthy around the house.

'Ninja.'

'Yep.' Emma giggled.

'That's the spirit. Smile. Make a deal with Mum. If she lets you go to the party, you'll do the dishes.'

'Ewww,' Emma said, 'no thanks. Can you tell her to put me in karate? Maybe then she'll actually let me do stuff like you can.'

'I'll tell her,' Cynthia promised. 'You should get to bed before she catches you. Ninjas never get caught, right?'

'I'm nine, not five, Cynthia.'

'I know, I know. Give Mum a kiss for me.'

'M'kay. Good night.'

'Good night.'

Cynthia smiled as she tapped out a message to her mum, then tossed her phone on the pillow beside her. She and Emma fought like cats and dogs most days, but it was nice to hear her sister's voice.

Footsteps clunked up the stairs, and a moment later Brigitte knocked on the floor and her head appeared.

'Everything alright? I heard voices.'

'Yeah, I was just talking to my sister.'

'Okay.' Brigitte paused for a moment. 'Wilhelm and I are going to bed. See you in the morning.'

'Yeah, goodnight.'

The next morning, Cynthia set off for Potsdam. The sun had been displaced by clouds and sticky humidity, heralding yet another storm, but as she travelled further west it cleared up steadily, and by the time Cynthia was disembarking from the train in Potsdam, the sun was shining again.

She felt free. Brigitte had been working from the office that morning, meaning she'd dodged the usual morning inquisition into her plans that day. She could do what she wanted today, and her expenses would be paid, and she felt like she was doing something meaningful. Even better, Nathan was being positively chatty via text, an obvious attempt to make up for disappearing for two days.

It was a good day.

For the first half of the day, Cynthia roamed the gardens and explored the lavish palaces which had housed centuries' worth of Prussian kings, princes, and emperors. After lunch, she took a bus to Schloss Cecilienhof, the youngest palace, and also the only one she'd been familiar with before arriving; it was the site of the Potsdam Conference of 1945, in which the Russians, Americans, and British had decided the fate of Germany. She'd learnt about it in history at school.

Supernaturals, Nathan had said via text message when she pointed that out, *have a sense of irony.*

If Nathan's intel was correct, then all three branches of the KUA used this as their meeting place. The equivalent in Oxford was the Sheldonian Theatre. Unlike Oxford, neither the witches nor the vampires seemed to have any other haunt, at least, not according to official records. In Oxford, both had had their own private headquarters, alongside the official meeting place, rather like the hunters had their office here.

Nathan suspected that their intel was simply out of date.

However, if the local hunter intel was correct, then Cynthia was about to find absolutely nothing.

'Well, we'll know soon,' she said to herself as she clambered off the bus.

Cecilienhof Palace was built in the style of a Tudor country house. The gardens sported red flowers arranged to resemble a star, a relic of the Russian inhabitants during the USSR's occupation of East Germany. Cynthia nosed around the gardens for a few minutes, looking for any secret entrances or high-level illusions that would indicate supernatural activity, but all she ended up with was a headache. It hurt her eyes to keep up her magical sight for too long.

Another thing Nathan and Monica didn't have trouble with.

Finally, after earning herself her third irritated look from tourists trying to take selfies, Cynthia forked out a few euros to gain entrance to the palace.

> **Cynthia:** No sign of magic outside
>
> **Nathan:** Jeremiah says security guard in study is usually a witch, password is permittitis intrare
>
> **Nathan:** Same as Oxford
>
> **Cynthia:** Thanks

Inside was dim and cool. Cynthia roamed from room to room, checking each with her magical sight. None of the staff seemed magical; there were no colourful auras indicating witchcraft, nor the deadened air which would indicate vampirism. The only trace of magic she found was in a display cabinet in one of the halls. A silver box gleamed red to her second sight. To her regular vision, it was old and slightly tarnished, and otherwise innocuous. She couldn't get close enough to read the little plaque, and the security guard watching like a hawk deterred her from climbing over the cordon.

Eventually, after checking each room, she made her way back to the study. The security guard was young-ish, and decidedly non-supernatural, but Cynthia had promised she'd try. Nervously, she approached him.

'Kann ich Ihnen helfen?'

'I, um, permittitis intrare?' Cynthia asked.

The guard stared at her as though she was a total weirdo.

'Can I help you?' he repeated.

'I'm, uh, I'm Cynthia Rymes. I'm here from the Council in Oxford?' Doubt engulfed her. 'I'm sorry, I'll go.'

'I don't know what you're talking about,' the guard said. 'Maybe try the front desk?'

'Okay… thank you.' Cynthia sidled away, embarrassed, and looked around for the exit.

Well, that was a wash.

Outside seemed very bright as she emerged from the palace. She fumbled her phone out of her bag.

> **Cynthia:** Nothing inside

Nathan: For real?

A second later, her phone rang.

'Seriously?' Nathan asked by way of greeting. 'No signs whatsoever?'

'I checked every room. I tried permittitis intrare. The guard looked at me like I was stupid.'

'That's weird. Did you see anything off?'

'There wasn't a trace of magic, except some stupid box in a display cabinet.'

'Got a photo of it?'

'No photos allowed, but I can describe it.'

'Hold on,' Nathan said, 'I'm putting you on speaker so Monica can hear.'

A moment later, Monica's voice came over the phone, 'Hi.'

'Hey, Monica.' Cynthia sighed. 'Has Nathan told you?'

'The mysterious case of the missing vampires continues.' Monica sniggered. 'Can't say I'm sad. If I were you, I'd stop looking and let them be gone.'

'We can't stop looking,' Nathan said. 'Whoever did this, they're powerful.'

'And dangerous,' Cynthia chimed in.

'Dangerous to vampires,' Monica said.

'Dangerous to witches, too,' Nathan pointed out, 'seeing as the witches have also abandoned their HQ.'

'Ugh,' Monica muttered, 'you two are so responsible. Fine. What do you need me for?'

'The box?' Nathan asked.

'It was about thirty centimetres long, and twenty centimetres deep. Silver. There was a pattern on the outside, which looked a little bit like… not quite like the hunter runes Nathan uses.'

'Hold on, I'm sending you a picture,' Nathan said.

Cynthia's phone buzzed a moment later. She put the call on speaker and opened the picture. It depicted a series of runic alphabets.

'Can you tell which one?' Nathan asked.

'Yeah, Norse.'

'Elder or Younger Futhark?'

'Elder, I think.'

'Anything else you could see on it?'

Cynthia put the phone back to her ear. 'Nothing, not even a lock. I don't think the box was important. It looked old.'

'What colour was the aura?' Monica asked.

'Red.'

'Blood magic.' Monica sighed. 'It could be anything, Nate. For all we know, the blood magic was used to seal it because it doesn't have a lock.'

Nathan made a noise of disappointment. 'Was there a lot of magic? Did it look fresh?'

'I don't know. My magical sight's not that good,' Cynthia said in frustration. 'The aura was noticeable. But it was in a display cabinet. I mean, it could have been there for years, right?'

'Probably,' Monica agreed.

Nathan sighed. 'Fine, the box is a dud. And the palace is a dud. So where are the vampires?'

'Hibernating?' Monica asked.

'Hiding?' Cynthia suggested.

'Guys…'

'No, she might be right,' Monica said. 'If there is a threat in Berlin, they might have gone to ground.'

'Point,' Nathan conceded. 'Where, though?'

'Somewhere underground?' Cynthia suggested.

'Somewhere protected,' Monica said, 'with an easy food source.'

Food… Something tickled at Cynthia's brain suddenly.

'The bus! Nathan, do you remember that bus crash?'

'Of course,' Nathan said.

'Was the Council involved?'

'It wasn't a supernatural incident, was it?' Monica asked

'Wasn't it?' Cynthia replied. 'Lola works for the police. A colleague of hers told me all the victims had been drained of blood.'

'Okay, that is weird,' Monica said. 'Nate?'

'A human colleague?' Nathan asked.

'No, a mage. He had a weird aura, electric blue and green.'

'Seriously?' Monica asked. 'My God.'

'Is that bad?'

'He's a technician!' She sounded excited. 'I've never met one before. They're super rare.'

'A technician?' Cynthia asked.

'Techno-mages. They can control computers with their minds. It's really cool. Just, like, maybe switch your phone off if you see him again. He could hack it.'

'Hack my phone?' Cynthia repeated in alarm. 'What would someone like that be doing working for the human police?'

'I dunno,' Monica said. 'Could be a good place to get information, though. Ooh, that's so cool. I'm jealous. I'd love to pick his brain.'

'I'll let you know if I meet him again.'

'Oh, do!'

'Sure.' Cynthia glanced around. It was getting to closing time, the hordes of tourists ebbing. 'I should probably head back into the city.'

'Yeah,' Nathan said. 'I'm going to look into a few things. I'll try the hunters again, try and light a fire beneath them. And I'll try the KUA in Bonn, though I doubt they'll be useful. I'll get back to you, okay?'

'Alright.'

'Don't sweat it, though. This is obviously bigger than what we realised, and I don't want it to take up your entire holiday, so I'll bring someone in who knows Berlin.'

'Alright,' Cynthia said, disappointed in spite of herself, 'but if there is anything I can do, let me know.'

'I will,' Nathan said. 'Go for a drink tonight, on me. As thanks.'

'Maybe you'll find a vampire out and about,' Monica suggested. 'They've got to eat eventually.'

Cynthia wrinkled her nose. 'Yuck, Monica!'

They all laughed.

After saying goodbye, Cynthia hung up. The gardens were almost empty, and the sun had dipped towards the treeline, sending long shadows over the grounds as she walked towards the bus stop. The back of her neck prickled, and she paused, glancing back.

Was there someone between the trees?

She blinked, and the impression was gone.

Weird.

Cynthia carried on walking, but she couldn't shake the feeling that someone was watching her. Every time a bird twittered, or leaves rustled, she jumped and looked over her shoulder.

But there was never anyone there.

CHAPTER SEVEN

LOLA INVITED CYNTHIA TO dinner that evening, so instead of making her way back to the Deckers' apartment, she headed into the city. Lola lived in an inexpensive, studenty area, not far from the police station she worked at. Her apartment was at the back of a courtyard, on the fifth floor of a building with no lift.

'Hey,' she said brightly when she opened the door. 'Sorry to drag you out here. I thought we ought to talk, you know, somewhere where no parents or weird colleagues can overhear.'

'Like Anton?' Cynthia asked, looking around curiously. 'This is really nice, by the way.'

'Thanks.' Lola grimaced. 'Yeah, I'll tell you about Anton. Come into the kitchen.'

The kitchen was a narrow room with all of the workspace down one side. At the far end, a table and two chairs were crammed beneath a tiny window. Cynthia sat there, watching as Lola threw together pasta and tomato sauce.

'So, what is the deal with Anton?' she asked.

'Like I said, Anton's my boss,' Lola replied, passing her a beer, 'but only for some things.'

'Like?'

'Anything where we think the supernatural might be involved.' Lola frowned. 'You know, I shouldn't tell you this stuff, but it's better to tell you than you go asking questions to other people, I think. So, anything where we might have to cover up part of the story. Like the bus.'

'That vampires were involved,' Cynthia said.

'We think so. It was difficult to keep that one quiet, actually. The KUA used to have a couple of vamps who would compel the right people to keep things out of the news, but there are no vampires around

Berlin anymore.'

'Do you know why?'

'No one knows why.' Lola shrugged. 'Last year, there was a period of about a month or two before Christmas, where we had at least a dozen burnings. We think someone was poisoning the vampires. They got scared and hid. There hasn't been a single vampire out and about, since.'

'Right.' Cynthia filed that away for later. 'Why did Anton tell me about the bus story, then?'

'He wanted to see if you knew about vampires.'

'And what did he figure out?'

'Oh, I'm sure he guessed.' Lola leaned over to set the table. Her face twisted into a frown. 'You should… be careful of Anton. He has a way of knowing things he shouldn't.'

'Monica, my friend in Oxford, called him a technician,' Cynthia said.

'Yeah, that's what he calls it.' Lola turned the stove down and came to sit opposite Cynthia. 'I don't know how his magic works, but it doesn't matter what security you have… passwords, encryptions, firewalls… whatever. He can get past all of them. Whatever you had on your phone when you met him, he probably saw it. And he investigates anyone new in the city.'

She meant any supernatural. The thought sent a shiver down Cynthia's spine. She'd never been important enough to be investigated like that before. The thought wasn't flattering.

'So that's what he was really doing? The rest was just an excuse.'

'Probably.' Lola shrugged again and took a long sip of her beer. 'Anyway, I can't think that you'd have anything to make him suspicious, so you probably won't see him again.'

'Yeah,' Cynthia agreed guiltily, thinking of her text conversations with Monica and Nathan. 'I hope so.'

'Me too. The last thing we need is him digging too much into the shifter community.'

Lola got up to finish off the dinner. Cynthia sipped her beer, watching a bunch of toddlers playing in the courtyard far below. What had Anton read into her phone data? It wasn't as if she was doing anything bad here. But maybe she ought to minimise how much she chatted to her friends, just in case…

'So,' Lola said, setting the pans down on the table and gesturing for Cynthia to serve herself, 'tomorrow night, we'll meet in Kreuzberg. I invited Fritz and the others. There's a bar we always go to. You'll like it—it's very… Berlin.'

'I love that you use that as an adjective.'

Lola shrugged. 'There's no other way to say it. Don't dress up. It's a really casual place. I'll meet you at the station at nine PM.'

'Sure.'

'Great.' Lola grinned. 'You'll love it. It'll be a nice break from sightseeing.'

'I don't mind sightseeing. It's nice to just enjoy travelling for a change, rather than feeling like I'm constantly on the run.'

Lola's smile grew tight. 'Yeah, I suppose… What did you do today?'

Cynthia took a mouthful of pasta to stall for time. Tell her, or not? Would Lola know the significance of Cecilienhof palace? How much did Lola know about the KUA?

One way to find out…

'I went to Potsdam.'

Cynthia knew it was a mistake the moment she said it. Lola's expression closed off entirely.

'Seriously? Just like that? I thought Mum warned you of the places to avoid.'

'You were quite cool about it before,' Cynthia pointed out.

'Yeah, but it's one thing to bump into them in the middle of the street, and another to go looking for their headquarters!'

'I wanted to see the palaces. Anyway, I didn't see a single vampire or witch. I don't even think they're there anymore.'

'Don't be naïve.'

'I'm not naïve! You said yourself, they're hiding.'

'Not the witches!' Lola snapped.

'I haven't seen a single witch either—except Renata!'

'Renata's dangerous too. I'd have never left you alone at the barbeque if I knew she'd come and talk to you.' Lola made a noise of frustration. 'You're going to get us all in trouble.'

'Not all witches are bad!'

'Not all—do you even hear yourself?' Lola put her fork down, fixing Cynthia with an incredulous look. 'You just said that you spent your entire life running, and now you want to, what, hug them and be friends with them? You have got to be joking.'

'I never said that. Anyway, I haven't run for two years now, since I've been in Oxford. And things are different now. I know how to deal with witches.'

'Hah, yeah, we all go through that phase.'

'It's not a phase!' But something had clicked into place all of a sudden. 'Is that it, then? Was Renata your 'phase'?'

'No,' Lola said quickly.

'Really? Because I saw her again yesterday, and she mentioned the same name you did. Santiago? Who was he?'

Lola's face had gone very white, and Cynthia realised she might have gone too far. 'Lola, I—'

'Santi—' Lola interrupted in a choked voice, 'Santi was a shifter. He… he was half-German, half-Portuguese, and he came to stay in Germany for a while, to finish school. He lived with us.'

'Oh,' Cynthia whispered.

'He was like you,' Lola said. 'Idealistic. He thought vampires and witches and shifters should get along. He used to say, 'We're all supernatural. Why should we fight? We all protect the same secrets.' He had witch friends, Renata… he and Renata dated…'

No wonder Renata had been so angry, so miserable.

'What happened to him?'

'He disappeared,' Lola said. 'We never found out. Probably, the witches got him. Renata was still in with her coven, then. I don't think she is now. She probably took him home, and her parents decided he'd make a nice sacrifice. Mum and Dad wouldn't let me investigate. They said it would bring trouble down on all of us. So we never found out.'

'And after that you decided to go into the police?' Cynthia guessed.

'Pretty much. It wasn't only that. Also because… Renata is studying art.'

'She told me.'

'When did you see her?' Lola asked.

'I bumped into her when I went to the memorial in Kreuzberg.'

Lola frowned. 'The one in Viktoriapark? You should be careful there. That's—'

'Witch territory, I know,' Cynthia said in exasperation. 'Look, I am being careful, I swear, but I also can't live just hiding. I won't.'

'And what does that mean for the rest of us? Once you leave, we stay here. We deal with any trouble you make.'

'I know,' Cynthia said guiltily. 'Look, maybe I should find somewhere else to stay whilst I'm here. It's just… I can't stop going to these places, not yet. There's someone I have to find.'

'Someone like who?' Lola asked quietly.

'My father.' The words lingered in the air between them. 'He's a mage,' Cynthia added.

'I always thought he was one of us.'

'I know, that's what I thought too.' Cynthia fiddled with her fork. 'Eventually, Mum fessed up. He's a mage. I just… want to know. I want to know why. And it's so weird to think that he's out there and that he... I don't know.'

Lola was silent for a long time. Finally, she said, 'You think he's in Berlin?'

'I know he is. I saw him.'

'And you never said.'

Cynthia shrugged. 'You'd have been angry.'

'I am angry. Cynthia! You should have warned us. You'll put us all in danger.'

'I won't, okay, I can ask my friend if I can stay in her dad's apartment. If I stay away from you guys—'

'Then what? You don't think the damage is already done?'

'No! No, I don't. I went all around Potsdam and saw no one. Not a vampire, not a witch. And if I didn't see them, and I was looking for them, then they didn't see me.'

Lola looked away, biting her lip.

'I think you should go home.'

'That's not your choice to make,' Cynthia said.

'It's not your place to endanger our community, either.'

'I won't. I'm one stupid tourist. And the witches and vampires clearly have bigger problems.'

'You don't know that.'

'Pretty sure I do, actually. Or where are they? Maybe you know, and you just don't want to tell me.'

'If I did,' Lola snapped, 'then I certainly wouldn't tell you now.'

'Easy for you to say, seeing as you have both of your parents. You've never lost any family members to the witches, have you?'

'I lost Santi.' Lola gripped the edge of the table so hard her knuckles went white. 'How dare you?'

'How dare I what?' Cynthia couldn't believe herself. Her hands shook from adrenaline. 'Dream of a better world? If I had known him, I'd want justice. I'd at least want to know what happened. Your safety is an illusion—'

'Don't you think we know that?' Lola slammed her hand down on the table, making the plates rattle. 'I know, alright! Damn it, Cynthia. I miss him every day. I spend all my time at work trying to make sure the witches can't do it again. Just—tell me your father's name and I'll make enquiries. If anyone can find him, Anton can. But stop looking for witches and vampires, or we'll lose you, too.'

Her words made Cynthia feel sick with guilt.

'I'm sorry,' she said softly. 'I didn't realise…'

'No, of course not,' Lola said bitterly. 'Our people, we come and we go, and we affect other people's lives, and then we leave them behind and don't think of them again. You're right, it's a horrible life, always running, and very selfish, but it's the best one we have.'

'Or we fight.'

'Against witches?' Lola asked. 'What use is shifting against their magic?'

'I don't know.' Cynthia cleared her throat. 'His name is Justin. Justin Gastrell. Two Ls.'

'Okay,' Lola said, 'I'll see what I can find.'

They finished their dinner mostly in silence, and Cynthia left for home right after. On the way, she texted Lily.

> **Cynthia:** Hey, I really hate to be presumptuous, but Monica said Damien has an apartment here in Berlin. If it's empty, is there any chance I could stay there? Things are… complicated with my host family, and it might be better if I get out of their hair
>
> **Cynthia:** If not, though, I totally understand. I'll look for a hostel
>
> **Cynthia:** Thanks and I hope you're enjoying the US

She slept uneasily that night, haunted by Lola's words. By morning, Lily hadn't replied, and Cynthia found herself on the phone to Monica instead.

'I think you're reading too much into it,' Monica said once Cynthia had explained the situation. 'If they were really worried the witches were going to scoop them off the streets, they'd have left four years ago, after Santiago disappeared. That's what your mum would have done, right?'

'For sure,' Cynthia agreed, 'but I still don't want to be responsible for putting them in danger.'

'No, but you also want to find your father, right?'

'Right.' Cynthia sighed, sprawling back on her bed. 'So it's a catch-22.'

'Mm,' Monica said. 'Well… not entirely. I mean, Lola agreed to help you, which is a win. And you still have non-potentially-fatal options.'

'Such as?'

'How about you go bother the hunters again? I bet they know something. Having a dark mage in town is exactly the sort of thing hunters would want to know about, right?'

'I guess.' Cynthia sat up. 'Yeah, maybe you're right.'

'Course I'm right. I'm always right.'

Cynthia snorted. 'Sure, you keep believing that.'

'Rude.'

'Pshhh. What should I say to them?' Cynthia asked, pulling her shoes on.

'Bullshit them. Tell them the Council wants to know.'

'I can't do that. If Jeremiah finds out, he'll—'

'Thank you for doing him a favour?' Monica laughed. 'Tell him it was my idea. He'll laugh it off and tell you that I'm always coming up with bad ideas, and it would be better for your health to ignore me.'

'See, when you say that, it's funny. But if Jeremiah says that it's a threat.'

'Pshhh,' Monica mocked. 'Go on. You'll feel better for bullying a few hunters. They're so bully-able.'

'Why am I friends with you, again?'

'Because Nathan's so nice. You need someone to balance out his influence.'

'That sounds about right.' Cynthia rolled her eyes. 'Alright. I'm going to head out. I'll let you know how it goes.'

'Good luck!'

The hunter office was unchanged from Cynthia's previous visit. The air-conditioning was still too cold, the TV still wasn't working properly, and the receptionist was sitting in the same position, reading a magazine. Cynthia cleared her throat as she walked up to the counter.

The receptionist looked up, her expression closing off the instant she recognised Cynthia.

'Guten Morgen.'

'Guten Morgen,' Cynthia replied courteously, 'I'd like to make an enquiry.'

'We are closed.'

'I don't need to speak to a hunter. You should be able to look it up from your computer there.'

'I don't have the authorisation.'

'You don't know what the question is, yet.'

The receptionist pinched her lips together. Cynthia leaned her elbows on the counter and tried to channel Monica a bit less. Reading the woman's name badge, she tried, 'Look… Evelyn, I—we'd really appreciate it if you could check if a man named Justin Gastrell is in your database. He should be residing in the city.'

Evelyn frowned. 'Does the Council think we know every citizen of this city personally?'

'Of course not. He's a marked dark mage and a person of interest—' Cynthia hesitated, trying to think of an excuse, '—he's wanted back in Oxford.'

'For?'

'Practicing dark magic?'

Evelyn's expression was one of supreme disbelief, but she typed the name into the computer anyway, her manicured nails clicking against the keys. After several pregnant moments, she said, 'That name isn't in the database.'

'Are you sure? Gastrell with double L?'

'I'm sure.' Evelyn turned the monitor. The message was in German, but the meaning was unmistakeable. No search results.

'Look,' Cynthia twisted her fingers into her hair, fighting an overwhelming wave of despair, 'I lied, alright, this has nothing to do with the Council. I just really want to find him. He's my father, and he won't speak to me, and I'm worried if I don't find him soon I'll never see him again—' She cut herself off sharply, taking several deep breaths to dispel her tears.

Evelyn's expression had morphed into one of pity, which was no better, really. 'I am sorry,' she said. 'I can give you the phone number of the KUA in Bonn.'

It was the nicest thing she'd said to Cynthia, but conversely also the most useless.

'Thank you.' Cynthia sniffed. 'Yeah, why not? May as well exhaust all avenues before I give up.'

Evelyn produced a business card, which Cynthia accepted with a small, 'Thanks.'

'I will see you again, I'm sure.' Evelyn sounded rather droll. 'Goodbye, Miss Gastrell.'

Cynthia had to laugh. Miss Gastrell. That was a new one. It sounded utterly bizarre. 'Thanks,' she repeated. 'Bye.'

She descended the stairs battling tears. It wasn't fair. Why did Berlin have to have supernatural drama right when she was there? Why did no one keep records of these things? If they had been in Oxford, Jeremiah would have bashed their heads together for being so negligent.

He's a fucking criminal. How can they not know where he is in the city? For all they know, he could be the one murdering vampires—what did Lola say? Poisoning them.

Actually, that sounded like something a dark mage would do.

Cynthia kicked the pavement angrily, turning towards the U-Bahn. She had a whole day to kill before meeting Lola. If she was still meeting Lola tonight. Lola had been pretty angry. Another thing to worry about. Monica and Nathan never seemed to worry about these things. Monica would have just carried on prodding people until she got what she wanted. And no one ever got upset at Nathan. He could get away with the most outrageous things, just because he was nice, and somehow everyone still liked him. Cynthia couldn't seem to be nice enough or nasty enough, and so she was stuck in the middle, never quite managing to get along with anyone.

And it sucked.

And she'd been so lost in her bloody thoughts that it had taken her this long to realise there was someone behind her.

Following her.

Cynthia had been followed before. She remembered being seven years old, in Athens, and her mother explaining to her what to do if she thought someone was following her. *Stay calm. Don't run. Find a crowded place. Find a mother with children, ask to borrow her phone, and call for help.*

That had been years ago, before Nathan had taught her self-defence.

Anyway, Cynthia wasn't in the mood to hide.

Keeping her pace even, she scanned her surroundings. Spying a likely alleyway, she veered abruptly to the left. She was in luck: there was a row of bins against one wall. She sheltered behind the last one, waiting.

A moment later, a figure turned into the alley, glancing around. Cynthia jumped out, tackling him, and they both fell against the wall. He twisted like a snake beneath her, pushing her to the ground. Cynthia managed to swipe her leg at his, tripping him, and he fell on top of her legs.

'Scheiße! Ouch!'

'Who are you? What do you want?' Cynthia scrabbled for the knife she kept in her bag.

'It's me! Honestly, are you crazy? I thought you weren't a hunter!'

Her would-be attacker sounded young, and spoke with a German accent. After a moment, Cynthia managed to get her fingers around the knife, but when she looked up, she let go of it again with a laugh. It was the trainee hunter she'd met the last time she visited the hunter office.

'Gunther? Why were you following me?'

'I was waiting until you were away from the KUA to speak to you. You weren't meant to see me!'

'It might help if you were stealthier! A five-year-old would have caught you!'

'I'm not that bad!'

Cynthia snorted. 'Um, yeah, you really are.' She kicked her legs. 'Get off me.'

Gunther scrambled up, eyes wide. Cynthia had to laugh again. His jacket was askew, his hair a mess. He didn't look much like a dignified hunter. Scowling, he held out a hand and pulled her to her feet.

'How did you know I was following you?'

'My ex is a hunter. He taught me a few tricks.'

'He told you about the supernatural?' Gunther looked shocked. 'That's illegal. He could get kicked off the force.'

'He didn't tell me. I already knew.'

'But you're not supernatural.' Gunther squinted at her. 'Are you?'

'If you don't know, I'm not telling you.'

'Oh, come on!'

'No,' Cynthia said.

'I'll help you.'

'No.'

'I might know how to find your father.'

That brought Cynthia up short.

'What? How?' She frowned. 'You shouldn't eavesdrop.'

'Uh, hypocrite. You're here to spy on us.'

Cynthia crossed her arms. 'That's not true. I really am just on holiday.'

'On holiday, looking for your dad?'

'Yeah, exactly.'

Gunther stared at her pointedly. Cynthia met his gaze dead on. It wasn't hard. Either his growth spurt was late, or he just wasn't that tall, because he was only a few inches taller than her. After several seconds, Gunther looked away.

'I really do know useful stuff.'

'You'd be breaking the hunter code to tell me,' Cynthia pointed out.

'Look around. Have you seen a single vampire since you've been here? We don't need a code. We don't even need hunters anymore.'

'And you know why?' Cynthia guessed.

'No, of course not. They just disappeared. Stopped feeding. No one knows why, not even the witches.' Gunther shrugged. 'But I know a safe place you can go to ask questions.'

That was an offer too good to refuse.

'Fine.' Cynthia headed for the main road. 'Come on, then.'

'Where are you going?'

'I'm not revealing all my secrets to you in an alley full of smelly bins!'

Gunther sprinted to catch her.

'So, you'll tell me?' he asked as they started down the street. 'Really?'

Cynthia weighed her options. 'You have to swear not to tell anyone. And to stop following me.'

'I will, I will.'

'Say it properly.'

'I promise I won't tell anyone or follow you again.'

'Fine.' She paused dramatically. 'I'm a shapeshifter.'

'A what?'

'You know, like a person who can turn into an animal.'

'A werewolf?'

'No, not like a werewolf. I can turn into any animal. The last animal I looked at.'

'I've never heard of that.'

'No, well we keep ourselves secret, don't we?' Cynthia rolled her eyes. 'I'll show you, but not here. Now it's your turn.'

'Where?'

'Give me your mobile number, and we can arrange it. If your information is good.'

'That wasn't the deal!'

'Sorry, did you think I was going to give you a free show?'

Gunther huffed, but pulled his phone out. Shortly, they'd swapped numbers. Cynthia gave him an expectant look.

'Fine, fine,' he said, 'so, there's this bar.'

'A bar,' Cynthia said sceptically.

'It's called MIX. It's an illegal bar. We're not supposed to know about it.'

That sounded promising, actually. Witches and vampires loved illegal places.

'Where is it?'

'I'll text you the address, after—'

'Now.' Cynthia glared.

'No way. I'm not giving you it for free!' Gunther shifted his weight uneasily.

'You don't know it, do you?'

'What? Of course I do!'

'No, you don't.' By the look on his face, Cynthia knew she was right. 'You overheard someone talking about it—'

'Fine! So what if I did? I know it's real. It's in Mitte. The supes consider it neutral territory. Anyone can go there, and they're not allowed to hunt.'

'And you think I can get information there?'

'Well, it's better than sniffing around Potsdam, isn't it?'

Cynthia gave him a piercing look. 'Fine,' she said, pulling her phone out to text Nathan. 'I'll see what my contacts say. And if the information is good, then—and only then—I'll show you how I shift.'

'That's not fair!'

'Life isn't fair,' Cynthia said smugly. 'Better get used to it.'

CHAPTER EIGHT

LOLA WAS IN A BETTER MOOD when they met for drinks that evening. She was waiting outside the U-Bahn station in Kreuzberg with a smile on her face, dressed in jeans and a tank top that showed off the wolf tattoo on her back.

'I didn't know you had a tattoo,' Cynthia said.

'I got it as soon as I turned eighteen.' Lola stroked her shoulder and grinned. 'Dad was furious.'

'I bet.' Wilhelm didn't seem the type to approve of tattoos.

'Listen,' Lola said, 'I'm sorry about last night. I was… that stuff with Santi and Renata, it brings up old memories. I miss him a lot.'

'It's okay. I'm sorry I pushed,' Cynthia said, relieved.

'No, I'm sorry. You had a right to know, I mean, you should know that the witches are dangerous here. Shifters have gone missing before. That's why Mum and Dad are so scared, too. And if we'd have told you that earlier, then maybe things would have been… well, you'd have understood.'

'Maybe,' Cynthia said. 'But now, I think it's for the best if I find somewhere else to stay. I don't want to put your family in danger. That was never my intention.'

'I know.' Lola smiled. 'Did your friend get back to you?'

'Not yet. I'll give her until tomorrow, then try calling her.'

'Cool.'

The bar was a short distance from the station. Its front entrance was so covered in graffiti and old posters, that Cynthia would have totally overlooked it if Lola hadn't stopped and said, 'This is it.'

'Okay, I see what you mean by 'so Berlin',' Cynthia said.

'It is, isn't it?' Lola laughed. 'They do like fifty different kinds of beer. Come on.'

The inside followed the same theme as the outside; graffiti covered every inch of the wall except for the shelves behind the bar. They found Fritz, Luisa, and Klara in a cramped booth in the back.

'Hey-hey!' Fritz greeted. Luisa jumped up to hug Cynthia and Lola.

'I'm glad you made it,' she told Cynthia. 'We're going to have so much fun!'

'I hope you have a good alcohol tolerance,' Klara said, 'because this lot can drink all night.'

'I do,' Cynthia said. Shifters couldn't get drunk. 'I've never been out all night before.'

'We have to introduce you to Berlin-style nights out.' Fritz grinned. 'Beer?'

'Yes, please.'

In short order, Cynthia was a good deal poorer and severely testing her supernatural alcohol tolerance. Lola's friends drank beer like they were the ones who had supernatural healing. Even the vampires Cynthia knew back in Oxford hadn't drunk this much.

She was a good few in when she realised her phone was ringing. Digging it out, she saw it was Nathan.

'I have to take this,' she muttered to Lola. 'Be right back.'

Lola glanced at her phone and nodded. Cynthia slipped out of the booth and hurried away from them as she answered.

'Hey!' She darted a glance over her shoulder at Lola's friends. 'I wasn't expecting you to call back so quickly.'

'Sorry, did I catch you at a bad time?' Nathan's voice danced with amusement. 'Sounds like you're out somewhere. I hope it's not somewhere your mum would disapprove of?'

'No…nope. None of that.' Cynthia smiled. 'I'm being perfectly well behaved. All you can hear is, um, the TV.'

'Right.' Nathan laughed. 'So, what's the supernatural bar called?'

'*MIX*, apparently.'

'*MIX*. Hmm…' Nathan hummed quietly under his breath. 'Sorry, the hunter database is kinda slow.'

'That's okay.' Cynthia fiddled with her bag strap, studying the graffiti as she waited, feeling very out of place. Everyone seemed so relaxed and cool, and she was a ball of anxiety, hoping Lola wouldn't realise she was chatting to a vampire hunter on the phone.

She glanced over her shoulder again.

'Got it,' Nathan said. 'There's an address. I'll text it to you. It might be tricky to get in, though. Did your hunter friend tell you how?'

'No, I don't think he knew.' Cynthia had to laugh, remembering Gunther. He had nothing on Nathan. 'And he's not my friend.'

Nathan snickered. Cynthia's phone buzzed.

'Okay, I've sent you the address,' he said. 'But the database says there's a passphrase to get in.'

'What is it?'

'It's not recorded. You'll just have to try. Or ask someone. Would Lola know?'

'I doubt it. I don't think that's the sort of place she goes, and anyway, she'd be mad if I told her I wanted to go to *MIX*. You know how shifters get about other supernaturals. We just argued about it yesterday.'

'Yeah, Monica said. Hmm...' Cynthia heard Nathan's fingers clacking on his keyboard. 'Nope, nothing. Okay, either you can ask the hunters, or I can see if any Council contacts know. I'll text you what I find out, okay?'

'Sure.'

'Enjoy your TV programme.'

Cynthia giggled. 'I lied. It is a bar.'

'Of course you did.' Nathan laughed. 'I'm glad you're having fun. Ciao.'

'Bye.'

Cynthia hung up, still smiling. It was getting easier to talk to Nathan now there were a few hundred miles and a good bit of sea between them. She shoved her phone back in her bag.

'Didn't take you for the sort of person to break promises.'

Cynthia yelped and spun around. Lola was standing right behind her, leaning against the wall with her arms crossed and her hip cocked. Her expression was aggressive.

'What... what are you talking about?'

'Don't play dumb with me. I heard you talking to your friend.'

'I wasn't... I'm not...' But Cynthia's mind had gone blank. She couldn't summon up a single convincing excuse. 'Look, I know I said, yesterday... but this place is supposed to be safe.'

'I know all about MIX,' Lola said. 'Sure, you're safe whilst you're inside. But there's nothing stopping them from following you home, is there?'

'I won't go straight home,' Cynthia started.

'You won't go to MIX at all!'

'Has Anton found anything out yet, then?'

Lola made a face. 'I haven't asked him yet. I do also have a job to do, you know?'

'When, then?' Cynthia pushed. 'The day before I leave, so I don't have time to look?'

'It's not like that.'

'I'm only here for another week and a half!'

'Plenty of time for you to do damage, clearly,' Lola sneered. 'Where did you even find out about MIX? Were you already planning this when you spoke to me last night?'

'No! I found out about it today!'

'From who? Renata?'

'Of course not. I spoke to the hunters.' Cynthia crossed her arms. 'Ordinary humans. You didn't tell me I couldn't speak to them.'

'Ordinary *dangerous* humans!'

'They're not dangerous to us. Anyway, the one who told me isn't dangerous to anyone. He's just a kid. I knocked him flat on his back—' A slight exaggeration, not that Lola needed to know that. '—without any effort. He's barely trained.'

'And that changes things how?' Lola demanded. 'He has friends and family on the force. He only has to tell one of them.'

'I made him swear not to.'

'Oh, wow, you clearly thought of everything.' Lola rolled her eyes. 'That'll stop him.'

'I'm not going to stop looking. Anyway, you know about MIX, too. You know Renata.' Cynthia recalled Monica's point from that morning. 'Sometimes, I think you exaggerate the danger. If you were so scared, you'd have left.'

Lola looked away, studying the graffiti on the wall. Someone had doodled a series of cats committing suicide in creative ways.

'Okay, you know what? Fine. Let's go to MIX.'

'What?'

'You and me,' Lola said, 'together. I can make sure you don't do anything stupid. But you have to do something for me in return.'

'Okay.'

Lola smiled grimly. 'Seeing as you're so keen on being friends with witches, you can make friends with Renata. And find out what she knows about Santiago. Because I bet she knows what happened to him.'

'I don't think she does,' Cynthia cautioned.

'Someone in her coven does,' Lola replied, 'and if you want me to speak to Anton, and if you want to go to MIX, then you'll find out who.'

'I could just go to MIX on my own.'

'But this is better,' Lola said.

Cynthia chewed her lip, thinking it over. It wouldn't be bad to have backup—and someone who spoke German. 'Do you know how to get in?'

'Of course I do.'

'Fine. I'll speak to Renata. But we have to go to MIX tonight.'

Lola narrowed her eyes. 'Fine, we'll go tonight.'

They spent another hour with Lola's friends. Cynthia was sceptical, thinking that Lola was trying to postpone, but it turned out to not be a problem. They took a night bus to the city centre, disembarking in a residential area.

'This doesn't look right,' Cynthia said as they walked down a street of dirty art nouveau-style apartment blocks.

'This is correct. Trust me.'

Honestly, Cynthia trusted Lola less and less as time went on—so much for thinking Lola was nice—but she bit her tongue and trailed beside her friend until they stopped in a recessed gateway that led to a courtyard. In the light from the streetlights, the courtyard's cobblestones were cracked where tree roots had torn through them. Most of the apartment blocks were missing doors, and some of the windows had been boarded over.

'Charming,' Cynthia observed, pulling out her phone to crosscheck the address Nathan had sent. It matched.

Lola rang the bell for number thirty-seven. As they waited, Cynthia studied the graffiti around the gateway. Cramped between illegible loopy letters and an anarchists' A was a martini glass with the word MIX written inside the glass.

The intercom crackled. A female voice asked, 'Bloody Mary oder Red Russian?'

'Snakebite,' Lola replied confidently.

'Ein Moment bitte.' The intercom went dead.

'What was that?' Cynthia asked.

'Bloody Mary for vampire. Red Russian for witch.' Lola rolled her shoulders. 'The Red Russian was a witch who killed a bunch of people in the 1800s.'

'Snakebite for shifters?'

'Exactly.' Lola paused. 'Look, be careful of the bartender.'

'Why?'

'I don't know what she is. And that's always…'

'Worrying?'

'Yeah.'

'I'll be careful,' Cynthia said. She seemed to be saying that a lot, lately.

A short while later, an elegant woman approached from across the courtyard. She was tall and slender, dressed in jeans and a black T-shirt despite the heat, with brown skin and thick black hair. Something about the way she held herself reminded Cynthia of Monica. She guessed the woman to be about in her thirties, but she had a sort of agelessness about her.

'Lola, lange nicht mehr gesehen,' she greeted.

'Anjali,' Lola replied, 'this is Cynthia. Cynthia, Anjali is the owner and bartender of MIX.'

'English?' Anjali asked. She spoke with a fluid accent that was hard to pin to a single language. 'Welcome, Cynthia. Has Lola explained the rules to you?'

'Not yet,' Lola said.

'I will explain as we walk. Come in.' Anjali held the gate for them, then led them across the courtyard. They entered a stairwell that had been stripped of everything of value. Even the light fittings were gone. As they climbed, Anjali said, 'MIX has simple rules. Respect everyone. No fighting. All species allowed. Don't tell anyone how to get here. Access is by invitation only.'

'Whose invitation?' Cynthia asked. Had she broken a rule already?

'Mine,' Anjali said.

They had reached the second floor. A door stood open, spilling music and chatter into the hallway. Anjali turned to them. 'Do you agree to abide by the rules?'

'I agree,' Lola said.

'I agree,' Cynthia echoed.

'Very good. First drink is on the house.' Anjali's smile was cold. 'Lola did me favour once.'

Cynthia glanced at Lola, who looked a little uncomfortable.

'Come on,' she muttered, following Anjali inside.

Beyond the doorway was what had once been a simple two-room apartment. The walls had been knocked out, leaving a large open space. The bar was obviously handmade and sat against one graffiti-covered wall. The rest of the room was filled with mismatched tables and chairs, occupied by an eclectic mix of supernaturals. There were witches of all shapes and sizes, several people with no auras whatsoever, and a group of burly men with strangely energetic auras. In the corner, a singer sat playing the guitar and crooning in what sounded like Spanish. His aura, when Cynthia checked, glowed a dull lilac and seemed to pulse in time with the music.

Anjali had slipped behind the bar. Lola and Cynthia approached her, and she passed them each a beer.

'Empress Bernadette is performing at three, Die Zwinger at four. You came on a good night.'

'I'm not sure we'll stay that long,' Lola said, sipping her beer.

'You know I can't give you information if this is police business,' Anjali replied, looking busy wiping down the bar with a cloth that was dirtier than anything else in the room. 'The customers won't like it.'

'This isn't police. It's witch business.'

Anjali tilted her head, her hand still moving rhythmically back and forth across the counter. Cynthia took a moment to study her. Anjali had no aura, which ought to have meant she wasn't magical. But even without Lola's warning downstairs, Cynthia wouldn't have believed her own eyes on this one. Something about Anjali said that she was dangerous.

'You know the witches won't like you prying.'

'I know that someone needs to go and give the branches a good shake and see what falls out,' Lola replied.

'The information you seek will not win you any favours. That way lies only misery.' Anjali turned her gaze on Cynthia. 'For both of you.'

'You don't know what we're looking for,' Cynthia said.

Anjali smiled, her eyes empty. 'A name, yes?'

'Don't tell her,' Lola said. 'She'll only answer you in riddles and bargains.'

'You should have warned your friend better,' Anjali said. 'Feel free to look around. I can't stop others from talking.' She went back to wiping the bar.

'Come on.' Lola tugged Cynthia away, and they settled on a bench near the singer. He winked at Cynthia before going back to mouthing barely audible lyrics. 'Don't mind her. It isn't always clear if she's talking about things that have already happened or things that might happen.'

Cynthia shivered. 'She gives me the creeps.'

'That's intentional. She's trying to get rid of us.'

'Why?

'She doesn't like me coming here,' Lola replied. 'It was okay when I was still in school, but now I'm police. This place isn't licensed.'

'Oh.' Cynthia turned her beer around and around in her hands. She had loads more questions, but she wasn't sure how to ask them. 'So, what now?'

'Mingle, see what people know,' Lola said. 'You were the one who wanted to come.'

'I'm not good at this stuff.'

'No, you'd have taken Anjali's bargain. And she knows it. Stay away from her.'

Lola's scolding made Cynthia feel like a child. Annoyed, she stood. 'Fine, let's mingle.'

They drifted around the room, chatting to people, but it soon became obvious that there was nothing to be found. Too many people knew that Lola was with the police, for starters. The rest of them eyed Cynthia hungrily, studying her. It was awful, being a shapeshifter in a room full of witches.

After about half an hour, Cynthia muttered, 'Do you want another beer?'

'Yeah.' Lola passed over a few coins. 'Don't let her charge you more than two euros per beer.'

'Okay.'

Cynthia wove between the tables and approached the bar again. One of the stools had come free, and she settled on it.

'Can I get two more beers, please?'

Anjali set two bottles on the counter, accepting the coins. She rolled a euro coin between her fingers thoughtfully.

'Care for a wager?'

Cynthia darted a glance back at Lola, who was chatting to a stout man with a grey aura.

'What kind of a wager?'

'Heads or tails?'

'Tails.'

'Tails for the shifter.' Anjali flicked the coin into the air, caught it deftly, and slapped it against the back of her other hand. She lifted her fingers. 'Tails. You get your first favour free. The man in the window. He knows everything and everyone.'

Cynthia twisted around to look. 'Who?'

But Anjali was already moving on to serve another customer. Cynthia grabbed the beers and hopped off the stool. Two seconds later, Lola marched up.

'What are you doing flipping coins with Anjali? I just warned you!'

'It was just a game of heads or tails.'

'Sure, where you barter bits of yourself! Memories! Cynthia, you need to be careful.'

Cynthia swallowed, suddenly uneasy. 'I won,' she said.

'What did you win?'

'She told me to speak to the man in the window.' They both looked at the window overlooking the courtyard, where a man lounged, his legs propped up. As though he'd heard them, he looked up suddenly, swinging his legs down. His expression turned smug, like a cat that had just caught a canary.

He was tall and rather slender, with messy blond hair. Cynthia studied his aura. It was red, and it refracted light the way a precious gemstone might. It made his skin shimmer and hurt her eyes. She looked away, blinking.

'I don't know him,' Lola murmured.

'I've seen his aura before,' Cynthia said. She hadn't realised it until she said it, but it was familiar.

'Where?'

'I don't remember.' It was on the tip of her tongue, but the more she reached for it, the more it seemed to slip away. 'It'll come back. I'm sure I've seen it before.'

The man flicked his fingers, beckoning them over. Cynthia took a step towards him, but Lola stopped her.

'Remember what I said about trusting Anjali? We ask around first.'

'Fine.'

Lola steered her to the table of burly men, prodding one of them in the shoulder. 'Hey, Rolf.'

'Hallo,' the man returned.

'How's it going?'

'Alright. We don't want any trouble, yeah?'

'No trouble,' Lola promised. 'The guy in the window? You know him?'

The men around the table exchanged glances. 'Nah,' Rolf said finally, 'but he's always there, lately. Doesn't drink much. Anjali lets him be.'

'Thanks.' Lola glanced at Cynthia, her expression wary.

'I'll speak to him,' Cynthia said. 'How bad can it be?'

'Bad.'

'He's just a warlock. I've handled warlocks before.'

'They're never just warlocks,' Lola said. 'Fine. Want me to come with you?'

Cynthia shook her head. Leaving Lola to canvas the rest of the room, she approached the mysterious stranger. He watched her like a fish he was reeling in, curious, hungry. Cynthia stopped a few paces in front of him.

'Hi.' Up close, he was rather intimidating. His age was impossible to tell, maybe twenty, maybe thirty. He had cold green eyes and a sort of otherworldliness to him that she'd only seen in a few people before. Monica, in the midst of a complicated spell. Jeremiah or Damien, who were both ancient vampires. The Witch Council in Oxford.

'Hello, Cynthia,' he purred.

'How do you know my name?'

'You've introduced yourself at least three times since I got here.' His smile was feral. 'I know everything about you.'

'I doubt that.' Cynthia's heart seemed to be trying to beat right out of her chest. 'Why were you listening in on my conversations? How could you hear from that far away?'

'I have many talents,' he drawled. 'We don't get a lot of your species around here.'

'I wonder why,' Cynthia said.

The man chuckled. 'Anjali thinks I can answer your question. So, go on. Ask.'

'Shouldn't you already know? If you've been listening in?'

He smiled, leaning back. 'You've been circumspect. Maybe I want to make sure we're on the same page.'

Cynthia frowned. 'I'm looking for someone. A dark mage named Justin Gastrell.'

'And you think you can find him in a city of some million, with only a name? Seems a little ambitious.'

'You'd know him if you saw him, trust me.'

'I've seen many people, shapeshifter.'

Cynthia was starting to get annoyed. Mind games, always mind games. 'Have you seen him?'

'What's it worth to you?'

'I'm not making bargains. I don't even know you.'

He smiled again, dark and cold.

'Leon.' He took Cynthia's hand and brushed his lips against her knuckles. A shiver ran down Cynthia's spine. 'At your service.'

Cynthia yanked her hand back, her heart feeling as though it was about to leap out of her throat. Leon laughed.

'Jumpy shifter. What are you afraid of?'

'I'm not a fan of unknown men kissing my hand.'

'But you know me now.' He tilted his head, studying her like she was a puzzle.

Cynthia wiped the back of her hand on her skirt to get rid of the feeling of his lips. 'You think I'm going to trust you when the only thing I know about you is your name? Seems a little ambitious.'

For the first time, Leon smiled a genuine smile. 'Is that how it is? In that case, I should relish the opportunity to get to know you better. Go out with me? I'd love to hear the perspective of a shapeshifter.'

'No thanks,' Cynthia said tersely. 'I don't date creeps. Seeing as you obviously don't know where Justin Gastrell is, I'm going to find someone else to speak to.' She turned away.

'I never said I didn't know where he was.'

Cynthia spun back. Leon's gaze was entirely too smug. She could've kicked herself for taking the bait.

'If you knew, why bother playing mind games?'

'Mind games?' Leon asked innocently. 'Why would I play mind games?'

'Why is the earth round? Why do vampires drink blood?' Cynthia glowered at him in frustration. 'Do you know, or don't you know?'

Leon's eyes danced with mirth. 'Do vampires drink blood? Is it the blood that nourishes them, or the magic? Could the magic not come from another, more efficient source?'

'Of course not. Everyone knows vampires have to drink blood.' Even Cynthia, who had not, technically, been aware of the existence of vampires until she was sixteen. 'Can we get to the point?'

Leon slid off the windowsill. Standing, he was much taller than she was. He brushed his fingers through the hair that was sticking to her face, the pads of his fingers soft against her skin. Cynthia shuddered and stepped back.

'Stop it.'

'You never answered my question,' Leon said.

'What question?'

'What's it worth to you?'

'I told you, I'm not making deals with people I don't know.'

'You know me as well as any other person in this room, English girl.' Leon smiled. 'And you'd have bargained with them. Am I special?'

'Do you know where he is?'

Leon dipped his head a little. 'I don't know Mr Gastrell.'

'Fine, in that case—'

'But,' Leon continued, 'I may know where a Mr Gastrell would make his residence, if indeed, as you say, he has made his residence in Berlin.'

Cynthia's head was starting to hurt, quite a feat, considering she had supernatural healing.

'So you do know? Or you don't know?'

'Now it's your turn. What's the information worth? The tears of a virgin?'

'I'm not—' Cynthia felt her cheeks heating up.

'The kiss of a lover? A date with a mysterious stranger?'

'You are so full of crap.' Cynthia took another step back. 'I can find out on my own, thanks.'

'Suit yourself, Cynthia Rymes.'

She turned and hurried away, the back of her neck prickling under his heated gaze. When she reached Lola, Cynthia muttered, 'Come on, let's get out of here.'

'Finally!' Lola jumped up, darting an uneasy look towards Anjali. As they entered the stairwell, Cynthia glanced back. Leon was watching her, framed by the window. There was something ethereal about his features, but not in a good way. Predatorial.

Dangerous.

Cynthia turned away.

'Did you get anything useful?' Lola asked.

'Not in the slightest. Just mind games and more mind games.'

'I could have told you.' Lola sighed. 'Anton will be a better bet. Come on. You can crash at my place.'

They crossed the courtyard swiftly and let themselves out the gate. It was already almost dawn, the sky just lightening on the eastern horizon. Cynthia stared at it in surprise. Where had the night gone?

'Cynthia?' Lola called. She was already a few steps ahead. 'Come on, the trains should be opening soon. It's easier than the night bus.'

Cynthia jogged to catch her up. They rounded a few corners, and suddenly she was in an area she recognised, near Rosenthalerplatz, where she'd gone to a museum the day she'd seen her father. The uneasy feeling, which manifested as a tension between her shoulders, began to ebb. Lola was right. Supernaturals were bad news, and the more time Cynthia spent around them, the more she missed ordinary, simple human concerns.

As they approached the stairs to the U-Bahn, Lola paused. She reached for her belt, pulling out her police badge. Cynthia hadn't realised she had it on her.

Following Lola's gaze, she saw a man and a woman, talking on the steps.

'Lola?'

'It's probably nothing. Come on.'

They were still a couple of metres away when suddenly the man jumped at the woman, grabbing her shoulders. He was babbling in broken German; Cynthia couldn't make out a word. She understood the woman, though, shouting in a mixture of English and French.

'Get off—arrête! Laisse-moi! Get off me!'

'Sie müssen mir helfen! Ich muss die Hexen finden!'

'Get off!' the woman screamed. She shoved him with supernatural strength, and the man lurched back. In a flash, the woman had run off down the stairs, the air shimmering around her with magic. A witch. The man turned, his gaze fixing on Cynthia and Lola. His eyes glowed an unnatural red; his skin was so pale it was almost translucent.

A vampire.

'Gestaltwandlerinnen?' Faster than the eye could track, he lunged towards them. Cynthia stumbled backwards, consumed by fear, but the vampire never reached her. As he left the shadow of the stairs, the sun rose above the horizon and lit his skin reddish-gold. He screamed, an unearthly, chilling scream, as his body caught fire. In a matter of seconds, he had burnt away to nothing but a pile of ash.

CHAPTER NINE

LOLA WAS ON THE PHONE, and Cynthia's insides were still dancing the tango as they caught the U-Bahn home.

She'd known about vampires for two years now. Before that, she had thought shifters and witches were the only supernaturals. Her mother had hidden knowledge of vampires and werewolves, hunters, and a myriad of other groups, from her, ostensibly for her safety. Not that knowing about vampires had really changed anything for shifters. The witches still posed the main danger to them.

In those two years since Nathan had broken the news, Cynthia had never seen a vampire burn. She had known, objectively, that they did burn if they didn't drink blood. Official statistics said they could go around a week, maybe a little longer, before they combusted in sunlight.

But Cynthia had never seen it happen.

The U-Bahn swayed, making her stomach slosh about again. She'd puked, embarrassingly. Lola had been pretty calm about the whole thing. She'd brushed the dust away with her foot, made sure no one else was around to see, hustled Cynthia into the U-Bahn, and called Anton. Anton would make sure no one had filmed it and put it on Twitter. That was his job.

'Shouldn't we tell the vampires?' Cynthia had asked. Lola had just laughed.

'There are no vampires around to tell.'

It left a sour note in her stomach.

Now, Cynthia played with her phone. It wasn't the first death she'd seen, but they never got easier. Nathan or Monica would have been calm, but Cynthia wasn't cut out for this. Once again, she was the one who felt too acutely. She couldn't stop herself from wondering if he'd had friends, a family. Had he been recently turned? What had made him go without blood for so long?

What had he wanted? *Hexen* meant witches, the single word Cynthia had understood. He'd been looking for the witches.

She glanced at Lola, but her friend was still engrossed in her phone call. Cynthia opened up the map Nathan had sent her and found the rough area they'd been in. Rosenthalerplatz was right near Hackescher Markt, and that whole area was shaded red. High supernatural activity. It was where she'd seen her father, too.

Coincidence?

Or was that where the witches were hiding?

Lola hung up the phone. 'This is us.' She gestured to the doors.

Cynthia hastily closed the map. 'Is Anton taking care of it?'

'He said that probably no one saw. We're lucky it was so early.'

'That's good.' Except it wasn't, was it? Because a life had been extinguished, and she and Lola were the only ones who knew.

'What could cause him to burn like that?' Cynthia asked in a small voice as they disembarked the train and headed above ground.

'Lack of blood,' Lola said. 'Try not to obsess. Put it out of your mind.'

'I've never seen…'

'Cynthia, it will haunt you if you let it.'

'I know, I know.' Nathan had warned her of the same thing.

'Before you sleep, message my mum,' Lola said as they entered her apartment. 'She'll be worried if she wakes up and you're not back.'

'Okay.' Cynthia pulled her phone out to do that. 'Can I take a shower before I sleep?'

'Sure.'

'Thanks.'

She felt slightly better after a shower. Wearing a pair of Lola's old pyjamas, Cynthia curled up in the bed in the spare room, staring at the ceiling. That had been the first vampire she'd seen in this city, and he'd died. What was going on with the vampires in Berlin? What could affect every vampire in an entire city? There had to be hundreds of them in Berlin alone, and vampires were strong, immortal. What could make all of them hide?

She reached her hand over to her bedside table, grasping her phone.

To text Nathan, or not?

The thought made Cynthia's stomach curdle. Even several countries away, she was still dependent on Nathan. Every time something went wrong, she picked up the phone. He was going to start getting annoyed. No, she'd wait until she had proof. Calling him just because a vampire was dead, well, what could he do about it? The vampire was dead. She didn't even know his name.

Cynthia turned on her side, pushing the covers down to cool off. Things would look better after she slept.

She awoke to her phone ringing insistently right beside her ear. Cynthia sat up groggily, swaying with dizziness. She was exhausted.

What...?

Oh yeah. It all came back in a rush; *MIX*, the vampire, falling asleep holding her phone. *Oops.* She fished it out of the sheets and answered without looking.

'Hello?'

'Cynthia?' It was her mother. 'Where have you been? You haven't called me in ages. I was worried.'

'Morning, Mum.' Her voice came out as a hoarse croak. *Shit.*

'It's afternoon. I called Brigitte; she said you never came home last night.'

'I stayed over at Lola's. I texted Brigitte.'

'That's not good enough. Do you know how we worry? Berlin is a big city, Cynthia. You could find all manner of trouble, and we wouldn't know about it.'

'Ugh.' Cynthia lay down again, waiting for her body to adjust to its new state of being awake. What time was it? She definitely needed another few hours of sleep. Was Lola up yet?

Her mother, heedless that she wasn't listening, continued full-steam-ahead.

'...we really need to know that you're safe. How do you think Brigitte will feel if something happens? She agreed to be responsible for you—'

'She's not responsible for me. I'm an adult,' Cynthia cut in.

'Don't take that tone with me.'

'Well, it's true!' Cynthia took another shot at sitting up, this time with more success. Her stomach churned. Her tongue tasted like stale milk. Water. Breakfast. In that order. 'I'm eighteen. I've been here two weeks, and I haven't found any trouble. When are you going to let go? What will you do when I move out of home?'

None of this was new. They'd had a thousand arguments on this same topic over the last few months. Cathy Rymes's overprotectiveness had only become more stifling as she grew older. And the more she pushed back, the harder her mother clung on.

'You're not moving out yet, therefore you still live by my rules.'

'Mum, let it go. None of my friends have to report their every move back to their parents. What are you going to do, anyway? You're a thousand miles away.'

'It's not quite that far. I'm less than two hours away by plane.'

Cynthia rolled her eyes. 'I'm not texting you on demand. I budgeted a certain amount for my phone for this trip, and I'm already over—' Her own fault, for calling Nathan and Monica so often. '—I did text Brigitte, so really, you're panicking over nothing. All we did last night was go out drinking, you know, like normal teenagers, and I can't even get drunk.'

'I don't like it when you're out late at night.'

'You won't be satisfied unless I promise to stay living with you until I'm thirty. Sometimes I think you want Emma and me to grow up with severe social anxiety.'

'Cynthia, that's not on.'

'No, you're right, that's *not* on.' Cynthia crawled out of bed, annoyance lending her strength. 'Call me back when you can think straight. I'm going to get breakfast. Lunch. Whatever. Bye, Mum.'

She hung up, her annoyance a living, breathing thing. This was the problem in her life, summed up in one single phone call. She couldn't live. She couldn't explore things for herself, figure out who she was. Who was Cynthia Rymes, away from her family? Well, if her family would leave her alone for five minutes, maybe she'd be able to figure that out.

Tossing her phone onto the covers, she searched for yesterday's clothes. A moment later, there was a knock on the door.

'Come in!'

It was Lola, fresh out of the shower and armed with a stack of clothes.

'Hey, I heard you talking.'

'Yeah, my mum called.' Cynthia rolled her eyes. 'Overprotective Mama Shifter Syndrome.'

Lola laughed. 'It gets better once you've moved out, and they realise they can't call you every second of the day.'

'I sure hope so.'

'Here.' Lola tossed her the clothes. 'You can borrow those and give them to Mum to wash.'

'Thanks.'

'Shall we go get ice cream? Fritz thinks it's a good hangover cure.'

Cynthia laughed. 'May as well.'

A fun day out with Lola and Fritz turned out to be just what Cynthia needed. They got ice cream, then trekked deep into the old area of East Berlin, where all of the apartment blocks were tall, utilitarian, and distinctly Soviet. There, Lola took her around the museum in the old Stasi headquarters, and for a few hours, Cynthia forgot about vampires, witches, and other supernatural drama.

It would have been the perfect day, if not for the fact that she couldn't shake the feeling she was being followed. Her neck would prickle at the funniest of times, and whenever she looked back, there seemed to be someone there, a dark figure who was always just out of sight.

But when she blinked, he was gone.

Paranoia, it was probably just paranoia because of what had happened last night.

Still, she took a roundabout route to get home. The last thing she wanted was to lead anyone back to the Deckers. As she climbed the stairs to the front door, a black cat darted past her.

A black cat crossing your path from right to left was bad luck, right? No, wait, was it the other way around? Cynthia had to laugh at herself. *Now I really am being ridiculous,* she thought as she unlocked the front door. She took two steps before she realised something and glanced back. The cat was gone, of course.

But looking at it, Cynthia hadn't picked up its form.

That only happened in two cases: one, the animal was too far away. Cynthia had a range of about ten or so metres. Two, the animal in question was a shifter. You couldn't steal the form of another shifter.

'Who…?'

When she entered the apartment, she immediately called out, 'Brigitte? I'm home.'

'In the lounge, dear.'

As she turned the corner, Cynthia found both Brigitte and Wilhelm sitting there, watching TV.

'Good evening,' Wilhelm said.

'Hi.' Cynthia glanced around, but there was no evidence that someone else had been here. Maybe the cat had just passed her by too fast?

'Did you have a good time out with Lola?' Brigitte asked.

'Oh, yes thanks. But, uh, what did you tell my mum? She called me earlier. She was really worried.' Cynthia frowned. 'I didn't mean to worry anyone.'

'That's okay,' Brigitte said. 'We spoke to Lola just now.' She patted her phone. 'Next time, maybe text us the night before if you're going to be out all night?'

'I will. I am sorry. I didn't realise I'd be out that late.' Cynthia darted a glance between the two of them. Brigitte was at ease, but Wilhelm looked rather displeased.

'Do you need help with dinner?' Cynthia asked finally.

'That would be good. Thank you.'

Somehow, though, the matter didn't seem resolved. Both Wilhelm and Brigitte were distracted during dinner. Much later that evening, Cynthia climbed down the stairs from the attic to go and use the bathroom. The apartment was dark, but light was shining beneath the door to the Deckers' bedroom. Cynthia crept past, her footsteps halting when she heard soft voices.

'...genau so wie Santiago, sie hört uns nicht zu—'

'Sie ist nur ein Kind,' Brigitte replied.

Cynthia stood dead still in the hall, listening to their whispers, but she couldn't pick out anything more. Heart pounding in her throat, she slipped into the bathroom. If only she could understand. They'd mentioned Santiago. What had they been talking about?

She was fiercely curious, but she didn't dare tell Brigitte she'd overheard. Still, with no new information, there didn't seem to be much Cynthia could do. She spent that weekend by the lake, sometimes with Brigitte and other times alone. Doing nothing was frustrating, but it kept her host family happy.

On Sunday, she'd just headed upstairs after dinner when her phone buzzed.

Gunther: Hey, this is Gunther Ditka

Gunther: Did you go to MIX?

Gunther: You promised to show me your shifter form

Cynthia: Sorry! I had an eventful weekend

Cynthia: Let's meet tomorrow?

They arranged to meet at two PM the next day, after Gunther finished training. Cynthia wanted somewhere neutral; Gunther suggested an area a little out of the city from where the Deckers lived. When she arrived, she found more lakes and greenery. Gunther looked smaller somehow without his uniform. He was in shorts and a T-shirt, leaning against a railing, waiting for her.

'Hey,' she greeted awkwardly.

'Hi.' Gunther grinned. 'So, somewhere private.'

'Somewhere we can't be seen.'

He gestured off down the road. As they started walking, he asked, 'Did you go to *MIX*?'

'Yes.'

'Where is it? What's it like?'

His enthusiasm was rather cute.

'It's in Mitte, like you said. My friend gave me the address.'

'Your hunter friend?' Gunther asked.

'My hunter friend.' Cynthia considered what to tell him. 'It's very basic. Lots of graffiti. There were all different sorts of witches there, and I think maybe werewolves, too.'

'Wow! And did you find out about your father?'

'No,' Cynthia said disappointedly. 'Everyone just wanted to mess me around.'

'I'm sorry.' Gunther touched her arm, smiling sincerely. 'I'm sure you'll find him.'

'You don't know anywhere else like that, do you?' Cynthia asked.

'No, they don't tell me anything.'

'Oh,' she replied dejectedly. It was just like Nathan; he'd always complained of the same thing before he graduated.

'I might be able to find out, though.'

She glanced up in surprise. Gunther shrugged uncomfortably. 'Look, promise you won't tell anyone?'

'I swear.'

'I know how to get on my dad's computer. I could look in the database. See if there's anything else.'

'You'd do that for me?' Cynthia asked, torn between suspicion and hope.

Gunther shrugged. 'You seem… nice? It's not like you're going to hurt anyone, right?'

'I won't.' Cynthia's mind was racing. She felt hopeful, all of a sudden, and it was intoxicating.

'I was thinking, though… two's safer than one, right?' Gunther avoided her gaze. 'I'm decent at self-defence.'

Cynthia's instinct was to say no. She'd only end up being responsible for him. But then, hunters knew a lot of useful stuff. And this was far too good an opportunity to pass up.

'Alright. If you find me more places I can look, I'll take you with me.' *If it's safe, she added in her head.*

'Really?' Gunther's face lit up. 'Thanks! I won't make you regret it.'

'You better not,' Cynthia said, only half-joking. 'I expect you to look after yourself.'

'Hey! Just because you got me that one time…'

'Uh-huh, that one time. You've been training for years!'

They ribbed each other back and forth until they found a spot in the trees, away from any roads or paths. Almost immediately, Cynthia's nerves made a reappearance. 'So, um, maybe turn your back?'

'Why?'

'I have to get naked!'

'Oh!' Gunther went an interesting shade of red. 'Oh, right.' He turned his back hastily.

Cynthia began pulling off her clothes. She'd tried picking up Gracie's form for this, but it wasn't to be. There'd been three different dogs on the train, and since they'd been in the trees, she'd seen all manner of squirrels and birds. It was pretty annoying changing forms that quickly; it was almost impossible to keep a specific form for too long. Now, she absorbed the form of a sparrow, taking in how it twittered, the way its wings moved, how fast its little heart was beating. The knowledge slipped into her brain, filling up all the empty corners. She gave in to it, and it displaced her human self seamlessly.

The smaller your form, the harder the shift. It wasn't just getting your mass that small—which involved a lot of poking, prodding, and squeezing—but it was tough to maintain, as well. There was actually a shifter community on Facebook that ran competitions to see who could maintain small forms for the longest. Cynthia's personal best for a sparrow was about thirty-five minutes.

It took her a few moments to figure out how her wings worked. Finally, she managed to flutter up and land on Gunther's shoulder. He yelped loudly.

'Hey, hau ab—wait, Cynthia?'

Cynthia chirped at him, almost overbalancing when he moved. Gunther reached for her, and she managed to manoeuvre onto his fingers. Controlling wings was *hard*.

'That's so cool! Can you become any animal? How long can you stay like that? Wait, show me how you fly! I want to film it.'

No filming!

Cynthia pecked him sharply. Gunther swore in German.

'Alright, alright, no filming. I get it. But fly around anyway.'

After a few false starts, Cynthia managed to get the hang of flying. She flitted around Gunther for a few minutes, then almost fell out of the air when a sudden buzzing cut through the stillness of the forest.

Danger!

'I… I think it's your phone.' Gunther rifled through her clothes and lifted it, waving it at her. 'Want me to answer?'

No! Cynthia chirruped furiously, flying down to her clothes and immediately starting the shift back. Gunther turned away, his cheeks bright red. Once she was standing, Cynthia lifted her wings—no, arms—and grabbed her T-shirt, tugging it on.

'Who is it?'

'Uh, it's a German number.' Gunther turned back just enough to pass her the phone. Still dressing one-handed, Cynthia answered.

'Hello?'

'Cynthia Rymes? Is this a bad time?'

'Um, no, not at all. Just a sec.' She balanced the phone between her ear and shoulder and managed to get her knickers and shorts on. 'Sorry about that. Who's speaking?'

'This is Anton Matussek.'

'Anton?' Cynthia echoed in surprise. 'Oh. I wasn't expecting you to call.'

'No? So you didn't know Lola was putting your case to me?'

'No, I mean yeah, I knew.' Cynthia shut up before she could dig herself a hole. 'Can you help?'

'Perhaps this is a conversation best had in person?'

'Um… sure. I don't mind meeting up.' Cynthia managed to get one sandal on and shifted her balance to work on the other. 'What were you thinking?'

'I'll text you an address. Are you free tomorrow night?'

She was now.

'I think I can make that work.'

'Excellent, I'll see you there.'

CHAPTER TEN

ON HER WAY HOME, Cynthia called Lola.

'Hey,' Lola greeted when she picked up. 'Good timing. I just got off work.'

'Yeah, hey.' Cynthia studied a few of the ads on the opposite wall of the train. 'Thanks for speaking to Anton.'

'Oh, he got hold of you?'

'Yeah, about an hour ago.'

'Great, well, I hope he helps.' Lola paused. 'Just be careful with him. He's effective, but he's hardly a nice guy. If you want me to come along with you…'

'I'm sure I'll be okay,' Cynthia replied. She wasn't really comfortable sharing the gritty details of her father's past with Lola. The Deckers wouldn't be pleased to know she was the daughter of a dark mage and known murderer. 'Anyway, I just wanted to say thanks…'

'When are you meeting him?'

'Tomorrow.'

'Good.' Cynthia could hear traffic faintly on Lola's end. 'Have you called Renata yet?' she asked.

Immediately, Cynthia's mood turned sour. She'd been trying to forget about that particular agreement. 'Not yet.'

'Just remember, you promised.'

'I know, I know.' Cynthia sighed. 'I'll call her right now.'

'Great,' Lola said. 'Anyway, I need to go to the supermarket. I'll see you soon. We should do dinner again before you leave.'

'Yeah.' Cynthia chewed her lip. 'About that. What would you say if I extended my trip?'

Lola was silent for what felt like an indecently long time. 'Are you thinking of doing that?' she asked cautiously.

'Nothing's set in stone yet,' Cynthia assured her. 'Depends on what

Anton comes up with.'

'Oh… well… I can't obviously say yes on behalf of my parents.'

'No, I mean, I'd find somewhere else to stay.'

'Right. Well, that might be okay.' Lola didn't sound too sure. 'You'd better speak to Mum and Dad. They can advise you on hostels.'

'I will. Thanks.'

'Alright, well… bye.'

'Bye.' Cynthia hung up, frowning. For the first time, she found herself doubting her friendship with Lola. They were friends, right? She had always assumed they were. If the roles had been reversed, Cynthia would have been more enthusiastic about the prospect of her friend staying.

Maybe something else had been distracting Lola?

Weird.

She'd made a promise, though, so she put it out of her mind and instead found the number Lola had texted to her. That Lola had Renata's phone number was another oddity. Lola remained adamant that they had never been friends, so how had she got it? And why hold onto it when they were no longer at school together?

Renata took a long time to pick up.

'Renata Friedemann.'

'Hi, Renata, this is Cynthia.'

'Cynthia?' Renata echoed in obvious confusion. 'Who?'

'The shapeshifter. We met at the memorial in Kreuzberg.'

Renata was silent for a long time. 'Oh,' she said finally, 'how did you get my number?'

'From Lola. I was wondering if you would be willing to meet up.'

'Why?'

That was a good question. Cynthia was no good as espionage. One of the reasons why she'd delayed calling Renata was because she had no idea what to tell her.

'Maybe it's better to discuss that in person,' she deferred.

'Is that so?' Renata asked sceptically.

'Please? I—Lola doesn't know I'm calling—I want to ask a favour.'

'Alright.'

'Really?' Cynthia asked in relief.

'Really, but only because Lola doesn't know.' Renata snorted. 'And maybe it'll get you out of Berlin sooner.'

'Um, that's maybe what I wanted to talk about?'

'Meet me back at the memorial,' Renata said. 'Tonight. Sunset. I get off work late.'

'Okay, thanks.'

'Don't thank me, Dog-Girl. I'm hardly doing you a favour.'

Kindness just didn't pay off with some people. 'Fine. See you tonight—oh!'

Renata had hung up.

Rolling her eyes, Cynthia texted Monica.

> **Cynthia:** I've found your soulmate
>
> **Monica:** Are they hot?
>
> **Cynthia:** She is the bluntest person I've ever met
>
> **Monica:** Does she speak English? Pass me her number

There was just no winning with some people.

That evening, Cynthia made her way to Kreuzberg and climbed the hill. The rush of water down the waterfall was a great accompaniment to her racing thoughts. What to tell Renata? Why did Renata hate Lola? Did Renata know who had killed Santiago?

Was Cynthia walking into a trap?

There was a smattering of people at the top of the hill, but Renata wasn't there yet. Cynthia climbed onto the podium and walked around the memorial, looking for traces of magic. It was only the one side of the memorial that transformed from her proximity. She stood close enough to keep it from transforming back, and pulled out her phone to translate the German.

'What are you doing?'

Cynthia lowered her phone, twisting around. A man was standing behind her, his face in shadow. A moment later, she recognised him. It was the warlock from *MIX*, the one with the red aura.

'Leon.'

'Hello, Cynthia Rymes. We meet again.'

'So we do,' Cynthia said suspiciously. 'What are you doing here?'

'What does one do in the presence of a memorial?' Leon asked. 'Remember.'

Cynthia glanced sceptically back at the memorial. 'Denkmal für die in den Hexenkriegen verlorenen Vorfahren. 749 – 1179 AD,' she read out clumsily. 'I'm no expert in German, but how can you remember something that happened a thousand years ago?'

'I don't know.' Leon smiled, but there was something sad about his mien. 'Can you?'

'Of course not.'

'But you're here too,' he pointed out.

'I'm meeting someone.' Cynthia glanced around again, hoping Renata would appear to rescue her. No luck. She hadn't texted either. Cynthia tucked her phone away, taking the moment to covertly study Leon. He was staring at the names on the memorial. There was something unchanged about him, and she realised suddenly what it was: his clothes. He was wearing the exact same jeans and long-sleeve T-shirt as he had been at *MIX*.

'Do you come here often?' she asked.

'Often enough, I suppose.' Leon turned away from the memorial. 'It's a good place to think.'

'Do you know what the memorial is for?'

'Of course.' Leon seemed surprised. 'Don't you?'

'I don't speak German.'

'Really? It's not that dissimilar from English.'

Cynthia gave him an incredulous look. 'It's completely different. I only understand one word.' She pointed to the memorial. '*Hexen* is witches.'

'So it is.' Leon smirked. 'But none of the names on this list belong to witches.'

'How do you know?'

'You really don't know what it's for?' He studied her face, as though he thought she was joking. 'Translate it.'

Cynthia pulled her phone out again. Painstakingly, she typed out the phrase in Google Translate.

'Memorial for the ancestors lost in the witch wars.' When she looked up, Leon was smiling.

'Remarkable.'

'What is?'

'Nothing.' His smile grew. 'You don't know who the ancestors are?'

'No.'

Leon turned away, amusement radiating from his every pore. Cynthia felt a spur of irritation.

'Don't play games! I bet you don't know, either.'

Leon laughed. It melted years off of his face; suddenly, he didn't look too much older than Cynthia. After a few seconds, he sobered.

'You're funny.'

'Not intentionally,' Cynthia snapped.

'Don't be angry. I didn't mean to offend you. The ancestors were vampires.'

'Oh—'

'Cynthia?'

They both turned. Renata emerged at the top of the stairs, her face flushed from the climb. Her gaze flicked from Cynthia to Leon, and her eyes narrowed, her posture turning aggressive. 'What's he doing here?'

'Huh?' Cynthia glanced at Leon. The amusement was gone from his gaze. 'He was here when I got here.'

'Oh.' Renata stared at him. 'We arranged a private meeting.'

'I shall leave you to it.' Leon bowed stiffly, a proper eighteenth-century style bow. 'Well met, witchling, Cynthia.' He sauntered off. Oddly, Cynthia missed his company. For a second, he'd relaxed, even teased her. And now, she was back to politicking with witches.

'Sorry,' she said to Renata. 'I genuinely didn't know he'd be here.'

'It's fine.' Renata busied herself tying her hair back into a ponytail, under the guise of which she glanced around suspiciously. Cynthia didn't blame her; she'd done the same, but it was odd to recognise the same paranoia in others. 'Do you know who he is?'

'Leon?' Cynthia asked. 'No, do you?'

'No one does.' Renata shrugged. 'He just turned up last year and stayed.'

'Wouldn't he be registered with the KUA?'

Renata pulled a few cartons out of her bag. 'If he is, the vampires aren't telling.'

'I thought he was a warlock?'

Renata looked up suddenly. 'Hmm? Of course. But the vampires take new registrations in the city. They always have.' She held out a carton. 'You want? I work in the kitchen. They give me leftovers.'

It turned out to be Chinese takeaway. Deliberately dismissing her qualms about taking food from a witch, Cynthia sat beside Renata on the memorial. She was supposed to be befriending the other girl, and that meant gestures of trust. Not refusing food because it might be poisoned.

'So?' Renata asked at length. 'What's so secret that you stole my phone number from Lola?'

'I wanted to apologise. For getting angry last time.'

Renata snorted. 'You think I care about that? You're strange.'

Cynthia shrugged. 'My mum always told me not to pick fights with people unless I can shout at them in their own language.'

Renata laughed. 'It's not hard to tell someone to shut up in German. Halt die Klappe. Halt's Maul. Hau ab. Verfick dich. I'm sure you'd manage.'

'Alright, alright.' Cynthia fiddled with her chopsticks. 'Lola told me about Santiago.'

Renata tensed. 'Did she?'

'That you and he were… well, I'm sorry, anyway. I must have brought up bad memories.'

'You really are soft. How have you not been eaten yet?'

'Luck?' Cynthia shrugged. 'Powerful friends?'

'Some friends, leaving you here all alone. Berlin's a dangerous place.'

'It wasn't meant to be,' Cynthia said. 'I'm from Oxford. I didn't think Berlin would be worse.'

'Oxford is Council territory. They see everything. We're a long way from the Council, and a long way from the KUA. They don't care about Berlin,' Renata said cynically.

She sounded really upset.

'Did you try and find out who did it?' Cynthia asked cautiously.

'Of course. But no one fucking cares about one dead shifter, yeah? And your people keep to yourselves. It's selfish. You don't work with other supernaturals, and when one of your own dies, you just pretend it never happened.'

'That's not true.'

'So the Deckers know what happened to Santi?'

Cynthia frowned. 'No… no, Lola said she wasn't allowed to investigate.'

'Exactly.'

She was right, of course. Cynthia had never seen it that way before. 'We always look out for ourselves.'

'You look out for the living shifters. But animals don't care for their dead.'

The hurt in Renata's voice was as much a blow as the actual words. Cynthia flinched. 'I'm not an animal. We aren't animals.'

'No? Zebras leave their dead for the lions, don't they?'

'It's not like that. Anyway, does that mean the witches are the lions?'

Renata glared at her food. 'I didn't kill Santi. Is that what Lola told you?'

'No, but she thought you might know who did.'

'Lola's a fucking bitch. She blames me because she doesn't want to admit the truth.'

'What is the truth?' Cynthia asked.

'Your lot don't look after your own people. Santi wasn't the first shifter to go missing in Berlin.'

'Really?'

Renata looked up, but her gaze was miles away. 'Why did you call me?'

'I—' Cynthia looked away. 'I was hoping you'd help me. I need to speak to the Witch Council.'

Renata laughed. 'You're crazy. What would they want with you? We have enough problems with the covens here.'

'I'm trying to find my father.'

'Still? Have you tried a phone directory?'

'Piss off.' Cynthia put her food aside, suddenly not hungry. 'You think I'm stupid? You do this thing; you hide behind your anger. I know people like you. You're just afraid.'

'Of you? Fuck off.' Renata snorted.

'Not of me, but of someone.'

'Pah,' Renata spat. 'You're full of crap.'

'I'm not trying to be.' Cynthia fiddled with her bag strap. 'I want to be your friend.'

'Witches and shifters aren't friends, Dog-Girl.'

'Cynthia.'

Renata shrugged. 'What do I care for your name? The more I learn, the more it'll hurt when you go missing, too.'

'What makes you think I'll go missing?'

'That's exactly it!' Renata's voice came out louder than Cynthia had expected. 'You're just like Santi, naïve. We aren't friends. You fucking call me up and want to hang out, like I'm a normal girl, like you're a normal girl, like there aren't people in this city who would kill both of us!'

With anger came truth, Monica always said.

'Is there anyone in this city trying to kill you?' Cynthia asked.

Renata's expression closed off, hiding everything: the anger and the pain. 'No, of course not. No one would dare.'

'Why not?'

'They just wouldn't.' She stood suddenly, shrugging. Her aura rippled, green and blue and grey, then settled again. 'I'm going. This was a waste of my time. Don't call me again.'

'I'm sorry.' Cynthia stood as well. 'Please. Look, we don't have to talk about supernatural stuff. I really would like to be your friend.'

'Lola can be your friend. I don't need any dogs in my life.'

Renata picked up her bag, turned away, and stomped down the stairs. Cynthia remained behind, a carton of cooling cashew chicken beside her, guilt in her heart. She wished she hadn't accepted Lola's bargain. Whoever Renata was, she wasn't a criminal. She didn't deserve to be saddled with false friends.

CHAPTER ELEVEN

PLAGUED BY GUILT, Cynthia avoided three phone calls from Lola the next day, and spent the day doing scrupulously non-supernatural activities. She finally visited Checkpoint Charlie, wandering around the museum and imagining what life must have been like during the Cold War. She was doing a good job of it—the avoiding supernatural, not the imagining—when her phone rang.

'Hello?'

'Hey, it's Gunther.'

'Oh, hi,' Cynthia said, her guilt resurfacing. Another false friend. How did Monica and Nathan stomach it? She wanted to confess all her guilt to him, and Gunther was basically a stranger.

'How are you?'

'Fine, and you?'

'Good.' He sounded excited. 'Are you free? I found something out.'

Cynthia perked up. 'What kind of something?'

'A possible location, but I think we have to go at night.'

'Hold on.' She took the phone away from her ear and checked the time. 'I can't, not tonight. I'm meeting someone after dinner.'

'Damn.' Gunther wore all his emotions on his sleeve. Even down the phone, Cynthia could hear his disappointment. 'Tomorrow?'

'Yeah, sure.'

They arranged to meet after dinner the next day. Once she hung up, Cynthia tried to get back into the sightseeing mindset, but the supernatural had intruded once more. Instead, she headed out and found a place for dinner, from where she called Monica.

'Long time, no speak,' Monica said.

'I texted you yesterday!'

'Yeah, but you haven't called. Nathan's out of his mind with worry.'

'He could have called me.'

Monica just laughed. 'He thinks he's doing you a favour not calling you, giving you time. Can you please just put him out of his misery? I know you two still like each other.'

'It's not like that.' Cynthia stared unenthusiastically at her salad. 'I don't… I don't know…'

'I thought you did still like him.'

'Even if I did, I can't just be me around him.'

'So, tell him that,' Monica said. 'The tension is killing me.'

'I did try. But Nathan just laughs things off and goes on as usual. It makes me feel like I'm overreacting.'

'You can't do that. If you let people influence how you feel, you'll never be happy,' Monica said.

Monica was one to talk. Cynthia scowled. 'I can't just switch it off. Anyway, I'm not getting back together with Nathan. Maybe we were just too young. Maybe in a few years it'll be easier. Or maybe we'll both meet people who are better for us.'

Monica made a noise of disappointment. 'Your relationship was good, though.'

'Most of the time, when he wasn't busy with work.'

'True.'

Cynthia ate a few bites, waiting for Monica to add whatever was on her mind. Finally, Monica said, 'It would be better if you talked it out. Letting it fester won't help. And Nate wants to help you. Don't deny him that.'

'I did speak to him the other day. But he's also busy with work.' Cynthia paused. 'I'll text him just now,' she allowed.

'Alright. Anyway, how are you?'

'Fine. I thought you'd want to know that I'm meeting that mage again.'

'The technician?'

'Yeah, that's the one.'

'Don't trust him,' Monica said. Cynthia laughed. 'I mean it! He's probably checked your internet history already.'

'Yuck!'

'Stalker-mage.' Monica sniggered. 'Why are you meeting him?'

'Lola asked him about my father.'

'Oooh, good call.'

'I hope so,' Cynthia replied. 'Because I also spoke to Renata. She won't help.'

'You asked her about your father?'

'And about the Witch Council.' Cynthia took a sip of water. 'She told me to get out of town. Too many missing shifters apparently.'

'And a witch warned you about that?' Monica asked.

'Yep.'

'Iiiiiinteresting.'

'I know.'

'Tell Nate. In the text which you were totally lying about sending.'

'Monica!' Cynthia rolled her eyes. 'I wasn't lying. Why would I lie?'

'Obfuscating. You'd have texted him eventually. I'm telling you to do it now. Forewarned is forearmed,' Monica sang.

'Why would Nathan need to be forearmed?'

'Hmm…'

'Monica…'

'Fine, fine, Nate's thinking of coming to Berlin. But I didn't tell you that. He'll be unhappy. He was going to try and time it for after you left.'

That hurt. 'Great, now he's avoiding me, too?'

'You told him you didn't want him there!'

'Yeah but not like that! Not so much that he can't come here on business. Not so much that we can't avoid each other. It's a big city!'

'You're kinda being a hypocrite, here.'

'Speak for yourself,' Cynthia snapped. 'You're the queen of hypocrites.'

'Nice.'

Fuck. 'Monica… sorry.'

'No, it's fine,' Monica said airily. 'Look, I'll speak to you soon. I'm trying to organise a call with Lily for sometime soon. I'll let you know.'

'Okay.' Guilt churned in Cynthia's stomach. 'But I am sorry. It's not you I'm mad at. It's me.'

'Sure. See you.'

Monica hung up without waiting for Cynthia to say bye. Cynthia set her phone down, annoyed at herself. Why couldn't she stop picking fights with her friends?

Texting Monica now probably wouldn't help, so she sent a message to Nathan instead.

Cynthia: Hey, how's it going?

Nathan: Good, you?

Cynthia: Fine, except I may have just upset Monica

Nathan: Oops. She'll get over it

Cynthia: I hope so. Something weird came up, though. Seems like there might have been more than one missing shifter in Berlin?

Nathan: I'll look into it

Cynthia: Thanks. Hey, do you know what a red aura means?

Nathan: Blood magic. Why?

Cynthia: A warlock I met had that aura. I thought I'd seen it somewhere before

Nathan: The box at Cecilienhof

Cynthia: No, that's not it. Somewhere else

Cynthia: Never mind. I'm heading to the centre to meet someone soon. Might have info on my dad

Nathan: Good luck!

Nathan: What's the warlock's name?

Cynthia: Anton Matussek

Nathan: The one with the red aura

Cynthia: Oh, Leon. He seems nice. Bit creepy

Nathan: Thanks

Nathan said nothing further. Cynthia finished her dinner before heading to the station. She was a bit early, but there wasn't enough time to go home, and anyway, Brigitte and Wilhelm would ask questions.

In the end, she was glad she'd arrived early. Anton's directions were deceptively simple: she was to meet him at a bar named *Verzaubert*—German for *bewitched*—beneath the Hackescher Markt S-Bahn station. Unfortunately, Anton's directions led her to a plain black service door, not to a bar.

Cynthia stared up at it for several seconds, before pacing back to the square and looking around doubtfully. This did seem to be the place. At least, according to the internet, there was a bar here, or maybe there had once been a bar here. The internet didn't seem sure whether the place was still open.

Spying no likelier places, Cynthia strode back to the door and double-checked her instructions. *Tell them you're meeting me.*

She knocked.

For several seconds nothing happened, long enough for Cynthia to worry that she had got the wrong place. Finally, the door swung open to reveal the most enormous man she'd ever seen. He had to be at least six and a half feet tall, as wide around as a tree, and all muscle.

'Guten Abend.'

'Um… guten Abend,' Cynthia replied cautiously. 'I'm looking for *Verzaubert*?'

'This is *Verzaubert*,' the bouncer said. 'We're not admitting anyone at the moment.'

'Oh.' Cynthia's confidence faltered. 'I'm meant to be meeting someone here.'

'You don't sound too sure.'

'I…' She steeled her shoulders. 'No, I am sure. Anton Matussek. He told me to meet him here.'

That got an obvious reaction. The bouncer put a finger to his earpiece and murmured something in German. A moment later, he stepped back.

'Welcome to *Verzaubert*.'

Cynthia edged past him, her heart thumping with nerves. Within was a boxy entrance, mirrors on the walls making it seem larger. The floor was chequered black and white, and a bench against one wall was upholstered in red velvet.

The door slammed, making Cynthia jump. She turned, but she was alone. The bouncer had stayed outside.

I guess the only way is forwards.

Straight ahead was a doorway. Beyond it, Cynthia descended a short flight of stairs and came out in a long, narrow room. The bar extended down one wall, and the rest of the room was seating. The décor had a minimalistic, industrial feel to it: exposed brick walls, furniture in burnished metal and brown leather, dim lighting. A single sign in neon pink lit the wall opposite the bar:

ONE CANNOT THINK WELL,

LOVE WELL, SLEEP WELL,

IF ONE HAS NOT DINED WELL.

—Virginia Woolf

On the far side of the room were two archways. One led to another staircase, going even deeper. The other to the toilets. The room was largely empty, except for a small group of middle-aged ladies at one end of the bar. As Cynthia wandered over to the bar and settled herself on a stool, a door swung open in the back wall, revealing the bartender. He was somewhere in his forties, and he immediately stood out. His biceps bulged against his T-shirt, and his shaggy brown hair, tanned skin, and neat beard gave him a slightly leonine air. He strode towards Cynthia and stopped dead after about two steps, his expression flickering with shock. He'd noticed her aura.

Worse, he pegged her for a tourist. When he finally stepped over, he spoke in English, his tone hostile. 'Shapeshifter. Interesting choice to stop for drinks.'

Cynthia checked his aura and found nothing, not even a flicker. Of course, some humans could see magic. Or he might be a mage who knew how to hide his aura.

'I'm meeting a friend here.'

That didn't seem to impress him in the slightest. Gruffly, he asked, 'What can I get you?'

'Um…' Cynthia scanned the line of bottles on the wall behind him. She didn't know what half of them were. 'Can I see a menu?'

Unimpressed, the bartender set a brown leather booklet in front of her. 'Take your time.' He walked off, vanishing back through the door into the kitchen.

Right, then. Clearly, shapeshifters were not welcome here.

Cynthia looked through the menu, darting frequent glances towards the stairs. She was early; Anton probably wouldn't be here for a while. But she wished he'd hurry up, anyway.

She was deliberating between a coke and a glass of wine when someone said, 'You should try the old fashioned. It's a house favourite.'

Cynthia looked up in surprise. The bartender had returned, his footsteps surprisingly silent considering his size. He looked to be in a better mood.

'I'm not much of a cocktail drinker,' Cynthia said.

'On the house.'

'Well, okay then,' Cynthia said shyly. The bartender stepped away, deftly reaching for bottles, and in short order, he'd begun assembling her cocktail. He didn't use any tools; instead, he crushed the sugar by clicking his fingers and stirred the drink by moving his hand clockwise over the glass. He garnished it with an orange twist and served it to Cynthia with a flourish.

'The magic makes it extra special,' he said proudly.

'Oh, really?' Cynthia had to smile. Despite his gruff first impression, he seemed okay.

'Really.' He held out a hand to shake. 'I'm Gideon.'

'C—um, Cindy,' Cynthia replied, shaking his hand. His grip was firm and steady.

'Nice to meet you, Cindy.' If Gideon noticed her slip, he didn't comment on it. He nodded at the cocktail. 'Try it.'

Cynthia sipped the drink tentatively. The whiskey burned her throat, but it wasn't awful.

'You really aren't much of a cocktail drinker, are you?' Gideon chuckled.

'Uh… not really. But it's nice.'

'Maybe it'll grow on you.'

'Maybe.' Cynthia took another careful sip and pulled out her phone, pretending to fiddle with it. The bartender lingered, watching her.

'Your friend must not like you too much, if he's letting you sit in a place like this alone.'

'Oh, that's my fault. I'm early.'

'I see.' Gideon didn't seem convinced. 'I was surprised they let you in, to be honest.'

'Because I'm a shapeshifter?'

'The witches don't like trouble. They've enough in-fighting, without inviting shapeshifters through their doors.' He smiled wryly. 'But I suppose you stood outside for long enough. Too much risk of attracting attention.'

'You saw that?' Cynthia could feel her cheeks heating. Hopefully, he'd attribute it to the alcohol.

'CCTV on the door. We get trouble, sometimes. This place used to be a popular human bar, before we took it over. Some people don't take no for an answer.'

'Oh.' Cynthia checked her phone again, wishing Anton would arrive.

'Been stood up?'

'Not yet.' Cynthia grimaced. 'I'm sure Anton will be along soon.'

'Anton? Anton Matussek?'

'You know him?'

'Everyone knows him, don't they? There's a man with his fingers in every pie.' A woman down the bar flagged him. Gideon frowned. 'I have to go. Don't trust Anton. He's bad news.'

He hurried off, glancing back twice. Cynthia stared after him. Well, that had been weird. Witch in-fighting? Renata had mentioned something like that, too.

First the vampires, now the witches. What's going on in this city?

Her phone vibrated.

Anton: I will be there shortly

What would Monica do? An ironic question to ask, seeing as Cynthia had just argued with her. Sending mental apologies to her friend, Cynthia slid her phone back into her bag, waved to Gideon, and mouthed, 'toilet.' He nodded and pointed down the bar.

She got up and slipped into the darkened hallway, watching the bar area. Gideon strode back over to her things, and for a moment, Cynthia really did think he was going to rifle through her bag. Then he wiped his hands down on his apron and turned away.

Anton arrived a moment later, glancing around. He approached the bar, and Gideon gestured to the empty spot next to her bag. Cynthia made a show of coming out of the hall, wiping her hands on her trousers, in time for Gideon to say, 'Interesting mark. Thought the Council had enough trouble on their hands.'

'Keep your nose out of my business, old man.'

'As long as you do the same.' Gideon nodded to Cynthia. 'Mind the rules. No trouble on witch territory.'

'Of course.' Cynthia smiled tremulously. Anton turned to her, a political smile in place. He'd changed after work, and looked rather handsome in jeans and a white button-down shirt.

'Good evening, Cynthia.'

'Hi.'

'Shall we sit somewhere more private?'

'Actually,' Cynthia said, climbing back onto her barstool, 'I'd prefer to stay here, if you don't mind.'

Better the devil you know than the devil you don't.

'Very well.' Anton settled beside her. 'Can I offer you another drink?'

'I've still got, thanks.'

Anton nodded. To Gideon, he said, 'Whiskey sour, please.'

'Coming up.'

As Gideon moved away, Cynthia asked, 'The bartender's English?'

'I didn't think you spoke German,' Anton replied.

'I don't.' He'd spoken English for her benefit. 'Thanks,' she added.

'You're welcome. Shall we get down to business?'

Gideon returned with Anton's drink, side-eying them suspiciously. Anton nodded his thanks and Gideon retreated to serve a group of women with toxic yellow auras who'd just entered. Cynthia watched him go.

'Did he say something to you?' Anton asked.

'No.' Cynthia squared her shoulders. 'Business?'

'Have you figured out what I am?' Anton asked. 'Or Lola told you.'

'Another friend, actually.' Cynthia felt guilty, as though she was telling on Monica, which made her feel a bit stupid. 'She told me you were a technician.'

'That's what we call ourselves,' Anton said agreeably. 'I have the ability to control technology. I won't bore you with the details.'

Cynthia's gaze went to her bag, where her phone was. Anton laughed. 'Indeed. Your phone history reveals many interesting things. Don't worry. I prefer to limit my investigations to criminals.'

'Well, I'm pretty sure that doesn't include me.'

'I assure you, we wouldn't be sitting here if it did.'

Cynthia smiled nervously. 'Well, that's good to know.'

Anton picked up his drink, swirling the glass before taking a sip. 'So, tell me.'

'I'm looking for someone. Justin Gastrell.'

'Your father.'

'Yes.'

'And you think he's in Berlin?'

'He wrote me from here,' Cynthia said uncomfortably. Instinct told her not to reveal too much, but then, Anton probably knew most of this already. 'I saw him. Briefly.'

'I see.' Anton sipped his drink again. 'To my knowledge, there is no one called Justin Gastrell living in Berlin.'

Cynthia's heart sank. 'Oh.'

'However,' Anton drawled slowly, 'that is not to say that Mr Gastrell doesn't live in Berlin. He may simply have taken a different name.'

'Right.' Cynthia plucked at her straw, disappointment swirling in her stomach. 'Can you find him?'

'Few people are beyond my reach.' Anton sipped his whiskey.

'But?'

'How do you know there's a caveat?'

Anton seemed amused. Cynthia rolled her eyes. 'Experience. You're a warlock.'

She felt stupid, suddenly, for coming here and just expecting him to help because—what? Because he was Lola's colleague? Out of the kindness of his heart? But Cynthia was rapidly realising that kindness was in short supply amongst Berlin's supernatural community. Anton, like every other warlock, would have some wicked bargain that would trap her soul for all eternity. She ought to leave, but she was here now. She may as well find out what he wanted.

'Just tell me.'

Anton smiled. 'You aren't at all what I was expecting.'

'Sorry to disappoint.'

'Hardly a disappointment.' Anton glanced up at Gideon. Following his gaze, Cynthia realised that the bartender was watching them rather closer than he ought to be, as he poured several beers from the taps. Unnerved, she looked back at Anton. 'I find it rather intriguing, actually.'

'Really?' Cynthia asked sceptically.

'Shouldn't I?'

'You're a police officer and a warlock. I'm just an eighteen-year-old girl.'

'An eighteen-year-old girl who has managed, in the space of only two weeks, to crack the surface of Berlin's supernatural underworld. How goes your search for the vampires? I have to say, it never occurred to me to send a shifter to search for missing people, but it seems a rather inspired choice.'

'Excuse me?' Cynthia demanded, certain there'd been an insult somewhere in that last sentence.

Anton gave her his usual political smile. 'Some people move better through our ranks than others. Some of us attract too much attention from the wrong sort of people, you understand?'

'And I get the right sort of attention?' The only attention Cynthia ever seemed to receive was the lascivious type; it was hardly flattering.

'Precisely.' Anton sipped his drink. 'Do the names Anya Bakker and Natasha Murphy mean anything to you?'

'No?' Cynthia asked, confused at the turn the conversation had taken.

'A shame.' Anton set his drink down. 'I would propose an alliance. You are clearly able to collect information that I am not—that of a more... human variety, I suppose. Computers can tell us many things, but they are no substitute for real interactions, and supernaturals are rarely trusting of the police.'

'You don't say.'

Anton smiled vaguely. 'I suggest we combine our information. Perhaps you can assist me with a few things I'm working on.'

It was a surprisingly tempting offer. Bring criminals to justice? Figure out what in heck's name was going on in Berlin? It was Monica's advice that stopped her from taking the leap. *Don't trust him,* she'd said. *He's probably already checked your internet history.*

And what had he seen? That she had an in with the Council in Oxford?

I'm useless to these people, Cynthia thought bitterly, *but my friends aren't, are they?*

'And in return, you'd lead me to my father?'

'Correct,' Anton replied.

'Right.' Cynthia's heart felt oddly heavy. 'What would I be giving you information on?'

Anton considered that. 'A choice, I think... both active cases, which someone, somewhere, doesn't want me digging too deeply into.'

'What are the cases?' He was stalling, and the more he stalled, the less Cynthia liked this.

Anton paused, thinking deeply, swirling his glass slowly.

'What do you know about the family you're staying with?'

'The Deckers? They're—' Cynthia paused. 'Why do you want to know about them?' she asked suspiciously.

'They're surprisingly well-connected, for shapeshifters,' Anton said.

'Surprisingly? You just said more or less the same thing about me,' Cynthia pointed out. Her heart was racing, and her palms were clammy. She hid her hands in her lap. There was no way she could trade her father's location for the Deckers. No way at all.

'In a different way than yourself.' Anton paused, studying her. 'Very well, I can see that I've offended you. Let's discuss something else. Does the name Leon mean anything to you?'

He was watching Cynthia too carefully for her to be able to hide her surprise. Leon seemed to be popping up everywhere, these days.

'What about him?' she asked.

'You've heard of him?'

'Yes, but… I don't know anything about him,' Cynthia replied warily. She suspected a trap, but she couldn't figure out what it was. Leon was a warlock, like Anton. If they had a problem with one another, that was for them to resolve. Witches didn't usually involve anyone else in their business. 'Why?'

'He's a person of interest.'

'For you, maybe.' Cynthia shrugged. 'Isn't that witch business? I'm not in Berlin to get caught up in some witch feud.'

'Hmm.' Anton studied her with sharp brown eyes. 'So, you don't want to find out about your father?'

Frustration blossomed in Cynthia's chest. 'Of course I do. But I don't know anything about Leon to tell you.'

'I suspect you know more than you think you do.'

'I'm pretty sure that's not true.'

This had been a mistake. Before Cynthia could figure out how to extract herself—preferably without being roped into some witchy turf war—Anton said, 'It interests me that you've managed to meet Leon. Do you make a habit of poking your nose in places other people can't get to?'

Cynthia froze. 'What? How do you know that?'

'Lola told me,' Anton said. 'You told Nathan Delacroix—an interesting name indeed to have in your phone contacts. Does Lola know you're friends with such dangerous people?'

'Leave Lola out of this!' Cynthia was starting to panic. She'd lost control of the conversation in an annoyingly short period of time.

'Why? Afraid I'll reveal your secrets?'

'No.'

'I think you are.' Anton smiled. 'And for such an ordinary girl, you truly have many secrets. You didn't tell Lola who your father was, did you?'

'I told her enough,' Cynthia said uneasily.

'Did you tell her that you can recognise him by the tattoos on his arms? Did you tell her what they meant?'

Cynthia didn't have an answer for that.

'Do you know who Leon is?'

'No. I only met him twice.'

'More times than most of us have met him,' Anton replied.

'I don't see what this has to do with anything. If you want to meet the guy, I bet you could find out his phone number and call him.'

'But that's just the thing, isn't it?' Anton steepled his fingers beneath his chin, radiating smugness. 'He doesn't have a phone.'

'Everyone has a phone.'

'Not Leon.' Anton picked up his glass and studied it, the liquid glimmering in the low light. 'Let me explain something to you, Cynthia. I track people by their digital paper trails: bank transfers, emails, gas bills, SMS conversations. Now, there's someone in this city who has no trail. That makes me uneasy. Where does he live? Work? Where does he buy his food and how does he pay for it? These are things I can find out about every person in Berlin—except him. He's a digital ghost. Do you understand?'

'No.'

'Let me give you an example.' Anton gestured to her bag. 'You arrived in Berlin two and a half weeks ago. The first thing you did was withdraw five hundred euros in cash. Once you pay cash, I can't track your payments. However, your phone pings each wifi and satellite it connects to. I know you were in Potsdam. I know you've been to the hunter office. I know where you are staying, and who else lives there.'

'That's creepy.'

'I don't need most of that information, so I don't look for it.'

'Except you did.'

Anton shrugged. 'In this case. As in Leon's case. But in his case, there is nothing to find. No phone, no home address, no bank accounts, no CCTV footage. He doesn't exist.'

'Except you've seen him.'

'Me? No, he's not stupid enough to be seen by me.' Anton laughed. 'If I see him, I know he exists. No, I only know his name from conversations—like yours, with Nathan Delacroix. Mentions. But does that mean he exists? How many mentions make a person real? But then he made a mistake.'

'Lola saw him.' Cynthia surreptitiously wiped her palms down on her legs. She was curious, in spite of herself. She ought to get out of there, but Anton seemed in a mood to share. *Monica would say to keep him talking.*

'He must not have known she worked for me. Or perhaps, he was too fascinated by you.'

'He wasn't fascinated by me,' Cynthia said. The thought made her uncomfortable. Actually, Leon had looked rather interested, that first night in *MIX*. 'Anyway, you make it sound as though he's personally hiding from you.'

'A person with no paper trail has something to hide,' Anton said. 'It's my job to find out what.'

'That's not the same thing as him hiding from you, personally,' Cynthia pointed out.

'Perhaps. The difference is irrelevant at the moment.'

'I don't see how.'

Anton drained the last of his drink. 'Seeing as you are unwilling to help me, there's no need for you to know, is there?'

Damn it. Cynthia scowled. 'I'm not helping you betray anyone, not without a good reason.'

'Then perhaps you aren't as desperate to find your father as I thought you were. A shame.'

Cynthia gripped the edge of her stool, warring with herself. Who was Leon, anyway? Just some guy she'd met twice. Some guy who had seemed sad and a bit lost, and much less threatening than Anton. But she didn't know that. She knew more about Anton than she did Leon; Leon could be anyone, really. She could be projecting her own feelings onto him.

'I—'

'Is that how the Witch Council operates these days? Blackmailing teenagers?'

Cynthia jumped. Gideon had crept up on them. Anton tipped his head back and laughed, though Cynthia couldn't at all see what was funny.

'Don't be a hypocrite, old man.'

It was the second time he'd said that. To Cynthia, Gideon looked in his forties. Monica had said mages could live longer than ordinary humans, and you couldn't always tell. Was he one of them?

'Mind you don't overstep, Matussek.'

Anton's eyes narrowed. 'Nothing comes for free, Gideon. I don't do favours, not even for teenagers.'

'There are better ways of getting information than blackmail,' Gideon replied coldly. 'I suggest you get out of my bar before you find trouble.'

Anton's demeanour had changed entirely, all the friendliness draining away. 'It's not your bar.'

'I don't recall it being your name on the lease, either.'

For a moment, the two men stared at each other, and the air practically crackled with their hatred. Anton looked away first.

'Let me know your decision, Cynthia.'

He stood, slid his hands into his pockets, and sauntered off. Cynthia watched him go, disappointment mixing with annoyance in her chest.

'You should mind who you trust,' Gideon said.

'If I had to pick, I think I'd choose the police officer over the dodgy bartender,' Cynthia replied tersely. Gideon flinched.

'That's your decision.' He picked up a serviette and casually used it to wipe condensation from the bar counter. 'Just remember, Anton is only a police officer for nine hours a day.'

'You're only a bartender for nine hours a day,' Cynthia replied.

'Less than that, I assure you.' Gideon smiled coolly. 'Wonder what he does for the other fifteen hours?'

'I don't.' Cynthia stood. 'I'm tired of witches in general, actually. They're all shit. You, him, Renata, my bloody father. I'm going home.' She slapped twenty euros on the bar counter. Gideon waved it away.

'If you won't take the advice, at least take the drink. I said it was on the house.'

It didn't sit right with Cynthia, but she wasn't in the mood to press the issue.

'Sure. See you around, then.' She headed for the door, for the streets of Berlin, for human company. For once, she was rather pleased to cross Berlin and not see a single other supernatural.

CHAPTER TWELVE

'I'M SORRY,' THE RECEPTIONIST SAID, 'we haven't got a Justin Gastrell on record, and we are not able to give you information on the Decker family, as you are not related to them.'

Cynthia suppressed a sigh. It had taken her fifteen minutes to get through to the KUA in Bonn, she'd been on hold for another five, and now this. Luck was not on her side.

'Thank you anyway,' she replied.

'Can I help you with anything else?'

'No… no, wait, there is something else.' Cynthia took a deep breath. 'Do you have any information on a mage named Leon? Residence place Berlin.'

'One moment, please.'

The hold music, some tinny rendition of a classical piece, began to play again. Cynthia picked at a thread that was coming out on her shorts. A short moment later, the receptionist picked up again.

'Hello, Ms Gastrell?'

'Yeah, hi.'

'I'm sorry, that information is not available to the public. If you would like to request it anyway, you can fill out a request form in our office and present yourself to the committee for consideration.'

Go figure.

'No, thanks. I can't get to Bonn at the moment. Thank you for your help.'

'Is there anything else?' the receptionist asked in a tone that strongly discouraged further enquiries.

'No, that's it. Thank you.'

'Goodbye.' The receptionist hung up. Cynthia lowered her phone with a sigh.

She had a choice. Option one was to take Anton's deal. Option two was to fess all to Nathan and let him deal with it. Option three… She eyed her phone thoughtfully.

Cynthia: Can I come over to your place? I'd like to see you
Gunther: Now?
Cynthia: When your parents aren't there
Gunther: You can come now

Guilt swirled in Cynthia's stomach as she navigated to the address Gunther had given her. It wasn't too far from the Deckers' place, and turned out to be a reasonably modern apartment block on a main road, with a large kids' play area. Gunther buzzed her in. She climbed the stairs and found him in an open doorway on the second floor, a big smile on his face.

'Hey.'

'Hi.' Cynthia sighed deeply. Gunther's smile dropped.

'You don't seem happy.'

'It's complicated. Can I come in?'

He stepped back. It reminded her rather of Nathan, who also would never invite anyone in verbally; vampires needed that to get past your wards. Cynthia felt the tingle of their wards over her skin as she entered.

Gunther poured them both a glass of sparkling water, and they sat in the lounge with the balcony door open.

'So?'

'Yeah…' Cynthia stared at the bubbles in her glass. 'You said you had access to your dad's computer. Could you look someone up for me?'

'A person?' Gunther asked.

'A few people.'

'Why?'

'I… I don't know.' Cynthia shrugged. 'I thought it'd be simple, coming here, you know? Hang out for a bit. My host family are nice, I've known them for ages. I wanted to just be me. And then maybe ask around a bit about my dad. But instead, the vampires are missing, and the witches are sketchy, and now I think the shifters are sketchy too. And everyone seems to want something from me. I'd like to figure this stuff out on my own, not end up with bargain after bargain with dodgy mages, but for that I need information.'

'Uh…' Gunther frowned at her.

'Never mind. Someone said something that made me suspicious. I'd like to make sure the people I'm staying with aren't doing anything illegal.'

'Okay.' He shrugged. 'Dad will be out until four. You want to do it now?'

Cynthia nodded, relieved that she hadn't had to resort to snogging to get him to agree. This sat badly in her stomach, but she followed him to the office anyway. Mr Ditka's office was neat and sparsely decorated. A photo sat on the desk, showing Gunther with a man and woman, all in hunter uniform.

'All-hunter family?' Cynthia gestured to it.

'Mum's retired now, but Dad's still practising.'

'Where is he now?' Cynthia asked.

'He keeps an eye on a few places, but yesterday and today he was in Leipzig to teach a class.'

'Cool.'

Gunther sat at the desk and logged onto his father's desktop. Cynthia pulled up another chair, watching over his shoulder.

'First, let me show you this one place I found.'

'Okay,' Cynthia said, resting her hand on his shoulder. Gunther typed in a few things in German.

'So, Dad's watching a bunch of places where there have been incidents. Loads are in this area, Rosenthalerplatz to Hackescher Markt.' Gunther pointed to a map. 'Dad thinks the vampires might be hiding out here.'

'Oh,' Cynthia said in disappointment. 'I went there.' She checked herself. Turning the witches over to the hunters was not a smart policy.

'Damn,' Gunther said. 'I was hopeful for you.'

He was so sweet. Cynthia felt even worse.

'Will you get in trouble for this?' she asked.

'Nah, Dad will never even know.' Gunther pushed his sleeves up. 'So, who am I looking up?'

'Start with Anton Matussek.'

She watched closely as Gunther typed the name in. 'One S or two?'

'Uh… don't know.'

'I'll start with two, I think it's the more common spelling.' Gunther hit enter. It took a few moments, and then the search results were in. There was a list of names that were close matches, each one with a photo. Cynthia pointed to the first one.

'That's him.'

'Great!' Gunther clicked the link. A second later, the window went white, with a red exclamation mark in the middle. The text proclaimed, *Sicherheitsfreigabe 5 benötigt.*

'What does that mean?' Cynthia asked.

'Security clearance level five required,' Gunther translated. 'Who is he?'

'He works for the police. But he's a warlock.'

'Guess that would do it. I bet he knows all sorts of stuff, working for the police.'

'I guess.' Cynthia frowned. 'Try Leon.'

'Leon? Last name?'

'I don't know it.'

'Okay.' Gunther typed it in. They scrolled through a list of at least a dozen names, Cynthia examining each photo.

'He's not there.'

'You're sure? This would be easier with his last name.'

'No, I'm sure.' She sighed. 'Anton's right, he's a ghost.'

Gunther gave her an odd look. 'How do you know these people?'

'I don't, not really. I just keep meeting them.'

'Just like that?'

'Pretty much.' Cynthia shrugged uncomfortably. 'Wilhelm Decker.'

Wilhelm Decker had a file. It was sparse and neat: there was his address, his place of work, his immediate family members.

'He's boring,' Gunther remarked.

'I'm starting to think that's a good thing.' Cynthia stared at the page, frowning. If Wilhelm was so ordinary, why had Anton hinted that he wasn't? 'Try… try Santiago Carvalho. C-A-R-V-A-L-H-O.' She'd found his full name scribbled in an old phonebook in Lola's room.

This yielded only one search result. The boy in the photo looked around Cynthia's age. He was handsome, with shoulder-length brown hair and tanned skin. Gunther clicked the link, and the whole thing unravelled into a massive mess.

'What the…' Gunther whispered.

'What does it mean?' Cynthia asked.

'This,' Gunther gestured to a banner across the top, 'means missing, considered deceased.' He scrolled down. 'Last known address is the same as Wilhelm Decker's. And this means that there are a few security flags. I can open these. Dad has security level four; these are three.' He opened the first one, and the page expanded, showing another profile.

Jacek Dabrowski

He, too, was marked as missing, considered deceased. One by one, Gunther opened the other flags.

Anya Bakker

Courtney Stein

Hans Zimmermann

Natasha Murphy

'They're all shapeshifters like you,' Gunther said.

'Holy shit,' Cynthia whispered. 'Six. Six shifters have gone missing… in…'

'Ten years,' Gunther filled in.

'That's…'

The phone cut through the air. Gunther jumped and looked around. 'Uh, I better take that.'

Cynthia nodded distractedly, and he hurried out of the room. She sat there in shock for several seconds.

'Hallo?' Gunther asked in the hall.

Cynthia forced her shock away. She couldn't waste this opportunity. Hastily, she pulled her phone out and snapped a few photos of the screen. This was evidence. Then she opened a new tab and clumsily typed in the words she'd looked up earlier: *Vampirzentrale.*

Several locations came up, each one with a level five security flag, but the addresses were visible. She photographed them and closed the tab just as Gunther finished his call.

He came back into the study.

'Sorry about that. Just my mum. Do you want another drink?'

Cynthia took a deep breath, let it out slowly, and hoped she just looked scared, not guilty. 'Yes, please.'

CHAPTER THIRTEEN

'RIGHT,' NATHAN SAID, 'I might have something for you.'

Cynthia was sitting in a coffee shop, an iced latte in front of her, her legs curled up to her chest. All around her were ordinary people with ordinary concerns. She felt like there was a target painted on her back.

'Yeah?'

'So, I've crosschecked the addresses you sent me with the data I got from the KUA in Bonn. It seems like for a while, back in the twenties, the vampires used to have another HQ. It's one of the addresses. Clärchen's Ballhaus.'

'The hunters know about this?' Cynthia asked wearily. She wasn't ready to dig into the amount of obfuscation going on in the hunter records. 'They just didn't tell me.'

'If it makes you feel any better, they should have told me, too, when I asked.' Nathan laughed bitterly. 'And I ought to report you for breaking into our database, but frankly, I'd like to give you an award. What are you going to do about the other thing?'

'I don't know yet.'

The knowledge of six missing, dead, shifters weighed on her like a physical pressure. She felt sick from it. And from the need to tell someone. But who?

There were two people involved in this: Lola and Renata. But who to trust?

Last known address is the same as Wilhelm Decker.

'I'm going to try and ask the vampires about my dad, then decide,' she said. 'If they don't know, I'm going to give up and get out of town.'

'Before you become the seventh name on that list,' Nathan said.

'Basically, yeah.'

With Nathan's knowledge of German, Cynthia had managed to decipher the rest: none of the missing shifters was native to Berlin.

They'd all been there for various reasons; work, holiday, visiting family. If that wasn't a compelling reason to be afraid, then Cynthia didn't know what was.

'Listen,' Nathan said, 'I could be on a plane tonight.'

'Or I could.'

'Let me help you.'

'I'm not—' Cynthia swallowed. 'I'm not ready.'

'To see me,' Nathan said, frustrated. 'You really would rather be in danger than around me? We had a good relationship.'

'We did when you were committed to it, but work always came first—'

'—No—'

'—and now you're trying to turn me into your job!'

'Cynthia, it's not like that! I mean…' Nathan sighed. 'It was never meant to be that way, okay? I know I'm not perfect, but you aren't my job. You're my friend, first. You mean a lot to me, and if you're in danger I want to help. Monica wants to help. Heaven knows she's bored stupid hanging out here. Give her an excuse, and she'll help you.'

'I want to help myself.'

'The best way to help yourself is to admit when you need other people.'

Cynthia glared at the wall. Einstein, the mascot for the coffee shop, glared back.

'I have other people. The Deckers, for one. Shifters. My people.'

'Your people who didn't tell you there were six missing shifters in Berlin.'

Nathan was right, as always.

'I'll speak to them. Maybe they were just trying not to scare me.'

'Maybe.'

A tinny beep cut through the phone line, once, then again. Nathan cursed. 'I have to take this call.'

'Here we go again.'

'Cynthia, don't. I'll call you back straight afterwards.'

'Yep.' She grabbed her coffee. 'Sure. Later, then.'

'Bye.'

Cynthia hung up and downed the last of her coffee, imagining she was swallowing down her irritation. *Clärchen's Ballhaus.* She had an address for that.

And that was all she had needed.

Returning to the Deckers' apartment made her uneasy. She ate dinner with Wilhelm and Brigitte but found herself jumping at every stray noise. Gracie in the hall, Wilhelm clanking his knife against his plate.

'Are you okay?' Brigitte asked.

'Mm-hmm.' Cynthia thought about it. 'I might call Lola after dinner, see if she wants to meet up tonight.'

'That sounds fun.'

It had just been an excuse, but after dinner, Cynthia found herself actually doing it. Lola picked up on the second ring.

'Hey, how's it going?'

'Uh, do you want to hang out tonight?' Cynthia asked. 'I'm... thinking of cutting my trip short. Maybe we could spend an evening together before?'

'Sure.' Lola sounded surprised. 'Is everything okay?'

'I'll explain when I see you.'

'Okay. Come over.'

She packed an overnight bag, bade Brigitte goodbye, and took the train over to Lola's apartment. When she met Lola at her front door, the older girl looked her over worriedly.

'What happened?'

'Nothing happened.' Cynthia slipped inside. 'I just... did you know that there were six shifters who have gone missing?'

Lola's expression flickered, so quickly Cynthia might have missed it if she hadn't been watching closely.

'You did know. Why didn't your family leave?'

'This is our home.' Lola shifted her weight from foot to foot. 'Did you just come here to ask that?'

'No. I just... found out and wanted to reassure myself, I guess.'

'Right.' Lola eyed her suspiciously. 'Want a beer?'

'Yes, please.'

They sat in the lounge, which doubled as Lola's bedroom. Lola put music on, then joined Cynthia on the sofa.

'How did you find out, anyway?'

'My hunter friend checked the database for me.'

'You told shifter secrets to the hunters?' Lola asked. 'Why?'

'I didn't tell him any secrets. I was tired of everyone dropping hints and not having any information. So I went over to his place, borrowed the computer, and looked everyone up. Anton, Leon, your dad, Santiago.'

'My dad? Why would you look him up?' Lola asked.

'You tell me what reason I might have,' Cynthia said.

'You think he's involved in the disappearances? What the fuck, Cynthia?' Lola stood up abruptly. 'You have no right!'

'I'm not saying he is, but someone thinks he is.'

'Who?'

Cynthia stood up as well, but then she didn't do anything. It felt wrong to tell on Anton. 'Why did you tell Anton I knew Leon?' she asked instead.

'I knew Anton was looking into him, so I mentioned him. Why's that important?' Lola asked defensively.

'I don't know. But Anton thought it was.'

'Did Anton mention my father?'

Cynthia hesitated. 'No.'

'You're lying.'

'I'm not.'

'I don't believe you. Someone did.'

'Renata,' Cynthia fibbed.

'For fuck's sake! And what? You'd rather believe her, a witch, than your own people?'

'No. But I had to be sure.'

'But you aren't sure,' Lola said. 'You think Dad did it. Fuck you.'

'I don't. I just think it's suspicious. We'd have left, Mum, me, and Emma. We'd never have stayed.'

'This is our home! You said yourself that you hated running.' Lola shook her head. 'I can't do this. Get out.'

'Fine.'

Cynthia took a long slug of her beer, grabbed her bag, and marched to the door. 'I told my friend on the Council. If your dad is hiding something, he'll find out.'

'Fuck you,' Lola snarled. 'You're ruining everything.'

Cynthia let herself out, shaking with adrenaline. As soon as she was out of the stairwell and back on the street, she pulled her phone out and called Lily. It was about time she spoke to her friend; Lily didn't usually ignore text messages.

The phone rang quite a few times, enough that Cynthia was worried Lily wouldn't pick up. Finally, it connected.

'Hey, Cynthia, I'm soooooo sorry.' Lily sounded groggy and a bit out of it.

'Lily? What's up?'

'Nothing. Well, lots of parties and a few hot guys. But that's no excuse.' Cynthia could hear movement, and Lily's voice became clearer. 'I meant to reply to you ages ago.'

'It's okay, it's just… I maybe need that apartment now. I think I just… forget burning bridges with my host family. I might have just blown the bridge up.'

Lily laughed, bell-like and delicate. That was Lily, all over. Delicate and sweet. And a half-vampire. But that was easily ignored.

'Okay, the apartment is on Bleibtreustraße. I'll give Roswitha a ring. She's the housekeeper. She can pass you the keys.'

'It's alright, though, right?' Cynthia paused in a recessed gateway. 'I don't want to impose.'

'You're not imposing. Nate stayed there last year, and Adrian's used it before, too. Don't worry. How is Berlin going?' Lily asked.

'It's a disaster.'

'Really?' Lily's voice turned sympathetic. 'Why? Anything I can do to help?'

'Too much to go into over the phone.' Cynthia sighed. She felt like crying. 'Do you know anything about the Vampire Council here? I think I might have an address for them, finally, and I'm going to go there tonight.'

'Oh yeah, I know loads about them,' Lily said, 'but aren't they in Potsdam? That's where Damien always goes to meet the KUA when he's in Berlin.'

'Nope. They up and vanished recently.'

'Wow, okay, I missed a lot.' Lily laughed. 'I've met a few of them. Julianus is the head, acting head, actually. He's the one you want to deal with. The others are just annoying.'

How bloody ironic. She'd gone in circles, and here Lily had all the information she needed. *Should have called her a week ago.*

'Is he old?'

'Maybe 400?' Lily didn't sound too sure. 'I doubt he's really Roman. A lot of vampires change their names, to make themselves sound older, or younger, or just because it's a fashion. Damien is really Damon. Jeremiah is Jeremias. This guy might just be plain Julian.'

'Okay. And the others?'

'Twins. Ceren and Aysun. They're Turkish originally. They arrived with the Ottoman legation in 1763.'

'Thanks.'

'Seriously, though,' Lily said, 'if there's anything I can do…'

'I have missing vampires, seriously freaky witches, dead shifters, and nowhere to stay. You can solve one of those problems.' Cynthia smiled wryly. 'You're doing great.'

'Okay,' Lily said uncertainly.

An idea popped into Cynthia's head. 'Do you know who the Witch Council are?'

'No.' Lily perked up. 'But I can text Damien and find out.'

'Thanks. And an address, if you've got one.'

'They were also in Potsdam. But I'll ask.'

'Thanks.'

'I'll text you as soon as I've spoken to Roswitha,' Lily promised.

'Great.'

It only took fifteen minutes for Lily to text Cynthia. She was on the S-Bahn, on her way back to Hackescher Markt. The vampires appeared to have holed up near the witches, surprise, surprise. Everything was starting to make sense in a funny sort of way. Vampires got scared, witches got scared, they both retreated. Lots of supernatural incidents in that area. Some kind of turf war?

Clärchen's Ballhaus was an unassuming building on Auguststraße. A blue sign announced its name, and a smaller sign advertised a mirror hall.

When Cynthia entered, a woman stopped her. 'Heute ist eine Privatveranstaltung.'

'I…Ich muss mit Julianus sprechen,' Cynthia stammered. 'Permittitis intrare?'

The woman mustered her for about ten seconds, making Cynthia squirm.

'Hinten bei der Band.'

'English?' Cynthia asked hopefully.

'At the back by the band. On the left. Tonight is a private event, so keep to yourself,' the woman replied.

'Thank you.'

Cynthia slipped inside, feeling instantly out of place. Everyone was dressed up, men in suits, women in dresses. She looked strange in her jeans. Still, she persevered, examining the room as she crossed it. The walls were hung with streamers, and a live band was tuning their instruments on a small stage. Next to the band, her eyes fell on the second vampire she'd seen in Berlin. He wore a suit and tailcoat with a blue and white polka-dotted bowtie, and leant against the wall, surveying the room disinterestedly.

Cynthia stepped up to him. 'Are you Julianus?'

'Who wants to know?'

'I'm a new supernatural in town. I'd like to make an enquiry.'

The man tilted his head, studying her. He was exceptionally pale, his skin contrasting starkly with his very dark hair.

'Shapeshifter. We don't get many of your kind around here.'

'I can't imagine you get many visitors of any sort here,' Cynthia pointed out. 'It's taken me two weeks to find you.'

'And yet, find us you did.'

'I'm determined.'

'I see that.' He gave her a cold, fangy smile. 'Your kind are no friends of ours. Why should we give you safe passage?'

Heart in her mouth, Cynthia recited the words Monica had taught her aeons ago when they'd planned this trip. 'I am a friend of the Vampire Council in Oxford. I was promised I'd be greeted with the same courtesy here.'

'The Vampire Council should know better than to make promises on our behalf.' The vampire raised a hand and clicked his fingers. 'Friedrich will take you to Julianus.'

They were joined by a boy who looked easily three or four years younger than Cynthia, if not for the fact that he was also a vampire. He was dressed as a waiter and had the same pale skin as the first vampire, although his hair was much lighter. Under the dim light, it looked as though there were shadows moving under his skin.

'Take the shapeshifter to Julianus,' the first vampire ordered.

'Yes, sir.'

Friedrich led Cynthia across the room and up a flight of stairs. 'I haven't seen one of your kind around here before.'

'It's hard to be sure of our welcome,' Cynthia said.

'You're an exception.'

'I guess.' She didn't feel like answering questions about that, not after what she'd found out today. 'How did you get turned so young?'

'That's a personal question,' Friedrich said.

'You asked me a personal question.'

'I didn't ask any questions. You volunteered the information.'

Nathan and Monica were much better than Cynthia at these political games. Cynthia chewed the inside of her lip, a nervous habit she'd never been able to shake.

'Why is your skin so pale? I've never seen a vampire as pale as you.'

'If Julianus deems you worthy, he will answer your questions,' Friedrich said gravely.

At the top of the stairs, he opened a door and ushered Cynthia into a large room with antique mirrors lining the walls. The ceiling was gilded in gold, and the bottom half of the walls were panelled wood. On the far end was a small stage with four golden chairs on it. Three of them were occupied.

'Eine Gestaltwandlerin meldet sich bei uns,' Friedrich said. 'Sie bittet um ein Audienz mit Julianus.' He bowed deeply.

The three vampires lounged like kings on their thrones. It was immediately obvious which of them was Julianus; he was wearing a deep purple toga. He seemed tall, although it was hard to tell when he was sitting down. His hair shone red and gold in the candlelight and, like Friedrich and the other vampire, he too was painfully pale.

The other two vampires were twin women, perhaps in their forties. They had olive-toned, strangely sickly-looking skin and dark hair, worn so long it covered their legs as they sat. They were both dressed in identical ballgowns, one white, the other black. The effect was eerie.

Cynthia turned back to Julianus and attempted a clumsy curtsey.

'Kommen Sie näher.' Julianus smirked. 'Wir beißen nicht.'

Even without understanding, Cynthia sensed the threat behind his words.

'Sie spricht Englisch,' Friedrich said.

'Ah.' A shark-like smile played about Julianus's lips. 'Come closer, shapeshifter. I don't like shouting across the room.'

The moment he said it, Cynthia could think of nothing she wanted less than to approach him. She shook the thought away. She was going to handle this. She was *not* scared of Julianus.

She lifted her chin, steeled her shoulders, and stepped closer.

Julianus's feral smile grew. 'Very good. Friedrich, leave us.'

Friedrich slipped through the door and shut it behind him with a thud that seemed deafening. Cynthia watched him go. When she turned back, the twins were right in front of her, staring at her with unabashed curiosity. Cynthia blinked and stumbled back a step.

'E—excuse me.'

'How curious,' cooed one twin. 'I've never seen one up close before. Will you transform for us?'

'Oh, please do show us,' said the other. 'We had a werewolf once, he howled so prettily on the full moon.'

'He howled so beautifully when we ate him.' The black-clad twin sighed wistfully.

'I—I would prefer not to,' Cynthia stammered, feeling a little nauseous.

'Aysun, Ceren, that's enough,' Julianus interjected. 'We are civilised creatures.'

The twins pouted, flouncing back over to their chairs. Julianus beckoned to Cynthia. Hesitantly, she stepped closer to him. He, at least, seemed sane.

'Tell me, English shapeshifter, what can we do for you?'

Cynthia took a deep breath, pushing away her fear. You should never show fear to a vampire. 'I'm looking for someone,' she said. 'A dark mage.'

'A mage?' Julianus raised an eyebrow. 'Would that not be a request for our witch brethren?'

'The Vampire Council in Oxford assured me of your expertise.' Her words prompted a wave of giggles from Aysun and Ceren.

'She's from Oxford!' one twin screeched.

'One of Jeremiah's pets,' the other crowed. 'Perhaps he keeps her around for a midnight snack.'

'If she were my pet I'd not have let her out of her cage—'

'Ladies, enough,' Julianus interrupted. 'Temper yourselves.'

The twins returned to pouting prettily, though with a distinct undercurrent of hunger. Cynthia missed the Vampire Council in Oxford fiercely, all of a sudden. Staid and old, brutal and terrifying… but at least they were sane, and the few times she'd met Jeremiah, he'd never given any indication that he was planning on eating her.

'I'm not a pet,' she said belatedly, 'just a friend.'

'I wasn't aware the Oxford Council tendered friendships; they've certainly never extended the privilege to the rest of us,' Julianus said flippantly. 'Are you in their employ?'

'No.'

'So you conduct your search independent of their authority?'

'Um…' Julianus's speech was hard to follow. Cynthia was pretty sure he was deliberately trying to tie her in knots. 'They're aware.'

'Very well.' Julianus's smile was smug and cruel. Cynthia had the impression she was being led into a trap, but she couldn't figure out what it was. 'And what is the name of the dark mage you seek?'

'Justin Gastrell.'

For a fraction of a second, Julianus's smile dropped, just long enough for Cynthia to notice. Then it was back.

'Regretfully, I am not familiar.' He glanced at the twins. 'Mesdames?'

'Never heard of him,' they chorused.

'I was told that the vampires took all new registrations in the city,' Cynthia said.

Julianus waved that away disinterestedly. 'Do you really think I involved myself in the day-to-day affairs of common witches?'

'He's hardly a common witch. You'd know him if you saw him,' Cynthia said. 'Or do you mean to say that you're allowing a threat to go untracked in your city?'

It was a comment Monica would have been proud of. All three vampires bristled.

'You doubt our authority?' Julianus said. 'If the man were a threat, we would have found him.'

'So you know him?' Cynthia challenged.

'Is he a threat?'

'Yes.'

'So the Council of Oxford knowingly allowed a threat to move into our territory, and now they wish for us to clean up their mess?' Julianus leaned forwards. 'My, Jeremiah is slacking, these days.'

Nathan was going to kill her. Scrambling, Cynthia said, 'Jeremiah has larger concerns than a single dark mage.'

'So do we.' One of the twins tittered.

'Ceren,' Julianus snapped. To Cynthia, he said, 'Jeremiah can't think very fondly of his pets, if he sends them unprepared into enemy territory.'

'Are you saying you're Jeremiah's enemy?'

Julianus withered. *Nailed it!* Cynthia thought in triumph. Pressing her advantage, she asked, 'Where's the fourth member of your council? I'd have thought you'd all want to be present to meet a messenger from Oxford.'

Julianus's face seemed to tinge a bit green at that. 'Indisposed,' he said shortly. 'Perhaps with greater warning…'

'Really? How long has he been indisposed for?'

'Not long. Nothing for Jeremiah to concern himself with.'

She was onto something, but she didn't know what. Before Cynthia could think of her next move, Julianus spoke.

'The dark mage, perhaps the name is familiar.'

Cynthia looked up sharply, hope blossoming like roses in her heart. 'You know him?'

'I didn't say that.' Julianus tilted his head, studying her. 'But negotiations could be made.'

'I don't negotiate with vampires.'

'A shame.' He leaned back. 'Our needs are considerably simpler than witches'.'

'I'm not interested in making a deal. This is your job.'

'You have little understanding of my job.' Julianus seemed angry, suddenly. A moment later, faster than Cynthia could track, he appeared in front of her. She jumped back, and he caught her wrist, gently stopping her from falling.

'Let me go!' She yanked her hand back.

'Forgive me.' Julianus's eyes glittered with cruel amusement. 'My deal is not so onerous. I'd never dream of hurting one of Jeremiah's pets. A single taste…'

An odd look came over his face. Cynthia took several seconds to realise what it was.

Hunger.

Panic engulfed her. She stepped back again, too terrified to take her eyes off him. How far away was the door?

'Absolutely not!' she snapped.

'Come now. One sip and Jeremiah's little mistake could disappear.'

'No, no thank you!'

'Are you *sure?*' Julianus leaned in, his eyes glowing an eerie red. He was trying to compel her. Once before, she'd had a vampire compel her, to test if it worked. It had, and it was the scariest thing she'd ever felt. Not just the loss of free will, but the fact that she had enjoyed it. Wanted to do whatever he told her.

But with Julianus, there was no pull. She felt no desire to comply.

'No,' she repeated, this time with more certainty.

Julianus leaned even closer. Cynthia hardly dared to breathe. He veered to the side suddenly, and inhaled deeply beside her neck. Cynthia stumbled back.

'I—I thought we were civilised creatures,' she choked out.

The twins laughed, though their eyes were glowing red, too.

'Oh, she's delightful. Are you sure we can't keep her?'

Julianus stepped back, straightening his toga. 'My apologies. We are, naturally, creatures of habit. But even bad habits can be broken.'

He returned to his chair, sitting stiffly. 'Tell Jeremiah his request is denied.'

'It's not his request.' Cynthia willed her racing heart to calm down.

'In that case, my terms are simple. Your blood for the information. If not, you are naturally welcome to seek out the witches. It's your decision. You may find them less accommodating.'

'Accommodating?' Cynthia echoed incredulously. 'I'm not your evening snack.'

Julianus's expression didn't waver. 'You may go.'

'I'll tell Jeremiah about how… *accommodating* you were,' Cynthia said angrily.

'Be my guest. And do remind him of my last. Jeremiah owes a few debts he has not yet paid.' Standing, Julianus bowed courteously. Cynthia glared at him. Keeping her eyes firmly on the insane vampires, she backed to the door and opened it.

'I hope you reconsider,' she said.

But Julianus had turned away and was murmuring something to the twins. Cynthia shut the door and stomped down the stairs, barely glancing at Friedrich when he melted out of the shadows to escort her.

'You should not have come alone.'

'I know how to hit you where it hurts,' Cynthia snapped. 'Don't talk to me.'

Friedrich sniggered. It was the youngest he'd looked since she'd met him. At the door, he glanced wistfully outside, then turned away.

'Until we meet again, shapeshifter.'

'Whatever,' Cynthia muttered. She slipped outside, relishing the cool air. Bloody vampires. What now?

Checking her phone, she found the address and phone number Lily had given her. Was it too late to call Roswitha? Only one way to find out. She dialled the number. A few seconds later, it connected.

'Guten Abend, Roswitha Beckmann.'

'Roswitha?' Cynthia asked uncertainly. 'Hi. This is Cynthia Rymes. Lily von Klichtzner gave me your phone number.'

'Of course. Good evening, Ms Rymes. Fraulein von Klichtzner asked me to pass you the keys to the Bleibtreustraße apartment.'

Roswitha was brisk, reasonable, and rather human-sounding. Cynthia felt herself relax a little. 'That's right.'

'I can meet you at the apartment in circa half an hour?'

'That would be excellent. I'm in the centre. Will that be enough time?'

'I should think so. What's your nearest station?'

Roswitha gave her instructions to get to Savignyplatz, promised to meet her outside, and hung up. As she stashed her phone back in her bag, Cynthia sighed. What a mess she'd gotten herself into.

'Nice part of Berlin.'

Cynthia shrieked and whirled around. Standing behind her, not three steps away, was Leon.

'Oh my God! Leon!' Cynthia gasped and pressed a hand to her chest. 'What are you doing here?'

Leon chuckled.

'Hello, Cynthia. We meet again.'

Cynthia frowned. 'Are you stalking me?'

'How can I be stalking you? I was here first.'

'Here?' Cynthia looked around pointedly. 'Spying on the vampires for the witches?'

'Perceptive, aren't you?' He smiled, closed-lipped. 'What might you want with the vampires?'

Cynthia crossed her arms. 'It's none of your business.'

'Really? You don't think they're going to lead you to Justin Gastrell, do you?' Leon shook his head patronisingly. 'Come now, you saw them. They couldn't lead a babe to its mother, let alone find a mage in this city.'

'What's wrong with them?'

'No one knows.' Leon gestured for her to walk, falling into step beside her.

'Everyone has an opinion,' Cynthia said.

'True.'

'So? What do you think?'

Leon considered the question for a while. Cynthia studied him. His hair fell in his eyes a little. He was dressed in the same clothes she'd seen him in twice before. How old was he? She'd originally guessed late twenties, but suddenly, he seemed younger.

'I think they've been cursed,' he said finally.

'Who could curse every vampire in the city?' Cynthia asked.

'A good question. Who would want to?' Leon replied.

'Also a good question.' Cynthia shrugged. 'I don't know Berlin.'

'Interesting that you say that. You seem to have found all the main players, already. Matussek, the Friedemann girl—'

'Renata? Wait, you know I met Anton?' Cynthia stopped short in a puddle of light from the streetlights. 'How do you know that?'

'Did you tell him anything?' Leon asked. 'Did you tell him about me?'

'No, my question first. How does everyone in this city seem to know everything I do?'

'I know everything. This is my city.'

'Don't talk shit. No one person can know everything in an entire city,' Cynthia snapped.

'Such language,' Leon replied mockingly. 'I use the same tricks you do. Information is just a matter of overhearing the right conversation, isn't it?'

'No!' Cynthia took a deep breath. 'Were you in *Verzaubert*, listening in?'

'Of course not. Would I be so foolish?'

'I don't know. I don't know anything about you.'

The words struck Leon harder than she'd meant them to. His face fell; he turned away and began walking towards the S-Bahn.

'You don't let anyone close. It's hardly my fault.'

'That's rich.' Cynthia hurried after him. 'You answer my questions with more questions. How am I supposed to get to know you?'

'I offered you a date.'

'Is that what you call offering? I'm not going on a date in exchange for information.' Cynthia crossed her arms. 'How do you know where I'm going?'

'Savignyplatz is accessed via the S-Bahn. You repeated the instructions back over your phone.'

Cynthia huffed in annoyance. 'Is that what you do, then? Listen in on conversations? Look, why are you even here? Why are you talking to me? Who are you? What's your full name?'

'Leon is my full name.'

'Surname.'

'I don't know it.'

That brought Cynthia up short. 'How can you not?'

'I don't remember my parents.' The moonlight struck Leon's face as he looked down at her, turning his profile to a statue of sadness.

'I—I'm sorry.'

'It's fine.' Leon shrugged it off, as though he'd done it a thousand times before. 'What else do you want to know? Why am I talking to you? Knowledge is power. I find things out by talking to people.'

'But not Anton Matussek.'

'Anton is dangerous. You should stay away from him.'

'You're not the first to say that.' Cynthia sucked in a breath. 'Can you slow down? I can't walk that fast.'

'Sorry.' Leon halted at the entrance to the S-Bahn. 'We're here, anyway.'

'We are.' Cynthia stared up at him. 'How old are you?'

Leon frowned. 'Older than you think I am.'

'I don't know, or I wouldn't be asking.'

Leon shook his head slightly. 'Ask another question.'

'Fine. Did you grow up in Berlin?'

'For a while. I was born in a small town in the North. Brandehuse.'

'I don't know it,' Cynthia admitted. 'This is my first time in Germany.'

Leon smiled. 'It's on the Baltic coast, in Holstein. Small. It was a trading port, years ago.'

He sounded fond. 'Sounds nice,' Cynthia said.

'Maybe, if you like fish.'

It was a joke, the first that Leon had told. Cynthia smiled tentatively.

'Do you?'

'I'm more partial to people, actually.'

'Me too.'

They exchanged grins. Cynthia felt a lurch in her stomach. Leon looked at her like she was the only person in the world. No one had ever looked at her that way.

'I…' she said reluctantly, 'I have to go. Roswitha is waiting for me.'

'I know. I'll find you again,' Leon promised.

'How?'

'I always know where to look. You stand out.'

'How?' Cynthia repeated. 'I'm not special.'

'You are,' Leon said, 'more than you know.' He paused, and when he spoke again, his voice was pained. 'You… shouldn't trust the vampires. They won't lead you to Justin Gastrell.'

'No one wants to lead me to him, even you. I'm going in circles.' Cynthia's frustration reared up like a familiar friend.

'I could.'

'But you want something from me.'

Leon shrugged. 'No,' he said, 'not much, at least. You… intrigue me. Pretty shapeshifter. You're not scared of me.'

'A little.'

'Yes, but the other animals run and hide in the woods.' He bent down, his gaze on her lips. 'I may know an address. Schulze-Boysen-Straße number thirty-seven.'

It was exactly what she'd been looking for, and yet, at that moment Cynthia couldn't care less. Leon leaned in. Cynthia's heart skipped a beat, then began racing. Was he going to…? He was, he was going to kiss her. Her palms felt clammy. Should she let him? Leon closed the distance, his lips millimetres from hers.

He froze, his breath ghosting over her lips.

'You were followed.'

'W—what?'

Leon stepped back and turned. A figure appeared from the shadows, a boy. He stepped under the streetlight, and Cynthia recognised him.

'Friedrich?' She felt sick, all of a sudden. The Vampire Council had had her followed, and she hadn't even noticed. 'What are you doing here?'

The orange light made Friedrich look even paler, sick and frail.

'Julianus is a fool, letting you walk away.' His voice was harsh, choking out of his throat. 'Such a tasty morsel—'

He got no further. In the blink of an eye, Leon had crossed the pavement and slammed him against the wall. Friedrich's feet came away from the floor. He scrabbled for purchase, trying to pull Leon's hand away from his throat. Cynthia stifled a gasp. Leon was *strong*.

'Stop! Halt! Lass mich!' Friedrich sobbed.

'Do you know who I am?' Leon asked, his voice a deadly whisper.

'Yes! Yes, I do!'

'Then go, go and tell Julianus to leave the shapeshifter alone.' Leon pulled his hand away, and Friedrich fell to the floor in a heap. 'Go!'

The vampire jumped up and stumbled away. He ran half-human, half-vampire, sometimes blurring and disappearing, other times staggering like a wounded deer. Halfway down the street, he stopped and looked back.

'Go,' Leon repeated, quiet and angry. Friedrich vanished from sight.

CHAPTER FOURTEEN

ROSWITHA WAS BRISK AND reasonable, but not human. Her aura rippled with almost violent energy, like the very air particles were repelling one another. Cynthia studied her aura for a few moments before she had to look away and let the second sight go. It hurt her eyes, up close.

She followed the woman into the entrance of an attractive art nouveau building. In design, it was not dissimilar to where Lola lived, but it was obvious that this apartment sold for a considerably higher price. The street outside was leafy and filled with expensive boutiques and restaurants. The building was clean, and the décor was understatedly elegant.

Roswitha brought Cynthia to the top floor. She was in her seventies, at least, with steel-grey hair and a kind smile. At the top of the stairs, Cynthia finally caved.

'Are you a werewolf?'

'So you do recognise the aura,' Roswitha replied as she unlocked Damien's front door. 'Yes, I am, but at my age, I'm tired and old. Herr von Klichtzner supplies me with his blood. It eases the pain around the full moon. In return, I can live comfortably on a salary and clean an apartment that is only lived in one week a year.'

'He should rent it out.'

'I told him that.' Roswitha chuckled. 'He is a stubborn old man.'

'Old?' Cynthia coughed. Damien didn't look a day over thirty.

Roswitha laughed. 'Older than I will ever be. Come.'

She led the way into the apartment. It was large and spacious. Big windows were open, letting in the evening air and the noise of the city. The furniture was modern, with hardly any wear and tear.

'If you let me know what you need, I will do the shopping,' Roswitha said.

'Oh, that's very kind.' Cynthia stepped back from the bedroom she'd been peering into. 'You don't have to do that.'

'I'm paid to do it.' Roswitha pointed to a door. 'Fraulein von Klichtzner's room.'

'Thanks.' The last thing Cynthia wanted was to accidentally sleep in Damien's room.

Roswitha fussed around for a few minutes, before sticking her head through the door. 'I will go now. Here are the keys.'

'Thank you.' Cynthia accepted two keys. 'See you tomorrow?'

'I'll bring you breakfast.'

'Thanks.'

A moment later, she was alone. Cynthia lay on the bed for a few seconds, staring up at the distant ceiling. Finally, she got up. She was sweaty, and the bed was clean. She needed a shower.

The water system clanked a bit when she started it up, the only sign she'd had so far of the age of the apartment. As the water cascaded over her, Cynthia finally allowed herself to think through everything that had happened that day.

Six missing shifters. That ought to be the work of witches. It was hardly the first time Cynthia had heard of something like that. It ought to be a sign that she should get out of town.

But…

The weird thing wasn't the missing shifters. The weird thing was that every one of them had been a visitor to the city. The local shifter population remained intact—and safe. So, were the visitors doing something stupid that tipped off the witches? Or were they being betrayed?

But why?

No, Cynthia pushed the thought out of her mind. She trusted her people. They'd have no reason to turn their own in. There had to be something else going on here.

The sensible thing to do would be to get out of town. Tell the Council, see if they could investigate. Come back when it was safe.

But then her father might have moved on. She might lose his trail entirely. Especially as he probably suspected she was looking for him by now. There'd be no more postcards, and the only hint she'd have of his existence would be the occasional information turned up through the hunter database.

And then there was the address Leon had given her.

Was it possible that he knew where her father was staying? Could it really be that simple? If she went there tomorrow, would she find him?

Thinking about Leon brought up all sorts of other thoughts. He'd been about to kiss her. Cynthia was no blushing virgin. She'd only had the one boyfriend, but she knew when a guy was about to kiss her. She knew when a man found her attractive. Leon liked her.

But he's a warlock.

Yet, he was also handsome, intriguing. And she was only here for a short while. If it didn't work out, she'd be leaving again soon.

So… extend my trip, look for my father, see where this goes?

Cynthia shut the shower off, resolved within herself.

Why not? What harm could it do?

She slept like a log that night. Maybe things had been weighing on her more than she'd realised, or maybe it was just because she seemed to be staying up late every night, but she was woken the next morning by Roswitha entering the apartment.

'Guten Morgen,' the woman sang when Cynthia crept out of Lily's bedroom. 'Sleep well? I brought croissants.'

'Morning.' Cynthia stifled a yawn. 'You didn't have to. I'd have managed.'

'Nonsense.' Roswitha waved dismissively. 'I also brought bread, pasta, some sauce I made at home. For you tonight. You can text me a shopping list. Plans for today?'

Roswitha's attentions were efficient; she hustled Cynthia into a seat at the little kitchen table and served her tea, English style, and croissants with apricot jam. As Cynthia ate, she explained that she needed to go back to her host family to say goodbye and fetch her things.

'But first I want to do a short trip,' she said. 'A… friend gave me a possible address for my father.'

'Your father?'

'He's a mage. I think he's staying in Berlin. I've been looking for him.'

'What's the address?' Roswitha asked.

'Um… number thirty-seven… Schulte-Boysen-Straße number thirty-seven.'

'Schulze. I know it. It's in the east.' Roswitha passed her a glass of water.

'Thanks. I hope he's there.' Cynthia sighed and spread more jam on her croissant. 'I've certainly asked enough people.'

'Witches love their mind games.'

'It's not just the witches!' Cynthia peered at her. 'What do you think is up with the vampires in Berlin?'

Roswitha's face closed off. 'I try not to concern myself too closely with supernatural politics. It tends to reduce your life expectancy.'

Cynthia laughed. 'I'm starting to agree.'

'You should be careful. You're young. People will try and take advantage of that.'

'I think I'm doing okay.' Cynthia shrugged. 'Anyway, Leon, the guy who gave me the address, I think he's just lonely. And that's more okay than people asking me to spy on people in return for information, or whatever.'

'Leon?'

'You know him?'

Roswitha looked pensive. 'No, it can't be the same person. Don't mind me.' She smiled affably. 'Finish your breakfast. It'll take you longer than you think to get to Schulze-Boysen-Straße.'

It was a fair day out. Cynthia took an extra croissant for the journey and rode the S-Bahn east, before switching into the U-Bahn. When she arrived, she found a street full of tall apartment blocks. Number thirty-seven was the tallest of all and housed over fifty apartments.

'I was wondering if I'd see you here.'

'Is this a joke?' Cynthia turned to face Leon. 'You're playing me for a fool.'

He was lounging in the shade of a tree, his shirt sleeves rolled up to show off slender, strong forearms. He looked more human than she'd ever seen him look before.

'That's not my intention at all.' Leon pushed off the tree and sauntered over. 'Maybe you're just not looking properly.'

'I don't find this funny,' Cynthia muttered, turning away. She had an idea of what he meant, though, so with a little focus, she activated her second sight and examined the street. It was to no avail. The only magic visible was Leon's aura, glittering like rubies. Cynthia studied it for several moments before she finally blinked and let herself see normally again.

'What kind of magic do you have?'

'An old kind,' Leon said. Cynthia pursed her lips.

'This is the address you told me.'

'Apparently.'

'Apparently?' Cynthia groaned in frustration and turned back to the apartment block. German apartment blocks always had rows of neat post boxes beside the door, each one with a name and number. *Eckelmann* and *Buchholz, Hüber* and *Müller, Volker* and *Klein.* Most of them had peeling stickers requesting *kein unadressiertes Werbematerial* — no advertising. Unfortunately, none of them announced the presence of a dark mage named Justin Gastrell.

'What am I doing here?' Cynthia asked finally.

'I don't know. Why look for someone who doesn't want to see you?'

'How do you know he doesn't want to see me?'

'Why hasn't he told you his address?' Leon asked.

'Maybe he can't.'

'Maybe.' Leon scuffed his foot against a weed growing between the paving stones. 'I wanted to see you.'

'I have a phone. You could have asked for my number.' Instead, he had vanished after Friedrich, as though it were his personal responsibility to ensure the vampires left her alone.

'You can give it to me now. Next time, I'll call.'

Cynthia ran her fingers through her hair and sighed. 'I'm never going to find him.'

'Tell me about him?' Leon asked.

'What's the point?'

'He seems important to you.'

'I've never even met him,' she muttered bitterly, 'except once for ten seconds. There's nothing to tell.'

'We don't have to meet people for them to be important to us,' Leon said.

'True.' Cynthia watched a car driving by. 'He's my father.'

'But you're animal-kin.'

'What?'

'A shapeshifter,' Leon clarified.

'I've never heard it called that.'

He looked uncomfortable for a second. 'Maybe I made that name up. Your father isn't like you?'

'No, I get it from my mum. She said you can only be one or the other. Clearly, the shifting was stronger.' Cynthia looked up at the sky. 'The weather's going to change. Let's find somewhere to get coffee.'

'Can you tell?' Leon seemed fascinated.

'A bit. It's not perfect. I just get a feeling, sometimes.'

'Like animals. They hide to shelter from the rain.'

'I guess.' Cynthia started towards the U-Bahn. Leon trailed behind her. 'Where are we going?'

'I don't know,' he said. 'You choose.'

Cynthia knew one coffee chain in Berlin, the one Lola had said was best, so she took Leon back to the place where she'd had her row with Nathan the previous day. The memory weighed heavily on her. She ought to call him and apologise. But then, that was what she'd always done: apologise to him. Maybe she should just leave it. Maybe the world wouldn't end if she didn't let Nathan be right this time.

Maybe Nathan wouldn't even notice. He had his own life, nowadays.

Cynthia bought them both lattes, and they sat by the window. Leon, when he was sitting still, was a fiddler. He fiddled with his sleeves, with a tarnished bronze medallion that hung around his neck. He watched the passers-by. Outside, it began to drizzle.

'You were right.'

'It's a sixth sense.' Cynthia grinned. 'I always used to say that if none of my other career options work out, I could always be a weather reporter.'

Leon laughed. 'They'd be confused by the accuracy.'

'I know!'

She caught his eye. Leon grinned shyly, and Cynthia found herself smiling in return. She picked her coffee up and took a sip.

'So… a year and a half ago, this thing happened. You know I'm from Oxford, right?'

'I had heard. Jeremias's Council, yes?' Leon asked.

'I don't work for the Council. I suppose it's my fault people got that idea, but I really don't.' Cynthia took another sip. 'We don't usually stay long in one place, me and my mum and my sister—Emma, she's nine. Anyway, in Oxford some stuff happened, I met this guy, he's a hunter. Because of him, I guess we managed to get in with the Council, and since then they've stopped witches from hunting us on their turf. So we've been safe. But a year and a half ago, before they started protecting us, something happened with a group called the Sahir.'

Cynthia glanced up at Leon, but his gaze remained blank.

'Dark mages? It's Arabic,' he remarked.

'Yeah, I guess. They kidnapped me and my mum. They wanted to use our magic in a dark ritual to overthrow the Vampire Council, but the hunters and vampires stopped them. Anyway, that was when my mum told me about my father, and that he was one of the reasons she moved us around so often when I was little.'

'She didn't want him to find you.'

'Right.' Cynthia trailed off, staring outside. It wasn't that it was hard, talking about these things, just uncomfortable. It felt like someone else's life, almost. Some other girl was sitting in a coffee shop with a handsome warlock, who apparently didn't have three euros twenty for a latte.

'When did you meet him?' Leon asked.

'The same day.' Kicking her shoes off, Cynthia curled her legs up in her armchair. 'That same day, the Sahir tried to strike against the Vampire Council. When we went to save them—' She paused, grimacing. '—well, I didn't do much saving. That was the others. But when we went to save them, the Sahir were waiting. A man appeared out of nowhere and killed two of them, saved my life. Then he disappeared again. He had—' She gestured to her arm. '—he had an invisibility ward, which he could activate so he could come and go.

'About three months later, I got a postcard in the mail, from London. It had Big Ben on the front. He'd written me an apology, basically. He confirmed that it was him, and that wasn't how he would have wanted us to meet. And he said that he had tracked us as we moved around, so Mum was right, but he never meant to hurt us. He always tried to keep us safe.' Cynthia shook her head. 'But he doesn't want to meet, or for me to look for him.'

'But you are anyway.'

'I don't follow instructions very well, as it turns out.' Cynthia shrugged. 'Your turn. What deep dark secrets are in your past, Mr Mage?'

'I—' Leon looked stricken for a moment. 'What do you want to know? I'm not that interesting.'

'Everyone's interesting,' Cynthia said. 'Come on, you've got to have something. Tell me about your magic.'

'It's not really… magic,' Leon said in a pained voice. 'Not like… not like witches. I can call people to me, do other things, but not really useful stuff.'

'You could call me through magic, instead of by phone.'

'No! No.' He shook his head. 'It's not what you're thinking. It doesn't work that way.'

He really didn't want to talk about it. Cynthia cast about for a different question.

'Do you have any siblings?'

Leon shook his head. 'It's just me.' He picked at his sleeve again.

'Where do you live?'

'I have a place in Friedrichshain.'

'I don't know Berlin that well,' Cynthia reminded him.

'South-east of here. It's… different.' Leon shrugged. 'People are different there.'

'Can't be that different. It's all Berlin.'

'No… it's like a… maybe you'd call it a commune.'

'Like hippies?' Cynthia asked, intrigued. 'I've never met anyone who lives in a place like that.'

Leon shrugged.

'Do you have a job?'

'I do odd jobs,' he said.

'For the KUA?'

'Yeah.' He picked his latte up and took a few tentative sips. Evidently, he didn't find it wholly distasteful because he drank the rest pretty quickly. 'What are you going to do now?'

'I'm not sure,' Cynthia said, running her finger around the edge of her cup to catch the foam. She licked it, then looked up to see Leon watching her. 'Sorry.'

'No, don't be.' He smiled.

'I have to, um, go make nice with my host family,' Cynthia said. 'Things are complicated. All my stuff is still there, but I'm moving to another place, today hopefully. All this… poking my nose into things has made them uncomfortable. And I don't want to put them in danger.'

'Naturally.'

'Once I've done that…' She shrugged. 'The only people I haven't asked are the Witch Council.'

'They aren't the helpful sort,' Leon said. 'There are lots of small covens in Berlin, and they don't get along.'

'Yeah, that's what I've heard. *In-fighting.*' Cynthia leaned back, considered her options. So many people to ask, and all of them wanted something. What was the deal with the lowest risk? 'Who would you ask?'

Leon was staring out the window, stroking his medallion slowly. 'Everyone. Anyone. One of them will let something slip eventually.'

'You mean… wait for someone to make a mistake?' Cynthia shook her head. 'I'm not good at those games.'

'You did okay with the vampires.'

'You think so?'

'Well, only the little boy came after you. Maybe you scared the others off.'

Cynthia snorted. 'I doubt it!' She dug through her handbag and found a pen. 'Here.' She scribbled her number on a napkin and passed it over. 'In case you get over your phobia of phones.'

'I don't have a phobia!'

'Tell that to Anton.'

Leon's expression twisted. 'I'd rather not tell Anton anything. Do you know who he is?'

'Deep in with one of the Councils. I'm guessing the witches.' Cynthia had deduced as much. Leon nodded gravely.

'Don't trust him. Stay away from him entirely. He knows things no one should. And people around him don't tend to last long.'

'I'll bear it in mind, but to be honest, I doubt I'll see him again.' Cynthia was pretty sure she'd burnt that bridge when she'd argued with Lola.

'Good.' Leon glanced outside again. 'I should go. You should go.'

'Unfortunately.' Cynthia stood. 'Call me?'

'Of course.' Leon grinned cheekily. 'I have to, now, to prove I don't have a phobia.'

Cynthia laughed.

CHAPTER FIFTEEN

COFFEE WITH LEON HAD been a pleasant interlude in the mess that Cynthia's life had become. She arrived at the Deckers' apartment to find all three members of the family waiting for her, even though it was the middle of the workday.

'Where have you been?' Wilhelm asked when she entered the living room.

Cynthia hesitated for several seconds, studying the scene, trying to figure out the right thing to say. All three of them looked grave; Wilhelm was furious. The real question was, had she done anything wrong?

No, no she hadn't. She hadn't hurt anyone.

If only her heart agreed with her brain.

'I stayed the night at a friend's apartment. And this morning I went to East Berlin, to investigate an address where my father was staying.'

'Your father, the mage,' Wilhelm sneered.

'Lola told you.' Cynthia turned her gaze on her friend. Lola looked at once ashamed and furious. It was an unpleasant combination.

'Lola told us many things, most of which she should have told us a long time ago,' Wilhelm said. 'I was right, you are trouble.'

'I'm trouble?' Cynthia asked. 'You don't look like you're in trouble.'

She couldn't believe her own bravery. Her hands were shaking, but she continued anyway. 'Actually, you seem pretty comfortable. It's everyone else who gets in trouble.'

'I provide for my family,' Wilhelm snapped. 'What are you implying?'

'Nothing.' Cynthia's heart was racing. 'Nothing except that you clearly didn't consider Santiago family. Other shifters provide for the whole community—'

'How dare you?'

Before Wilhelm could work himself up into a froth, Brigitte jumped in. 'Let's all just calm down and not leap to conclusions.'

'I'll not allow her to come in here and disparage us,' Wilhelm said. 'She has no right—we put her up!'

'You act as though you own Berlin!' All of Cynthia's frustration and rage was bubbling to the surface. 'You were constantly suspicious of everything I did, prying into everything and acting as though I was a threat to you. If you didn't want me to come here, you needn't have offered for me to stay with you!'

'We were right to pry! You were a threat!'

'I only became a threat because you kept prying,' Cynthia snapped. 'Anyway, it's ridiculous. Six shifters, *six*, have disappeared in Berlin. That would be enough to scare most people. You're still here. How am I a bigger threat than the witches?'

'You'll lead the witches right to us—'

'I don't need to! You're in the KUA's database!'

Wilhelm's expression was closed off, but it was Brigitte who gave the game away. Her face told a story of guilt. Cynthia felt suddenly certain that she was on the right track.

'You're not in danger at all, are you? Not from the witches.'

Silence.

'How'd you get the witches off your back?'

'We didn't—'

'Brigitte!' Wilhelm interrupted.

'We didn't,' Brigitte continued. 'They have enough problems between the covens. But that's not the point. If you stir up trouble, all you do is draw attention—'

'Really?' Cynthia asked. 'Because I find it kind of suspicious. I mean, Renata probably knows where you live, too. How much attention do you need before it becomes bad—'

'That's enough!' Wilhelm roared. 'How did you find out about the other shifters?'

'I searched the hunter database.'

'You mean you betrayed our secrets to hunters?' he demanded.

'Of course not. It was in the database. They already knew.'

Wilhelm glared at her, obviously struggling to find an answer. After a moment, he demanded, 'Who have you told about this?'

'What's it to you?'

'You'll bring trouble down on all of us! This is the problem with children, they never think about the bigger picture, they never care about the good of the community.'

'Of course I care about the good of the community!' Cynthia cried. 'But this is the community! Someone's killing shifters in Berlin, and I'd have thought you'd care. I'd have thought you'd want to warn people, find out who was responsible, make it safe! You're the ones who don't care about any community outside of yourselves! Shifters from other places don't matter.'

'Of course you matter! But if you come in here and make trouble for us—why should we put your needs over our own?'

'Because that's what a community means! It means the good of all, not the good of the Deckers!'

'You have some nerve!'

'So do you! Santiago deserved justice as well!'

'Santiago was a monster! He ran around and did drugs and fucked witches—'

'Wilhelm, Wilhelm, stop!' Brigitte grabbed his arm, but Wilhelm shook her off.

'—Don't do that. He fucked witches and hung out at vampire bars and took my daughter with him and taught her all sorts of bad habits. And it was my job to pick up the pieces when it turned out badly!'

'It wasn't like that, Papa!' Lola cried. 'It was once, with the drugs.'

Wilhelm turned his glare on her. 'And that witch girl? She still sniffs around and sticks her nose into things—'

'Because she wants justice for him too,' Cynthia said. 'Just because you can't imagine a witch having feelings—'

'She doesn't want justice, she wants someone to blame. And she doesn't have to look far, just in a mirror,' Wilhelm sneered. 'All witches are murderers. You're naïve if you think that isn't the case.'

'I know plenty of witches who aren't murders,' Cynthia said.

'You know witches who *say* they aren't murders,' Wilhelm replied. 'In my experience, that's no guarantee.'

'Rich, considering the attitude the shifter community here takes to outsiders!'

The moment, she said it, Cynthia knew she'd gone too far. It was one thing for there to be dead shifters, quite another to accuse the shifter community of wanting them dead. Wilhelm's expression turned black with anger.

'You will leave.'

'Fine,' Cynthia replied, 'I just have to get my things—I've made arrangements to stay at a friend's place.'

'No,' Wilhelm said, 'you will get out of town, if I have to drive you out myself.'

'Fine!' Cynthia thought fast. 'Fine, but I just need to—to make some phone calls. Make arrangements.'

'Do that,' Wilhelm snapped. 'But quickly. I want you out tonight, before you get my family killed.'

That evening, the whole Decker family accompanied her by bus to Hauptbahnhof, Berlin's central station. The trip was made in cloying, uncomfortable silence. Outside, the sunset turned Berlin red and gold. It ought to have been beautiful, but Cynthia was too weighed down by guilt to enjoy it.

The bus dropped them outside the front of Hauptbahnhof. The station itself was a large glass building, ultra-modern. There was a large concrete plaza in front of it. People milled about, waiting for buses or trains, some with suitcases, others talking on phones. Someone had erected a memorial next to one of the bus stops, covered to protect it from rain, filled with flowers, photos, and a few sputtering candles. Cynthia lingered as they passed it; it was for the bus accident. Of course, that had happened near here, hadn't it?

'Hurry up,' Wilhelm said tersely.

'I'm not going to miss my train. I have half an hour,' Cynthia replied. She wanted to be polite and make nice, but at the same time she was furious. The fury was winning.

The station was a maze of walkways and escalators. People moved in purposeful streams, and there was a constant rumble of trains arriving and departing. Cynthia paused in front of the huge board, looking for her train.

'Which one?' Lola asked.

'It's the train to Dessau. I'm changing there for Leipzig.'

'The regional train?'

'I couldn't get a direct train on such short notice,' Cynthia said defensively. 'It was too expensive.'

Lola looked away. 'Fine. Come on, it's this way.'

Cynthia was permitted to buy herself food before she was herded onto her train platform. After a short wait, the train pulled in. She gathered her bags to board.

'So, I guess this is goodbye.'

Wilhelm's expression said it was more like good riddance.

'Thanks for everything,' Cynthia added awkwardly. She felt nauseous. Picking up her backpack, she slung it over her shoulder.

'You dropped this.' Lola held out a flyer. Cynthia grabbed it.

'Thanks.'

'You're welcome.' Lola avoided her gaze. 'See you around.'

'Not in Berlin,' Wilhelm said.

'Wilhelm, stop,' Brigitte said. 'Let's not part on bad terms.'

You don't own Berlin, Cynthia thought, but she bit her tongue and hugged Brigitte instead.

'Thank you for letting me stay.'

'I'm sorry for the way things turned out.'

'No, I'm sorry. I never wanted to make things difficult for you,' Cynthia replied.

Lola hugged her too, but briefly, pulling away all too soon. Then Cynthia was boarding the train. She found a seat and peered through the window. The Deckers huddled together, as though danger might come at them from any side, but there was nothing on the platform except commuters, heading out of Berlin for a long weekend.

Cynthia waved once and received an unenthusiastic wave from Brigitte in return. Then she sat back, put her headphones on, and waited for the train to depart.

The Deckers remained on the platform, vigilant against any possibility that she'd try to stay, but Cynthia was resolved. She was leaving their lives. For good.

Ten minutes out of Hauptbahnhof, her phone rang.

'Hey.'

'Did the train work out?' Renata asked. 'Or did they insist you take the direct train?'

'No, it worked out. I think they were too concerned about me leaving to care.' Cynthia leaned back, finally relaxing. 'All clear on your end?'

'All clear on my end,' Renata confirmed. 'I'll see you in Seddin.'

The train trip seemed to whistle by, as Cynthia wrestled with her guilt. Somehow, nothing had turned out the way she'd expected. Had she acted prematurely? Had she made a mistake approaching Renata? It all seemed so confused.

Should she call Nathan?

But Nathan had been silent since yesterday, and Monica since the day before, and Cynthia couldn't shake the feeling that she'd offended her friends. It seemed like she was burning bridges left, right, and centre.

Before she knew it, she'd arrived at a tiny station, little more than a building, a bridge, and a parking lot. The plaque read *Seddin* in gothic letters. When Cynthia descended the stairs, halfway concerned she was in the wrong place, Renata was waiting, leaning against her car. She waved jauntily.

'You found it.'

'So I did,' Cynthia said, still looking around curiously. There was nothing to see. She felt a bit nervous at the thought of being in the middle of nowhere with a witch.

Renata's car was surprisingly nice, for a twenty-year-old art student. It was a sedan, and there was a kid's car seat in the back.

'You don't have kids, right?'

'This is my parents' car,' Renata replied.

'Younger siblings?'

'Two younger and an older brother, all half.' Renata rolled her eyes. 'Don't worry, they're in Berlin. You won't see them.'

'I wasn't worried. Just curious.'

'You're much more a cat than a dog.'

Cynthia had to laugh. 'I actually have a cat, back home in England. The dog is Lola's.'

'I know.' That short reply carried a depth of loathing and hurt which Cynthia was still not sure she wanted to wade into. But Renata had answered her frantic phone call, helped her with the trains, and even agreed to pick her up. She'd even suggested a place to stay overnight so that Cynthia wasn't immediately returning to Berlin.

Just in case.

It was the old paranoia. Cynthia was surprised how easily she slipped back into that mindset: picking up, running away, avoiding notice. Trusting Renata was a necessary evil, but Cynthia was moderately sure that Renata didn't have it in for her.

Once they were away from the little station, navigating small roads through the forest, Renata said, 'You said you had evidence.'

'I said I might have evidence,' Cynthia replied cautiously, 'but I need a promise, first.'

'As if I haven't helped you enough.'

'No promise, no evidence.'

'Fine.' Renata steered them through a crossroad. 'What do you want?'

'Promise me you won't report the shifters to the head of your coven, or the KUA until we have proof.'

'Still loyal to your people?'

'Aren't you?' Cynthia asked.

'Not really. What's the point?'

'I thought witches liked their covens.'

'For protection.' Renata indicated and turned them onto a new road. Abruptly, the trees opened up on one side, and a lake was visible. 'For communal magic. My magic isn't communal, and my protection comes from other sources.'

'Like?'

'My magic.'

'Your *non-communal* magic.'

'Yes.' Renata gestured left, to the lake. 'Seddiner See. We're close.'

'Already?'

'Yes. This is a holiday home. It belongs to the mother of my older brother. She won't mind if we stay the night.'

'Is she also a witch?' Cynthia asked nervously.

'Everyone in my family has magic,' Renata said, 'but not all magic is dangerous. Are all shifters this jumpy? Should I bother asking?'

'Yes and no.' Cynthia shrugged. 'Shall we say, not all of my family are shifters? My father is a mage.'

'The dark mage, Justin Gastrell.'

'Yep.'

'How dark?' Renata's smile was audible in her voice. 'More dangerous than me, I bet.'

'Let's talk about Santiago instead,' Cynthia said evasively. Renata laughed.

'Fine, it's up to you.'

A moment later, she pulled into a cul-de-sac of modern houses and stopped in front of one of them. It was closed up, the curtains drawn.

Cynthia felt nauseous, just looking at it. A witch's house. Her mum would kill her.

The inside was neat and reasonably modern. Renata opened all the curtains and directed Cynthia to a guest bedroom.

'I'll be in this room,' she added, gesturing through a doorway into a room filled with computer gear.

'What's all that stuff?' Cynthia asked.

'Uh, no idea. It belongs to my brother. He's always building computers and stuff.'

There were more computer knickknacks in the guest room Cynthia had been assigned. She left her bags and joined Renata downstairs in the kitchen.

'So...' Renata prompted once they were settled with cokes and crisps. 'Evidence?'

'Your promise?' Cynthia replied.

Renata rolled her eyes. 'I promise I won't betray your people without good cause.'

'Okay.' Biting her lip, Cynthia passed over her phone. 'I got this from the hunter database.'

Renata looked impressed. 'You are well-connected, for a shapeshifter.'

'My friends are well-connected,' Cynthia said.

'What's the difference?'

Cynthia shrugged. 'Makes it sound less intentional. Here.'

Renata took the phone and skimmed each of the photos. Finally, she summarised, 'Six missing shifters.'

'It looks like it.'

'And so? What do you want me to do with that?'

'I...' It felt wrong to share her suspicions out loud with Renata, but Cynthia pressed on anyway. 'The thing is, most of the shifters I know would have... run... if that many people had gone missing in one place.'

'But the Deckers didn't.'

'Right.' Cynthia fiddled with her glass. 'I think it's suspicious. But... I don't know. It doesn't prove anything, does it?'

Renata shrugged. 'It's enough that you could take it in front of the Council. I don't know what they'd do with it. Who'd want to kill shifters in Berlin?'

'Usually, we assume it's witches doing it.'

Renata snorted. 'In Berlin, witches kill witches. What do we want with shifters?'

'Magical power?'

'Well.' Renata tossed her ponytail over her shoulder. 'I can't use your power.'

'Really? I thought all witches could channel other supernaturals,' Cynthia said.

'Depends on the magic.' Renata passed the phone back. 'You friends with a lot of witches? Back in England?'

'One or two,' Cynthia said.

'Good enough to know what type of magic they do?'

'Um…' She thought about it. 'Monica… I guess she's my closest witch friend… I've only ever seen her do ritual spells. With the elements and magic circles. No, that's wrong. Very occasionally she does other spells.'

Renata waved a hand dismissively. 'That's witchcraft, standard stuff. Spells and invocations. Probably, she can do a lot of useful things, but not many specialised magics.'

Cynthia shrugged helplessly. 'I don't know. We don't discuss it.'

'What colour is her aura?'

'Grey.'

Renata chuckled. 'You have interesting friends. Grey witches and dark mages.' She laughed again. 'All magic needs a source. Her magic comes from inside herself. When that's not enough, she can borrow from other people. Or give to other people. Or take from the earth. But not all magic draws from the earth.'

'Where does yours draw from?' Cynthia asked.

'We don't know each other that well,' Renata replied. 'Where does your power come from?'

'We're born this way,' Cynthia said. 'It doesn't come from anywhere. It's genetics.'

'But how do you determine what you turn into? Is it only the last animal you saw? Any animal? How long can you hold a form?'

'Didn't Santiago tell you these things?' Cynthia replied, uncomfortable with the interrogation.

Renata shifted. 'Sure,' she said, her face twisting with sadness. 'Is it different for every shifter?'

'I don't think so.' Cynthia sipped her drink as she considered. 'It's always the last animal you saw. Any animal.'

'Insects? Warm-blooded or cold-blooded?'

'No insects. No fish, either. Mammals are the easiest, large animals are the easiest.' Cynthia paused. 'Different people can hold forms for longer or shorter. I can hold a cat form the longest. It's what I'm most used to. My sister likes birds the best.'

'You don't have spirit animals? Santi loved bears,' Renata said.

'I'm not sure I'd call it spirit animals,' Cynthia replied, 'but sure, we all have favourite forms.'

'What's it like, shifting?'

'Uhhh, uncomfortable when you shift. But then, fine. You sort of become the animal mentally as well. I mean, you can still think like a human, but it takes more effort.'

Renata nodded. She held out a hand. Tentatively, Cynthia took it. Renata focused, but after a few seconds she shook her head.

'I can't channel you. Only people with similar powers.'

'Good,' Cynthia said. Renata laughed.

'Tomorrow, I'll take you back into Berlin and then I can speak to the KUA witches,' she said.

'About the shifters?' Cynthia asked warily.

'I won't mention any of the living shifters,' Renata said. 'One of the members of the council owes me… let's say a favour. If I tell her I want to find out about Santi, she'll look into it.'

'Right.'

'I can also ask my brother, but he'll probably be annoying about it.' Renata rolled her eyes.

'And… what do you want in return?' Cynthia asked.

Renata hummed. 'If the shifters are at fault, you have to let KUA deal with it.'

'I…' Cynthia stared at her drink. 'I really don't want anyone to get hurt.'

'Six people are already dead.'

'Yeah, but the Deckers… they're not bad people.'

Renata scowled.

'Lola's the same age as you,' Cynthia added. 'That's… come on. She's not a bad person. She misses Santi, too.'

Renata snorted. 'It's a good thing you weren't there after he died, you might not say that.'

'Grief makes people do crazy things.'

'*I* didn't do crazy things,' Renata snapped. 'Most of us just get on with it, yeah? We don't go accusing other people of being murderers, or stalking them online, or—'

'Or going up to their friends and insulting them?' Cynthia asked sharply.

Renata looked away, something like shame creeping onto her face. 'Fine, I saw you, and I thought of him. But okay, you're not the same as Santi, because Santi was trusting. You're… different.'

'Everyone's different,' Cynthia said. 'You don't want us to judge every witch the same, but then you can't judge every shifter the same.'

'I know.' Renata frowned at her coke can. 'Fine. I'm sorry I was a bitch to you. Even if you were totally using me to get information.'

'A bit,' Cynthia said, relieved that it was out in the open. 'But you'd have done the same.'

'Probably.' Renata stood and stretched. 'We have to leave really early tomorrow. I need to be at the uni for classes at nine.'

'Okay.' Cynthia followed her lead, finishing her drink and chucking the can away. 'By the way, Renata?'

'Yeah?'

'Thanks for this. It means a lot.'

Renata scowled, though beneath it she seemed pleased. 'You're welcome. Cat-Girl.'

'I'll take that.' Cynthia laughed.

CHAPTER SIXTEEN

RENATA DROPPED CYNTHIA BACK at the Bleibtreustraße apartment the next morning. She was suitably impressed by Damien's address.

'Who lives here?' she asked as she double-parked outside.

'Damien von Klichtzner.'

Renata raised an eyebrow. 'You know Damien von Klichtzner? Well enough to borrow his apartment?'

'His daughter is one of my best friends,' Cynthia said. 'How do you know him?'

'Everyone knows him. He's like an urban legend.' Renata shook her head. 'You are strange, for a shifter. Next, you're going to tell me you know the Oldenburg Vampire.'

'Who's that?'

Renata laughed. 'Another urban legend. Don't worry about it. Go unpack, I'll text you when I can meet up.'

That left Cynthia twiddling her thumbs. She sent a reminder to Lily to please check the Witch Council names—which went ignored—and finally caved and sent apologies to Monica and Nathan. Nathan was as silent as usual, but Monica replied promptly.

> **Monica:** No worries
>
> **Monica:** How are things going?
>
> **Cynthia:** Let's say I've burnt a few bridges
>
> **Monica:** Following my advice? Got to burn the bridges to build new ones
>
> **Cynthia:** Jeremiah is right, your advice is bad for my health
>
> **Monica:** LOL

Reassured that she hadn't completely ruined all her friendships just yet, Cynthia decided to head out into the city. She didn't make it far before her phone rang.

'Hi Mum,' she greeted.

'What have you done?'

Cynthia's heart sank.

'What do you mean?'

'I spoke to Brigitte Decker. Cynthia, what are you thinking? Where are you?'

'I'm… staying at a friend's apartment.'

'What friend? Lola?'

'No… Lily von Klichtzner.'

'Cynthia—' It was rare moments when Cynthia managed to stun her mother speechless. They almost always spelt trouble. Cynthia felt sick.

'Look, Mum, I know what you think, but just hear me out.'

'Oh, I'd love to hear what your explanation is,' her mother snapped. 'I've been friends with the Deckers since before you were born — Cynthia, I cannot believe you. Did you really accuse them of murder?'

'No… not as such.'

'*Not as such?* That's it. I want you on a plane today.'

'No.'

Cynthia was as surprised as her mother by the vehemence behind that word. She hadn't realised her own frustration until that moment.

'No? I'm your mother—'

'No. I'm eighteen. I'm paying for my trip. I'm staying here.' Cynthia took a deep breath. 'Someone's killing shifters in Berlin, and someone needs to find out who and bring them to justice. So I'm going to.'

'Are you insane? You'll get yourself killed!'

'I won't.'

'You can't possibly know that.'

Cynthia's heart was racing, and her breath felt short. She said, 'We're in danger all the time. We learn to live with that. I can take care of myself.'

'Absolutely not.'

'I have to stay,' Cynthia said, 'and I'm tired of you trying to control me all the time. It's got to stop. The spying on me and checking my phone when you think I'm not looking and making me text you all the time when I go out. I'm not as helpless as you think, Mum.'

The other end was so silent, Cynthia thought for a moment that her mother had hung up. Then, abruptly, she heard a choked sob.

Shit.

'Mum—don't cry.'

'I—I—Cynthia, you're only eighteen. Please come home.'

'And if I died, Mum? Who would avenge me? Lola's right, shifters are selfish. We abandon our dead. I need to see this through.'

'I don't want to lose you. You're… you're so like I was, Cynthia. Thinking you're right… you're stubborn.'

'Wow, thanks.'

'I just don't want you to make the mistakes I did.'

'I'm in contact with Nathan,' she said. 'I'm not alone, Mum. And I'm not stupid. I'm not going to run into trouble. I'm working with the hunters here.'

'Even so…' Her mother blew her nose loudly. 'Please come home.'

'One more week.'

'What will I tell Emma?'

'Tell her I'll bring her a chocolate bear.'

Mum gave a watery laugh. 'Oh, Cynthia.'

'I'll be fine, Mum. You know I will. You taught me how to run away. I'm good at it. And no one knows I'm in Berlin right now.' *Except Renata,* she added mentally.

'Just be careful.'

'I will, I promise.'

'Text me every night.'

'I will, Mum.'

'I love you.'

'Love you too, Mum.'

They hung up. Cynthia found a bench to settle on, trying to swallow down her nausea. She was a terrible daughter, wasn't she? A liar. She really ought to go home.

But then… who would investigate Santiago's death? Who would bring the murderer to justice?

She rubbed her fists against her temples.

'This is so messed up.'

What to do now?

Finally, Cynthia stood up from the bench and started walking again. This was what Nathan or Monica would do, so she was going to do the same. Be brave. Face her demons. Find out the truth.

She took the train west to the Deckers' apartment. Their car was gone from the parking lot, and the apartment looked empty. It was Friday, so Wilhelm was probably working. Brigitte might be at the shops, or on a similar errand. The apartment would be empty.

A plan blossomed in Cynthia's mind.

Before she could think the better of it, she set off hunting for a bird to shift into. Something small.

Sparrow. Gotcha.

She took shelter behind the hedge, stripping her clothes off and folding them neatly. Her heart pounded as she did it. This was different from shifting in the woods with Lola, showing off for Nathan, or playing with her sister. This was dangerous, illegal. Mum would kill her.

This is the right thing to do.

Taking several deep breaths, Cynthia reached inside herself for the sparrow, letting it displace her human consciousness. She felt the familiar pushing and prodding as her body was rearranged. Feathers took shape, a beak, the world seemed to grow larger around her. Finally, the magic settled. She flapped her wings experimentally, and managed to take to the air.

Flying always took practice. The sparrow was so jumpy, too. Every twitch in the bushes was a cat stalking it, every rustle in the trees was a larger bird coming to snatch it out of the sky. The sparrow was ruled by its fear.

Once Cynthia had got the hang of it, she managed to manoeuvre herself to the top floor of the building, flitting around until she found a window that was cracked open. She settled on the sill, peering in worriedly.

Please let the apartment be empty.

Everything seemed still. Finally, Cynthia fluttered in, settled on the ground, and transformed back. She was standing in the living room. Her breathing sounded terribly loud in the silence.

Where to look?

She started with Brigitte's papers, lying on the dining room table. A cursory glance through showed they were mostly to do with local tours. Anything that might have been more interesting was in German, and Cynthia's phone was with her things outside, so she couldn't take photos. After that, she crept up to Lola's room, but she'd already searched through most of the things there: detritus of Lola's teenage years. Sketches, notes from school, old books and comics. Nothing Cynthia could use.

The last place she looked was the most terrifying: Wilhelm's study. She'd never been in before. He usually kept the door shut. A sofa bed stood against one wall, the desk against the other. There was a desktop computer, plenty of books and folders, and stacks of papers. Most of it meant nothing to Cynthia: spreadsheets with detailed financials, bar graphs, ominous headings in German. She wiggled the mouse, but the computer was off.

Claws against the floorboards caught her attention. Cynthia straightened in alarm, squeezing her eyes shut. Gracie. *Crap!* If she saw the dog, her shifter form would change, and she'd have no way out.

Gracie woofed loudly, excitedly, and then Cynthia felt a soft head butting against her bare leg.

'Gracie, no! Nein! Shit, Gracie, you need to go!'

Blind, she nudged the dog away and stumbled towards the door. She stretched an arm out and managed to find the doorframe. Gracie, thinking it was a game, got under her feet, barking enthusiastically and tripping her up.

'Gracie, stop! Sit!'

Cynthia gripped the doorframe, edging forwards. Her feet moved from carpet to wood as she reached the hall. Where was the dog? Could she look? She tried to visualise the hallway, stumbling forward another step. Claws skittered, and Gracie knocked into her. Cynthia's hand brushed something on the wall and there was a crash and the sound of glass shattering.

'Fuck!'

Cynthia froze instinctively, her heart racing. Of course, there was no one here to hear the crash. She felt silly. But what to do? She couldn't pick the glass up, couldn't leave it here.

Footsteps and a voice echoing in the stairwell made her freeze all over again. Was that…? It was. *Brigitte. Crap!*

Throwing caution to the wind, Cynthia opened her eyes and crouched down. She grabbed the largest shards of glass, the back of the frame, the photo. Keeping her eyes on the ceiling, she stood and ran for the open window. She threw everything outside, then transformed as fast as she could.

Faster, faster, faster, she urged, hearing the key turning in the door.

Gracie was barking. The shift finished, and Cynthia found her wings, flapping them desperately. *Fly!*

Then she was airborne. She lurched out the window and plummeted towards the ground, pulling up at the last moment and darting behind the hedge. Her little sparrow-heart beat a frantic rhythm as she touched down beside her clothes and began to shift back. That had been close. Far too close.

Cynthia kept her gaze on the window high above her as she dressed hastily, but nothing stirred. She ought to fetch the picture. Hide the evidence.

Sucking up her courage, she darted back to the house. The glass had shattered to a fine dust, which ground beneath her shoes. She picked up the frame and backing and looked around for the photo. It had drifted a little way away. As Cynthia picked it up, writing caught her eye. Someone had scribbled on the back, just like her mother used to do on analogue photos.

Lola Decker und Tasha Bakker, 2010 (Foto von Anya)

Heart in her mouth, Cynthia flipped the photo over. Two preteen girls peered back at her. One was undoubtedly Lola. The other had dark hair in pigtails and braces.

Bakker.

Anya Bakker.

The Deckers had known another of the missing shifters.

Well, crap.

CHAPTER SEVENTEEN

'SO THE DECKERS ARE linked to two of the missing shifters,' Renata said grimly, turning the photo over and over in her fingers. 'Suspicious.'

'I still don't think they're murders,' Cynthia insisted. She felt a little like she was flogging a dead horse. But whatever was going on here, she couldn't imagine Wilhelm and Brigitte Decker murdering someone. Murdering shifters. No way.

'Don't be naïve,' Renata said haughtily.

'It's not naïve!' Wilhelm had said the same thing. The words flooded Cynthia with anger. 'It is NOT naïve to believe the best of people.'

'When faced with evidence, yes it is!'

'This isn't evidence! I know dead people. Does that make me a murderer?'

Renata rolled her eyes and reached for her drink. 'Don't take it out of context.'

'I'm not,' Cynthia said stubbornly, picking up her own drink. The alcohol sat funny in her stomach.

'Fine,' Renata said, 'so a photo doesn't make them murderers, but you have to admit it's suspicious.'

'Maybe.' Even that one word felt like a betrayal. Renata fixed Cynthia with an incredulous look, and Cynthia hunched her shoulders. 'Okay, it's suspicious.'

'Thank you.' Renata pulled her phone out. 'I'm going to see if I can find Tasha Bakker's phone number.'

'What? Why?'

'To see if she knows anything.'

'I don't think that's a good idea,' Cynthia said.

'Why not? It's her mother. I'll bet she investigated.'

Cynthia tried to imagine how she would feel if it were her mother, and she got a call from a witch about it seven years after the fact. *No, nope. Bad idea.*

'At least let me make the call.'

Renata's expression was eloquent. 'If you must.'

Cynthia wouldn't have known how to go about finding someone's phone number if she'd never met them, but Renata made short work of the job, and finally rattled off a +41 number.

'What country is that?' Cynthia asked.

'Switzerland.'

'Oh.'

Renata rolled her eyes. 'I thought you were well-travelled.'

'I thought so too,' Cynthia muttered. She plugged the number into her phone and listened nervously as it rang. A moment later, someone picked up.

'Tasha Bakker.'

'Hi, um, Ms Bakker. This is Cynthia Rymes. I—' *Have no idea what I want to say.* 'I'm calling from Berlin.'

'I don't know a Cynthia Rymes.' Tasha Bakker's voice had gone distinctly cool. 'What's this about?'

Cynthia took a deep breath. 'I'm a shapeshifter. I'm investigating the disappearances—'

'I have no interest in speaking to you,' Tasha interrupted. 'Please do not call me again.'

'No—wait!'

The silence on the other end was practically deafening, but the call was still connected. 'Please,' Cynthia said, 'I want to know what happened.'

Across the table, Renata was laughing.

'You think I want to discuss that with a random stranger? You have some nerve!'

'Don't you want justice—'

The call dropped. Cynthia groaned. Renata, still sniggering, shook her head.

'Like I said, naïve.'

'It's not naïve!' Cynthia snapped. 'Why does everyone think that wanting the best, wanting to see the best in people is naïve?'

'Because people aren't good,' Renata replied. 'We're all doing what we have to do to survive. Everyone for themselves.'

'You were angry with me because the shifters took that attitude about Santi's death.'

Renata scowled. 'That's different. There was no threat to anyone else, was there?'

'Maybe. We don't know that.' Cynthia chewed her lip. 'What if the shifters are being blackmailed?'

'By who?'

Cynthia almost said *the Witch Council,* but then she thought the better of it. That was a sure-fire way to piss Renata off. 'I don't know. But there could be someone. I hardly know every witch in the city.' She thought of Anton. 'But I do know warlocks who try to blackmail shifters.'

'Here?' Renata asked. 'We have enough problems of our own.'

'Maybe you do. But that might not be true for everyone.'

Renata pressed her lips together. Finally, she said, 'Let me try calling the Bakker woman.'

'If you call right after me, she'll just hang up,' Cynthia said.

Renata shrugged. 'Tomorrow, then. But then we have nothing more to discuss this evening.'

Cynthia let her gaze drift to the singer in the corner. 'Call her tomorrow and let me know what you find.'

Renata nodded and stood. 'Let's get out of here.'

That left Cynthia at a loose end again. Breaking into the Deckers' apartment was not exactly what she'd call a success, so instead she wandered around Berlin the next day. She had just finished lunch when her phone rang. It was an unknown number, German. Cynthia answered cautiously.

'Hello?'

'…Hello?' The voice was male and vaguely familiar.

'Who is this?'

'It's Leon.'

Cynthia smiled. 'You got over your phobia of phones.'

'I don't have a phobia!' he said sniffily. 'I don't know where you got that idea.'

Cynthia laughed. 'What's up?'

'I thought you had left the city. But then you came back.'

That threw Cynthia. 'Wait, how'd you know I left? Are you stalking me?'

'I had to make sure you were safe.' Leon sounded defensive. 'You can't trust the witchling.'

'So you followed me?'

'I didn't follow you. The wolf came back to the apartment with food, so I knew you must still be staying there—'

Some days Cynthia felt like she was the only human in the room. Supernaturals just had such strange logic.

'Leon…' Cynthia sighed. 'You make no sense, you know that?'

'Can we get coffee again? I'll pay this time.'

At some point, she was going to hit her maximum quota for weirdness.

'Alright. Where?'

'The same place?'

'Fine. I'll see you there.' Hanging up, Cynthia saved his number to her phone. Did that mean Anton was wrong? Did Leon have a phone? Was she betraying him by saving the number? Well, only if Anton went hunting through her phone history again… but Cynthia doubted she'd be seeing the man again, so it was probably fine.

When she reached the coffee shop, Leon was waiting, all ripped jeans and old shirt and boyish enthusiasm. He lit up when he saw Cynthia.

'You came.'

'I said I would.'

Leon looked embarrassed. 'I have money this time.'

'It's okay.' Cynthia patted him on the arm. 'I've had boys do worse than ask for cash for a coffee.'

'I'm not a boy!' Leon said indignantly.

Cynthia laughed.

They got their lattes and sat on the last unoccupied sofa, knees almost brushing.

'What did you want to see me for?' Cynthia asked.

'No reason. I mean—' Leon paused. '—I just wanted to see you. Is that okay?'

'Oh!' Cynthia said, surprised and rather flattered. 'Yeah, that's alright.'

'Good,' Leon said. 'Great.'

They sat in silence for a few moments, until Cynthia couldn't bear it any longer.

'I did leave,' she said. 'I had a fight with my host family. They wanted me out of the city. So I went.'

'And came back.'

'Renata picked me up at Seddin and brought me back.'

'Renata Friedemann.'

'You know her?' Cynthia brushed her hair away from her face and studied him. Leon had beautiful blue eyes, but they didn't give away any of his secrets. 'Everyone seems to know everyone, round here.'

'Maybe.' Leon hesitated. 'The supernatural community… it has quite a small core.'

'Similar to Oxford, I guess.'

'Maybe? I've never been to Oxford.'

Cynthia turned so she was facing him properly. 'Have you lived in Germany all your life?'

Leon nodded. 'You haven't. You've travelled a lot in a short time.'

He didn't say it like a question. Cynthia wondered if she was that obvious.

'Mum moved us around a lot, like I said before. I've lived in America, England, Sweden, Greece…'

'I've never been out of Europe,' Leon admitted. 'You know more about the world than me.'

'I doubt that. At least…' Cynthia sipped her coffee, thinking. 'I know different stuff to you. I'll bet you know all the best places to go in Berlin. I don't know any one place that well, just a lot of places… okay.'

'I could show you,' Leon said.

'You could…' Cynthia looked up at him. He shifted a hand onto her knee, putting his coffee down. She felt a sudden thrill. Leaning forwards, careful not to displace his hand, Cynthia put her coffee next to his.

'Leon…'

Leon leant in and brushed his lips against Cynthia's cheek. He pulled back, his throat working furiously as he struggled to find words. 'I… Can I kiss you?'

'You're asking permission?' Cynthia whispered.

Leon's expression twisted. 'Don't you want me to ask permission?'

'I… yeah, actually.' A little smile crept across Cynthia's face. 'Yes, you can kiss me.'

He leaned in again, and then his lips found hers. It was a terribly gentle kiss. Cynthia caught his shoulders, trying to pull him closer, but Leon was unmoveable. He kissed her slowly, finally sliding his tongue between her lips. His hands came up to stroke her cheeks, her hair, unhurried. Cynthia sighed against him.

Leon moved back, his hands cupping her face, studying her.

'Was that alright?'

'That was lovely.' Cynthia gave him a coy smile. 'You could do it again?'

'I could.'

He captured her lips again, this time a little more forcefully. Cynthia lost herself in the kiss, wrapping her arms around Leon's shoulders. She could feel the strength in his arms and shoulders. He pulled her onto his lap, skimming his hands over her back.

When they parted, Leon's face was alight with enthusiasm.

'Wow,' Cynthia whispered. 'That was…'

'Will you…' Leon caught her hand, tangling their fingers together. 'I'd like to show you something. Can I take you out?'

'Sure,' Cynthia said breathlessly, 'I'd like that.'

Still gripping her hand, Leon stood and pulled Cynthia to her feet, almost knocking over their discarded coffee cups. Cynthia laughed and reached down to right them. His enthusiasm undiminished, Leon tugged her out of the café and led her to the S-Bahn.

'Where are we going?'

'You'll see.' He grinned.

'Is it a date? Am I dressed okay?'

Leon looked down at her, and then at himself. 'I'm sure the locals won't complain.'

'What does that mean?'

But Leon just laughed and led her on, refusing to give anything away.

They travelled forever, further and further east, to a part of Berlin Cynthia had never seen before. Once again, the city seemed to fall away; apartments and houses interspersed with greenery. From the S-Bahn, they walked until they reached a street running parallel to the river. Abruptly, Leon took Cynthia's hand again and pulled her off the road, along a fence beside a boarded-up building. He stopped in front of a collapsed portion of fence.

'This is it.'

'You want to go in there?' Cynthia asked suspiciously. 'It looks abandoned.'

'It's been abandoned for years.' Deftly, Leon scrambled over the fence and turned back to hold out a hand. Cynthia eyed him warily.

'I don't think we're allowed in there.'

'No one cares. Only vandals and squatters come here anymore.' Leon wiggled his fingers. 'Come on. It's safe.'

Reluctantly, Cynthia took his hand and let him help her over. They crossed the grass and rounded the back of the building. The river lapped sluggishly against the banks, and the rear windows of the building were smashed in.

'I'm really not sure about this,' Cynthia said as Leon climbed the stairs.

'We're not going to get in trouble. Come on.'

'Isn't this illegal?'

'This is Berlin.' Leon shrugged and vaulted over the windowsill. 'Climb up. I'll lift you down.'

The windowsill was full of splinters, and chunks had even broken off in places where other people had obviously also climbed in. Inside, there was further evidence of other people breaking in: the walls were covered in graffiti, cigarette butts and broken bottles littered the floor, and the whole place smelt of urine.

'Charming,' Cynthia remarked, examining a series of racist slogans on the wall.

'Through here.'

Leon led the way through the rooms, gracefully dodging rubbish and debris. Cynthia held his hand and eyed the ceiling warily; it didn't look structurally sound. The walls had suffered water damage, and the floorboards were dark with rot. Leon led her into what must have once been a ballroom. There were the remnants of intricate paintwork, mirrors, and chandeliers.

'What is this place?' Cynthia asked as they paused in the middle.

'Ballhaus Riviera,' Leon replied. 'It used to be a ballroom. It closed down, I suppose. It's what they do. Close old things down, let them fall apart, get rid of them, and build something new and ugly.' He shrugged. 'That's Berlin, these days.'

'I think Berlin is beautiful,' Cynthia said. 'Like a mix of old and new, and everything in between. People can be themselves here.'

Leon smiled sadly. 'I like your Berlin better.' He turned to face her and bowed, a neat, unostentatious movement. 'Dance with me?'

'What, here?' Cynthia eyed the decaying building sceptically. 'I don't know how to dance.'

'It's not hard.' Leon hummed a few bars of a piece which Cynthia vaguely recognised. He wiggled the fingers of his outstretched hand. 'A lady should know how to dance.'

Cynthia giggled.

'I'm surprised you know how to.'

'Of course I do.' Leon pressed a hand to his chest, feigning offence. 'I am a gentleman.'

'Of course you are.' Cynthia took his hand and gasped when he tugged her closer. 'Leon, careful! Are you sure the ceiling won't collapse on us?'

'Relax,' Leon whispered, right next to her ear. 'Trust me? If it does, I'll protect you.'

'That's not reassuring.'

'It should be.' He pulled back and grinned. 'I have magic, remember?'

'You said it wasn't useful.'

'Well, it would be if the ceiling collapsed… but how often are you in buildings where the ceiling collapses?'

'Not too often, I guess. Alright, alright, you've convinced me.' Cynthia smiled up at him. 'Show me how to dance.'

Leon slid his other hand to her shoulder, holding her close, and led her in a slow circle. Cynthia stumbled along with him.

'Close your eyes,' Leon whispered.

She let her eyes fall shut. He hummed the same tune again, adding the next few bars, and for a few seconds, Cynthia imagined being there with live music and other people dancing around them.

'Open them.'

They had stopped in front of one of the mirrors. It, too, had suffered water damage. Their reflections were distorted and oddly monstrous.

'Can you see?' Leon asked.

'Um…' Cynthia glanced at him uncertainly. He grinned and reached out, sticking a hand through the mirror. Cynthia gasped.

'What?'

'It's an illusion. The magic has almost worn off. Does your phone do light?'

'Sure.' Cynthia pulled it out and switched the torch on. Leon clambered over the bottom of the mirror's frame, vanishing entirely for a moment, like he'd stepped into a pool of mercury. Then he leaned back and offered Cynthia a hand. She climbed cautiously after him.

Inside was a small room, narrow enough that it probably didn't appear on the floorplan, and no one would notice the space was missing. Something moved and Cynthia swung her phone around, yelping.

'It's just a rat.' Leon chuckled.

'Thanks for the warning!' Pushing away the awareness of the rat— not an animal Cynthia was planning on shifting into, thanks—she moved her phone slowly around, taking in the peeling walls and the ornate gold chair, its red velvet cushions torn through. 'What is this place?'

'Hunting room.' Leon's grin bordered on creepy in the low light. 'Revenants used to sit back here. Whenever someone came close enough, they'd—' He made a snatching gesture.

'And eat them? Wait, revenants?'

'Vampires.'

'Why do you call them that?' Cynthia asked.

'It's from French, *revenir*? Because they came back from the grave.'

'Oh.' She moved towards the walls. There were traces of a rust-like substance on them. Up close, Cynthia realised it must be blood. Yuck. 'People died here?'

'I doubt it. The vampires can persuade their victims to forget, right? I imagine it was entertaining for all.'

'That is… vaguely creepy. I have to say. Not how I imagined our first date would go.'

'Oh, is this a date?' Leon smiled. 'May I kiss you again?'

'Are you going to ask every time?' Leon leaned in. 'Leon! Maybe not here!'

Leon laughed. 'The building's stood for this long. It will handle us kissing.'

'No! No!' Cynthia yelped as another rat skittered by. 'Ugh, even the rats don't like us hanging out here. Can we go back in the light, now?'

'Of course.'

It was a relief to climb back out into the ballroom and head out into the dim afternoon light. Cynthia rubbed her arms, feeling as though the dirt from the abandoned building was clinging to her.

'How did you know about that hunting room?'

'There are places like that hidden all over Berlin.' Leon helped her back through the fence. 'The vampires are lazy.'

'You really don't like vampires, huh?'

Leon smiled. 'I like you. Can I take you someplace else? Tomorrow or the next day?'

'Okay,' Cynthia said, 'I'd like that. But maybe somewhere with less dirt?'

'Dirt optional,' Leon replied. 'I'll bear it in mind.' He leaned in. 'I want that kiss now.'

'Alright.' Cynthia giggled a bit. Leon swallowed the sound as he pressed open lips to hers, his tongue tangling with hers. Cynthia tipped her head back and ran her fingers over his neck and into his hair. It was soft. Leon's teeth scraped her bottom lip, and he pulled back.

'Let me walk you back to the station. You shouldn't linger out here on your own.'

'Alright.'

They held hands back to the station, where Leon saw her onto the train. Cynthia felt strange crossing Berlin that evening, a mixture of elated and a bit terrified. Today had been perfect in the oddest way. Leon was like no other man she'd ever spent time with — creative, a bit weird, definitely not the sort of guy her mother would approve of.

Then again, her mother didn't approve of anything she was doing right now.

It was Saturday. She was supposed to have flown home today, but… she'd cancelled her flight, and now the future opened up before her, unencumbered and free. She felt as though she could do anything. She'd stay here, find out what was going on, see where her father was at… She'd be strong, like Nathan and Monica.

She smiled the whole way home, ate the food Roswitha had left in the fridge for her, and climbed into bed.

Hours later, Cynthia awoke to her phone buzzing in short, sharp bursts. Someone was texting her.

Lily: I'm soooo sorry

Lily: I really meant to get back to you

Lily: Damien's been AWOL

Lily: Anyway
Lily: KUA witches
Lily: Walter Gehring
Lily: Jürgen Strohkirch
Lily: And Karolin Friedemann
Lily: I hope that helps
Lily: How are you doing
Lily: Crap, I just realised it's 5AM in Germany. Sorry!

Cynthia felt cold as she read the last name. Friedemann was Renata's surname. Why hadn't Renata told her she was related to a KUA witch?

There was no further sleep to be had that night.

CHAPTER EIGHTEEN

'YOU HAVE REACHED THE voicemail service of Nathan Delacroix. Sorry, I'm not available at the moment. Please leave a message after the beep, and I'll get back to you.'

'Nathan…' Cynthia hesitated. 'I think I might have a problem. Please get back to me ASAP? Thanks.'

Sighing, she hung up the call and thumbed through her contacts. Who to call? Who would be able to help her find out what was going on? Her finger lingered over Leon's name. *What the heck? May as well try.*

She dialled the number, mentally plotting out what she'd say to the elusive mage. Leon seemed to know everyone. Maybe he could just straight out tell her who Renata was and whether she was a threat? Maybe he already knew what was going on? Or maybe he was also playing her. He had, after all, fessed up to doing odd jobs for the Council. Was she just an odd job?

The dial tone switched over to a message in German. Cursing her inability to understand, Cynthia hung up. Who else could she call? Monica? But what would Monica do? Lily? Lily was in the US.

Monica would say to go straight to the source.

She took the train to Hackescher Markt. Although it was unchanged, the square seemed somehow sinister under the light of the waxing moon. The shadows beneath the bridge were like a dark hole, waiting to swallow her up. Cynthia almost laughed at her own jumpiness.

She marched over to the black service door, knocking firmly. A bouncer opened the door and looked her up and down disdainfully.

'Guten Abend,' Cynthia said. 'I'm meeting someone.'

'I know.' He stepped aside. 'No trouble, yeah?'

'No trouble,' Cynthia agreed. She descended the stairs. *Verzaubert* was busier than it had been last time. It was Sunday, later, and dozens of witches and warlocks lingered in small groups, drinking and chatting. A group of teens with neon auras, women who had fluid auras like smoke, two men whose auras were dark blue like luxurious velvet. It was like being in a club with the lights flashing. Cynthia had to blink away the second sight, but the colours remained seared into her retinas.

Witches were so colourful.

Renata was waiting at the bar. She'd dressed up. Her hair was plaited in a series of complicated braids, with all manner of ribbons and beads threaded between them, and she wore a short black dress. Her expression was one of a Viking going to war.

The same bartender was there as the last time. Gideon seemed unsurprised to see Cynthia. He was rinsing glasses under a pressure tap, and signalled one minute to her. Cynthia nodded and slid in beside Renata.

'Hi,' Renata replied, setting her phone aside.

'Hey.' Her mouth felt dry. Cynthia wished she could down a shot and draw courage from it, like people did in films, but she'd have to drink a lot and fast to get tipsy, and she didn't have the money for that sort of thing.

'So?' Renata prompted after a while of silence, 'do you have new information?'

'No.'

Renata arched an eyebrow. 'Then what are we doing here?'

'You…' Before Cynthia could figure out the right words, Gideon approached.

'What can I get you?'

'Whiskey sour,' Renata ordered. Gideon glanced expectantly at Cynthia.

'I liked the old fashioned,' she said.

'Coming up.'

'Didn't take you for that sort of girl,' Renata said.

'I don't think you know me very well.' Cynthia gathered her courage. 'I know your mother is on the Witch Council.'

Renata gripped the edge of the bar. Cynthia noticed her fingers were trembling.

'Who told you?'

'A friend got their names for me.' Suddenly, Cynthia didn't feel like giving away any information to Renata. 'Why didn't you tell me?'

'Why does it matter?'

'Of course it matters! After everything—' Cynthia cut herself off angrily. 'I trusted you.'

'And the name of my mother changes that? She sits on the Witch Council, yes. I don't live with her. I hardly talk to her. Will my father's name change things too? Do you need to know my whole family tree to be friends with me?'

'It's not like that,' Cynthia snapped. 'I told you about my father.'

'Yes, and I didn't care!'

'Well, I do,' Cynthia replied. 'Did your mother know Santiago? Why am I investigating the Deckers? Is this what you wanted? To throw suspicion off your family?'

'Of course not!' Renata sneered. 'It was your idea to investigate the Deckers. I never told you to go to their house or look them up in the hunter database.'

'That's not the point right now.'

'Then what is the point?' Renata demanded. 'Why am I suddenly under suspicion, just because you don't trust witches?'

'You lied to me!' Cynthia cried.

'I never lied. You never asked. But you knew my full name. How am I to know you didn't realise what it meant?'

'You should have made sure,' Cynthia insisted. She felt crushed and angry but mostly frustrated with herself. 'If you weren't making a secret of it, why didn't you tell me?'

'Because I knew you would care!' Renata spat. 'Typical fucking dog, the moment you find out—I hardly speak to my mother. She has another family now! But all you care about is the name! Of course!'

'Don't call me a dog! I'm tired of everyone calling me that like it's funny!'

'If you don't want to be called one, then stop acting like one!'

A bang startled them both. Gideon had set their cocktails down.

'Is there a problem, ladies?'

'No.' Renata snatched her drink and took two deep sips. 'No, no problem. The stupid shapeshifter is just throwing around accusations as usual. That's all they're good for.'

'Mind your tongue,' Gideon said pleasantly. 'No matter your status,

I do expect all customers to be polite.'

'You have no authority over me.' Renata stood up, taking her drink. 'Don't call me again,' she snapped at Cynthia, before marching off down the bar. She vanished down the steps into the lower room, leaving Cynthia with anger prickling over her arms like static electricity.

'Fuck,' she muttered.

'I would say,' Gideon said.

'I messed that up, didn't I?'

'Hmm…' He considered her. 'If I might venture an opinion?' At Cynthia's nod, he continued, 'It doesn't do to tar all witches with the same brush, just because you've had bad experiences in the past. You never know what leads people to keep secrets. Renata's not that much older than you… And I think you've… shall we say worldlier concerns than most people your age. Don't assume they do too.'

'You mean Renata's just an ordinary girl, she's not plotting against me,' Cynthia said. 'You could just say that.'

'Diplomacy is a forgotten art,' Gideon lamented. 'Renata has a complicated relationship with her family, and it's been well documented by the local gossips.' He nodded to the witches down the bar. 'Probably, she was hoping you would look past that.'

'Damn it, that makes me feel worse.'

Sulkily, Cynthia sipped her drink. Gideon wandered off to serve two men who'd just entered. A little while later, he came back.

'I'm going off shift, soon. Would you like another drink before then?'

'Yeah, same again.'

'If I may be so bold, this isn't the safest place to drown your sorrows.'

'I suppose.' Cynthia finished the dregs of her first drink. 'I don't know where in this city is safe, though.'

'Have you considered going home?'

'Yeah.' Gideon began mixing her a second drink. After a moment, Cynthia said thoughtfully, 'Why do you suppose people do bad things?'

'I suspect that would depend on the individual and the nature of the bad deed.'

'Killing people,' Cynthia said.

'I can think of a few reasons,' Gideon replied, 'some selfish, others nominally noble.'

'What's a nominally noble reason for killing someone?'

Gideon slid her drink to her. 'Protection, perhaps?'

'Is protection really worth killing someone for?' Cynthia prodded her straw, watching it swirl around in the glass. 'Thanks.'

'Not a problem.' Gideon signed something to another bartender, who had just appeared out the back room. 'I would hope you're too young to be worrying about that sort of thing.'

'Supernaturals don't seem to care about age too much.'

'No, that is the trouble with vampires and witches. Maybe we live too long.' Gideon shrugged. 'Will I see you tomorrow? Or will you manage to stay away?'

'I hope I'll stay away,' Cynthia replied.

'Alright. Goodnight.'

'Night.'

Gideon vanished in back, and there must have been another exit because he didn't emerge again. Cynthia finished her drink slowly, but as the bar began to fill up, she grew uncomfortable. Gideon's presence had been more protective than she'd realised, apparently. Finally, she relinquished her spot to someone else and headed back to the street. It was dark and cool out. She shivered as she pulled out her phone.

> **Cynthia:** Hey Renata, look, I'm sorry. I was really rude and you're right, it actually doesn't matter
>
> **Cynthia:** Heaven knows my father's done shit things, I shouldn't judge

She watched the screen for a few moments, but Renata didn't reply. Sighing, Cynthia went to put her phone away, and at that moment it vibrated in her hand.

'Hello?' she asked, keeping her voice quiet, suddenly unnerved by the stillness in the air.

'Cynthia?'

'Leon?' Cynthia asked, surprised. 'What's up? I expected you to call earlier.'

'Where are you? You're not at the Bleibtreustraße apartment.'

'No,' Cynthia replied slowly, 'I had to go out. I'm at *Verzaubert*.'

'No,' Leon breathed. Cynthia felt her chest grow tight at his tone. 'You need to leave.'

'Why?'

'It doesn't matter, just go.'

Cynthia was fed up with witches who thought they could boss her around and give her no information.

'Actually, I'm not doing anything until you tell me why.'

'Cynthia—' Leon inhaled sharply. When he spoke, his tone was rife with desperation. 'You need to go home.'

'I don't understand. How can you know—' A movement in the shadows brought her up short. 'I have to go.'

'No, wait!'

She hung up as the man slithered out of the shadows. He was deathly pale, tall, and stick-like.

'Cynthia Rymes, your presence has been requested.'

Cynthia took a wary step back.

'Who are you?'

'You can come peacefully, or I can take you by force.'

The vampire followed her, step for step. Cynthia was almost at the square when he darted forwards. She shoved her knee up, catching him between the legs. He staggered and crumpled.

A movement behind her caught her eye. Hands raised defensively, she turned until she could see out of her peripheral vision.

Three more people slunk out of the shadows.

She was surrounded by vampires.

All the vampires were identically pale. Now that she had seen several of them, Cynthia could tell it wasn't just their skin tone that was affected by the sickness; they were weak. They had none of the usual grace of vampires, little of the speed. She should never have been able to land a blow on the first vampire. There was undoubtedly something wrong with all of them.

It didn't stop them from surrounding her.

Cynthia backed into the wall of the bridge, her hands held aloft, her mind racing.

'What do you want? Who is requesting me?'

'The Vampire Council has spoken,' a female vampire said. 'You must come with us now.'

'What if I don't want to?'

'We will take you by force.'

That was clear enough. This was less of a request and more of an order. Cynthia's mind raced. If she went compliantly, maybe they'd be kind. Then again, the Vampire Council in Berlin hadn't struck her as the nicest bunch. What they did want was blood, very obviously. She wasn't the usual target for vampires—vampires didn't drink the blood of other supernaturals; they didn't like the taste—but these ones didn't seem to be of a mind to be fussy.

'Why have I been requested?'

'That is for Julianus to explain.'

'Does Julianus think I'll do what he wants if he threatens me?'

The first vampire, the one she'd kneed, said, 'You won't have a choice.'

She had to get out of here. Grasping in her bag for her knife, Cynthia looked around desperately for a way out. Vampires could only be killed with three things: stakes, fire, sunlight. Cynthia had none of those available. Could she outrun them?

Outrun a vampire? The idea was laughable.

But these vampires were sick.

'I'm not sure I like Julianus's terms,' Cynthia said, her heart racing. 'I think I'd like to renegotiate.'

'Renegotiation is not—'

Cynthia dived between two of the vampires. One reached for her and missed entirely. The other lunged, hitting her with the force of a small car, and they both crashed into the opposite wall. Cynthia's right side exploded in pain—she was definitely bleeding. She stumbled, and her foot hit something—something which moved—

The vampire snarled as Cynthia stamped on its foot. Cynthia didn't hang around. She sprinted for the marketplace. People, crowds—that was her only chance. She ran like she'd never run before, heading for the busy centre of Berlin. The tram rattled in front of her, and she veered off course abruptly, into a side street.

Shit, this was so bad.

She chanced a glance over her shoulder. Two of the vampires were giving pursuit, but none of them seemed to be gaining on her. They ran like humans.

They're sick... all of them are sick...

Cynthia wasn't going to question her luck. Turning back to the front, she sprinted as fast as she could, taking corners haphazardly and praying she didn't hit a dead end. All of the streets around here doubled back eventually; Berlin didn't seem to like cul-de-sacs. All she needed was people to hide behind, enough people that the vampires would give up. A bar. There were loads around here.

She ran and ran, hoping she was angling towards the centre of Berlin, but the streets became less recognisable and less populated, and Cynthia knew she was in trouble. She sprinted through an alleyway and emerged onto a main street, just barely stopping herself from running into the road. Where was everyone? Left or right? She picked right at random and got lucky at a crossing; the light went green as she approached.

Where to go?

She took another right and found herself in a small, quiet street. *Damn.* Her footsteps echoed, frightening her. She darted a look backwards—the vampires were gaining on her. She plunged into another alleyway, this one dark with shadows. Her foot hit something, and she fell to the ground with a scream. A moment later, the vampire was upon her, dragging her back by the ankle.

'Stop, please! I'll speak to Julianus! Don't hurt me!'

She clawed at the cobblestones, her fingers slipping and sliding. The vampire hauled her over onto her back. His face was a rictus grimace of hunger, more monster than man. His eyes glowed red.

He lunged, latching onto Cynthia's neck. She screamed in pain as his fangs pierced her skin. It burnt like poison, and she couldn't help but remember what Leon had said—that they were cursed—would she be cursed now?

The vampire tore at her neck, drinking clumsily, spreading blood. He bit her again, again.

Then, suddenly, he was ripped away and thrown against a wall, collapsing into a boneless heap. Cynthia stared up in fear at her rescuer—shadowed face, dark eyes. For several moments, no one moved, the only sound was her panted breaths.

She scrambled to her feet.

'D—don't hurt me!'

'It's okay.' The man shifted and the shadows fell away from his features. It was Leon.

'Leon? What are you doing here?' Cynthia's voice broke on a sob.

'I came as soon as I could.' Leon's tone seemed apologetic. Or maybe she was imagining it. The whole world was starting to shift out of focus.

Footsteps rang out and Leon spun around. Cynthia stumbled dizzily, grabbing his arm to keep herself upright.

'No.' Leon half turned, steadying her. 'Cynthia? You have to hold on.'

'They—they were chasing me.' Three vampires. The fourth was still crumpled on the floor, but righting himself slowly, like an ancient beast unfurling its limbs after a long sleep.

'Give her to us,' the female vampire rasped.

'Please,' Cynthia sobbed. 'You have to help me!'

'I'm sorry,' Leon said. 'This is my fault.'

He was going to kill her. Cynthia choked on a sob, and in the space of that single heartbeat, Leon was gone. A scream rent the air, and something hot and sticky splattered over Cynthia's front. She stumbled forwards, her knees giving out, and Leon caught her.

'What—what—' She grappled herself upright, gripping his arms, trying to see past him. Leon pulled her face to his chest. His shirt was damp.

'Don't look. Not yet.'

'Leon—'

'It's okay. Shh. It's okay. You're safe now.'

Slowly, he released his grip, though his hands remained on her shoulders. Cynthia managed to find some vestige of strength, enough to stand on her own and look past him.

The alleyway was empty.

'What did you do?'

'They're gone,' Leon said, 'I promise.'

There was something on the floor, something grey and papery. Ash. Cynthia turned to look at Leon's face. It was as impassive as always, unreadable, impossible. He couldn't have.

'How?'

'Don't,' Leon whispered. 'You're weak. You need help.'

'I...' She had nowhere to turn. 'I can't go to hospital.'

'It's okay.'

Leon kissed her gently, his lips sliding over hers, velvety soft. Cynthia gasped gently, and his tongue slid into her mouth, tangling with hers. Every movement was slow, gentle, as though to hurry would shatter the moment. Leon ran his fingers through her hair.

'Cynthia, Cynthia,' he murmured against her lips, a prayer. It was without a doubt the most magical kiss of her life.

Finally, Leon pulled away, his mouth moving to her ear. 'You must drink,' he whispered. 'The venom from the bite is preventing you from healing. The vampires will smell your blood. More will come.'

'Drink?' Cynthia asked shakily, euphoria from the kiss warring with her ever-fading consciousness.

'My blood.'

Leon leaned back, raising a wrist to his mouth. His eyes glowed an eerie red, and then he sank his fangs into his own arm.

CHAPTER NINETEEN

A GENTLE BREEZE WAS stirring her hair. Cynthia cracked her eyes open slowly. She was in her room—Lily's room—in Damien's apartment. The window was open, making the curtains flutter. She could hear cars far below, a dog barking.

What happened?

Yawning, she sat up and stretched. Her eyes were crusted from sleep, and there was a terrible taste in her mouth, metallic and stale, almost like…

Blood.

Memories of the night before came rushing back. Cynthia slapped her hand to her throat, wincing before she realised that there was no pain. No bite. No blood. She jumped up, stumbling dizzily, and rushed to the bathroom to look in the mirror. Her face stared back at her, a healthy flush in her cheeks, her blond hair messy from sleep. There wasn't a single mark on her neck. The wound was gone.

'Did I dream it?'

Her voice came out a hoarse rasp. Cynthia ran the tap and bent over to drink long mouthfuls, dispelling the taste. But her mouth remembered. Coppery and slimy and hot.

Blood.

She'd drunk Leon's blood.

Either she'd dreamed the whole thing, or…

'He's a vampire.' Cynthia looked in the mirror again. Her eyes were wide with fright. 'He's a *vampire.*'

How?

Cynthia knew vampires. Well, she knew one vampire: Nathan's uncle, Adrian. Peripherally, she was also acquainted with a few others: Lily's father, Damien; Jeremiah, who sat on the Vampire Council; and Nathan's mentor, Aodhán. But she didn't count any of them. They were old and… what interest would they have in an eighteen-year-old shapeshifter? None whatsoever. It wasn't as though Cynthia was going to go asking them questions or anything.

She'd talked to Adrian, though, a little. He was a bit… scary. Vampires were scary, in general. Shifters were taught to be afraid of witches, but Cynthia found vampires more terrifying by far. They had something ageless, timeless, unchanging about them. It just screamed supernatural, like they weren't part of the same world as Cynthia. The way they moved, talked, even their manners, were just out of this world.

Leon wasn't like that.

So, maybe I did dream it.

She splashed water on her face and dried it with a towel, trying to calm her racing heart. It was a dream. She'd stayed in last night. None of it had happened. The memory of the pain in her neck was just an illusion.

But if she'd dreamt the whole thing, did that mean she'd never spoken to Renata?

The entire logic threatened to collapse. Cynthia pushed the thought away. She could check her phone. She'd texted Renata, right? So… no messages meant it was a dream.

And if she had texted Renata…

Bang!

Cynthia jumped, yelping. She clamped a hand over her mouth. *Crap! What was that?* Was there someone in the apartment?

Trembling, she crept into the hall. Noises were emanating from the kitchen; quiet voices and clattering. Cynthia edged over to the door and peered around it, then sighed in relief.

It was Roswitha.

She had the radio on and was preparing breakfast. Cynthia sighed again, and Roswitha glanced over.

'Good morning.'

'Hi,' Cynthia replied uneasily, still trying to master her own fear. 'Um…'

'You're dressed already.' Roswitha gestured to her crumpled clothes. 'Are you going anywhere today?'

'Actually, no, I…' Cynthia had no idea what to say. 'How long will breakfast be? I think I might take a quick shower.'

'Ten minutes.'

'Thanks.'

The shower improved matters considerably. Once she'd dressed in fresh clothes, Cynthia checked her phone. The text messages to Renata were there.

If x equals yes, then y equals yes, she thought bitterly.

So what did that mean? Leon was a vampire. Except, he didn't behave like a vampire. He didn't look like a vampire. He had an aura.

He wasn't pale and cursed and mad with blood lust.

I should text Nathan.

Cynthia shoved her phone in her pocket and headed for the kitchen. She was done being the damsel in distress who always called her friends for help. She'd figure this out on her own.

Maybe there was a simple explanation.

Roswitha's practical cheeriness might have been welcome on any other morning, but this morning it seemed to grate on her. After breakfast, Cynthia rattled around the apartment, unsure what she should be doing. She was a bit scared to go out. The apartment felt safe—truth be told, it was safe. Leon oughtn't to be able to get at her here because there were wards which should keep him out.

But then, how had she got back in the apartment last night?

Her memory was a blank between drinking his blood and waking up this morning.

Could drinking blood do that to you?

Nathan would know.

Or maybe the answer was entirely innocent. She had drunk his blood and passed out. Leon had brought her home. He knew where she was staying.

She'd drunk his blood.

Her hands shook.

He's a vampire. I trusted him, and… he's a vampire.

Why hadn't he told her? She'd out-and-out asked him about his magic. They'd spoken about vampires. Witches. He'd lied.

'I don't remember my parents.'

All of the missing clues slotted into place. Leon was a vampire. He wouldn't tell her his age—because he was old. How old? Old enough to have forgotten his parents? Was Leon an old name? Had he changed his name?

Why wasn't he cursed like the other vampires?

I trusted him.

Cynthia kicked her foot against her suitcase and cursed under her breath. She wasn't a fan of swearing, at least, not out loud, but some situations just called for it.

'Sort your shit out,' she said to the walls. 'Fine. I'll call him.'

Her phone was practically dead; she'd had to put it on to charge this morning. There was still no reply from Renata—another bridge burnt—but Cynthia wasn't too sad about that right now.

Berlin was filled with liars, apparently.

She had two numbers for Leon. The one she'd saved under his name, and the other he'd used last night. She tried both. One went to voicemail, and the other got an automated message in German and English.

'This is Clärchens Ballhaus. We are not open to take calls until four PM. Opening hours are eight PM until one AM. Thank you for your understanding.'

He'd called her from the office. Cynthia barked out a laugh, bitter and angry. From the fucking Vampire Council.

I trusted him.

She chucked her phone on the pillow and lay back on the bed, staring at the ceiling high above. She needed to think. What should she do now? Renata was in with the Witch Council. Leon was a vampire. Who did she trust?

Anton? No way.

Gunther? But Gunther was young and inexperienced. What would he even be able to do?

Gunther's father?

I should call Nathan.

She glanced at her phone and gnashed her teeth. It was the same story over and over again. When she was in trouble, she called for help.

Maybe it was time to go home?

That thought grated even more, but Cynthia forced herself to consider it. She was in way over her head. She hadn't even started to think about what had happened last night. The Vampire Council had had her followed. They'd tried to kidnap her. What if they did it again?

She'd only seen vampires at night, Cynthia realised suddenly. During the day, she was safe. Of course, that didn't account for the witches.

Or Leon.

But she was safe from the Vampire Council during the day.

Except that she couldn't just hide in the apartment whenever the sun went down. Eventually, the vampires would find a way to get at her. Compel a bunch of humans to fetch her. Threaten someone she cared about. Anyway, if she was hiding, she wasn't finding out anything new.

So she was stuck.

She picked up her phone and sighed deeply.

Stuck, out of options. Except for the one option, the one it always came down to.

She rang Nathan.

The phone rang.

And rang.

And rang.

And clicked.

'You have reached the voicemail service of Nathan Delacroix. Sorry, I'm not available at the moment. Please leave a message after the beep and I'll get back to you.'

'Nathan…' Cynthia swallowed against the lump in her throat. 'You know what, I don't even know how to put this into words, so, uh, call me back as soon as you get this. Please.'

She hung up and let her arms flop onto the bed. Voicemail, again. She was starting to worry. Nathan could be bad about replying, but he was never unreliable, just busy. Normally, he'd call her back as soon as he finished work or whatever thing he was doing. This was unusual behaviour.

Had something happened back in Oxford?

She texted Monica.

> **Cynthia:** Nate around?
> **Monica:** Nope, busy with something, didn't say what
> **Monica:** Something the matter?
> **Cynthia:** More like, is anything going right?
> **Monica:** Anything I can do?
> **Cynthia:** I don't know
> **Monica:** Want to call? I'm on break in 30
> **Cynthia:** It's okay, but thanks

Where did that leave her? Nathan was busy, but Monica wasn't worried. So, Cynthia shouldn't be either. That was good, but it didn't solve her problem.

For something to do, she began pulling her clothes together to put in the wash. She either needed to decide to go home or commit to staying here. Too bad she'd never been great at making big decisions. What were the pros and cons?

Pros of going home—I don't get eaten. She laughed. *That's a big one. Cons—I don't find out who murdered Santi, nor where my father is.*

She tried to think of more.

I don't get to apologise to Renata.

And she did want to apologise.

Con of staying—Leon is dangerous.

But was he? He'd saved her from the vampires.

But he was a vampire.

She was going in circles. Cynthia switched the washing machine on and went back to her room. She'd managed to make a mess. Her things were strewn over the bed and floor. She picked up a couple of things, tossing them into her suitcase. Nathan would have been neater. He was also fairly unsentimental. He didn't collect flyers and tickets and random scraps of paper. Cynthia picked up a flyer for the old Olympic Stadium to add to her binder.

Wait. She'd never been there.

It had been on her to-do list, but Lola had said it was out of the city, and it'd be easier to plan a day trip and see several places out that way...

Lola.

Lola had given her a flyer at the station. Cynthia had completely forgotten about it.

Fingers shaking, Cynthia unfolded the flyer. A scrap of paper was tucked inside. *I might be able to help you find out what happened. Call me. – Lola*

Her breath left her in a rush.

If only she'd found this days ago. Why hadn't she checked?

I was too caught up in being angry at Wilhelm.

Fuck.

There was no time to waste. Cynthia grabbed her phone and, heart in her mouth, dialled Lola's number. The phone seemed to ring forever, and yet all too soon Lola picked up.

'Cynthia.'

'Hey.' Now that she was on the phone, Cynthia had no idea what to say. 'I… uh… I'm sorry.'

Lola took a deep breath and let it out in a long sigh.

'Shit got fucked up fast, hey?' She sounded like she was moving, then she stopped and sighed again. 'Look, I don't agree with what you said, but I do agree that we need to find out what happened.'

That wasn't the response Cynthia had been hoping for, but she knew better than to argue. 'You asked me to call you.'

'Yeah. Are you in Berlin?'

'Is that a problem?'

Lola was silent for a long moment. 'As long as you stay away from my family, no.'

'Good.'

Neither of them spoke for a while. It was Lola who finally broke the silence. 'I pulled a few police files. They're all closed cases, but they show the last movements of the missing shifters. Maybe it will help.'

'Can you show that to me?' Cynthia asked.

'No, of course not.'

Lola was agreeing to break the law for her. Cynthia swallowed. 'I don't want you to get in trouble.'

'Then make sure you keep this to yourself, yeah?'

'I will.'

'Fine, let's meet up. I'll text you an address. Come alone. Seven PM tonight.'

'Thanks,' Cynthia said.

'Don't thank me. I still think you're stupid and reckless and out of your fucking mind for accusing my dad.'

'I won't do it again,' Cynthia said. 'No more accusations until I'm sure.'

'You better.' Lola hung up. A moment later, Cynthia's phone buzzed with a message. She checked the address. It wasn't too far from Lola's apartment.

Great.

The day progressed slowly. Another summer storm was brewing, and Cynthia felt the tension in the air. Roswitha was off, too: an animal instinct that shifters and weres seemed to have in common.

That evening, Cynthia dressed for war. Black leggings and tunic, knife strapped to her wrist beneath her jacket. Nathan had given her the knife, but she'd never used it before. She knew the theory, though.

Please don't let tonight be the night.

She took the U-Bahn to Lola's place and found the bar. Wood counter and stools, old posters and mirrors on the walls. It could have been any other bar in the city. Lola was sitting at the counter, looking much the same as she usually did: jeans, tank top, fierce expression. Her tattoo was on show. Cynthia slid in next to her.

'I'm sorry,' she said immediately.

Lola's lips twisted. 'Let's just forget about it.'

That didn't make Cynthia feel any better. Her guilt was like a living thing, making her chest ache and her stomach churn.

'Okay,' she said through a tight throat.

They sat in uneasy silence until the bartender came by. Lola ordered two beers in terse German; Cynthia wasn't particularly talented at languages, but she was starting to get an ear for German. The beers were cold and bitter, which sort of matched the mood.

'So,' Lola said finally.

'So?'

'Look, don't let it go to your head, but… you were right about… about Santi needing justice. And the others. I didn't know about all of them, and I did some digging…' She trailed off. 'Fine, we need to do better as a community, alright?'

'I don't hold it against you,' Cynthia said. 'I'd protect my family, too.'

'We sound like the fucking shifter mafia,' Lola grumbled. Cynthia giggled, and for a second everything felt normal.

'I always thought vampires were more of a mafia. And the witches—'

'Don't get me started on the witches!' Lola groaned.

'Did you know Renata's mother is part of the KUA?' Cynthia asked. Lola looked at her askance.

'No, must be a recent promotion.' She frowned. 'Anton should have warned me. Who are the other members? Still Strohkirch, and—what's his name?'

Cynthia checked her phone. 'Strohkirch, Gehring, Friedemann.'

'I wonder what happened to the other guy.'

'What other guy?'

'Uh, I think his name was Dieter Weber. Something like that. He used to liaise with the police, but I only met him once or twice.' Lola shrugged. 'Witches disappear all the time in this city. I don't pay attention unless it's to cover it up. They kill each other.'

'I've never really known witches to do that.'

'Yes, well, your witches don't seem to be much like our witches,' Lola said.

Her words cut through the friendly conversation like a knife. Cynthia shuffled awkwardly and sipped her beer. Lola pulled a few sheets of lined paper out of her bag and unfolded them.

'I looked up all the cold cases for the last few years. These are the ones that I'm—' She hesitated. '—at least seventy percent sure are shifter deaths. These two I know are, Santi and Anya Bakker.'

She flipped pages. The next sheet was a map, with several crosses marked. 'These are their last known locations.'

Two were in an area which Cynthia knew was where the Deckers lived, but the others were scattered around. A dotted line encircled an area of north-western Berlin.

'What's that?' Cynthia asked.

'The area where they all likely disappeared,' Lola explained. 'It's the territory of the Margraf Coven—Renata's coven.'

'She told me she wasn't in a coven.'

'I think she fell out with them.' Lola shrugged unhappily. 'When I was at school with her, she was still a coven member.'

'Okay.' Cynthia stared at the map, trying to consider it from all angles. 'What does it mean? Margraf?'

'It's just a name, probably the surname of one of the founding members.'

'Oh.'

Lola folded the papers together again and pushed them towards Cynthia. 'I don't know if any of this will be useful… but maybe it will help.'

'I hope so.'

Lola grabbed her beer, downing it in a few gulps.

'Thanks,' Cynthia added. 'I appreciate it.'

'You're welcome. Stay away from the other shifters, yeah?' Lola put her bottle down. 'And mind the witches. Even if they're not behind this, that doesn't make them trustworthy. They'll kill you if it helps them win their petty squabbles with their neighbours. You'll be dead just the same.'

'I know.'

They parted a few minutes later. Cynthia found herself once again weighed down by guilt. Had she made a mistake in fighting with the Deckers? Her mother always accused her of being too stubborn, wilful, argumentative. Had she jumped to conclusions?

Her phone rang, drawing her out of her thoughts. When she checked the screen, she smiled in relief.

'Nathan,' she greeted. 'I've been worried.'

'God, Cynthia, I'm so sorry.' Nathan groaned. 'I feel like a jerk. I meant to call you, I swear I did, and you were in trouble, and things have been chaos. I'm a shit friend, aren't I?'

'It's okay,' Cynthia said.

'It's not. You don't have to say that for my benefit.' Nathan sighed wearily. 'It's not an excuse, but I've had a bloody long week.'

'Me too.' Spotting a bench, Cynthia flopped onto it. 'Where have you been, then? I even texted Monica.'

Nathan laughed. 'Don't kill me? I've been in Germany. Not Berlin, though. I had to go to Bonn, to the KUA headquarters. But I was thinking—'

'You're in Germany?' Cynthia's chest felt tight all of a sudden, from a mix of emotions she couldn't name. 'Since when?'

'Since yesterday,' Nathan said. 'I'm sorry I didn't tell you. Look, I know I've handled things badly. I was thinking, we have to take a trip up to the north, to the Danish border, and that should take two days, but after that, I fly home via Berlin. We could meet up? Clear the air.'

'I…' Cynthia swallowed. There was a lump in her throat. 'Yeah, okay, why not—'

She cut herself off abruptly as something moved in her peripheral vision. Two men stepped up to her, their movements intent. Cynthia stood up.

'Cynthia?'

'Sorry—I have to go.' She hung up and jammed her phone back into her bag. Two more men were approaching from further down the pavement. Cynthia didn't waste time on questions. She broke into a sprint.

'HEY!'

The men took up the chase. One of them fell away almost immediately, unable to keep up. Cynthia didn't break her stride, running for the U-Bahn station. If she could just get on a train…

Another man stepped out in front of her, and Cynthia slammed straight into him.

'Sorry, I—'

He grabbed her arms in a brutal grip, just as the other men approached. One of them barked something in German. Cynthia felt a pinch in her arm, and the world started to go dark.

CHAPTER TWENTY

SOMEONE WAS TALKING IN GERMAN, short bursts of speech that Cynthia couldn't understand, but they sounded angry. Cautiously, she cracked open an eye. Concrete room. Single, high window with bars in front of it. Plain metal door. Where was she?

More voices, closer to her this time.

She sat up. The room swam before her eyes. Her head throbbed in protest, before settling. Usually, she healed faster than this. What had happened?

It came back abruptly. The men. The injection.

She had been kidnapped.

Cynthia brought a shaky hand up to rub her forehead, trying to dispel the pain. What to do? First thing first: where was she? She managed to pull herself to her feet, pressing a hand against the wall, and stumbled to the window. It was high in the wall, with bars across it. Cynthia grasped them, pulling herself up, but the glass was frosted, and she couldn't see anything except a blur of green. Trees?

She looked around the room again, but there were no identifying features. *No, wait.* There was something on the floor. She shuffled over and crouched down to look. Dirty boot prints and a few dead leaves, which might have been stuck to the bottom of someone's shoe.

Wherever she was, it probably wasn't in the middle of the city, then. No one would have picked up that amount of dirt on their shoes in the city.

Cynthia moved to the door, straining her ears. There were still voices outside, but she couldn't understand anything, not even isolated words. Her head ached from the attempt. She examined the door, instead. The handle wouldn't move, and there was no lock on the inside.

She was trapped.

This was not good.

She looked around again, searching for inspiration. Her eyes landed on the window. If she could get it open, pick up the form of a bird… maybe she could escape. She hurried over, grabbing the bars. Her arms shook as she hauled herself up. Gosh, she was so tired. Her head throbbed.

The window had a latch. It took a few moments, but Cynthia managed to get it lifted and push the window open. It swung back as soon as she let go of it, clattering against its frame.

Damn it.

She needed something to wedge it open.

They'd taken her bag, of course, but it hadn't occurred to them to check for the knife on her wrist. Cynthia gripped the handle for a moment, feeling relief course through her, before shucking one of her shoes and, with renewed strength, reaching up to prop it beneath the window. That allowed her to peer out. She was, indeed, amidst trees. Tall and old, they looked rather like part of the forest where the Deckers had lived. Hopefully, that meant she was still in Berlin.

It didn't take long until a bird fluttered into view. Cynthia focused on it, hoping it was in range, but…

Nothing.

No form slid into her brain.

Was it another shifter? She couldn't grab a form from an animal that was really a shifter. Or it was out of range. But it wasn't that far away, maybe two or three metres, and Cynthia had picked up forms from further away than that. She strained her eyes, finding another bird, but that one had no form either.

Or…

Backing away from the window a little, Cynthia searched inside of her. Her current form was some kind of small dog, a terrier mix. She reached for it, but it seemed to slip away. Try as she might, she couldn't get the dog to take over.

They'd suppressed her magic.

Of course they had. They had to have known she'd try and use that to get away.

'Fuck,' Cynthia whispered. 'Fuck, fuck, fuck.'

Loud footsteps caught her attention. They seemed to be approaching. She grabbed her shoe, jamming it back on her foot. A second later, a key turned in the door, and it swung open. A man stood there, tall and burly, with an unpleasant look on his face. Cynthia clenched her fists, standing her ground.

'Who are you? What do you want?'

'Bring sie.'

Two more men filed into the room, grabbing Cynthia by the arms.

'LET ME GO!' She fought like a wild cat, trying to slip out of their grasp, but they lifted her so her toes barely touched the floor and dragged her out of the room. Beyond was a long corridor, with concrete walls and steel doors. Cynthia tried to grab the door handle, and one of the men almost wrenched her arm out of its socket. They marched down the hall, through a doorway, and burst outside into the light.

They were in the middle of the forest. Cynthia paused her struggling for long enough to look around. Several concrete buildings were grouped around an open area, their walls covered in graffiti. The ground was overgrown and covered in dead leaves. It put Cynthia in mind of an abandoned army base.

The men dragged her through the leaves towards the largest of the buildings. The door hung off its hinges. Inside, a few plastic chairs and tables were shoved against the walls of what might have once been a mess hall.

There were several people in the large room, but Cynthia's eyes immediately jumped to one man in particular: brown hair, leonine features, tall… It was Gideon, the bartender at *Verzaubert*. Like a bubble bursting in her chest, she felt a sudden sense of agonised nausea washing over her. She'd trusted him, but here he was, with her kidnappers. He turned to Cynthia, his eyes boring into hers, but she looked away.

Is there anyone trustworthy in this bloody city?

The men threw her to the ground. It was covered in pine needles, which stuck to Cynthia's hands as she clambered to her feet. When she turned around, two of the men had moved to block the door. The third approached the gathering of people at the far end of the room, murmuring to them in German.

Keeping them in her peripheral vision, Cynthia turned slowly, examining the room. Once again, the windows were set high in the walls. Apart from the rickety chairs and tables, there was no other furniture. Even if she did get out of here, she had no idea how she was going to get away. She couldn't shift, and her body was still weak from whatever they'd drugged her with. She'd never outrun the taller, stronger men.

Fear threatened to overwhelm her. Cynthia pushed it away, trying to channel Nathan. There was a way out. There had to be a way out.

A commotion caught her attention. The people on the far side of the room were starting to get angry; several of them had raised their voices. As Cynthia watched, one woman jabbed her finger into a man's chest. Cynthia wished she could see their auras. Without her magic, her second sight was blinded. She couldn't tell if the whole group were witches, or if there were other species involved.

No vampires…

None of them had the anaemic, waxy look to their skin. *Unless there are more vampires like Leon in the city…*

The argument grew louder and more frenetic, until finally one of the men clapped his hands firmly, cutting everyone off.

'She goes back in the cell until dark,' he said.

'I'll take her,' Gideon put in.

'No. We don't trust the witches.'

'You'll work with us, but you won't trust us?' a woman said with a laugh.

'Johannes and Arif can bring her.'

The two men by the door strode over. Quick as a flash, Cynthia darted around them, making for the door. She rushed outside into the twilight, stumbling over her own feet. The uneven ground seemed to be made of obstacles, dead branches and mounds of dirt trying to trip her up. She ran between two buildings, and almost crashed into a fence. She pulled back just in time; a large yellow sign warned that it was electrified.

'Fuck!'

Behind her, several people were crashing through the undergrowth. She chose a direction at random and began sprinting. A man stepped out in front of her—he'd come the other way around the building—he grabbed her arm and Cynthia fell against the fence, feeling not electricity, but the burning of dozens of wards—then she was being dragged back into the circle of buildings.

'LET ME GO! WHAT DO YOU WANT?'

Another man grabbed her other side. Her vision swam as she

struggled. Her whole left side burned from touching the wards. A voice in her ear murmured, 'Cynthia, can you hear me?'

Cynthia peered up blearily. It was Gideon.

'You fuck off,' she snapped.

Gideon frowned. 'I can get you out of here. I need you to be patient. The drugs will wear off, but if you keep fighting, they'll dose you again.'

The words flitted through her brain like moths around a flame, not finding purchase.

'I'm not doing anything you say,' Cynthia snapped.

'Shh!'

But it was too late. The other man barked something in German. Gideon pulled away, replaced by someone else, and together they dragged Cynthia back into the prison block. They threw her into her cell. She sprawled onto the floor, barely managing to catch herself. The door slammed behind her. Beyond it, she heard arguing in German again. One of the voices was recognisable: Gideon. Cynthia rubbed her temples, wishing she understood German. Why hadn't she ever bothered to learn? What were they saying? Why was she here?

Okay, think.

'Some of them are witches, I know that for sure.'

Speaking aloud seemed to help cut through the fog. Cynthia sat upright and tried to do a few stretches, wake up her body as well as her mind.

'So who else is there?' She thought back to the men who'd kidnapped her. It hadn't occurred to her to check their auras. Now she couldn't. But she did have one clue.

You'll work with us, but you won't trust us.

'So… if they're not witches and not vampires, then…' She paused, grimacing. To say it aloud would make it real. 'Then they're shifters.' So, it was probably true. The shifters of Berlin had turned on their own. And they'd made a deal with the witches for safety. Which meant…

'I'm witch bait.' Dropping her hands away from her ankles, Cynthia lay back on the concrete floor. 'They're going to hand me over to the witches.'

And that meant…

'I have to get out of here.'

With renewed vigour, she got up and began examining the room. It wasn't completely impenetrable. If she could only shift, she could get out, either through the window or a small vent at floor level. The window was less risky; with all the undergrowth outside, the exit from the vent might be blocked. Of course, that assumed she could shift. Gideon had said the drugs would wear off soon... but that meant trusting Gideon, which she didn't.

'Damn, this is a mess,' Cynthia muttered, trying to push the window open again. There were no birds in sight to test if she could shift. Worse, whatever the wards on the fence were, they'd really knocked her for six. Her head swam every time she made a sudden move, and her left side ached. It was hard to focus, too. The trees outside seemed to blur with movement, as though a wind had whipped them up suddenly.

A flash of colour caught her eye. Cynthia squinted. For a second, it looked as though there was someone between the trees, but before she could tell for sure, they were gone. Cynthia dropped back down to the ground and rescued the shoe she was using to prop open the window. It was almost dark; at this rate, she wouldn't be able to see any animals to borrow their form.

What were they waiting for?

She lay down, using her arms to prop her head off the floor. It was cold. Despite how tired she was, sleep was impossible. She jumped at every sound: distant voices, the scratching of mice in the walls, the rustling of the forest outside. Beyond the window, the light grew dimmer and dimmer. At some point, fluorescent lights flickered on in the cell.

The dark made Cynthia even more uneasy. You never knew what might be hiding in the dark.

An hour after darkness fell, she heard heavy footsteps in the hall outside. A moment later, the door opened. It was the same man from earlier. He hauled Cynthia to her feet, dragging her outside.

'Don't make trouble, don't try and run. There's much worse ways to die than what we have planned for you.'

Cynthia's chest felt too tight suddenly; her breath struggling to squeeze through to her lungs. Her fingers tingled.

I'm going to die.

'Why?' she croaked.

'You've made enough trouble for our community.'

'I haven't done anything!'

'Of course you have. Sticking your nose in where it's not wanted, attracting attention. We were fine before you arrived. Things were peaceful.'

'Peaceful?' Her stomach was roiling; Cynthia felt as though she was going to puke. 'People were dying.'

'What's a few sacrifices for the greater good?'

The words hit her like a punch in the gut. 'Those were people—they had families! I have a family!'

'You should have thought of that before you went meddling.' They'd stopped, a younger man standing in front of them. The first instructed, 'Take her to the vampires.'

'The vampires? I thought I was going to the witches?'

'What the fuck do we want with the witches?' The second man demanded. 'They're nothing but—'

At that moment, something hit them with the force of a wrecking ball. Cynthia was thrown to the ground. The shifter—if that was what he was—screamed in pain. Cynthia rolled over, pushing up, her hands slipping over the rotting leaves. A blur of movement rushed before her eyes, and then the shifter screamed again. Several people lurched out of the main building, but Cynthia only had eyes for the person in front of her. He'd stopped moving and was now fully recognisable.

It was Leon.

Blood was splattered across his face and arms. There was no question of his species in that moment. He'd never looked more terrifying.

BANG!

Before the gunshot had even registered, Leon was gone, moving too fast for Cynthia to track. Someone screamed behind her; she twisted around in time to see a man's head fly off and hit the wall; his body went in the opposite direction.

A cluster of vampires emerged from the doorway, noticeable for their sickly skin. For a split second, Cynthia's gaze met Julianus's: she saw him recognise her, saw his dread. One of the shifters shouted, 'VAMPIRES! TRAITORS!'

'Stop him!' Someone yelled.

But Julianus ignored that, and several other cries in German. Instead, he nodded sharply to Cynthia, snapped something to the other vampires, and vanished. In seconds, the other vampires were gone too, fleeing the site.

Leaving the shifters to their fate.

More screams echoed between the buildings. Someone grabbed Cynthia.

'Leave me alone!' she yelled.

But it wasn't Leon; it was Gideon. Ignoring her shouts, he pulled Cynthia to her feet. 'Come on, you have to go. Go!'

'Cynthia!'

The familiar voice brought Cynthia screeching to a halt. She spun around and came face-to-face with Wilhelm Decker. Of course he was here—he was the person who had betrayed her. And yet, Cynthia couldn't bring her feet to move. She couldn't run.

Leon would kill all of them.

Another body hit the ground with a thud. Leon was a dark blur against the night, wearing so much blood that it obscured his features. He flashed in front of Cynthia.

'LEON!' she screamed, 'STOP!'

The whole clearing seemed to freeze. Leon was the last to stop moving. He halted inches away from Wilhelm and turned to Cynthia. His face was a mess of blood and gore.

'Don't kill them,' Cynthia said.

'They deserve it.'

'Please. Please don't kill them.' She swallowed. 'You don't deserve it. To sink to their level. Please.'

Leon opened his mouth, his teeth a flash of white against his bloodied face. After a moment that felt like forever, he shut his mouth again without speaking. Then he nodded sharply and vanished.

For several moments, no one moved or spoke. All of them were afraid Leon would come back. But the air remained still; the violence didn't resume. Cynthia took a step back. One of the men turned on her.

'This is your fault!'

'You only have yourself to blame,' Gideon snapped before Cynthia could say a word. 'Julianus warned you what would happen.'

'The vampire is a coward!'

'We ought to kill the girl anyway! She'll expose us all.'

'Let it go,' Gideon said. 'It's over.'

The conversation switched to German, all the shifters shouting angrily. Amidst it, Gideon took Cynthia's arm.

'Come on, let's go.'

Cynthia snatched her arm away. 'Don't touch me.'

Gideon shrugged. 'This way.'

He led her towards a gap between the buildings. Beyond was a gate.

'I have a car,' Gideon said.

'Get fucked. I can make my own way home.'

'Frankly, I wouldn't be too sure of that.'

Cynthia wasn't sure either, not that she'd admit it to him. Her head pounded and her clothes were sticky with blood. And Leon was still out there. But she didn't want to take her chances with a mage, either.

'You were helping them.'

'I go where the KUA tells me to,' Gideon replied.

'Good little gopher.'

'Isn't that what you've been doing for the Vampire Council in Oxford?' Gideon asked.

Cynthia flinched. 'It's not like that! I don't work for them.'

'I don't work for the KUA.'

They had reached the gate. The wards fizzed over Cynthia's skin, ragged like something had torn them.

'Did the witches set the wards here?'

'Yes, but it seems like your friend has undone our work.'

'Who, Leon? He's not my friend.'

'He listened to you.'

'Yes, but…' Cynthia shook her head.

'The car is just here,' Gideon said.

'I'm still not going with you.'

'If you want to stay on your own in the middle of the forest, be my guest.' Gideon pointed. 'There's a train station a half hour walk in that direction.'

Cynthia clenched her teeth, but she followed him. It was dark. She had no idea where she was. She didn't have her phone.

The devil you know, or the devil you don't?

CHAPTER TWENTY-ONE

SOMEONE WAS SPEAKING IN a low, soothing voice with an American accent. Gradually, Cynthia was able to separate the sounds. There wasn't a person in the room—it was the radio. In between reporting on the New York traffic and weather, pop songs played. The sort of stuff Cynthia liked to listen to, though Monica would always scoff at her music choices.

It took an embarrassingly long time for Cynthia to realise what was wrong with this picture. She was in Berlin, not New York, and no one she knew would be likely to play an American radio station.

She opened her eyes.

Passing out and waking up in an unknown location was becoming a theme of this trip. Today, she found herself in a small bedroom, crammed with furniture. There was barely space to move between the double bed, cupboard, and bedside table. A chair was stuffed in the corner, clothes discarded on it. A pair of running shoes sat beneath the chair. Of the two doors, one was shut, with a jacket hanging behind it, and the other led to a bathroom.

She was alone.

Sunlight streamed between the gaps in the blinds. It had to be midday at least. Sitting up, Cynthia took stock of her own body. Mild headache, but no other pains. She was fully dressed, except for her shoes. She found those with her bag on the floor.

Her phone was missing.

Nathan would be proud of her for being so analytical, for not panicking. Smiling darkly, Cynthia slid out of bed. The world didn't end when her feet touched the floor. She managed to stand with minimal dizziness.

The door stayed shut.

Bathroom? Or face unknown enemies?

Cynthia stumbled to the bathroom and peered in the mirror. It wasn't a pretty sight. Her hair was plastered to her face, her eyes crusted with sleep, her clothes rumpled and splattered with blood. She washed her face and tried to finger-comb her hair, before finally giving up. Time to find out who'd decided to make off with her unconscious body this time.

There other door opened straight into the main room of the apartment. Unprepared, Cynthia almost walked straight into Gideon.

She shrieked in surprise. He grabbed her shoulder to steady her.

'Cynthia! I didn't expect you to be up yet.'

'What—where am I?'

'My apartment.' Gideon put his spatula down, and moved the frying pan off the heat, before turning to look her up and down. 'How are you?'

'What am I doing here?'

'I...' Gideon scraped his fingers through his hair. 'You fell asleep in the car. I didn't know where else to take you. That apartment you're staying in—I couldn't get past the wards without breaking them.'

'Right,' Cynthia said dubiously.

'It didn't seem like the most trust-inspiring action.'

'Bringing me to your apartment isn't really trust-inspiring, either. You could have woken me up.'

'I could have.' Gideon shrugged uncomfortably. 'The drugs were still in your system. I haven't touched you apart from to bring you upstairs, I promise.'

'Uh huh,' Cynthia said sceptically.

'I promise.' Gideon shifted his weight, frowning. 'Are you okay?'

'What's it to you?'

Gideon held his hands up. 'Okay,' he said slowly. 'Have a seat. I'm making food.'

'I'm not eating anything you make.' Cynthia crossed her arms.

'Please,' Gideon said, frustrated, almost desperate. 'You need food. You've expended a lot of energy trying to heal yourself recently—'

'Thanks to you and the bloody witches!'

'I've always had your best interests at heart.'

'Why?' Cynthia demanded. 'You don't know me. I'm just some girl who wandered into your bar.'

Gideon looked pained. 'You're right, but...'

'I want to go home,' Cynthia interrupted. 'Do you have my phone?'

Gideon nodded to a side table. Cynthia's phone sat there innocently, plugged into a charger. She snatched it, thumbing through her messages. Nathan, Monica, Mum, Renata.

Renata: You have some answering to do, dog girl

Nathan's messages graduated from worried to frantic. Cynthia sent him a quick text.

Cynthia: I'm fine. Had a run-in with the shifters. Escaped unharmed. Will call you shortly

The rest of the messages weren't urgent. Cynthia turned back to Gideon.

'Why are you helping me?'

'Call it a favour from your friendly neighbourhood bartender.' Gideon held out a plate of toast. 'I haven't poisoned it. If I wanted you dead, I'd have left you for the vampires.'

'Why am I special? You didn't help the other shifters.'

'I wasn't involved with the others. I'm new to the city.'

'That's convenient.' Cynthia stared him down. Gideon seemed to take up the whole apartment all on his own. He was dressed much the same as he did at work, all in black. He looked tired. After a moment, he waggled the plate at her.

'Please eat.'

'Fine.' Cynthia snatched the plate and held it so Gideon could heap scrambled egg onto the toast. 'But only after you do.'

Gideon scooped up a forkful of egg and ate it pointedly. Reluctantly, Cynthia took a seat at the little table that was squashed in the corner. She watched him for a few moments, but there was no indication the food was poisoned. She pulled her phone out and texted Nathan.

Cynthia: Update, some guy named Gideon (works for KUA) helped me. Name sound familiar to you?

Eventually, her stomach won out. Once she started eating, she couldn't stop. Gideon sat opposite her after a moment, watching with amusement.

'I didn't realise healing was such hungry work.'

'Everything to do with shifting is hungry work.' Cynthia scowled at him. 'Don't judge.'

Gideon raised his hands in surrender. 'No judgement here. Do you want something else? I have frozen pizza.'

Cynthia shook her head. 'This is fine. I really should go.'

'You know that apartment isn't safe, don't you? Plenty of people know you're staying there.'

'I'd rather know how you knew,' Cynthia said.

'The KUA is keeping tabs on you. You haven't been as subtle as you think.'

'I wasn't trying to be subtle.'

'Hmm.' Gideon got up and poked around the kitchen, coming back a moment later with two glasses of water. In short order, Cynthia had polished that off too.

'Maybe you should get out of town,' Gideon said. 'Berlin isn't safe for you.'

'Nowhere is safe for shifters,' Cynthia said.

'Seems a fair reason to leave, though. You aren't worried the vampires will try again?'

Cynthia fiddled with her fork, moving crumbs around her empty plate. 'What's it to you?'

'Are you going to disregard my advice just because I'm a warlock?'

'I'm not stupid,' Cynthia snapped. 'I'm also not going to tell you what I plan on doing now, in case you change your mind—or the KUA changes their minds. I haven't forgotten that you're their loyal gopher.'

'Not so loyal, or I'd have handed you over by now,' Gideon replied.

'Maybe you're just biding your time.'

'Maybe.' He smiled thinly. 'You're awfully suspicious, for a teenager.'

'You try being hunted by every witch on the planet, just for the crime of being born.'

Gideon's expression turned sad. 'I imagine it's rather lonely.'

'Something like that.' Cynthia put her knife and fork together and picked up her plate. 'Do you have a dishwasher?'

'Just put it in the sink. Do you want a lift back to the apartment?'

'No thanks.'

Cynthia crossed to the door. Gideon followed at a distance, watching her. 'I really can't persuade you to leave the city straight away? The KUA has a long reach, but they won't tangle with the Oxford Council.'

Cynthia glanced back at him. For a second, she thought she caught a glimmer of concern in his eyes.

'Do you have kids?'

'One,' Gideon said, 'but she's grown up now. Why?'

'Just a guess.' Cynthia shrugged. 'I'm not going to do anything stupid. Trusting you is on that list.'

Gideon smiled wryly. 'Good luck, then.'

'Thanks.'

She let herself out and took the lift to the ground floor. The halls were no more inspiring than the apartment itself; clean, but old. Cynthia exited the lobby into blinding afternoon sunshine. There was a large tree spreading shade across the street, and a couple of cars were parked on the side of the road outside several large apartment blocks.

She'd been here before.

It took Cynthia a second to place her sense of déjà vu.

She turned back and looked at the address: thirty-seven Schulze-Boysen-Straße.

The same address Leon had directed her to.

'Okay, that's just too weird.'

She glanced around the street. It was devoid of life.

No sign of Leon.

No sign of any witches.

But still…

Thoroughly creeped out, Cynthia made her way to the U-Bahn station. The street was deserted, but she still felt like she was being watched, and the feeling didn't leave her until she was safely on the train.

It was a relief to get home and unlock the apartment door. Damien's apartment was empty; it felt too still, like the owner had died. The shadows seemed too long for mid-afternoon; the air too cool for summer. Cynthia went straight into the shower, scrubbing herself until the water ran cold. When she came out her phone was ringing.

She caught it on the last ring, fumbling with her towel as she put it to her ear.

'Nathan, hi.'

'Cynthia! There you are!' Nathan said urgently. 'What happened?'

All of a sudden, Cynthia didn't feel the slightest bit ready to retell this particular story. 'I… uh… it's a long story.'

'I was worried,' Nathan said. 'You hung up so suddenly, and then I couldn't get hold of you. Do you need me to come down to Berlin?'

'No… no, I…' Cynthia trailed off, thinking. Was she safe? What should she do now? She needed to sit and think, figure out what clues she had, try to make a picture. 'I think I'm safe for now. But… there's something going on with the vampires and the witches and the shifters here.'

'I know,' Nathan said seriously. 'I'm looking into it. But your safety is my first priority. You know that.'

'Do you think I should leave town?' Cynthia sat down heavily on the bed. It was cool in the apartment; goosebumps crawled over her skin in the draught. Glancing back, she realised the window was open a crack.

Oops.

'Can you keep safe for another few hours? I can redirect and be there tonight. It's just the regional trains…'

'That's fine. I won't go anywhere.'

'Okay,' Nathan said, 'okay. We have a lot to discuss. Just… are you okay? Right now? You sound a bit…'

'Shaky? Yeah.' Cynthia laughed shrilly. 'So, I solved the mystery of the missing shifters. Dead shifters. But it's going to be easier to tell you in person. Anyway. Does the name Gideon mean anything to you?'

'Nope. Got a last name?'

'No.'

'Well, I'll ask around anyway,' Nathan said. 'Text me if you go out? Don't take any risks. I'll be there tonight, trains willing.'

'See you tonight.'

They said their goodbyes. Cynthia dropped the phone on the bed, cuddling the towel around her. A movement caught her eye, and she jumped—but it was just her shadow on the wall.

'It's official.' She laughed bitterly. 'I'm going mad. I'm done for.' She laughed again. Nathan would get there in time to lock her up, probably.

'Yep, you're going mad.'

She forced herself up off the bed. *Quit wallowing. Get dressed. Find paper and a pen. You have work to do.*

Roswitha had left a note on the kitchen table saying that she'd be by later with dinner. Cynthia helped herself to a coke and sat at the little table, window open, the sun warming her arms. She started by Googling military buildings in the Grünewald. It turned out to be trickier to find where she'd been taken than she had expected. Gideon would know; maybe Cynthia could put Nathan onto him. Find out where she'd been taken. Who had laid the wards?

The thing was, the shifters had been abducting shifters, but there had been witches involved. Shifters couldn't create wards. They had to buy them from witches. But Cynthia was supposed to be handed over to the vampires, if her abductor was to be believed, which meant that all three species were involved in this. And that was... weird and problematic. Bigger than just missing shifters.

Witches took shifters all the time, but what would the vampires want with them?

Tearing off a sheet of paper, Cynthia sketched a rough outline of Berlin and marked a few possible sites. Then she grabbed the map Lola had given her and compared them. There was no discernible pattern. But one of the possible sites was quite close to where the Deckers lived.

How critical were the Deckers in this?

There had been other shifters involved.

It didn't have to be Wilhelm and Brigitte alone.

It didn't.

Groaning aloud, Cynthia set the maps aside. She was torturing herself. Whether the Deckers were the sole perpetrators or not didn't matter. They'd still been sacrificing their own people for safety.

Lola was going to be gutted.

And I'm probably going to have to be the one to tell her...

Pushing that thought away, Cynthia grabbed a fresh sheet of paper and turned her attention to a new mystery: Gideon.

Gideon had lived at the address that Leon had given her. How had Leon got that address? Did Leon and Gideon know each other? Had Leon encountered the address by accident? What did it have to do with Cynthia's father?

Leon had emphatically disproven his own trustworthiness—Cynthia shuddered, unwillingly recalling the bloody scene he'd left behind last night—so he might well have just given her the address to manipulate her. The trouble was, no matter how she looked at it, Cynthia couldn't find the angle. What did Leon want with her? Why had he lied? What was in it for him?

She wrote each of their names on the paper, then, after a moment's thought, added the other two players she had: Renata and Anton.

Renata was related to the KUA. Anton seemed to work for them.

Gideon claimed to work for them. Leon had implied he worked for them.

And yet, none of them had any implicit links to one another.

How could both Anton and Leon work for the KUA, but never have met?

The longer Cynthia stared at the page, the less sense it made. Like a puzzle with missing pieces, and she didn't know what picture she was supposed to be making. The answer was right there on the page, but she couldn't seem to grasp it.

How had Leon known where to find her?

How had he known she needed finding?

Why had he given her the Schulze-Boysen-Straße address? And why did Gideon live there?

A loud buzzing shattered her train of thought. Cynthia jumped and glanced around, but it was just her phone ringing. Taking deep breaths to calm herself, she picked it up. Lola.

Oh no…

If there was ever a phone call Cynthia wanted to avoid, it was this one. But she couldn't evade Lola forever. With one last deep breath, she answered the phone.

'Hi.'

'What have you done?'

Cynthia flinched at the loud voice from the other end. 'What have I done?'

'My parents are going to be executed. This is your fault, you bitch! You went sticking your nose into things and now you've ruined everything and…' Lola's voice trailed off into wracking sobs. Cynthia tasted bile in the back of her mouth.

'Lola… Lola… I'm sorry,' she whispered.

'Sorry? Sorry won't save their fucking lives!' Lola snarled. 'You're going to fix this!'

'Fix what? They tried to have me killed!'

'Better you than them!'

'Wow.' A cold feeling settled over Cynthia, washing away her guilt. 'Thanks.'

'They're my parents! You had no right!'

'Your parents are murderers!'

'THEY ARE NOT!' Lola screamed. 'THEY AREN'T! They aren't…'

Then she was crying again. Cynthia swallowed hard.

'Don't they get a trial?'

'The witches don't do fucking trials. This isn't Oxford, okay?'

'I'm sorry…'

'Fuck your sorrys!' Lola snapped.

'What else am I supposed to say?'

'I DON'T KNOW! I don't know…' Lola trailed off. The silence between them grew. Cynthia felt sick to her stomach.

'Is there… is there anything I can do?' she asked finally, her voice tentative.

'I don't know…' Lola replied.

CHAPTER TWENTY-TWO

CYNTHIA TOOK THE U-BAHN to Lola's apartment. What else could she do? Lola might well turn her away after everything, but she deserved to have a friend with her in her time of grief.

Lola did answer the door. Her hair was unkempt and her eyes were red. She let Cynthia in without a word.

'Shall I make tea? Coffee?' Cynthia asked awkwardly.

'I don't care.'

Swallowing, Cynthia edged past her into the kitchen. She put the kettle on and found the peppermint teabags. Lola watched her from the doorway.

'Will you tell me what happened?' she asked, her tone monotonous, almost dead.

'Are you sure?' Cynthia asked softly.

'Yes.'

'Let me finish the tea, then.'

They sat in the lounge, Cynthia cradling her cup between her knees. Her hands were cold; actually, every part of her felt cold. She felt terrible. In a halting voice, she explained everything, from leaving the bar where she'd met Lola to Leon intervening.

'So, then I left with Gideon. I didn't have much choice—I had no idea where I was.'

'You just left them there? What if Leon had come back?'

Cynthia frowned. 'I don't know. But even if he had… what could I have done?'

'How did you know he would stop?' Lola asked.

'I didn't. But I had to try.'

'Fucking great,' Lola whispered.

'I never meant for this to happen,' Cynthia said weakly.

'Fuck your good intentions!'

Cynthia subsided. She had no idea what to say; she'd never been good with conflict. In any case, she couldn't shake the feeling that this was her fault. The guilt was like a sweet residue on her tongue: unpleasant, inescapable.

I never wanted it to end this way.

'I could call my contact with the Council in Oxford,' she suggested at length.

'To do what?' Lola demanded incredulously. 'They won't let them go. The punishment for murder is death.'

'It wasn't the shifters doing the murdering.'

'Exactly!' Lola spat. 'But they'll punish us because that solves their problem. Fuck. Fuck!' She jumped up, pacing furiously to the window and back again. Cynthia watched her nervously.

'What do you think we should do?'

'Get them out,' Lola said shortly.

'We can't do that!' Cynthia protested. 'They'll come after us, too!'

'As if you've never broken the law,' Lola sneered.

'I haven't—I don't know what you think of me, but—'

'So you didn't break into my parents' apartment?'

Cynthia flinched. Lola looked triumphant.

'I—'

'You're a hypocrite,' Lola said. 'If it were your family, you'd do it. And then you'd skip town and leave the rest of us to clean up your mess like you've been doing this whole time.'

'That's not true!'

'Pffft,' Lola said derisively. 'You came into our community and stirred up all sorts of trouble. What's this with Leon, then?'

'I don't know. Leon does what he wants.'

'Sure, *I don't know.* You think not knowing makes you not responsible?'

'So are you responsible for what your parents did, even though you didn't know they were doing it?' Cynthia snapped.

It was Lola's turn to flinch. 'I—that's not—'

'The same thing? Sure, it's not.' Cynthia crossed her arms, almost dislodging her mug. 'We're either both innocent, or neither of us is. You can't have it both ways.'

'*Fine!* So, what do you think we should do then?'

'I...' Cynthia stopped, her mind racing. What to do? 'Look, my friend's on his way to Berlin. We can stall the KUA. If we find out who was actually doing the murdering…'

'You think we can do that?' Lola asked incredulously. 'Us? And how long is that going to take? How long can your *friend* buy us?'

'He'll be here tonight. Look, just meet him before you make up your mind. When is the execution set for?'

'Tomorrow night.'

'Right, we'll meet Nathan tonight—'

Lola snorted. 'Your ex-boyfriend?'

'He's a Council hunter.'

'You are fucking weird and absolutely crazy.' Lola shook her head. 'Fine, I'll meet your friend. But he better have the power of God at his fingertips, or we're going to have trouble.'

Nathan didn't have any supernatural powers—unless you counted his ability to manage vampires and witches with minimal bloodshed as a superpower. Still, he could hardly make things worse at this point.

'I'm sure he'll do his best,' Cynthia replied.

They met Nathan at Hauptbahnhof. The last rays of the evening sun caught the glass roof, making it look like flames were licking over the building. The little memorial to the bus accident victims was still out front. Someone had replaced the flowers.

Nathan had beaten them there. He was waiting out front, eating a sandwich and watching the buses drive past. Cynthia caught sight of him immediately, recognising his black uniform. He looked like a soldier. She felt the familiar stirring of discomfort in her stomach. This was the guy she'd broken up with. Nathan was brilliant—most days, he seemed to exist in a whole different universe to Cynthia.

When he saw Cynthia, he lowered the sandwich and waved.

'Cynthia! Hey!'

'Hi,' Cynthia said awkwardly. 'Uh, how are you doing?'

'Good. Better question is, how are you?' Nathan pulled her into a hug. Cynthia hadn't expected it, and she stumbled into him. 'Sorry,' he added, releasing her. 'Didn't mean to knock you over.'

'It's okay. I'm okay. But we need to talk.' Leaning back on her heels, Cynthia gestured to Lola. 'This is Lola Decker. Lola, this is Nathan Delacroix.'

'Hi.' Nathan held out a hand. Lola shook it grimly. Nathan looked between them.

'Bad news?'

'Yeah,' Cynthia said.

'Fine, let's find somewhere to talk.'

They headed to Damien's apartment. Lola examined everything as they entered.

'Does Damien know you're staying here?' Cynthia asked as she let them in.

'Yeah, I checked with him.' Nathan kicked off his boots and shrugged out of his jacket. 'It's hot.'

'It was worse last week.' Cynthia fetched them water from the fridge, and they sat in the lounge.

'This is where you've been staying?' Lola asked.

'Yeah, it belongs to…' Cynthia glanced at Nathan awkwardly. '…a friend, well, her dad, actually.'

'Right,' Lola said. 'A friend. You have lots of *friends*.'

'Not really,' Cynthia said, 'but I have good friends. I thought we were friends.'

Lola scowled, clenching her fingers around her water glass. 'Yeah, before you got my parents arrested.'

'Your parents tried to have me killed,' Cynthia replied. Lola looked away.

'Run me through what happened,' Nathan said.

'Right.' Cynthia took a deep breath. 'So, it started two nights ago. I went out to meet Lola.' She narrated everything as quickly as possible. It felt like the fiftieth time she was telling the story, though it was only the second. It already seemed like it had happened a million years ago, instead of just last night.

Once she'd reached the point where her story was in real-time, Cynthia leaned back in her seat and gestured at the three of them. 'So, now we're here. And… I don't know. I know that the Deckers were doing something illegal, but on the other hand, it doesn't feel right to punish them before we figure out what's really going on.'

'Agreed,' Nathan said.

'Really?' Cynthia asked, relief bubbling up in her chest. 'That was easier than I expected.'

'It won't be.' Nathan smiled wryly. 'I'm not the one we need to convince. The KUA will want to sweep this under the rug. And…'

'Even if we do figure it out, they might still go ahead with the execution?' Cynthia guessed. She knew enough about witch-vampire-politics to know that was a risk.

Nathan sighed. 'Just don't get your hopes up.'

'We have to try.'

'I know. I'll put a call in tonight still, see if I can stir them up. You have the addresses where they're hiding out?'

'The witches are at a bar called *Verzaubert*, on Hackescher Markt. The vampires are at the ballroom.'

Nathan nodded.

'You found out a lot,' Lola said quietly.

'I suppose,' Cynthia muttered.

'Cynthia's pretty persistent,' Nathan said. 'I've never known someone to sniff out a lie the way she does.'

'Please no animal metaphors,' Cynthia groaned.

Nathan laughed. 'Alright, sorry. So, before I get on KUA's case, let's clear up a few things. One, what do we know the Deckers are actually guilty of?'

'Abducting at least seven shifters,' Cynthia said.

'No,' Lola denied immediately. 'Knowledge of seven abductions, and helping cover it up. But we don't know that they did the abductions.'

Nathan nodded. 'True, but they knew of all of them.'

Lola stuck her chin out stubbornly.

'Who's the shifter representative? Head of the community, or whatever you call it?' Nathan asked.

'Community,' Lola said. 'It's Thomas Fischer.'

'Thanks.' Nathan pulled his phone out to note that down. 'Got contact details?'

Lola nodded hesitantly. 'If you give me your number, I'll send them to you.' She passed her phone to Nathan so he could enter his number.

Once he had Thomas Fischer's phone number, Nathan added one more question.

'Do you know where Cynthia was taken when she was kidnapped?'

Lola shook her head immediately. 'I've never been to any place like what she described.'

'No idea?' Nathan was watching her closely. Cynthia studied Nathan, trying to figure out what he was thinking. Were these innocent questions, or did he suspect that Lola was hiding something?

'There are a lot of buildings in the forests around Berlin which could match her description, old police training places, airfields, military bases.' Lola shrugged. 'The forest reaches all the way into Brandenburg. Do you know how long it took to get back?' she asked Cynthia.

'No,' Cynthia admitted. 'I fell asleep pretty soon after we started driving.'

'Five minutes? Ten? Half an hour?' Lola asked. 'Did you recognise any landmarks, or were you still in the forest?'

Cynthia had to strain her memory. The drive last night was a blur. 'The car was parked out back. It looked military, and the area in the fence was pretty big. We walked for a while to get around it. Then we drove through the trees… I don't think I ever saw us reach a main road. Let's say it took me ten minutes to fall asleep.'

Lola nodded along pensively. 'There'd be an argument for it to be in the west of Berlin,' she suggested. 'Near where my parents live. There are several old military bases there. And that's where most of the shifter community lives.'

'Seems reasonable,' Nathan said. 'I'd like to meet this Gideon guy. You fell asleep suspiciously fast. You're not usually that trusting.'

Cynthia grimaced. 'True, but whatever they injected me with… it was pretty brutal.'

'The magic suppressant wears off after about two to three hours,' Lola said. 'Shorter, depending on how strong your magic is.'

'I was out for much longer than that,' Cynthia said.

'They probably dosed you more than once,' Lola replied. 'That would explain why it affected you so strongly.'

It made Cynthia uneasy, thinking back on it. She had a lot of missing time, and witches could do a lot with a little. Hastily, she changed the subject. 'Gideon is the bartender at *Verzaubert*. You can probably meet him there.'

Nathan nodded. 'I'll start with the hunters,' he decided. 'I'll have more clout stopping an execution if I have the Berlin hunters behind me.'

'Good luck getting them to do anything,' Cynthia muttered. Nathan laughed.

CHAPTER TWENTY-THREE

NATHAN WAS ALREADY UP, eating breakfast and talking on the phone in German, when Cynthia found her way into the kitchen the next morning. He waved as she entered.

'Good morning,' Cynthia told Roswitha, who was washing up and doing a poor job of hiding that she was listening into Nathan's conversation.

'Good morning. Tea?'

'Yes please.'

Cynthia sat opposite Nathan, nibbling a slice of toast. A moment later, he ended his call.

'I was speaking to my contact in the KUA.'

'And?' Cynthia asked, both hopeful and terrified of what she was about to hear.

'They'll postpone the execution.' Nathan was frowning, but for a second all Cynthia felt was a relief so light she thought she could just float away.

'That's great!'

'Yeah…' Nathan said slowly. 'It took a few favours, but I got there in the end.'

Cynthia's relief evaporated. Favours were bad news. Supernaturals had a knack for stretching your hospitality beyond any reasonable limits.

'What are they asking for?'

'Don't worry, I'll take care of it.'

Cynthia gritted her teeth. Nathan always did this. 'I can pay my own favours.'

'This is my favour.' Nathan's expression had closed off. 'Leave it. I'll sort it out. If I need your help, I'll let you know.'

There was no arguing with Nathan when he got this way. Cynthia would have to find out some other way. 'Fine. So, what now?'

Nathan relaxed a little. 'That's the other thing. The witches weren't going to just execute the Deckers. The vampires invoked Lex Talionis.'

'Lex Talionis?' If there was one thing Cynthia had learnt, it was that when supernaturals started going on about Latin, it wasn't going to be anything good.

'An eye for an eye. It's a vampiric thing—the Deckers would have had the same done to them that they did to the other shifters.'

'So...' It took Cynthia a second to follow his train of thought. 'They'd have been handed over to the vampires?'

'Looks like it. The vampires are going to be pissed off that we blocked them—which puts a deadline on us. Angry vampires are not patient vampires. And I think we need to find out what exactly the deal was that the Deckers had with the vampires.'

'How?'

'I guess by speaking to the Deckers.' Nathan frowned. 'We need a KUA witch, though. My guy can't get us into their prison.'

Cynthia stared at her toast. 'I might know someone... but I'll bet she won't be pleased to help us.' She glanced up at Nathan. He smiled wryly.

'Why am I not surprised?'

'Think Monica, only... younger and ruder.'

'Ruder than Monica?' Nathan laughed. 'Are we talking about the same Monica?'

'Nathan!' Cynthia snorted and kicked him under the table.

After breakfast, Cynthia called Renata. It was overdue; she'd never replied to the German girl's messages the previous day. Renata picked up almost immediately.

'My attendance is going to shit because of you and your fucking shifter drama.'

'Hello to you, too,' Cynthia said. 'Is this a good time?'

'No. What the fuck happened? My mum is going ballistic.'

Cynthia swallowed a laugh. 'I'd be willing to explain... in person?' she asked hopefully.

'What do you want?' Renata asked suspiciously.

Busted. Oops. 'Um... I need to speak to someone in the witch prison.'

'The Deckers. No. Fuck off!'

'Don't you want to ask them about Santiago?'

Renata was silent for a long time. 'Fine. I'll pick you up this afternoon. Five o'clock, from your apartment.'

'Thanks.'

'Don't thank me yet, Dog-Girl. And it better be a fucking good explanation.'

'Okay. I'll see you later.'

'See you.' Renata hung up. Cynthia caught Nathan's eye. He looked impressed.

'When did you get so… devious?'

'Devious?' Cynthia asked, feeling a little uneasy.

'I didn't expect her to agree so fast.'

'Oh.' Cynthia shrugged. 'That's Renata. I'm learning not to take offence to anything she says. She'll pick us up at five.'

'Good.'

'I'll let Lola know.' Cynthia scrolled through her contacts.

'Is that a good idea?' Nathan asked.

'Why not? We're doing this for her. Anyway, I'm sure she'd want to see them, hear what they have to say.'

'Hmm,' Nathan said. 'She won't try anything?'

'Like what? You'll be there. So will Renata.'

'True,' Nathan said. 'I suppose it would be worse if we went and didn't tell her.'

So it was that they met Lola and Renata that afternoon. Lola looked seconds away from vomiting, though she powered through it grimly. Renata pulled up a minute later and rolled her window down. 'You never mentioned *she* was coming.'

'You,' Lola snapped.

'Don't take that tone,' Renata sneered. 'You owe me an apology.'

'I owe you fuck all!'

'You went around for years telling people I was a murderer!'

'Just because you didn't kill Santi doesn't mean you're not a murderer!'

'Says the woman whose parents were abducting and killing shifters!'

'My parents didn't kill anyone!'

Renata snorted derisively. 'Sure, whatever. Cynthia can ride up front. I don't need you distracting me.'

They climbed in the car and set off. They were driving at the worst possible time. As they crossed central Berlin, the traffic slowed to a crawl.

'You know if they're smart, they won't tell you anything,' Renata remarked suddenly, cutting through the tense silence.

'The truth could get them acquitted,' Lola retorted.

'Telling on the vampires will only make things more painful for them in the long run.' Renata shrugged. 'The vampires have a taste for supernatural blood around here. As you should know.' She was smirking. Cynthia frowned. She didn't like this side of Renata, this vengefulness. She was almost smug that she'd been proven right.

'The witches would know,' Lola said. 'They started a war with the vampires, and now the vampires are killing them.'

'That's not how it went,' Renata denied immediately. 'The vampires struck first—there were two witches who died on that bus—'

'What's the bus attack got to do with anything?' Cynthia interrupted.

'That's when everything started.' Renata tossed her an odd glance before she had to look back at the road as they inched forwards. 'Didn't Lola tell you that?'

Cynthia twisted around to look at Lola. Her friend avoided her gaze. 'We can't be certain, but the timing is too convenient to be coincidental.'

'You didn't tell me!'

'It's none of your business,' Lola said. 'What do you care, anyway? Witches and vampires are at war all the time. It's the circle of life.'

Renata snorted. 'You would say that. You don't care too much when we're killing each other.'

'One more dead witch never hurt any shifter,' Lola said flippantly.

'No, it's the shifters who hurt each other,' Renata replied.

'Please stop,' Cynthia said. She glanced at Nathan. He frowned.

'What does the KUA know about the bus accident?' he asked after a moment.

'The same as what anyone knows,' Renata said. 'It was a vampire who did it.'

'They don't know who?'

'No.'

'The witches never looked into it?' Nathan pressed. 'I doubt that.'

'If they did, they didn't tell me.' Renata indicated and finally managed to pull them off the main road, onto a quieter side street. 'I'm not KUA. I'm not even in a coven anymore.'

'But you can get us into the prison,' Nathan said.

'Don't abuse the privilege,' Renata said. 'I know you work for the Vampire Council. Cynthia told me. I'm not going to tell you anything that will get my mother in trouble.'

'Of course not,' Nathan said. 'I don't expect you to.'

They wove their way east, the buildings becoming newer as they left the centre. It was Lola who broke the silence next.

'I thought the witches had their prison in the old factory.'

Renata took her time replying. When she did, her tone was brittle. 'We had to relocate to different facilities… temporarily.'

'How come?' Lola asked suspiciously.

Renata squirmed in her seat. 'It's none of your business.'

'I think it's my business,' Lola replied. 'I want to know where we're going. This could be a trap.'

'It's not a trap. We're going to an abandoned station in Pankow,' Renata said angrily. 'We had to move the prison into the city.'

'Why?'

But Renata pressed her lips together and refused to reply. Cynthia studied her profile, her thoughts twisting around one another like snakes. Renata was hiding something. What was going on now?

A short drive later, they pulled up outside a large fenced-in construction site. It looked mostly abandoned: several buildings on the verge of collapse, and a large turntable in the middle of it. It all seemed rather sorry.

A dour-looking warlock came up to the driver's side when they stopped at the gate. Renata lowered the window and greeted him in German, before passing over a few documents. The man scanned them and nodded, before heading to unlock the gate.

'How long do we have?' Nathan asked as they pulled up in front of a curved building.

'As long as we need,' Renata said, putting the car in park. 'No one comes here. The witches aren't taking a lot of prisoners at the moment.'

'Can't think why,' Lola muttered. Renata glared at her.

'Come on,' she said tersely. 'Let's get this over with.'

Renata led them inside, which turned out to be no more secure than the outside. Rubbish littered the floor; graffiti covered the walls. The doors were off their hinges, and weeds grew between the concrete and train tracks. The worst was the roof, which was so holey in places that Cynthia was worried it might collapse on them at any moment.

'Is this safe?' The question was familiar. She felt like she'd toured every abandoned building in Berlin this trip.

'We reinforced it with the blood of our enemies,' Renata said sarcastically.

'Witches and their blood,' Lola mumbled.

'Fuck off. It's just an old rune system.' Renata pointed to a graffitied woman making a crude gesture. She wore an elaborate necklace. On a closer look, Cynthia realised that the chain links of the necklace were actually runes woven together. As they stumbled their way across the tracks, she caught runes hidden away in several other works of art.

'Do the witches preserve a lot of buildings like that?'

'Some,' Renata said. 'The ones that are interesting to us.'

'Prisons, murder holes,' Lola said.

'Can you stop?' Renata demanded. 'I won't answer any more questions unless she shuts up.'

Cynthia glanced at Lola, who glared stubbornly back at her.

'Come on. Renata's helping us—she's not our enemy.'

'She might not be your enemy,' Lola said, 'but you have a strange way of picking friends.'

'So you've said,' Cynthia replied. She glanced at Renata. 'There's an old ballroom. I don't know what it's called. It was by a river.'

'Ballhaus Grünau?' Renata asked with certainty. 'It's famous. What were you doing there?'

'Exploring.'

'That one's not preserved by us,' Renata said. 'It's vampire territory. But, you know, where there are vampires, there are witches who'll work for them. KUA doesn't govern every witch in the city.'

'Does Gideon work for the witches?'

'The bartender at *Verzaubert?*' Renata paused with one foot propped on the rails, looking surprised. 'He doesn't work for anyone, I don't think he's even German. What do you want with him?'

'He was there when I was kidnapped.' Cynthia paused. 'He helped me get out—you know—after he helped them kidnap me.'

'Sounds typical.' Renata smirked. 'You won't take my advice anyway, but a warlock with no aura is a warlock who has a lot to hide.'

She jumped over the tracks and marched to the wall, pulling open a door.

'In here.'

They entered a corridor. This area was more overtly witchy: there were old chalk circles on the ground, partially washed away, and the remains of herbs and scented candles. Cynthia examined them as they crossed the hall, but she couldn't identify anything except the symbols for the compass points, which Monica had once said were derived from old Viking runes. Renata paused when they came across a complete circle with five candles burning around it. A woman in her thirties sat in a plastic chair next to a steel door.

'Fraulein Friedemann,' the woman greeted. She had protuberant eyes that made her look surprised and wispy hair.

'Jule,' Renata said, showing her papers again. They had a brief, whispered exchange before Jule moved to the door and began tracing her fingers over it.

'We can all go in,' Renata explained. 'We have to knock on the door when we want to be let out.'

'How do we know we won't get left in there?' Lola asked.

'You don't,' Renata snapped.

'Let's not fight,' Cynthia said. 'We need to work together.'

Lola and Renata both fixed her with looks that communicated emphatic disagreement, though Lola nodded sharply after a moment. 'Fine. Who's going to lead the conversation?'

Renata looked at Cynthia. Cynthia glanced at Nathan.

'You can do it,' he said. 'You know them.'

'I don't know what to ask!'

'You'll be fine.' Nathan smiled. 'We're right here with you.'

'Okay,' Cynthia said uneasily. What should she ask? Her mind went totally blank as they were let into some kind of old office. A rusted metal desk still sat against one wall, but the rest of the room was taken up by a large wooden table and chairs, which must have been brought there recently. They, alone, were free from decay.

It was obvious which side of the table was intended for them—that would be the side without the chains. Lola grabbed a chair, glaring at them as though daring them to stop her. Nathan ushered Cynthia into the other, a gesture which didn't go unnoticed by either of the other girls. They both watched Nathan warily.

Truth be told, he did look a little intimidating in full uniform, when the rest of them were in jeans and T-shirts. It was funny—Cynthia had never thought of Nathan as intimidating before. It felt as though she was seeing him through someone else's eyes since she'd been away from him.

Weird.

They waited about five minutes before the door swung open once more. The Deckers were led in by three tall, black-clad men, all of whom had unyielding steel grey auras. They made Cynthia shudder. She found herself reluctant to even share breathing space with them and was relieved when they were gone, even though that left her with the Deckers.

Wilhelm and Brigitte were both in a rather sorry state. They had been roughed up, and looked pale and frightened. Wilhelm, in particular, glared at the girls. Then his gaze fell on Lola. Brigitte began to cry.

'You should have left,' she sobbed.

'How could I have?' Lola asked.

'They'll take you down with us.'

'What is she doing here?' Wilhelm demanded, jerking his chin at Renata. He looked at Cynthia, expression cool, before his eyes slid to Nathan. 'Who are you?'

'Nathan Delacroix, Liaison for the British Council for Supernatural Affairs,' Nathan rattled off, pulling an ID card out his pocket and showing it to them. Wilhelm studied it disdainfully.

'What do the Oxford vampires want with us?'

'Nothing.' Nathan pocketed the card and motioned to Cynthia. 'I'm here as insurance.'

Wilhelm looked at Cynthia again. 'I see. You have some nerve coming back here.'

Cynthia felt jittery, but her voice came out surprisingly steady. 'Nathan has advocated to the KUA to get your execution postponed. So, actually, you could be a bit more grateful.'

Wilhelm's eyes narrowed. 'And what's the cost to us?'

'Information,' Renata said coldly.

'We're not speaking to you. You're a witch—'

'You'll speak to me, or no one at all!'

'Then I have nothing to say,' Wilhelm replied.

'Well, fuck you—'

'Stop,' Cynthia burst out. 'Stop it!'

Everyone looked at her. Renata was seething, Lola pleading. Cynthia felt their gazes like a physical weight. Nathan made this look so easy, but keeping everyone happy—or at least calm—might have been the hardest thing she'd ever done.

Cynthia took a deep breath. 'Renata stays,' she said. 'And I'm asking the questions. And you'll talk, because if you do, we might be able to get the bottom of this, and—and those shifters won't have died for nothing. If you stay silent, well, it'll just be two more dead shifters.'

Lola's breath hitched, and she turned away. Cynthia met Nathan's gaze, and he nodded slightly.

'Who put you in charge?' Wilhelm asked. 'You're eighteen. You have no authority here.'

'I'm an adult, and you almost had me killed,' Cynthia replied. 'I want to know why.'

'They wanted your blood for a spell.' To Cynthia's surprise, it was Brigitte who answered. Wilhelm immediately turned to frown at her, his chains rattling.

'Brigitte—'

'We may as well tell her,' Brigitte said, determined despite her tears. 'It could help.'

'It could get us killed all the sooner.'

'I'm willing to take that chance.' Brigitte smiled wanly. 'For Lola. The vampires wanted shifter blood for a spell.'

'How are the vampires doing spells?' Cynthia asked.

'They have witches working for them, just like we do. When we first lived in Berlin—Lola probably doesn't remember; she was very young, only two when we left—but when we first lived here, it was anarchy. The vampires were picking shifters off the streets. Berlin was terribly dangerous. But after we left Athens, we came back to Germany. Dresden. And at that time, we met a vampire who was… peaceable.'

Brigitte paused. The whole room was still, as though even the building was waiting anxiously to hear what she had to say.

'Her name was Irina, she… anyway, she was researching shifter magic, and she spoke to Wilhelm. By the by, she explained that she was from Berlin and that certain parties here would be interested in meeting us and hearing about our experiences.'

Brigitte stopped there, her expression regretful.

'You agreed,' Cynthia prompted.

'Not at first, but eventually… Berlin was always our home. Wilhelm and I both grew up here,' Brigitte explained. 'You know what it's like, that longing. To settle down, to not have to run.'

She did. The thought made Cynthia's chest ache. She hated that she empathised with them. *I would never go to those lengths to be safe,* she thought. *Never.*

'What did they want?' she asked.

'Shifter blood,' Brigitte said. 'A steady supply. In return, safety for the Berlin shifter community.'

'And you agreed?' Lola asked, horrified. 'Mama…'

'You have to understand,' Brigitte pleaded. 'It was the best way to ensure your safety. We could keep you in one school. You could have friends. A life. You'd be safe from the witches, too—that was part of the promise.'

'No one had to die for that!' Lola cried.

'Of course they did,' Wilhelm said. 'People die for that all the time. Ask your friend there, how many people have died for her safety.' He jerked his head at Cynthia.

'We haven't killed anyone,' Cynthia snapped.

'That doesn't mean people haven't died. Your stepfather, for starters.'

Cynthia felt a chill down her spine. It was something she tried not to think about too often. But Wilhelm was right; Daniel had died to keep her and Emma safe.

'That's not the same thing.'

'Perhaps not,' Wilhelm said. 'But dead is dead, at the end of the day. And shifters die all the time. This way, they died for a good cause.'

'Helping vampires is a good cause?' Renata snorted.

'What were they using the blood for?' Nathan asked.

'They didn't tell us,' Brigitte said. 'We can only speculate.'

'Speculate away,' Renata said darkly.

Brigitte frowned at her. 'Shifter magic is earthbound. Witches have been trying to use it to increase their power for as long as both species have been on this planet.'

'No witch can channel a dead power source,' Renata retorted.

'Some can, or how do you explain the massacre of our people?'

Wilhelm demanded.

Renata shrugged. 'It's not to increase their magic. They're using your magic to power spells.'

'I fail to see the difference,' Wilhelm said.

'Maybe Renata should explain,' Nathan said.

'I've heard enough from her—'

'Actually,' Cynthia said, 'I'd like to understand the difference. Seeing as I'm one of the persecuted species.'

Everyone looked at Renata. She scowled. 'Fine. Witches, most of them at least, can do two types of magic. The kind that comes from within, active spells, where the witch's magic is the sole power source. And external magic, rituals, for example, where the witch's magic is only the catalyst that starts the spell.'

Cynthia thought of all the times Monica did magic, trying to mentally classify them as one or the other. Rituals, obviously, would be the ones where she cast a magic circle.

'What does that mean for us?' she asked.

'I'm getting there,' Renata said impatiently. 'Active spells are harder because they are limited by how much magic you have in you. Weak witches can only do weak spells. To make themselves stronger, they can channel another person—but that person has to be alive and have magic.' She nodded to Cynthia. 'Like you and your witch friend.'

'Monica.'

'I don't care.' Renata rolled her eyes. 'With the other kind of magic, external magic, it doesn't matter how much magic the witch has. They only need a tiny bit, like a spark, and then the spell will draw from whatever power source you direct it to. The earth, a magic crystal, a person, etcetera. Blood is a potential power source. It's a link to the fifth element, spirit. The more magical the blood, the more potent a power source.'

'And shifter blood is particularly magical?' Nathan asked.

'I wouldn't know,' Renata said dismissively. 'I can't do external magic.'

'Convenient,' Wilhelm said.

'Absolutely,' Renata said. 'It rules me out as a suspect.'

'Let me get this straight,' Nathan said. 'You're saying because the shifters are being killed, that means their blood is an ingredient in a ritual.'

'Probably,' Renata said. 'And considering the amount, it has to be a very powerful ritual. Normally you'd only need a few drops.'

Nathan glanced at Cynthia, and she knew he was sharing her thoughts. This was seriously bad.

'How many shifters have the vampires taken in total?' Nathan asked.

'We don't know,' Wilhelm said.

'You know about at least two of them,' Cynthia said. 'Santiago Carvalho and Anya Bakker.'

'What's convenient,' Renata said suddenly, 'is that you don't know that, and you don't know what the blood is for, and I bet you also don't know if they're storing it or using it straight away. Which means that you actually know absolutely nothing useful. Maybe I'll call my mother right now and she can come and find out what's really hiding in those stupid heads!' She was breathing hard by the end of her tirade. Nathan put a hand on her shoulder, but Renata shrugged it off angrily.

Cynthia studied Brigitte and Wilhelm, searching for signs of deceit. Maybe they really didn't know any details. Vampires were notoriously closed-lipped when they wanted to be. On the other hand, the Deckers had everything to lose right now. And the rest of the shifter community didn't seem to be advocating for them.

Like animals, we leave our dead behind. Renata had been so right when she made that accusation.

'Please,' Cynthia said softly. 'I know it sounds… trite, but this could help you, and it could help all the shifters in the city. What will happen now that the deal is broken? What if the vampires go after the rest of the community?'

'Don't act as if you care,' Wilhelm said.

'I do care. I always did care.'

'If that were true, you wouldn't have stuck your nose where it wasn't wanted!'

'It is true. And wouldn't it be better if you could live safely without killing anyone?'

'Naïve,' Wilhelm spat. 'That's a ridiculous dream. Give it a few years. You'll see.'

Cynthia crossed her arms. 'So you'll condemn the rest of them to death. So much for dying for a good cause, right?'

Wilhelm glared. 'We've told you all we know. The vampires want to do a spell. They need a lot of power for it. If you want to know what they need a spell for, you're asking the wrong person. Even vampires are scared of something.' He nodded to Renata. 'Ask your friend there.'

'I'm not the local expert on murders,' Renata said.

'No? The witches and vampires have feuded over Berlin for decades.'

'We had peace for decades!' Renata said. 'It's only since your lot started stirring the pot that things have gone bad again.'

'Vampires were killing shifters left, right, and centre! You had peace at the expense of our people!'

'That's not true!' Renata tossed her head. 'If you ask me, the vampires were using shifter blood to curse the witches—and now they're trying to use it to undo the curse after it backfired on them.'

'That makes zero sense,' Lola said.

'What the fuck would you know? You know nothing, just like your stupid parents,' Renata dismissed.

'The curse only started last year!' Lola said. 'Shifters have been going missing for much longer than that—'

'How do you explain it, then?' Renata asked.

'I don't know, but this is a long-term plan. Revenge? An external threat?'

They both made good points but watching them argue was like watching a tennis match. Cynthia didn't know where to look.

'No external threat waits politely for ten years, whilst the vampires get their shit together—'

'Well, the curse only started now, so—'

'I know one other thing,' Brigitte interrupted suddenly. 'From something Irina originally said. The spell has to do with sealing something.'

'Sealing?' Cynthia repeated. She glanced at Nathan. He was frowning. 'Sealing what?'

'I don't know,' Brigitte said. She looked genuinely apologetic. 'They never told us much. The deal was simple. Safety in return for blood and keeping quiet about it.'

'Can you name any names?' Nathan asked. 'Who was involved?'

'They sent someone different every time. Since last year, meetings only took place after dark. That's it.' Brigitte shifted uncomfortably. 'I'm sorry.'

'After dark?' Nathan asked.

'They can't go out during the day,' Cynthia said.

'No blood,' Nathan surmised. Cynthia nodded. Blood deprivation was the main reason why vampires burnt in sunlight. Blood fuelled their magic.

So could shifter blood make them more powerful? Did it last longer than human blood?

Vampires didn't drink magical blood because it allegedly tasted foul to them, but if they were cursed, perhaps that was how they were keeping the curse at bay…

Nathan's phone ringing broke Cynthia out of her thoughts. 'We should go,' he said as he pulled it out. 'Regroup.'

Cynthia nodded reluctantly and stood. Renata banged firmly on the door.

'I'd like a moment with my parents,' Lola said.

Renata's lips thinned. 'No. That wasn't part of the agreement.'

'Let her,' Cynthia said softly. 'We'll be right outside.'

Renata scowled. The door opened, revealing the same witch as before. Renata muttered something to her, and after a short conversation, she nodded.

'Fine, five minutes,' Renata said. 'If you try anything…'

'You'll kill me.' Lola rolled her eyes. 'Piss off, witch bitch.'

'Creative,' Renata sneered. She turned and hurried out, Cynthia and Nathan following behind.

'Don't close the door fully,' Renata said to the other witch, who nodded.

'Let's go out by the tracks,' Renata added. 'I hate it in here. The wards give me a headache.'

Nathan had moved a short distance down the corridor. He signalled with his hands that he'd keep watch. Cynthia nodded and followed Renata out into the main hall. Gazing out across the abandoned tracks, Cynthia asked, 'Do you think the shifter blood is keeping the curse at bay?'

'Maybe.' Renata rubbed her arms. 'Who knows? Do you really think you can save them, by solving this? What are you, a detective?'

'I just want to help my friend,' Cynthia said.

'Giving her false hope is not going to help.'

'This is all I've got,' Cynthia said helplessly. 'I was raised to believe that the shifter community did whatever it took to help each other. I have a link to the Council. If I can help Lola and her parents—'

'Just don't forget what they did.'

'I haven't.'

They both stood in silence for a while. The shadows grew longer, making the building seem even more spooky.

'How long has it been?' Cynthia asked.

'Long.' Renata pulled her phone out. 'Seven minutes. I'm going to check. If she tried anything—'

'She won't.'

'Whatever.' Renata stepped inside again. Cynthia shifted her weight, suddenly anxious. It was quiet, too quiet. Where was Nathan? She heard something rustle and spun around. Nothing there. Turning back, she scanned the hall. A quiet thud made her turn again.

Brigitte stood before her, naked, a syringe held between her teeth.

'What—'

Cynthia stumbled backwards. Her back hit something—someone. She opened her mouth to scream, but a hand clamped over her jaw. She felt a prick in her neck, and the world went black.

CHAPTER TWENTY-FOUR

CYNTHIA CRACKED HER EYES open slowly, dispelling residual dreams of running and looming figures with glowing red eyes. Her head was pounding, and her mouth was dry. Near her, someone groaned, swearing quietly in German. After a moment, Cynthia's vision cleared, and she could make out the dank ceiling of the little office in the abandoned train station.

'Nathan?' she asked cautiously. 'Renata?'

'Hey,' Nathan said. Cynthia rolled on her side and managed to find him testing the wards on the door. 'You alright?'

'Feels like I got run over by a truck,' Cynthia muttered. 'That's the second time this week.'

'Sounds like a good week,' Nathan said, helping her up.

'God, I'm filthy.' Cynthia brushed her hands off on her jeans, not that it made a lick of difference. 'Of all the floors to end up unconscious on.'

Nathan sniggered. Cynthia shot him a token frown before taking stock. They were, indeed, back in the little office where they'd spoken to the Deckers. Lola and her parents were conspicuously absent, but Renata was sprawled on the floor.

'Renata?'

'Ughhh… yeah, I'm awake,' Renata grumbled. 'Fucking bitch.'

She sat up slowly, eyeing the room with distinct disdain. 'That is the last time I am trusting your judgement on literally anyone,' she told Cynthia.

'I'm sorry.' Cynthia's stomach churned uncomfortably. 'I really didn't think Lola would ever… I guess I didn't know her as well as I thought I did.'

'It happens to the best of us,' Nathan said.

'It seems to happen more to me,' Cynthia said bitterly.

'You learn.' Renata heaved herself up. 'Trust no one, and no one can hurt you.'

'Sounds lonely, coming from a girl who's also locked in with us,' Nathan remarked. Renata glowered at him.

'How'd she get you, anyway? I thought you were some hotshot hunter.'

It was Nathan's turn to look unhappy. 'I'm not invincible. Turns out even dating a shifter, I didn't learn all the tricks.' He glanced at Cynthia, who shrugged awkwardly.

'I've never used my abilities to ambush anyone.'

Nathan smiled weakly and turned back to the door.

'Is it locked?' Renata asked.

'Yes. Will unlocking it disengage the wards?'

'Should do,' Renata said. 'But I don't have a key.'

'I can pick it.' Nathan pulled a tool out of his jacket pocket and fiddled with the lock, an expression of concentration on his face. After what seemed like forever, he pushed the door open. Nathan grinned in triumph.

'And we're out.'

'Interesting skill for a hunter to have,' Renata remarked. 'What happened to law and order?'

'You're welcome,' Nathan said. 'If you want to stay here…'

'No thanks!' Renata was past him and out the door in a flash. Nathan stepped back and gestured for Cynthia to follow. It was dark in the hallway. Cynthia pulled her phone out to use as a torch, but the battery was dead.

'Here,' Renata muttered, cupping her hands. After a moment, she frowned. 'My magic's not working.'

'It's the drug she injected us with,' Cynthia said. 'It suppresses our magic. It'll wear off in a few hours.'

Renata pressed her lips together but pulled out her phone. By the light of the little torch, they examined the hallway. It was abandoned.

'You think they got the other witches?' Cynthia asked.

'Or they realised how much trouble they'd be in and ran off, leaving us to take the blame,' Renata said bitterly.

'Can you call someone and check?' Nathan asked.

Renata nodded and moved a little way off down the hall. Cynthia stuck with Nathan, who was also using his phone as a torch. He opened a few other doors down the hall, but all the rooms were empty.

'We were abandoned,' Cynthia guessed.

'Looks like it. I don't think the witches here are very loyal,' Nathan said.

'Funny enough, I got the same impression.'

Renata confirmed that when she came back over to them. 'The break-out has been reported.' Her expression was sour. 'I need to go and speak to my mother, I think.'

'Maybe we should come too,' Nathan said.

'Not Cynthia. She's one of them.' Renata darted a glance at Cynthia. 'My mother doesn't like shifters, and she'll be especially pissed off now. Better not.'

Cynthia nodded.

'Let's get out of here,' Nathan said.

'Alright.'

They crept through the darkened hallways. Outside, they finally found someone: a security guard who was fast asleep at his post. Renata prodded him awake, and he jumped comically when he saw her.

'Guten Abend, Fraulein Friedemann.'

Renata's look of displeasure was emphatic. 'The fuck do you think you're doing?'

'I—uh—'

'Honestly, go home. There's no one here to guard anymore.'

The guard looked absolutely horror stricken. He sprang up and raced inside to check. Renata liberated the witch light from beside his chair and raised it to illuminate the turntable and trainyard. Her car was gone.

'She stole my Mum's car!' Renata checked her pockets for her keys and came up empty. 'That bitch!' She looked like she didn't know whether to laugh or be angry. After a moment, she just shook her head. 'Gotta hand it to her, she got us good.'

'Yeah,' Cynthia said uneasily. She had the discomforting sense of having found herself on the wrong side of an argument by accident. It wasn't a nice feeling.

The gate had been locked again. Cynthia and Renata kept watch for the police whilst Nathan picked it, but all they saw was a group of young adults who'd snuck in from the back, looking for a place to have a party.

'I want what they're drinking,' Renata grumbled.

'At least you can get drunk,' Cynthia said. 'I wonder what they think we're doing here?'

'Getting high? Exploring? Thrill-seeking?' Renata shrugged. 'Squatting? We look like fucking squatters, right now.'

It was true; they were all pretty grimy from their date with the office floor. Self-consciously, Cynthia dusted her jeans down. A moment later, Nathan finally got the padlock open and unwound the chain.

'Sorry, that one was a bit tricky.'

'I'm not sorry. I wish they'd locked it earlier,' Renata said.

'You know it wouldn't have stopped them.' Nathan pushed the gate open enough for them to wriggle out, then locked it again behind them, whilst Cynthia checked anxiously for the police.

'Didn't think I'd ever be doing anything like this.'

Renata snorted. 'This is Berlin. People do shit like this all the time. Come on, the station's this way.'

They separated at Hackescher Markt, Renata and Nathan to go and plead their case with the KUA, and Cynthia to head home. She watched the others climb off the S-Bahn, slouching dejectedly in her seat. Everything had gone wrong—so much for her hopes of helping Lola. Had Lola planned this from the start? Enlisted her just to… to run off and leave Cynthia to take the fall? Some friend. Cynthia found herself suddenly doubting everything, every person she'd met on this trip. Was there anyone truly reliable?

I have Nathan.

At least, at the end of the day, she knew one thing: Nathan was a good person, and he always did his best for his friends. Cynthia was suddenly really glad that he was here with her. To think she hadn't wanted to see him—she didn't know what she'd do without him, right now.

I hope he gets lucky with the KUA…

The train pulled out of the station, and Cynthia felt a breeze over her skin. Goosebumps rose on her arms, as Cynthia suddenly sensed that she was no longer alone. The carriage looked empty, but still she reached into her bag, pulling out her knife. A gust of air whooshed past her, then a hand grabbed her wrist.

'That can't hurt me,' Leon said softly, releasing her and dropping to sit beside her.

'Leon.' Cynthia slid the knife into her lap and rubbed her arms, trying to dispel the goosebumps. 'What are you doing here?'

'What are you doing here? Alone, at night.' He blinked, his lashes fluttering over his cheeks. He was ethereally beautiful at night, and now that Cynthia knew what he was, she couldn't believe she'd never seen it before. 'Why didn't you stay with the hunter and the witch?'

'How do you know about them? You weren't in this carriage with us.' Cynthia's heart was pounding, and her fingers tingled.

'I was in the next carriage.'

'Listening in on us.' Cynthia thought back but couldn't remember them saying anything incriminating. They hadn't spoken much, each lost in their thoughts. 'I didn't expect to see you again.'

'Why not? I promised you would.' Leon tilted his head. His hands were splayed over his lap. Cynthia felt he was deliberately trying to make himself look unthreatening, and it set her on edge.

'You've told me a lot of things,' Cynthia pointed out. 'I don't know if any of them are true anymore.'

'I've never lied to you.'

'You didn't tell me you were a vampire.'

'No,' Leon agreed in a strained voice, 'but I never told you I wasn't one, either.'

The night vanished abruptly as they rushed into Friedrichstraße station, the train's brakes squealing, the fluorescents making their skin look sickly. Cynthia cast her mind back over their previous encounters. She couldn't say for sure if that was true, but she wasn't sure it was wrong, either. In hindsight, Leon had a way of manipulating words that made it impossible to be sure.

'I don't think lying by omission is any better than outright lying,' Cynthia said.

'It wasn't my intention to mislead you,' Leon murmured, turning to watch the few late-night stragglers move about in the station. Cynthia willed someone to get into their carriage, but no one did. The train pulled away again, enveloping them in night once more.

'Then what are your intentions? Are you going to kill me, too?'

'I was trying to protect you.'

'You murdered three shifters and two witches!' It took considerable effort for Cynthia to keep her voice low. Leon flinched.

'My methods could have been… different, I admit. But I wanted you to be safe.'

'How did you know where I was? That I'd been taken?'

'I...' Leon trailed off, avoiding her gaze. 'I... felt when the connection was broken.'

'Connection?'

'Because you drank my blood. As long as it's in your body, I can... sense your presence.'

Cynthia stared at him, aghast. 'Can you sense me now? Is that how you found me?'

'No, the connection broke. And anyway, it's been long enough that you would have neutralised it.'

Cynthia frowned. Even if she believed him—which she didn't—that was worrying. Nathan had never mentioned anything like this before.

'Can every vampire do that?'

'I don't know,' Leon said slowly. 'Not every vampire is born equal.'

'Vampires aren't born. They're turned.'

'Yes... but they were men once, yes?'

'Well, yes.' Cynthia turned that over in her mind. 'So, you're saying that vampires are different because they were different as humans?' She glanced at him out of the corner of her eye. 'Is that why you have a colourful aura, and the other vampires don't?'

Leon cast his gaze to the ground. 'My parents were witches.'

'I didn't think witches could be turned.'

'Some can.'

'Oh.' She was going to have to speak to Nathan. Either Leon was lying, or the hunters needed to update their information.

Or everyone knew and no one told me... as usual.

Cynthia pushed that thought away.

'Well... I don't approve of your methods,' she said cautiously, 'but thank you anyway. For saving me, I mean.'

'You're welcome.' Leon lifted his gaze, smiling tentatively. 'I'm sorry. About the shifters and witches. I was angry.'

Somehow, Cynthia couldn't picture Leon getting angry. He seemed too calm, almost disconnected from the rest of the world.

The lights of Hauptbahnhof shattered their bubble once more. Cynthia watched the people on the platform, but no one got into their carriage. Could the humans sense the presence of a predator? The train passed on, and she turned her gaze to Leon. He was fiddling with the bronze medallion around his neck.

'What's your medallion for?'

Leon looked down. 'Nothing. It belonged to my family.'

'It looks old.'

He smiled sadly. 'Older than me.'

'Which is?' Cynthia wished she knew more about history. Maybe then she could have made a guess at the age of the medallion. It was maybe two inches in diameter, tarnished from wear, the design almost worn away. There were symbols in a ring around the outside; Cynthia thought they might have been similar to the Viking runes that Monica sometimes used, but beyond that, she couldn't be sure.

'I don't know,' Leon said.

'How can you not know how old you are?'

'I don't remember.' He looked at the medallion. 'I remember this. I remember Brandehuse. I remember Berlin.'

'Do you remember the Berlin Wall?' Cynthia asked.

'No.'

The wall had come down in 1989. Of that, Cynthia was sure.

'That would make you less than thirty.'

Leon shifted uncomfortably. He had all of the grace and etherealness of an old vampire, but none of the mannerisms. Cynthia had never seen Damien or Jeremiah fidget. She'd never even seen Nathan's uncle, Adrian, fidget. And he was only around sixty years old.

'Why did you kiss me? Last time.'

'I like you.' Leon let the medallion fall against his ribcage with a weighty thud. 'You're refreshing.'

'Refreshing,' Cynthia quoted sceptically.

'Different from other supernaturals. More honest... upfront. You aren't playing games.'

'You are,' Cynthia said.

'I don't mean to. All I want to do is understand.'

'Understand what?'

'Everything. The things that go on around us. Why people do what they do.'

'Why don't you just ask?'

'When you ask, you give people the chance to lie,' Leon said.

'You give them the chance to explain themselves, too,' Cynthia said. 'People don't like feeling like they're part of some... game.'

'I'm sorry,' Leon said softly. His fingers went to his medallion again, tracing the circle of runes. 'Will you… may I still see you?'

Cynthia studied him. How could a person be so terrifying one moment, so sheepish and unassuming the next? She ought to say no: Leon was clearly dangerous. But then again, Nathan was dangerous. The vampires back in Oxford were dangerous. Monica was dangerous. In the supernatural world, danger was measured not by the ability or the deeds, but by the principles behind them. The most dangerous people were the ones who had no principles holding them in check.

Morality was a very fragile thing for people who had supernatural powers at their fingertips.

'I don't know if it's a good idea,' she said, torn.

'I won't harm you,' Leon said.

'It's not just about me getting hurt,' Cynthia said. 'I have to be able to trust you. You come and go. I never know when you'll be there, and… how do I know you won't hurt my friends?'

Leon's gaze dipped to his hands. He had long, slender fingers, Cynthia noticed.

'If they don't hurt me, I won't hurt them.'

'I'm not sure that's good enough for me.' *Especially after today.*

'I understand,' Leon said. 'We're… very different, aren't we?'

There was something in the way he said it. Cynthia felt her reluctance ebbing away. Under the harsh lights of Zoo station, in his same tatty jeans and shirt, Leon looked washed out, solitary, left behind. It was something Cynthia could relate to, that loneliness, feeling unable to connect to other people. Tentatively, she reached out and brushed her fingers against his hands.

'You shouldn't do that. You're wearing the design off the medallion.'

Leon glanced down, dropping it against his chest again. 'It can't be preserved. Time wears everything away. Makes space for new things.'

'Things can get better with time, too,' Cynthia said. She caught his little finger with hers. 'I don't want any more lies or half-truths.'

Leon met her gaze. 'Okay,' he whispered.

'You have to promise.'

'I… I promise.' He took her hand in his, squeezing it gently. Now that she knew what to look for, Cynthia could feel the immense vampiric strength, barely restrained in the gesture.

'Okay.' She tilted her head up.

'May I...' Leon asked slowly. Cynthia nodded, and he closed the distance between them, kissing her gently.

CHAPTER TWENTY-FIVE

'LET'S GO THIS WAY,' Leon said.

'What?' Cynthia glanced down the street. 'My apartment is that way.'

'I want to show you something.'

'Now?' She looked down at herself. 'I've been lying on a dirty floor. I need a shower… and sleep. I have a headache. Leon!' She laughed as he tugged her hand, pulling her in the wrong direction.

'I don't care,' he said. 'You don't need pretty clothes for this. You don't need pretty clothes, anyway. You're beautiful.'

Cynthia snorted. 'You need to work on your delivery. Flattery doesn't work when I know I'm covered in muck—and mould—and spent like three hours unconscious on a floor.'

'It wasn't flattery.' Leon grinned, the skin around his eyes crinkling. 'Can I carry you? It will be a long walk at human pace.'

'Oof.' Cynthia dropped his hand. 'Was that an insult? Sorry I'm too slow for you.'

'Not an insult,' Leon started seriously, but then he realised she was smiling. 'You're making fun of me. Fine, we can walk.'

'We can run,' Cynthia said. 'I don't mind. I've never, uh, been carried by a vampire before. I didn't know that was a thing.'

Leon regarded her curiously for a moment, before crouching down so she could climb on his back. It was less comfortable than Cynthia had expected. Leon was quite bony, and when he broke into a run, all of his bones seemed to dig into her body. The wind stung her cheeks. She shrieked loudly, but her words were whipped away as they moved faster than she could follow. She squeezed her eyes shut, terrified that any second now she was going to end up roadkill—

Leon set her down.

'We're here.'

'That was quick.' Swaying a little, Cynthia looked around. They were next to a chain-link fence, beyond which was an immense white dome. 'Where are we?'

'The gasometer.'

'The what?'

'It was built to hold gas. To light the city.' Crouching down, Leon lifted a loose section of the fence. 'Don't tell.' He held it up so Cynthia could wiggle underneath, before following her.

'I've spent this entire trip breaking into abandoned buildings.'

'What else did you want to do?'

'Oh, you know, museums, tours, not ending up unconscious on the floor of some grotty train station.'

'Pankow station has one of the only train turntables left in Germany,' Leon said solemnly.

'How do you know all this stuff?'

'I know Berlin.' He shrugged and gestured to the structure. 'Do you want to climb it? You can see the whole city.'

'You want to go up there?' Cynthia gaped at him. 'Are you insane?'

'There are stairs. They take tours up during the day.'

'Is it safe?'

Leon shrugged. 'I won't let you fall.'

'You won't die if you fall. I will!'

'I won't let you fall.' He took her hand. 'You can trust me.'

Cynthia shook her head. 'You're crazy, you know that? Fine, but this had better be safe.'

It turned out not to be as terrible as she had imagined. Okay, so touching the railing made flakes of paint and rust break off in her fingers—and looking down made her stomach turn—but Leon didn't let go of her hand. Vampiric strength was suddenly rather reassuring.

'How can you still have magic if you're a vampire?' Cynthia asked to distract herself from her burning thighs and aching lungs.

'I don't know,' Leon said. 'How can you have magic? You're not a witch.'

'I was born with it.'

'So was I.'

'Huh.' Cynthia turned that over in her mind. If witches could be turned, why should they lose their magic? She had always assumed that witch magic made the turn impossible, but maybe there were types of magic that were compatible with vampirism and types that weren't?

'Renata mentioned, um, external and active magic. Which type is yours?'

'I've never heard those terms before,' Leon said.

'Really?'

'Not all witches use the same language. Not all vampires do.'

'All shifters seem to,' Cynthia said. 'At least the ones that speak English.'

'Interesting,' Leon said.

'I guess.'

They climbed in silence for a little while. At length, Leon said, 'Can I ask you a question?'

'You don't have to ask permission for everything.' Cynthia giggled.

'I thought you liked it,' Leon said indignantly.

'Alright, alright. You can ask.'

'Do you know other vampires? How do you know the vampire who owns the Bleibtreustraße apartment?'

'How do you know it's owned by a vampire?' Cynthia asked.

'The scent, the traces of magic.'

'You can smell… he hasn't been there in ages!' Cynthia wrinkled her nose.

'Not like a smell,' Leon said. 'Traces. It's hard to explain. So it is a vampire?'

'Damien von Klichtzner, but I don't know him, not really. I'm friends with his daughter.'

'He has a daughter?' Leon asked.

'Lily. She's…' Cynthia frowned. Maybe she shouldn't reveal too much. 'She's a little older than me.'

'Also a vampire?'

'Half.'

'I see.'

They were almost at the top. Keeping her eyes fixed on the steps ahead, Cynthia said, 'I know one vampire personally. He's not that old. He's related to Nathan.'

'Your hunter friend.'

'Yeah. Adrian was a hunter before he was turned. He's easy to get along with. Fun. Then there's Lily, but she usually comes across as human. She's… like me.'

'I don't understand.'

'Awkward.' Cynthia chewed her lip. 'Lonely.'

'Loneliness is a curse that every species shares.'

'Yeah.' She'd been so focused on the conversation that Cynthia was surprised when she reached the top. She swayed. Leon caught her shoulders, steadying her. He stepped up beside her, draping an arm around her back. After a deep breath, Cynthia let herself look.

'Oh, *wow*.'

The view was absolutely stunning. The lights of Berlin stretched out around her like a carpet of stars. She could pick out the TV tower, standing tall above the rest, and Potsdamer Platz, with its modern glass-and-steel buildings. When she turned around, she found the gasometer. It was a huge dome, but in the dark it looked more like a gaping black hole. Staring into it made Cynthia feel dizzy.

'This is incredible,' she said. 'You can see the whole of Berlin.'

'I know,' Leon said quietly, his voice almost lost under the brisk wind whipping about. Cynthia turned to look at him. He was watching her, a small smile on his face. Impulsively, she went up on tiptoes and kissed his lips. Leon folded his arms around her, holding her tight.

When she pulled away, she was breathless and dizzy for a whole other reason. 'We should… probably find somewhere better to do this.'

'I won't let you fall.'

'Still.' Cynthia took his hand, tugging him to the stairs. 'Come on.'

They began to descend.

'Couldn't you turn into a bird if you fell?' Leon asked.

'Maybe.' Considering falling sent a shiver down Cynthia's spine. 'I'd have to see a bird or have seen one recently. And then I'd have to shift fast enough. So… probably not.'

'Fascinating.' Leon jumped nimbly down a couple of steps, landing with a clang. He turned back, taking Cynthia's hand as she reached him. 'I'd catch you.'

'There's no way you could get down the steps in time to catch me.'

'Of course I could.' Leon shifted to the railing. Cynthia pulled him back.

'Let's not. Come on, I need to get home.'

'Alright, maybe next time.'

Cynthia had to laugh. 'Where is this daredevil-ness coming from all of a sudden?'

'You bring out the best in me.' Leon smiled at her. 'Let's go. It's late.'

They descended quickly after that. Cynthia's thighs were burning by the time she reached the ground, and she consented quite happily to riding home on Leon's back. He deposited her at the front door to Damien's building five minutes later.

'This is as far as I go.'

'You don't want to come up?'

'Maybe not this time,' Leon said. 'Next time.'

'Alright.'

'I'll see you tomorrow.' Leon brushed his lips against Cynthia's, fleeting and gentle, before abruptly vanishing from sight, sending a breeze ghosting over Cynthia's arms. Still smiling to herself, she climbed the stairs and let herself into Damien's apartment.

'Cynthia?' Nathan emerged from the lounge suddenly, making Cynthia jump. 'Where have you been? I tried calling you.'

'Um…' Cynthia pulled her phone out of her bag. 'My phone's dead. Sorry.' She looked up, studying the worried lines of Nathan's face. 'Did something happen with the KUA?'

'They're convening a meeting in the morning,' Nathan said. 'I… I was just worried. I expected you to be here.'

'Sorry.' Cynthia scuffed her toe against the ground. 'I just… took the long way home, I guess. Did you need anything? I'm pretty tired.'

Nathan frowned, shifting his weight from foot to foot. 'No, we can talk in the morning.'

'Alright. Goodnight.'

'Night.'

Awkwardly, Cynthia shuffled around him and entered her room. It was a relief to shut the door behind her. What was that? Suddenly, things felt weird around Nathan, and she wasn't sure why.

Bed. It'll be better in the morning.

She showered quickly and climbed into bed, but sleep didn't come. She could hear Nathan moving around in the apartment, talking on his phone. Thoughts whirled around in her brain like leaves in the wind, as she tried to fit everything together. What was Nathan doing in Berlin? Had he really just come for her? For a moment, it sounded like he was shouting at something. Then the shower started up, the water clanking in the pipes. Cynthia slid out of bed, padding silently like a cat out into the hall.

Nathan was staying in the spare room, which was probably used as a study. His things were kept rigidly neat: overnight bag, hunter jacket, boots. Nathan was the opposite of Cynthia in so many ways, she was surprised they had managed to date for so long before their differences came between them.

His phone buzzed twice on the bedside table, the screen flashing on. Cynthia peeked at it.

Anton M. Mob: It won't be possible to block them forever

Anton? A chill ran down Cynthia's spine. Did M stand for Mattusek? Was that the same Anton she knew?

Before she could think the better of it, she picked up Nathan's phone and put his code in to unlock it. The screen opened to a WhatsApp conversation with Anton—the photo matched. Feeling sick, Cynthia scrolled back through the messages. They were mostly in English and went back as far as October of the previous year. The first message, dated October fourth, was from Nathan.

Nathan: I'm arriving tonight, 9PM. It was the first flight I could get

Anton M. Mob: Tegel? I'll arrange a pickup

So Nathan had been in Berlin last October? Didn't those dates coincide with the bus accident? She couldn't remember offhand... Cynthia flicked back through their conversation, lines jumping out at her. *Jeremiah offered his support... vampires are being stubborn... secrets upon secrets... say they have enlisted a witch...*

Anton M. Mob: I would not trust the vampires to guarantee the safety of your shifter friend

Nathan: That's non-negotiable

Anton M. Mob: I'll see what I can do

Shifter friend... That was her. Feverishly, Cynthia read through the other messages, trying to glean some kind of meaning from the disparate conversations. It was impossible. She only understood two things: one, Nathan had been involved in investigating the bus crash from the start, and he'd never told her, and two... he knew Anton. And it was the latter thought that made a feeling of betrayal blossom in Cynthia's chest. Nathan had known everything that was going on before she had, and he'd never told her. She felt played. Furious with herself, Cynthia put his phone back and slipped out of his room.

She had no idea what to do now.

CHAPTER TWENTY-SIX

KNOCK, KNOCK.

'Come in,' Cynthia called tiredly. She'd slept poorly the previous night, kept awake by a maelstrom of thoughts bouncing around her head.

Nathan poked his head around the door. 'Morning. You sleep okay?'

Cynthia sat up, brushing her tangled hair out of her eyes. She didn't know what to say to Nathan. 'What's up?'

'I just heard from the KUA. They want to speak to both of us.' Nathan's lips were drawn down into a frown, his shoulders tensed.

'What's wrong?'

'We have to go before the Council.'

'That's bad,' Cynthia guessed.

Nathan nodded grimly. 'Just... don't say anything that can incriminate us, okay? You should probably dress up, or something.'

'Got it.'

She didn't really have much in the way of smart clothes. Cynthia wore her only pair of trousers that weren't jeans, and a button-up blouse, and they took the train into the centre. Renata was waiting for them outside the station. She waved to Nathan first, before looking Cynthia up and down critically.

'You'll do.'

Nathan, of course, was fine in his hunter uniform. He'd gone from meeting Renata yesterday to apparently being best buddies with her, Cynthia realised sourly. Another person that was suddenly on Nathan's side.

'What would you have done if I wasn't dressed appropriately?' she asked.

'Nothing.' Renata shrugged. 'You want to offend them, it's not my problem.'

Some things never changed.

'Are we doing this, then?' Nathan asked.

'Yeah, let's go.'

Renata let them into *Verzaubert*. The main room was deserted, as the bar was closed during the day. They descended the second staircase. The room below was smallish and oppressively windowless, with a long wooden table down the middle.

Three people sat around one end of the table: two men and a woman. The woman had similar features to Renata, though Renata's face was softer. Of the men, one was fairly young, blond, with a very narrow face. The other was at least in his seventies, with feathery white hair and glasses. All of them were clad in long brown robes, and all wore identical looks of displeasure.

'Let me do the talking,' Nathan whispered as he and Cynthia took the seats they were directed to. Cynthia nodded uneasily. Behind them, the door slammed. Cynthia jumped. When she turned to see the latecomer, her heart sank even further.

It was Anton.

He slid into a seat next to Nathan, his gaze on Cynthia. She swallowed and looked away.

'You are Cynthia Rymes?' the woman asked.

'Yes,' Cynthia answered quietly.

'I am Karolin Friedemann. Beside me are Jürgen Strohkirch—' She indicated the younger man. '—and Walter Gehring.' The older man. 'You are charged with negligence resulting in the escape of the Decker family. As the Deckers were formally indebted to the KUA vampires, that means it falls to you to pay off their debt—'

'*What?*' Cynthia gasped.

Karolin Friedemann frowned at the interruption. 'However,' she continued coolly, 'your colleague here has requested the opportunity to plead your case.' She waved a hand dismissively. 'So plead.'

Cynthia looked at Nathan. He made a placating gesture, mouthing, 'It's okay.'

'It's not okay,' Cynthia hissed.

'Let me,' Nathan murmured. He turned to the witches and cleared his throat. 'With respect, Ms Friedemann, Cynthia was not at fault for the release of the Deckers—'

'So you say,' Walter Gehring interrupted, 'yet conveniently there are no witnesses.'

'Renata and Nathan were there!' Cynthia cried.

'Cynthia,' Nathan hissed. 'Let me!'

She scowled mutinously. Ms Friedemann's expression contorted with anger.

'We have witnesses,' she said coolly. 'The question is not of guilty versus innocent, but of who must now pay off the debt. If Cynthia Rymes is not going to repay the vampires, then who do you suggest in her stead?'

Cynthia's heart was racing in her chest. She glanced helplessly at Nathan, but he looked calm.

'I've spoken to Jeremiah. He insists that you call an intermission until he's able to adjudicate the situation.'

'Impossible,' Friedemann said. 'Jeremiah has no right to intercede in local judicial procedures.'

'Why should we allow him to protect the girl when the cost will fall to us to pay, instead?' Gehring demanded.

'You'd rather see a girl dead than find another solution?' Anton asked suddenly. 'My, how far the KUA has fallen.'

'Herr Mattusek is right,' Strohkirch spoke up abruptly. 'Why are we acquiescing to the vampires? We never have before.'

'Surely a solution can be reached that doesn't involve killing an innocent person,' Anton added.

'Hardly innocent; she's been sticking her nose into things from the start,' Gehring said bitterly.

'Children will do as they do,' Strohkirch started.

'I'm not—' Cynthia muttered.

'Unconscionable! The girl must pay!' Gehring cried.

'She's just a child,' Strohkirch protested.

'Surely,' Anton interjected smoothly, 'culpability should fall to—'

'The debt to the vampires must be paid,' Friedemann said. 'Why are we to take on the payment when it was not us who released the Deckers?'

'Cynthia didn't release the Deckers,' Nathan replied. 'She's as much a victim as the rest of us.'

'You are no victim.' Gehring sneered. 'As always, Jeremiah's Council saunters in and makes a mess and—'

'The Harz Coven does so love to throw around their accusations.' Strohkirch.

'Now, let's be reasonable—' Anton.

'—it is not a question of covens; this will fall on all of us—' Gehring.

'—if the hammer will fall, then let it fall. What can the vampires do to us anyway?' Strohkirch.

'—fighting like cats, the both of you!' Friedemann cut through it all. 'The girl is guilty—no, Jürgen, enough. The girl is guilty; therefore, she will solve the problem. Either she may turn herself over, or she can find a suitable alternative. But a solution must be found.'

'If I may suggest the ideal alternative for all of us,' Anton said smoothly. 'Cynthia is well-positioned to act as an informant—'

'Your problems are not the problems of the Witch Council,' Gehring said.

'I think you'll find that's not the case,' Anton replied.

'This is a courtroom, not a boardroom. You can make your shady deals elsewhere.'

'Walter, come, will we really put a girl to death to appease the vampires?' Strohkirch asked.

'The decision is made,' Friedemann said. 'Unless you can summon the Deckers back to Berlin to face trial, you can take their place,' she told Cynthia. 'You have three days. Now, leave.'

'Is this how justice is dispensed in Berlin?' Nathan asked coolly.

'Is this how the Council for Supernatural Affairs conducts its business?' Gehring replied. 'Sending children to judge us?'

'Jeremiah won't stand for it,' Nathan said.

'Then let Jeremiah come here and defend her case,' Gehring sneered. 'Ah, yes, I forget. He won't, will he? Because he, too, fears the curse that has befallen our vampires. No vampire will set foot in the city until it's lifted. We must solve our own problems.' He smiled coldly. 'Let the girl solve her own problems, too. What's good for the goose is good for the gander.'

Nathan's expression was very fixed. Cynthia had never seen him look that angry before. For her part, she felt numb with shock. She didn't realise it was over until Nathan took her arm, tugging her up. 'Come on.'

'But—'

'Not here. Come on, let's go.'

Nathan led her outside to street level. As soon as they emerged into the light, Cynthia pulled away.

'WHAT THE HELL?'

'It's three days,' Nathan started. 'I know it sounds awful. But Damien is on his way — we'll fix this —'

'It's not your life on the line!'

'I know, okay, Cynthia, I'm trying my best.' Nathan tried to take her hand, but she brushed him off. 'Can we please just get away from here, before they change their minds and hand you over now?'

'I can't believe this!'

Mind racing, Cynthia turned, looking for an escape. She felt like she needed to run, but she didn't know where to go. Instead, she came face-to-face with Anton, who had emerged behind them.

'The car's this way,' he said in a conversational tone.

'You!' The frustration welling up in Cynthia's chest finally exploded out. She whirled on Nathan. 'I know you're working with him! I saw the messages on your phone. He's been using me from the start!'

'Cynthia,' Nathan started uneasily. 'How… Anton's a colleague. You can trust him.'

'I mentioned him to you, and you didn't think to tell me that you knew him?'

'I couldn't — it's Council business…'

'Council business,' Cynthia spat. 'Your favourite excuse.'

Nathan frowned. 'You know I can't tell you things about my job — look, can we discuss this in the car?'

'Prove I can trust him. He was the first person in this awful city who tried to trap me in some kind of deal.'

'On the contrary,' Anton said, 'I was only ever trying to keep you safe.'

'*Safe?*' Cynthia spluttered. 'You call this safe? All you did in there was stir the pot.'

'You have no understanding of how politics works in Berlin. If I hadn't intervened, they'd have condemned you to die today. Now you have time.'

'Time? Time for what?' Cynthia snarled.

'Time to convince them they need someone else more than you,' Anton said. 'I know you're in contact with Leon. If you can —'

'Oh, so that's what this is about!' Cynthia laughed bitterly. 'Here we go. You can't stand there being someone in the city you can't track. You want me to trade his life for mine.'

'A life for a life is more than fair considering what you owe,' Anton replied. 'You should count yourself lucky.'

'Lucky? You're insane!' Cynthia snapped. 'There's no way I'm handing Leon over to be killed. I'd never do that!'

'That's up to you,' Anton said. 'Before you dismiss it out of hand, remember, I could free you and your fool father.'

'My father's a prisoner?' Cynthia felt lightheaded all of a sudden.

Anton chuckled derisively. 'In a prison of his own making, just like you.'

Fury filled Cynthia's chest. She was tired of being mocked.

'I'm not getting in a car with you.' She spun around and stomped off towards the S-Bahn station.

'Suit yourself,' Anton called. 'Just remember, most deals have time limits.'

'Fuck off,' Cynthia muttered.

She and Nathan rode in uneasy silence for their six stops. Cynthia was by no means calm, but she knew better than to pick a fight on the S-Bahn. Too much risk of exposure. That didn't mean she held back when they got home. The second they walked through the door of Damien's apartment, she rounded on Nathan.

'You lied to me about Anton. You know—you *know* that things would have gone differently if I'd known he was working with you.'

'Cynthia…' Nathan raked a hand through his hair. 'Look, Anton is… he works for the Council, but he's still a mage. I didn't want you involved with him, and, okay, maybe that was a mistake, but…'

'You dragged me into this in the first place! I'd never have gotten curious if you hadn't asked me to investigate!'

'I know!'

'And now, what—you think I should take Anton's deal? Hand over Leon to make my punishment go away? That's your grand solution?' Cynthia paced the length of the hall, fighting back tears.

'It's a solution. I'm not saying it's the answer—'

'It's not any sort of solution for me!' Cynthia cried. 'I like Leon! I like him a hell of a lot more than you or Anton, right now!'

Nathan flinched. 'Cynthia…'

Cynthia glared at him. Nathan sighed.

'If my job and your happiness conflict, then I have a problem,' her said. 'Don't you see? I'm trying to balance everything here, Cynthia, but the more pressure you put on me, the more risk there is of things falling!'

'You can't let them do this!'

'Cynthia!' Nathan reached helplessly for her hand, before dropping his arm back down. 'I'm trying my best to keep you safe here, okay? We've run afoul of people much older and more powerful than we are—'

'So you'll sacrifice someone else! They're lying about Leon!'

'You don't know that! Are you really willing to risk your own death on the chance that he's innocent?'

'I know he's innocent!' Cynthia's eyes filled with tears. 'You haven't met him, okay? Leon isn't evil!'

'People don't have to be evil to do evil things,' Nathan said. 'We don't know the whole story.'

'But you'd still rather condemn him!'

'No!' Nathan scrubbed his hands over his hair in frustration. 'I just—what do you actually know about Leon, Cynthia?'

'I know he's innocent. He's just lonely. He's never hurt me!'

'Those are opinions. Not things I can take in front of the Council.' Nathan shook his head. 'You don't know anything about him—I know you don't because no one does. I've checked with the Councils in Oxford, Paris, Bonn—'

'And you're willing to trust them over me! They've never met Leon either!'

'—and none of them had any information, Cynthia, none.'

'Maybe he doesn't have a file because he's not a criminal.'

'Or maybe he has a file and it's been erased,' Nathan said. 'All of them. Someone has tried to wipe Leon's name from all the databases that might have known anything about him.'

That brought Cynthia up short. She frowned, curiosity niggling at her. 'That doesn't mean Leon did it.'

'No, but who else would have?'

'Someone who did something that they wanted to hide?'

'Leon is the one hiding,' Nathan pointed out, his tone gentle. It annoyed Cynthia. 'Like it or not, he's the most likely candidate to have done it.'

'I don't like it,' Cynthia snapped. 'And I'm still not handing him over to keep myself safe.'

Nathan blew out an angry sigh. 'Look, Damien is on his way here, and I'm going to speak to the vampires this evening. Let me work on it.'

'Like you have so far?' Cynthia demanded. She knew she was being unreasonable, but she was so furious.

'I'm trying!' Nathan groaned. 'Please just—stay in. You're safe behind the wards. Don't go looking for Leon, and don't go looking for trouble. Let me handle it. I can buy us time to figure out a way out of the city without them noticing.'

'So—do nothing, let you solve it?'

'Please,' Nathan said. 'I don't want you to get hurt.'

Cynthia twisted her fingers into her hair. 'Fine. Fine, go run around and save the day and I'll just sit here like a damsel in distress.'

'It's not like that.' Nathan shook his head. 'Please, Cynthia.'

'Just go. I want to be on my own.'

Nathan stared at her pleadingly, but Cynthia just glowered at him. Finally, Nathan said, 'Alright. I'm sorry.'

Cynthia watched him leave, refusing to speak, but once he was gone, it was even worse. The apartment suddenly seemed tiny. She moved from room to room, restless, feeling like she was bouncing off the walls. She didn't want to eat, didn't want to talk to anyone, but didn't want to be alone, either. As the day dragged on, she got more and more stressed. She checked her phone compulsively as the hours slid by, but Nathan didn't contact her.

And why would he? He must be furious.

That was the kicker. This was Cynthia's fault, even if she hadn't meant for it to happen. The thought drove her crazy.

There's no justice to be had here.

Someone needed to die to appease everyone... it didn't seem to matter who.

What a bloodthirsty city.

By eight o'clock, Cynthia couldn't stand being alone with her thoughts anymore. She put her shoes on and, in defiance of Nathan's advice, went for a walk.

The streets of Berlin had emptied as night fell. Cynthia's flip-flops slapped the ground as she walked furiously, angry tears blurring her eyesight. She had no idea of her destination; she only knew that if she stayed in the apartment a second longer she was going to explode. So, she walked around the block, until she saw an elderly woman walking a border collie, and an idea occurred to her. She slipped into an alleyway, and within seconds had accessed the dog's form. It filled her skin to overflowing, pushing out all the human parts, until she was stretching and pushing and shoving into dogness. Once the shift had settled, she clumsily kicked her clothes to one side and set off at a trot.

I'm about to run through Berlin effectively naked.

Oh well, she'd done worse things. Anton could bail her out if she shifted back into human at a dog pound—it'd serve the bloody witches right.

Around the entrance to Damien's building, she stopped and sniffed around. *They'd stood about here...* shortly, she picked up her own scent and one that was... odd. Earth and blood and danger and human all rolled into one. The dog didn't like it at all, but it was easy to locate. Stronger than Cynthia had expected, as though Leon had stood in this place recently. Nose to the ground, she set off down the street.

Faster and faster, Cynthia ran through the city, tracking the scent, until her spine was tingling, and it was obvious where her destination was. Amidst the trees, she shifted back, the breeze cool over her skin, the stony pathway sharp beneath her feet, as she clambered beside the waterfall up to the war memorial in Kreuzberg.

A few people were scattered about the summit, drinking and smoking. Cynthia hesitated, nerves catching up with her. Where was he?

'Leon?'

Her voice was barely a whisper, yet moments later he was there, his expression stunned beneath the moonlight.

'Cynthia? What are you doing here?' He averted his eyes. 'Why are you naked?'

'I... sorry,' Cynthia said, belatedly embarrassed. 'I was shifting... the clothes don't come with... uh...'

'Here.' Leon pulled off his shirt and passed it over, still staring fixedly at a nearby tree. Cynthia dragged the shirt over her head, then threw her arms around him.

'Tell me it's going to be okay,' she cried. 'Tell me it'll all work out. This drama in Berlin has nothing to do with me. They're going to solve their own problems and leave me alone.'

Leon's hands fluttered over her shoulders, her waist, as though he didn't know what to do with them. 'I don't understand.'

'I got summoned before the KUA witches.' Cynthia's voice broke on a sob.

Leon's grip tightened around her. 'When? Why didn't you tell me?'

'Today.' A few tears escaped, trickling down Cynthia's face. 'They insist I have to trade—someone—for the Deckers. Because they survived. They wanted me, but now I h—have three days to come up w—with someone else—I can't let someone be killed! It wasn't even my fault! How could I know that Lola would—that she'd betray me—' A sob wrenched out of her throat. Leon lifted her, carrying her into the trees.

'Shh… shh, it's okay. We can fix this.'

'I can't!' Cynthia wailed. 'I've tried so hard… everything I do just makes things worse. All I wanted to do was help!'

'I can help,' Leon promised. 'Let me carry the burden. Cynthia,' he lifted her chin gently, 'may I?'

'Yes,' Cynthia whispered. 'Please.'

Leon's lips met hers. Cynthia clutched at him, deepening the kiss, pressing her body into his. She felt as though she could push all her worries onto him. She threw herself into the kiss, wanting to forget the rest of the world.

Leon gripped her shoulders, nudging her gently away. 'Cynthia—I don't want to hurt you.'

'Please,' Cynthia gasped. 'I want this. I don't want to think about… everything else. Not right now.'

Something flickered in Leon's gaze, something deep, rather like longing. His lashes dipped against his cheeks as he studied her. 'Here?'

'My place,' Cynthia whispered, tracing his lean, bare chest. 'It's empty.'

Leon carried her. The run that had taken Cynthia almost an hour as a dog was now reduced to a matter of minutes. Cynthia let them in, feeling a little drunk on her own recklessness. Nathan would kill her. She didn't care what Nathan thought. Screw him. He'd been using her. Sure, she could have handled things better, but if he'd been honest, she might never have ended up in trouble in the first place. She stepped inside, pulling Leon behind her.

'Come in.'

'Thank you,' he said formally. The wards tingled around them. Then Leon was inside, following Cynthia to her bedroom.

'Sorry—it's a mess.'

'I don't care.' Leon smiled beatifically, and Cynthia couldn't help but kiss him again. He was too tall. She had to grab his shoulders to balance herself. Leon crouched down, and Cynthia giggled.

'You're too tall.'

'I'm sorry.' Leon gripped her hips, lifting her and laying her out on the bed.

'Leon!' Cynthia gasped. He knelt at her feet, studying her intently.

'May I disrobe you?'

'You might have to.' Cynthia stroked his thigh with her foot, giving him a coy look. 'Unless you want to just—you know.' She felt a bit shy at the thought that he might *not* want to see her.

'No,' Leon protested. 'No, let me.' He crawled over her legs, grasping the hem of her shirt and sliding it up. Cynthia grimaced self-consciously, but Leon's expression was practically reverent as he exposed her stomach and breasts.

'You're beautiful,' he whispered, pressing a kiss to her hip. He sat up and wriggled the shirt out from under Cynthia's shoulders. She reached for his belt.

'Can I?'

Tossing the shirt on the floor, Leon crawled up to lay beside Cynthia. She traced her fingers over his chest, the fine scattering of hair above his waistband, then undid his belt and fly. Leon watched her all the while, drinking in her reactions. He lifted his hips so Cynthia could get his jeans off.

Every inch of him seemed sculpted from marble. Cynthia pulled his jeans down, studying him, and Leon drew her close, kissing her gently.

'Will you do something for me?'

'Now?' Cynthia asked, confused

'It has to be now.' His breath ghosted over her ear. 'Please?'

'Okay.' Cynthia leaned back so she could see his face. 'What is it?'

'Drink my blood,' Leon said. 'Just a little.'

'Oh...' The thought curdled Cynthia's stomach and dimmed her buzz a little. 'I don't know,' she said warily. 'That's not really... So you can track me?'

'Yes,' Leon agreed. 'But also... if you drink my blood, it will strengthen you. The witches will be much less able to hurt you.'

'I've never heard of that before,' Cynthia whispered.

'It's an old tradition.' Leon traced a line over the skin of her shoulder, his gaze heavy. 'Few practice the old ways anymore. But if the witches find you—it'll give me time...'

'Time to help me?'

'Yes. Will you drink my blood? Please.'

'I guess I could,' Cynthia said. 'Just a little.'

'It will be pleasurable,' Leon said.

'Are you sure?'

'I promise.'

'Okay,' she whispered. Leon raised his wrist to his mouth. Cynthia watched him closely, half-curious, half-disgusted, as his fangs slid over his bottom lip. Keeping his gaze fixed on her face, he sank his teeth into his wrist. Blood welled up around his mouth, trickling over his pale skin.

'This doesn't feel—uh—hygienic,' Cynthia started.

'Vampires can't transmit diseases,' Leon said. 'You must be quick, before it heals.'

He held out his wrist, the blood making an eerie pattern over his skin in dark red. Cynthia took it in shaking fingers. This was nothing like last time, which had been tainted by panic, blurred by her fading consciousness. She felt more alive than ever before, too focused to lack self-consciousness.

Leon tucked his other hand behind her head. 'Let me,' he whispered, guiding her face to his wrist. 'Drink.'

At first, all Cynthia could taste was the slimy, coppery flavour of blood. Then, slowly, heat rose in her belly and suffused through her veins. She threw a leg over Leon's thighs. He pulled her closer, closer, until her mouth fell away from his wrist.

'Leon—I need—'

'I know.'

He lay back, grasping her hips. Cynthia crawled over him, closing her eyes as he lowered her. They slid together, fitting one another perfectly. Leon rolled them over, settling above Cynthia so that he could gaze into her eyes.

'You're perfect,' he whispered.

'Please move,' Cynthia groaned. Leon began to thrust, setting an erratic pace. His eyes fell shut in ecstasy, a moan rising out of his throat. Cynthia scraped her nails down his back, trying to drag him closer.

'Leon… Leon… please.'

He dipped his head to her neck, breathing deeply. 'May I taste you?'

'Yes! Oh, please!'

Her neck stung briefly, then she felt the oddest sensation. Belatedly, she understood what he'd meant by taste. But the bite hardly hurt. On the contrary, Cynthia felt a tension building inside her, growing and growing until suddenly it snapped. Leon growled, the sound vibrating against her neck and through her chest. He thrust a few more times, hard, and both of them tumbled over the edge into orgasm together.

CHAPTER TWENTY-SEVEN

CYNTHIA AWOKE SUDDENLY. She was naked, the covers twisted beneath her, and the air had turned cool enough to make her shiver. It was dark. On the bedside table, her phone was vibrating.

'Leon?' she called.

There was no reply.

Cynthia grabbed her phone and answered.

'Hey… Lily?'

'Oh, hey, did I wake you? I didn't think it was that late.'

'Yeah, um…' Cynthia glanced at her phone. 'Almost eleven. No, it's fine. I was… napping.'

'Napping?' Lily giggled. 'Is that an excuse?'

'Um…' Cynthia felt her cheeks flushing. 'How bad will Damien kill me if he finds out I brought a guy back to his apartment?'

Lily laughed. 'Oh gosh. Usually, it's Damien bringing people back to that apartment.'

'Yuck!' Cynthia laughed too. Gathering the sheets around her, she stood slowly, stretching off the last of her post-coital sleepiness. 'Did you need something?'

'I was worried.' Lily hesitated for a moment. 'Have you heard from Nathan or any of the others?'

'Yeah… Nathan's here.' Cynthia paused. 'Maybe not right here. Hold on, I'll check.'

She headed out of her room, but the rest of the apartment was silent and still. The room Nathan was using was deserted.

'He's not here. To be honest, I've hardly seen him since he got to Berlin. He's been busy, and acting kind of sketchy and…' *Avoiding me.* '…we might have argued.'

'Oh dear,' Lily said sympathetically.

'Want me to call him for you?'

'I already tried. I can't get hold of him, nor Damien. Monica has no idea what's going on, and neither does Adrian, and usually Adrian knows everything Damien does.'

Lily sounded worried. Cynthia frowned.

'I'm sure they're just working on something big. And, you know how it is. They never want to involve us, right? We're *civilians*.'

'Yeah,' Lily said bitterly. 'Civilians, right.'

Cynthia couldn't help but agree with the sentiment.

'Anyway,' Lily said, 'I feel bad for waking you. Go snuggle with your guy.'

'I can't. He left.'

'Arsehole.'

That shocked a laugh out of Cynthia. Lily almost never swore.

'I don't think it's like that,' she said. 'He's complicated, Leon, he's pretty hard to pin down. Anyway, it's just a summer thing. I'll probably never see him again after I go home, right?'

'Even so, he shouldn't be sneaking out on you.'

'Don't worry, I'll get him to make up for it.'

Cynthia peered into the kitchen, the last room on her circuit, before settling in the lounge, with its antique maps. One of them caught her eye, a nineteenth-century rendition of Berlin. Kreuzberg was marked, and Cynthia suddenly thought of where she'd met Leon last night.

'Hey, before you go, there was something I was meaning to ask you.'

'Yeah?' Lily asked.

'Have you been to Kreuzberg?'

'Sure.'

'Do you know that memorial up on the hill?'

'In Viktoriapark,' Lily said. 'It's the Prussian memorial. What about it?'

'There's a supernatural memorial there, too.'

Lily was silent for a few moments, too long for it to be anything other than hesitation. 'You saw it.'

'So it is your family on there?'

'Damien's family. He took me to see it a few years back. It's his parents and siblings.'

'Damien had siblings?' Cynthia asked, shocked.

'A brother and a sister. They were both younger.' Lily hesitated again. 'They were killed, along with his parents. Damien escaped. He doesn't talk about it, so please don't ask him about it.'

'I don't think we have the sort of relationship where I can ask him personal questions,' Cynthia pointed out. Feeling guilty, she added, 'I didn't mean to stir up bad memories.'

'No… it's okay,' Lily said. 'It's not like I remember them. I don't even know if Damien really remembers them. It was centuries ago.'

It was hard to fathom someone measuring their life in centuries. The thought made Cynthia's chest ache.

'I'm still sorry,' she said quietly.

'It's alright,' Lily repeated. 'Anyway, will you let me know when you speak to Nathan? Even if it's three AM my time, just text me.'

'I will.'

'Thanks. Speak to you soon.'

'Yeah, bye.'

Lily hung up, and Cynthia lowered the phone, her mind still stuck on Damien. His family killed, their names on a memorial. Cynthia didn't even know if she had family members who'd been killed and immortalised on a memorial in World War One, a hundred years ago, let alone eight hundred years ago. Not that the memorial was eight hundred years old—more like one hundred and fifty. Who had created that memorial? Who had thought to recall the names of people who had died so long ago and carve them into a memorial?

Had the other people on the memorial been killed the same way as Damien's family? Were there other children amongst that list of names?

How old had Damien been when it happened?

Damien.

Something hit her at that moment, something she ought to have thought of weeks ago. Cynthia's heart plummeted, as though she'd missed a step going down the stairs.

Oh, shit.

Before she could think the better of it, she called Lily back. The phone seemed to ring a million times before Lily finally picked up.

'Hi. What happened?' Lily sounded out of breath.

'Damien,' Cynthia said. Her heart was racing a mile a minute. It took several moments for her to organise her thoughts. 'Damien's aura.'

'What about it?'

'It's red, right? Like, the colour of rubies, and kind of glittery. Hurts your eyes.'

'Yeah, sounds about right. Cynthia, what's going on?'

'I...' *Have no idea.* 'I think I've made a terrible mistake. I'm sorry, I have to go.'

'Wait, no, don't hang up—'

But Cynthia was already running for her room. She ended the call and threw the phone on the bed, scrambling for her clothes.

She had to go. She had to warn Nathan.

Five minutes later, she shoved her feet into her shoes and let herself out the door. On the stairs, she rang Nathan. The phone rang and rang and rang, before finally connecting.

'You've—'

'Nathan, thank God—it's him—I just realised—Leon is—'

'—reached the voicemail service of Nathan Delacroix. Sorry, I'm not available at the moment. Please leave a message after the beep and I'll get back to you soon.'

Beep!

'Fuck!' Cynthia cursed. 'Nathan, call me back as soon as you get this. It's urgent. Forget urgent. We've made a mistake. I've made a mistake. I need to speak to you RIGHT NOW!' She paused, trying to think how to put what she'd discovered into words, but she wasn't even rightly sure what she had discovered. Leon was like Damien. What did that mean? It meant that he wasn't a vampire like they'd thought—and—something—

Helpless, she hung up, shoved her phone in her bag, and sprinted down the stairs. Where to go? Where would Nathan be? He'd last said he was going to speak to the vampires, but that was hours ago. Who would know where he was? The hunters?

Anton?

As she set a course for the station, she pulled her phone out again and located Anton's number. After a few rings, he answered.

'Miss Rymes, how surprising.'

'Anton.' Cynthia swallowed a sigh of relief. 'I'm, um, sorry to bother you. I was wondering if you knew where Nathan was?'

Anton paused for a long moment. 'He has a phone, does he not?' His tone was mocking.

'Well, he's not answering it,' Cynthia replied crossly, 'so I'd appreciate it if you could just tell me straight if you know, or not.'

'I believe he's on his way to Clärchens Ballhaus,' Anton replied. 'Though you'd be prudent to just wait for him to call you back.'

'Thanks for the advice,' Cynthia said coldly. 'Goodbye.'

'As you wish. Goodbye, Miss Rymes.'

Anton hung up. Cynthia boarded the train, trying to breathe through her frustration.

Her panic was beginning to wear off. Maybe she should go back? But she hated the idea of staying home and waiting for Nathan to call. What if this was important? Damien was obviously a different species of vampire, capable of having children. Plus, Leon could do magic. She thought of the memorial in Kreuzberg, which had sparked this realisation. A memorial for the ancestors who were lost in the witch wars.

Ancestors.

But what did that *mean?*

Suddenly, Cynthia was thinking of all sorts of things that she should have told Nathan. Things she should have come clean about. She'd head for Clärchens Ballhaus, and maybe he'd call her on the way. Otherwise… well, she knew one thing: Leon wouldn't let the vampires hurt her.

Even if that came at a terrible price.

Guilt and confusion whirled in Cynthia's belly. The train ride seemed interminable, even though it was only twenty minutes. In short order, she was traversing the streets of central Berlin. Somehow, for the first time, they seemed rather spooky by night. Every shadow had a monster hiding in it, waiting to jump out at her.

But who was the monster?

She was a street away from the ballroom when a monster—of sorts—did step out.

'Good evening, Miss Rymes.'

Cynthia jumped. Lurking in the shadows, his skin glowing white in the moonlight, was Julianus. Instinctively, she stepped back.

'What are you doing here?'

'I thought to have a word. It seemed an opportune moment.'

'How did you know I was here?'

Julianus smiled, the rictus grimace of a corpse. 'Where else would you be?'

'At home? Away from you? I can think of plenty of places.'

Julianus's expression flickered. His gaze was hungry. It made goosebumps prickle on Cynthia's arms.

'Interesting,' he said finally. 'You haven't heard yet.'

'Heard what?'

'And here I thought your friends would have told you. So loyal. So determined to save you.'

Cynthia was feeling worse and worse; she had a sudden and desperate urge to flee. 'Told me what?'

'About your friend.' Julianus smiled. 'Leon.'

'What about Leon?' Cynthia's palms were starting to feel clammy. She wiped them surreptitiously. Was something wrong with Leon? Or should she be worrying about someone else? 'Is he okay?'

'Oh, I'm sure his conscience pains him greatly,' Julianus said. 'Physically, I expect he is fine.'

'Did Anton catch him?'

'Anton? Anton Mattusek?' Julianus chuckled. 'Such an impotent mage with his modern magicks cannot harm Leon. Don't be foolish.'

'Then what are you talking about?' Cynthia demanded.

'So impatient, the youth today,' Julianus said. 'Haven't you ever heard the saying give a little, gain a lot?'

'Is that a saying?' Cynthia asked sceptically, thoroughly irritated. Vampires, especially the old ones, just loved their word games. 'I think it sounds like a nice way of saying you want something.'

Julianus canted his head to one side, regarding her curiously. He looked like a snake considering where best to bite. It was extremely uncomfortable. 'A small favour, perhaps.'

Go figure.

'Why should I help you? You're trying to kill me.'

'All deals can be renegotiated.'

Here we go again.

'What renegotiation are you going to suggest now?' Cynthia asked. 'The last time I asked the vampires for negotiations, they chased me through the streets of Berlin and tried to eat me!'

Julianus's expression turned grave. 'That is true. I have not apologised for my lieutenants' behaviour yet. Their comportment was unforgivable.'

'Right,' Cynthia said cynically.

'Though perhaps the punishment did not fit the crime,' Julianus added.

'I didn't ask Leon to kill them.'

'No, and yet he did it for you. Does that absolve you of culpability?'

'I...' Cynthia chewed her lip, unwilling to commit to an answer. Whatever she said would be wrong. 'I'm still not really interested in negotiating. Maybe you should speak to the Council in Oxford.'

'Would that it were so simple,' Julianus said. 'But you already know that, do you not?'

'No?' Cynthia gazed at him, confused. What was he on about now?

'The reason the Council will not speak to us. Why they refuse to come to our aid,' Julianus said. 'You do know.'

'I don't,' Cynthia insisted. 'It's not as though Jeremiah and I have regular heart-to-hearts.'

Julianus considered her for a long time before he finally began to walk, slowly, rather like he was showing his age. He gestured for her to fall in beside him.

'Let me tell you a story,' Julianus said.

Brilliant. That was the last thing Cynthia wanted. Reluctantly, she said, 'Go ahead.'

'Do you know how old I am?'

That was a trick question, and Cynthia knew it. The silence stretched long, so she allowed herself to consider the answer.

'Forty, give or take. And I'd guess you were turned... more than a hundred years ago, less than five hundred.' She shrugged. 'At an estimate.'

'Most people assume I'm older.'

'But I know older vampires.'

Julianus's expression turned amused. 'I'm four hundred and twelve. A good guess, all around.'

'Great. What's that got to do with the story?'

'I'm coming to that. Mortals are so impatient.' He leaned against the wall, watching her like a cat watched a mouse. 'Are you aware that most vampires never make it to their first century?'

'Forty percent of all people who are turned go feral and get picked off by hunters,' Cynthia rattled off. 'Nathan told me.'

'That is indeed true. However, of those who survive, the sixty percent, the vast majority will die within the first decade or two. Vampires are most vulnerable in the early years, unused to their new life, hyper-sensitive to light, bloodlust… Many of them get caught by hunters, others are killed by witches or even other vampires. For that reason, a recently turned vampire is highly dependent on their sire for protection.'

That was news to Cynthia. She thought of Adrian—he'd never seemed too dependent on Damien, his sire. Maybe he'd aged out of the vulnerable period?

'How many survive?'

'At an estimate, no more than twenty to thirty percent,' Julianus said. 'The older the sire, the greater chance they have of protecting their children. Though, naturally, they must have the motivation to do so. And not all do.'

'Right,' Cynthia said. She'd have to check that with Nathan. 'Was your sire one of the good ones?'

Julianus laughed. 'Such personal questions. But I will answer—no, he was not. He cared little for his children, only what we could do for him. However, there was another vampire who was always kind. He would take in the city's strays, teach them, show them the best hunting spots. He found me, saved me from the witches, and I stayed with him.'

Cynthia could see where this was going. 'Leon can't be that old.'

'Leon is much older than I, I assure you.'

'No, no, that's not true. He told me—' She shook her head in frustration. 'He said he was thirty.'

'Did he?' Julianus asked neutrally.

'Yes, he did…' But even as she said it, Cynthia realised that he hadn't. He'd allowed her to assume that as the truth. 'Why?'

'It's what Leon does. Clever half-truths. He can't lie.'

'Everyone can lie. Maybe he's just honest enough not to.'

'Perhaps,' Julianus said, 'but he will never tell you the truth. As the fae, he will weave elaborate sentences until you're so confused, you forget your original question.'

'That's not the Leon I know.'

'And yet you've known him for how long?' Julianus challenged. 'Two weeks? A month? I have known him for four hundred years. Others may have known him longer—but there isn't anyone else left.'

'So he's killing everyone who knew him back then?' Cynthia asked cynically. 'Why would he do that?'

'A fresh start? Who knows?'

'He hasn't killed you.'

'No,' Julianus said, 'he never tried. I believed, foolishly perhaps, that I was special. That he valued me above others, enough to make me his equal.'

Equal. 'He's the fourth member of the Vampire Council,' Cynthia realised abruptly.

'Indeed. The oldest vampire in the city. He created the KUA in Berlin, long before there was a KUA, when we were just the Supernatural Committee. And when he did that, he selected me ahead of his other protegees, to rule beside him.' Julianus's voice took on a note of pride. 'We ruled Berlin together.'

Of course they had. It was the age-old story: powerful people wanted more power. Vampires were always warring over control of the cities. Resources. Money. People. Space.

Power.

'What went wrong?'

'Nothing, at first.' They had reached the river. Julianus paused at the railing, staring into the murky water below. 'We ruled peaceably for centuries. Leon scouted other vampires to join us—none of them as talented as I. None lasted. Some were killed by the witches; others disappeared. Perhaps Leon killed them, I don't know. He grew frustrated.' Julianus sighed. 'He changed, slowly enough that none of us noticed. At first, he desired to collaborate with the witches. But after a century of never-ending feuding, he began to take a harder approach. He became greedy; he killed them for lesser crimes. We broke the rules we had upheld. I didn't like that. The rules protected our species at a time when humans were becoming more and more dangerous. Leon and I started having disagreements. Finally, he turned on me.'

Julianus fell silent, his body bowed with sadness.

'You fought,' Cynthia guessed.

'We came to blows a single time,' Julianus said. 'He was... so powerful, you cannot possibly imagine. No mortal could fathom that power. He could have killed me in an instant... instead, he spared me.'

'But then why...'

'Am I ruling instead of he?' Julianus smiled bitterly. 'That is politics. I was peaceful, I sought a bargain with the witches. Leon had no friends amongst Berlin's witches; he'd killed too many of them. We pushed him out of the KUA. In return, he cursed us.'

'So there is a curse!'

'There is,' Julianus said gravely. 'Every vampire within the city boundary is cursed. Human blood no longer nourishes us; it turns to ash in our mouth and makes our veins burn with hellfire.'

'How?' Cynthia gasped.

'I don't know. Leon is unique amongst vampires. He does not follow the same rules as the rest of us. And in spite of no longer holding power, he still can sway the city to his will.'

'But...' Cynthia was putting everything together, faster than she wanted to. *Not Leon. No.* It seemed impossible, but now that Julianus was explaining, all the pieces were falling into place. 'The shifters...'

'The deal with the witches,' Julianus explained. 'There is no one in this city powerful enough to kill Leon. But to seal him away? That was a plausible goal. However, it required a power source.'

'Shifter blood.'

'Strong earthbound magic. Strong enough to counteract Leon's own magic. But we had difficulties. No such spell existed. It has taken time, and many lives have been lost needlessly.' Julianus gazed at her, his eyes holding the wisdom of millennia. 'Now, we are ready. All we are missing is the critical ingredient in the spell.'

'Blood?' A chill ran down Cynthia's spine. He couldn't be asking...

'The victim,' Julianus corrected. 'We need Leon.'

Suddenly, the story made sense.

'No.' Cynthia stepped back.

'No?' Julianus asked. 'After what I've just explained?' He gazed at her, surprised, perhaps.

'You think if you tell me a pretty story—how do I know it's true?'

'Look around you.' Julianus gestured to himself. 'The vampires are cursed.'

'Witches could have done that.'

'The witches suffer too. They are cut off from their power source, confined within the city borders. Their power grows weak. The only supernatural thriving in this city is Leon.'

'You're lying,' Cynthia said. 'Lying, because you want him, too. I'm not going to trade Leon's life for mine.'

'You will,' Julianus said. 'It won't be long.'

'It will be a long time before I betray Leon to you,' Cynthia promised. 'I would never do that.'

'Never is an awfully long time, Miss Rymes, especially for a creature such as myself. I'd hate for you to be proven wrong.'

Cynthia glared at him. 'What do you expect me to do, anyway? If you can't control him, how can I?'

'But he trusts you. It would be simple for you to persuade him to be at the right place at the right time—'

Julianus turned abruptly, something ugly flickering in his gaze. Cynthia's heart lurched as she turned as well. *Was Leon here?* But it was someone else approaching from the shadows, another familiar figure, another player in Berlin's endless game of chess.

Gideon.

'Let her go, Julianus,' he said coldly.

'I'm not holding her here,' Julianus said. 'She is bound only by her conscience.'

'Enough,' Gideon said. He met Julianus's gaze; for a moment, both of them were lost to the world, scorching each other with the fury in their eyes. Julianus looked away first.

'Remember our agreement, mage.'

'There is no agreement,' Gideon replied. 'Not if you renege on the terms.'

'You should have been more specific about your terms,' Julianus said stiffly. He turned to Cynthia. 'Please excuse me, Miss Rymes. I can see we have nothing more to discuss.' He bowed low before walking away.

Cynthia turned to Gideon; he was watching Julianus retreat with open hostility. 'What deal do you have with the vampires?'

Gideon's gaze snapped to Cynthia. 'It's nothing for you to concern yourself with,' he said angrily. 'I told you to get out of the city. What are you doing here?'

Anger surged in Cynthia's chest. 'It's nothing for you to concern yourself with.'

Gideon clenched his fists, his expression twisting, and his magic flared so strongly that Cynthia felt it, sticky and dirty like tar. She peeked at his aura: coal black. Then it was gone, and he'd mastered himself again.

'As you will,' he said coolly. 'On your head be it.'

He turned and left, leaving Cynthia feeling nauseous and quite like she'd made yet another fatal mistake. Clenching her fists, she swallowed hard and started for the train station. Bloody vampires, bloody witches. All of them, manipulative. Evil.

A buzzing in her bag distracted her from her angry thoughts. Cynthia pulled her phone out.

'Nathan!' she said. 'Finally! I've been trying to get hold of you. Where are you—'

'Cynthia? Cynthia, where are you?' Nathan demanded.

'I'm on my way home—I was looking for you. Nathan, you need to listen, there's something—'

'No,' Nathan interrupted. 'Cynthia, you need to go home right now. Get behind the wards, where you're safe. Go now!'

'Why?' Cynthia asked, her heart fluttering in fear. 'What happened?'

'It's the Witch Council,' Nathan said grimly. 'I know you trust Leon, Cynthia, but the evidence is—'

'Tell me what happened!'

Pause, silence. Nathan said, in a stilted voice, 'He killed them, Cynthia. He killed them all.'

Horror washed over Cynthia like a tidal wave. She stumbled, feeling as though all the strength had left her legs. 'What—no—he can't have—I was just with him—'

'What?' Nathan asked quickly. 'When?'

'I… I don't know. Three hours ago?'

'He's been busy since then.' Nathan took a deep breath. 'You need to go back. He can't get you behind Damien's wards.'

'No,' Cynthia whispered. 'No, you don't understand.'

'Understand what?'

'He's been in the apartment, Nathan. He can come in.'

'You invited him in? Cynthia, are you crazy? What if he…'

Cynthia.

Nathan's voice sounded like static. Cynthia could barely hear it over the panicked beat of her heart.

Come to me.

Her fingers were tingling. Her body swayed. 'Nathan—something's wrong—'

'Cynthia? Are you listening?'

Cynthia, come.

The world tunnelled around her. Cynthia stumbled a step forward.

Someone, somewhere, was calling her name. Their voice fell away, along with everything else.

Cynthia began to walk.

CHAPTER TWENTY-EIGHT

CYNTHIA'S PEACEFUL FEELING EVAPORATED slowly. She was lying down, a hand stroking gently through her hair. The room was pleasantly cool…

'Fiy mor mins, Mum,' she mumbled.

'Wake up, Cynthia.'

That wasn't her mother's voice. She dragged herself from the depths of sleep, finally managing to lift her head and open her eyes. She was in a dark room, lit only by a few lamps scattered around. Her head was pillowed on an antique cushion. Leon sat on a low table in front of her, and he was the one caressing her hair. His blue eyes gazed into hers.

'Hello, Cynthia.'

'Leon!' Cynthia sat up sharply. 'What's going on? Where am I?'

'Cecilienhof Palace,' Leon said. 'The city wasn't safe for us anymore, so I called you here. I'm sorry.'

'Called? What…' Cynthia felt as though she was half asleep. 'By magic?'

'It's not magic—not exactly.' Leon took her hand, gently tracing his fingers over her knuckles. Cynthia threw her legs off the sofa so she could sit upright.

'I don't understand.' Her brain was a tumble of thoughts—Lily's phone call, Julianus hinting, the dead witches, Gideon's disappointment…

'We shared blood,' Leon said softly. 'It forms a connection. It allows me certain… abilities.'

'Abilities,' Cynthia repeated numbly. She looked around. She was in Potsdam, where the old Prussian palaces were. How had she got here? 'Abilities like taking over my mind?'

'Not exactly. The mind is closed to me.'

'The mind is—you're speaking in riddles.' Cynthia pushed off the sofa, looking around anxiously. Leon followed her up.

'I can't control the mind,' he explained, his hands opening and closing into fists convulsively. 'Only the body. It's a brief control, it's not harmful, but I understand why you don't like it. I wouldn't have done it if it wasn't essential to get you away. The vampires and witches have hatched a terrible plan.'

He took a step towards Cynthia, but she skittered away from him. Leon paused, his expression twisting.

'You're afraid of me.' He sounded... not angry, exactly. Disappointed, or sad.

'Leon—I spoke to Julianus—he said—' Cynthia swallowed hard, words failing her.

'What did he tell you?' Leon asked urgently. 'You can't believe anything he says, Cynthia. Julianus is power-hungry. He'll tell you what you want to hear.'

'He said a lot of things—I don't know.' Cynthia shook her head, looking around again. She could see the exit, the neat green emergency exit sign catching the lamplight. But what would happen if she tried to leave? Would Leon stop her?

She still had her phone. She could feel it in her pocket. Could she get word to Nathan somehow?

'Leon, why am I here?'

'It's safe here. The witches can't leave the city. And the vampires won't risk it, not now.' Leon gazed at her, his expression fraught with sincerity. 'I didn't want them to hurt you.'

'I have to go back.'

'No! No.' Leon reached for her arm, his hands falling short as she backed away again. 'Whatever Julianus told you, it's a lie. Cynthia, please. You have to trust me.'

'I... I can't.' The words fell from her lips without her permission. 'Why did you kill the Witch Council?'

Leon turned away. 'You heard about that.'

'Nathan told me. Leon, why?' Cynthia stared at him beseechingly, unsure whether she wanted the truth, or... an excuse.

'Sometimes... sometimes renewal is essential,' Leon said, avoiding her gaze.

'Renewal? Leon, that's murder!'

'You have to get rid of the old to make way for the new. You've seen it yourself, that's how the city works. Always changing, evolving.'

'But who were you to decide that?' Cynthia asked, horrified. 'Those people had families! Leon, look at me.'

Leon turned to face her. His expression was blank, a book full of pages, every one of them empty. Somehow, it was more terrifying than if he'd been angry.

'What do you want me to say?' he asked. 'I did it for you. They mean to kill you.'

'I never asked for that.' Cynthia shook her head. She needed to think, but her brain felt too full up for clarity. 'I want the truth.'

'I've never lied to you.'

'How old are you?' Cynthia asked. 'You told me you didn't remember the Berlin Wall.'

'I don't.' Leon's gaze slipped away again. Now that Cynthia was looking for tells, she couldn't help but notice all of them. Leon wasn't exactly a great deceiver.

'Julianus said you were older than he is.'

'You shouldn't have spoken to him,' Leon said softly, insistently. 'Julianus lies.'

'Is he lying about that?'

Leon was silent.

'How old are you?' Cynthia repeated.

'I don't know.' Leon's voice had gone soft, fragile.

'Guess.'

'A… a thousand years… maybe more.'

A thousand years. For a moment, Cynthia was incapable of forming words. Her head swam. She had thought Damien was old, yet she knew he was born in the 1100s. Lily had told her. To be even older than that?

'A thousand…' Cynthia swallowed. 'That would be…' Why didn't she know more about German history? 'The Holy Roman Empire?'

Leon's gaze darted about, never settling on anything for long. 'I don't know the modern names… not in English.'

'How…' She was struggling to figure out what to ask. Lily could narrate Damien's history like a storybook, the parts of it she was willing to tell, anyway. How could Leon not know how old he was? Not know names or places? 'How can you not remember the Berlin Wall?'

'I…' Leon shifted his weight, his gaze distant, and slowly a change came over him. His features hardened. 'Why? If you already believe

Julianus, what does it matter?'

'Don't say that.' But suddenly, Cynthia was afraid. A sixth sense, located at the base of her neck, told her there was a predator in the room. 'Leon —'

'You're just like him, like the others, you don't understand.'

'Explain it to me!'

'Why? So you can pass your small, human judgement?' Leon's eyes blazed. He'd become someone else in the blink of an eye. Cynthia backed a step up.

'I don't want to judge you, I just want to understand why —'

'You have no *idea* what I've been through!' Leon roared. 'You could never understand!'

He took a step towards Cynthia. She reacted on instinct, turning and sprinting from the room. Leon's laughter followed her.

'You can't outrun me!'

'STOP IT!' Cynthia screamed.

'Coward!' Leon sang. Cynthia lurched into the next room, struggling to shut the heavy door. Finally, she gave up and went to the window. But even if she could get out, how would she escape? Leon would catch her.

But he wasn't in the room now. And he hadn't taken her phone. He didn't understand phones, Cynthia realised suddenly. Unlike Damien, Jeremiah, and other vampires who had adapted, Leon had no idea about modern technology. It hadn't occurred to him that she could call someone. She pulled her phone out. So many missed calls and messages, but she ignored them all. No time for that. She dialled Nathan's number, listening to it ring with her heart in her mouth.

In a flash, Leon was before her, his face a grimace of anger.

'Don't do that.'

Cynthia stumbled backwards. The call connected.

'Cynthia —'

Leon snatched the phone.

'NATHAN!' Cynthia screamed. 'I'M AT CECILIENHOF —'

Leon hurled the phone against the wall. It connected with an audible crack and fell to the floor, a shattered hunk of metal and glass. Leon's looked furious.

'That was a mistake.'

'Your mistake,' Cynthia said bravely. 'You should have taken it from me.'

'I trusted you! We were going to leave together!'

'I was never leaving with you, Leon. I have a family and friends.'

'Friends,' Leon spat. 'Friends who turned on you. They were going to hand you over to the witches. *I* was your friend.'

'If you're my friend, you'll let me make my own decision,' Cynthia said. 'If you're my friend, you'll trust me to make the right decision. Not hide the truth from me.'

Leon's face had closed off again. 'I don't lie.'

Cynthia remembered what Julianus had said. 'Don't... or can't?'

'I...'

'Why don't you want to tell me?' Cynthia pressed. '*What* don't you want to tell me?' Leon's gaze darted around the room uneasily, and Cynthia knew she was onto something. 'There is something, isn't there? What makes you different?'

'I...' Leon said. 'Please...'

'Tell me,' Cynthia said gently. 'Trust me.'

Leon shifted his weight, undecided. Finally, he pushed his sleeves up. 'I... I might be able to show you.'

'Show me?'

'I've seen it done once before.' He took a deep breath. 'There used to be others. Like me.'

'Ancestors?' Cynthia guessed.

'That's what they called us. The revenants.' He paused. 'The vampires. We created the vampires, they came from us.'

'You were the early vampires?' A whole lot of things were suddenly making sense. 'That's why you have magic. That's why... you were born, not turned?' It was a wild guess, but it made so much sense. Damien could have children.

'Yes,' Leon admitted. 'We didn't think of ourselves as vampires, though.'

'What then?'

'We were witches,' he said gravely. 'We did magic. We had covens. But we lived impossibly long. The other witches, the mortal ones, turned on us. They were jealous.'

'Oh, Leon,' Cynthia whispered. She could hardly imagine fifty years ago, let alone a thousand, but the pain in his voice was unmistakable.

'I knew a woman who could... share memories, share... thoughts,' Leon said. 'I might be able to recreate it.'

'You've never done it before?' Cynthia asked warily.

'No… but my blood can do anything,' Leon explained. 'As long as I will it.'

'Okay,' Cynthia said uneasily. 'Do you need my blood?'

'Only a small cut.' He reached for her hand.

'I have a knife,' Cynthia said. 'Where's my bag?'

'In the other room.'

They made their way back to the lounge and sat on the sofas. Leon took the knife and carefully cut across Cynthia's palm, and then his own.

'We need to be quick. I don't want to exchange too much blood with you… I don't know what it will do.' He grasped Cynthia's hand, pressing their cuts together. Gradually, she felt his pulse, or maybe his magic, beating in time with his heart. It throbbed against her palm.

'Leon, I don't like this.' She tried to pull her hand away, but he grasped it firmer.

'Wait.'

Suddenly, the room around them was gone. Cynthia gasped and twisted around. Leon stood beside her, their hands anchored together, his hair whipping around in a brisk wind. The rest of the environment was utterly unfamiliar: a long sandbank covered in scrubby bushes, shrivelled from the constant assault of the wind. Behind them, the land stretched away in rolling green hills with spiky grass. Above, the sky was the colour of steel. Ahead, the sea: a shade darker than the sky, the waves choppy and capped with white.

'Where are we?' Cynthia asked.

'Brandehuse,' Leon said. 'This is where I was born.'

'Is this a memory? Where's the town?'

'Maybe?' Leon looked around. He paused, tensing, and Cynthia followed his gaze. They were looking up the beach: smoke was rising, stark black against the sky, which was coloured orange.

'Fire?' she asked.

'The village.' Leon squeezed her hand. 'The Ascomanni. Come on.'

He set off at a brisk walk. Cynthia stumbled after him. The view blurred around them as they moved through the memory, and she found she had to stare at Leon's back to keep the nausea at bay. Suddenly, they stopped. They stood amidst the smouldering ruins of a village made of huts. A woman sobbed in a doorway, cowering and whispering words Cynthia couldn't understand. The straw roof of one hut was on fire.

Cynthia turned to Leon and a scream wrenched from her lips as an enormous man dressed in furs bore down on them. 'LEON!'

Leon didn't move. A moment later the memory was gone, and so was the town. They were in Berlin, a Berlin that Cynthia barely recognised, populated by women in ankle-length dresses and men in uniforms. There were no cars; instead horse-drawn carriages passed by them on the street. One came near enough for Cynthia to see inside. Leon and Julianus sat beside one another, both dressed in finery. Without warning, Julianus reached forwards and grabbed a woman from the seat in front of them, hauling her onto his lap, shoving her head to the side, and biting down on her neck.

Cynthia shrieked. The scene faded. They were in an ornate hall which Cynthia didn't recognise. Leon, dressed in an old-fashioned suit, strode past the two silent watchers and swung open double doors. When Cynthia saw the scene beyond, bile rose in her throat. Three bodies were strewn across the floor of the throne room beyond, little more than piles of flesh. Blood painted their clothes, their skin, the floor. A man knelt over them. When the doors opened, he looked up. It was Julianus. He seemed to look right through memory-Leon, to where Cynthia and Leon stood.

'Was hast du getan?' he asked.

The scene was already fading. Cynthia tried to pull away, but Leon held fast. 'Not yet.'

'What did he say?' she demanded shrilly.

'What did you do. Cynthia, you cannot let go!'

They had arrived at a place that was both familiar and foreign to Cynthia all at once. Beautifully painted walls and a large chandelier, with mirrors all around. It was the ballroom Leon had taken her to. Men and women twirled together in a waltz. Amidst them was a man, alone: Leon. He seemed impossibly lonely, as he walked the edges of the room. Finally, he turned and left. Cynthia and Leon followed him through to another room. Julianus was waiting with a glassy-eyed woman at his side.

The two of them spoke. Memory-Leon shook his head, and seemed about to leave, but Julianus lifted a hand and casually tore open the woman's neck.

'Du brauchst es,' he said.

'You need it,' Leon whispered, translating even though Cynthia hadn't asked him to. 'You cannot survive without.'

'I can go a little longer still.'

'Come, father. Consider it a peace offering.'

Memory-Leon stepped forwards, swiping his fingers through the woman's blood and bringing it to his lips. The moment he tasted it, his eyes grew wide. He stumbled, almost falling to his knees. Julianus grabbed him, forcing his face to the woman's neck. The more blood he got in his mouth and on his skin, the weaker he became. As he passed out, his eyes fixed on something in the corner of the room. Cynthia followed his gaze: it was a coffin.

The room went dark.

They were standing on a construction site. Looking around, Cynthia picked out a familiar glass building: Hauptbahnhof, Berlin's central station. Men in orange safety jackets were arguing, gesturing wildly. Leon squeezed her hand, and she followed his gaze.

A coffin, muddied and with a damaged lid, sat in a hole in the ground, about eight feet down. As Cynthia watched, a hand smashed through the lid. A dark blur sprang out. The men screamed, then abruptly fell silent. A figure rose above their dead bodies.

Leon.

He turned as if in a daze, taking in their surroundings. Blood covered his face and chest. He took one staggering step, then another, and Cynthia followed him automatically, across the paving, until he reached the road and stumbled into it.

Breaks squealed as a bus ground to a halt, hitting him with a deafening thud that made Cynthia's chest constrict.

He's fine—it didn't hurt him—

Then the screaming started, and she realised.

'It was you!' She turned to Leon, the screams ringing in her ears. 'You killed everyone on that bus.'

'It was an accident,' Leon pleaded.

'An accident? All those people!' Cynthia tried to drag her hand away.

'I was starving!'

'There were better ways!'

Leon shook his head. His face was contorted with misery. 'I'm sorry.'

He released her hand. Cynthia took a deep breath, feeling like she'd been underwater for too long. The world felt too sharp, too present. She blinked, struggling against a sudden tidal wave of sensations: a draught over her skin, the sound of the birds outside, even the roughness of her jeans and the smooth brocade of the sofa.

'What… what's going on?' When she looked at Leon, she could see every freckle, the specks of gold in his eyes, everything was in sharp relief. 'I feel weird.'

'My blood,' Leon said. 'It was too much. I'm sorry.'

'What was that?' Cynthia fought through the fog. She stood, and that made it easier to ground herself. 'How could you do that? All those people—'

'An accident, just an accident,' Leon whispered.

'No.' Cynthia shook her head. She needed to think, but she felt like her skull was filled with cotton wool. 'How long—they buried you, right? How long?'

'Ninety-four years.'

'Oh.' Cynthia clutched her stomach, nauseous. 'Why? How?'

'A potion in the woman's blood,' Leon said slowly. 'They tricked me. I…' He stood, suddenly agitated. 'Something's wrong. Can you feel it?'

'No.' As soon she said it, Cynthia realised she could. A deep tension in her belly. And the birds outside… she couldn't hear them anymore. Was this how it was for vampires all the time? This sensory overload? 'Yes.'

'Someone's here,' Leon said.

'I should thank you,' a new voice said. Both Cynthia and Leon turned in unison. Julianus appeared out of nowhere. An invisibility spell of some kind, Cynthia realised. 'Your little magic trick gave me enough time to sneak up on you. Or perhaps you've just grown sloppy in your old age.'

'Hello, Julian,' Leon said softly. 'Come to look me in the eye, at last.'

'Leonhard,' Julianus said. 'Returned to the scene of your crime?'

'My crime?' Leon asked. 'I am not the murderer amongst us.'

'Your count is far higher than mine.'

'I'm sure the many women you've slain to slake your thirst would beg to differ,' Leon said.

Julianus waved that away as though it were no more than a minor detail. 'Humans,' he said. 'You kill humans, the hunters get a little upset. You kill witches… well, we know what happens when you kill witches, don't we, Leon?'

'Still playing the same games, I see,' Leon said.

'It is not I who is playing games,' Julianus replied. 'Did you think I wouldn't figure out what you were doing? You should have made your interest in the shifter less obvious.'

Leon shifted, almost unnoticeably. Without her heightened senses, Cynthia was sure she would have missed it. But in a second Leon went from casual to ready to spring into action.

'What's he talking about?' Cynthia asked quietly. 'Leon?'

'Nothing,' Leon said. 'I swore I wouldn't hurt you, remember?'

'But did you swear you wouldn't kill her?' Julianus asked cruelly. His gaze jumped to Cynthia. 'Leon is a master at word games. He'll promise to protect you in the same moment as slitting your throat… which is what he intends to do.'

'No,' Leon said.

'And yet, here we stand,' Julianus said. 'I didn't realise it at first — we suffered so, we couldn't concentrate on anything else — but the curse weakens you. You can't power it forever. But with her blood… yes… I think the blood of a shifter would do it, wouldn't it?'

Cynthia turned to look at Leon. 'Leon, tell me that's not true.'

Even after everything, the betrayal hurt. She'd never expected that Leon might also want her for her blood.

Leon shook his head quickly. 'Cynthia, don't trust him, he's—'

'Lying?' Julianus laughed. 'You always were envious of the ability. But no, not this time. It's okay, Cynthia. I can help you if you let me.'

Cynthia stepped back, away from both of them. Her leg knocked against a table. 'Don't come near me.'

'It's alright. Soon we will all be free.'

But Cynthia was looking at Leon. He stared at her pleadingly. 'Trust me,' he said.

'That's right, Cynthia, trust him,' Julianus said. 'You'll go to the grave, just like everyone else who trusted him.'

'Shut up,' Cynthia snapped. Turning to Leon, she demanded, 'Tell me it's not true. You didn't want my blood. Tell me!'

'I…' Leon looked pained. 'I ingested your blood…' His face twisted.

'You cursed the vampires of Berlin,' Cynthia said.

'They deserved it,' Leon whispered.

'What could they possibly have done to deserve that?'

Leon shook his head. 'Don't—don't make me—'

'Tell me,' Cynthia insisted.

'Enough,' Julianus said. 'The time for talking is over. My witch has prepared the spell. There's no escape anymore, Leon.'

'You think you can kill me?' Leon's voice was deadly. 'The witches are confined to the city.'

'Only the ones who were bound to the Berlin covens. I found one that wasn't.' A cruel smile spread across Julianus's face. 'I should thank you, actually. We lost our first witch, thanks to you—but then you killed this one's mother, so she agreed to help instead.'

'Don't fool yourself,' Leon said. 'One witch alone couldn't do that spell.'

'They can with a strong enough power source,' Julianus said. 'And luckily for me, you provided one.'

Both of their eyes slid to Cynthia, and she finally understood the trap that had been laid. Julianus had never intended for her to turn Leon over. He'd wanted Cynthia close to Leon—so that when the time came, she'd be in the right place to power his spell.

'You can't!' she gasped.

'You owe the vampires a debt,' Julianus said. 'Tonight, it will be paid.'

Leon lunged towards Julianus. They both vanished from sight.

'Leon!' Cynthia shouted, suddenly alone. She heard a crash somewhere in the palace and spun around, but of course, there was nothing to be seen. Spooked, she crept into the hallway. 'Leon? Julianus?'

CRASH!

That had sounded like it came from outside. Cynthia ran to a window, peering out. Even with her enhanced vision, she couldn't see much more than a few shapes in the night.

'Hello, shapeshifter.'

She whirled around. Another vampire stood at the end of the hall, Friedrich, the unusually young one.

'What are you doing here?'

'Don't make this harder than it has to be,' Friedrich warned.

'Don't make what hard?' Cynthia asked. 'Whatever you're planning—'

'It has to be this way,' Friedrich said. 'It's the only way to free ourselves.'

'By killing me?'

Friedrich ran towards Cynthia. She turned and sprinted away, but he soon caught up with her.

'If you run, it will only make us want to hunt you!'

'GET AWAY FROM ME!' Cynthia screamed. 'LEON!'

Friedrich went flying, his body slamming against the wall before Cynthia's eyes even registered what had happened. Leon stood in front of her, breathing hard, his shoulders tense. 'Cynthia—you have to shift, shift and run.'

'I—'

'RUN!'

Cynthia raced for the doors, spilling out into the night, but it was too late. The grounds swam with vampires, all of them pale, all of them focused on her.

'The shifter!' one cried.

'Catch the shifter!'

'Catch the shifter!'

Like an eerie, deadly chant, the cry went up. Cynthia backed inside, her back touching Leon's chest. She turned to look at him. His expression was grim, his eyes sad.

They were trapped.

CHAPTER TWENTY-NINE

IF ONLY LEON HADN'T destroyed her phone... What Cynthia wouldn't have given to call Nathan for help right now.

As one, the sea of sickly vampires surged forwards, driven by a hunger beyond what Cynthia could comprehend. She and Leon had no chance to run. They were overwhelmed by the sheer number of vampires. Hundreds in front of her, and she could hear even more from behind. Cynthia clung to Leon, but dozens of hands clutched at her and dragged her, tearing her clothes, until she was pulled away from him into a crowd of pale skin and glowing red eyes.

'LEON!' Cynthia screamed, but she couldn't hear his reply. There was too much *noise*. Cynthia was carried by the crowd until they reached the open lawn outside the palace walls. A vampire hoisted her over his shoulder, and they crossed the lawn, Cynthia screaming as loud as she could.

'LEON! HELP ME! SOMEONE HELP!'

But wherever Leon was, this time he didn't come. They soon reached the water, where an area was lit by firelight. Cynthia was dropped unceremoniously onto the ground. She tried to roll to her feet, but the vampire put his boot on her chest, pressing down until she was scared her ribs would snap.

'Argh,' she wheezed.

'Try to run and we'll break your legs,' the vampire spat.

'Where's the witch?' someone asked.

'She'll be back. She went to her car.'

Cynthia lay as still as she could, trying to hear through the darkness. Where was Leon? Would he come for her?

A ripple ran through the vampires assembled around her, and they parted to make way for someone: a diminutive figure, hair piled on top of her head like coiled snakes. Cynthia's chest clenched with fear at the sight of the witch. Beside her walked Julianus. His gaze fixed on Cynthia.

'Sorry to have to do this,' he said, his tone almost conversational. 'If we had a choice... but the curse must be lifted.'

The pressure on Cynthia's chest eased a little. 'Fuck you,' she choked.

'You should be more respectful of your elders.'

'Fossils like you don't deserve respect!'

Julianus laughed. 'Enough. We finish the spell now,' he told the witch.

But the witch was standing as though petrified, staring at Cynthia. Cynthia watched her, waiting for the moment she'd start chanting, or pull out a knife, but the witch simply continued to stare. Julianus shoved her shoulder, and she stumbled forwards into the firelight.

It was Renata.

'Renata!' Cynthia cried. 'What are you doing here?'

'You!' Renata choked, her tone stricken. She turned to Julianus. 'What is this?'

'As I promised, the one responsible for betraying your mother.'

'That wasn't me!' Cynthia yelled.

'Of course it was,' Julianus replied. 'It was you who told Leon the Witch Council's demands. When he heard they wanted a shifter, and intended to use you, he took steps to keep you safe. It's not the first time he's taken drastic action. Leon can't abide people plotting against him.'

Cynthia shook her head. 'Renata, you have to believe me. I didn't know Leon would do something like that!'

She'd chosen the wrong words. Renata steeled her shoulders.

'I've heard enough excuses and apologies out of you,' she said.

'Please,' Cynthia said. 'I know you're hurting, but this isn't something you want to be involved in.'

'I can decide that for myself,' Renata snapped. She crossed the pool of firelight to something just out of Cynthia's view. Julianus watched them, arms crossed against his chest.

Something occurred to Cynthia.

'I thought you couldn't do this sort of magic,' she said. 'Ritual magic.'

Renata snorted derisively. 'I lied.'

'Why?' Cynthia gasped.

'My mother wanted you to trust me in case we needed you. I thought you'd feel safer if you thought I couldn't access your magic.'

Her words sent a stab of betrayal through Cynthia's chest. 'So that's all this was? You let me… befriend you just because the KUA needed a shifter?'

'Don't bother crying over it,' Renata said. 'You were using me, too.'

'Once,' Cynthia protested. 'After the first time, it was all genuine.'

'Yeah… well not for me,' Renata fired back. 'After you started sticking your nose into things, the witches knew the shifters might pull out. You were our backup plan.'

'You knew about this?'

Renata hesitated. 'Bring her over here. I need her blood. And the other vampire, Leon. Where is he?'

'He'll come when he smells her blood,' Julianus said.

'He'd better. We only have one shifter, so we can only do the spell once.'

The vampire finally took his boot off Cynthia's chest. A moment later, he reached down and hauled her up. 'Remember what I said. I can snap your arms right off.'

'Can you?' Cynthia asked. 'You don't look much up to snapping twigs, let alone—okay—okay!'

She held very still, but the vampire eased the pressure he'd put on her wrist. 'Behave,' he growled, dragging her towards Renata and throwing her towards the older girl. Cynthia stumbled on the uneven ground and caught herself against the barrel of flames. It seared her hands. She yanked them away and watched with fascination as they healed instantly, faster than she'd ever healed before.

Leon's blood.

It had made her stronger, faster to heal, just as he'd promised. But would it be enough?

Renata pulled out a wickedly sharp-looking knife. Avoiding Cynthia's gaze, she sliced her own hand and began dripping her blood along the edge of a circle of salt on the ground. As she did, she chanted under her breath, the language both guttural and melodious.

'Renata, please.'

Renata broke off her chant, looking angrily up at Cynthia.

'Just shut up, alright?'

'Why, so you don't have to face the fact you're going to kill me?'

'Because nothing you can say will bring my mother back!'

'I understand that,' Cynthia said desperately, 'but killing me won't bring her back either.'

'I don't care. She wanted to see this through, so I'm going to make sure it's done.' Renata returned to her chanting, dribbling blood over the last section of the circle. Abruptly, it flared a bright gold. Renata stepped back and looked at Julianus.

'I'm ready.'

'Then begin,' Julianus said.

'We need Leon.'

'He will come. Start now.'

Renata looked uncertain. After a moment, she steeled herself and turned to Cynthia. 'It's time.'

Cynthia took a step back, but instantly one of the vampires was there, pushing her forwards.

'Hold her still,' Renata said. The vampire gripped Cynthia's arms, pinning them behind her back as she tried to squirm away. Renata lifted the knife and pressed it to Cynthia's neck.

'Please!' Cynthia sobbed. 'Renata, don't do this!'

'I have to!' Renata snarled, but she didn't move the knife. Indecision warred in her eyes.

'What's the holdup?' Julianus demanded.

Trembling, Cynthia met Renata's gaze. 'Please,' she whispered.

'She was my *mother!* I advocated to her on *your* behalf.'

'I know.' Tears trickled freely down Cynthia's face. 'I know. I made a mistake. I didn't realise. But I'll make it right, I swear.'

'You're just saying that so you can run off with him again.'

'No,' Cynthia said. 'I was never going to run off with him, I promise.'

'Do it now,' Julianus snapped.

Renata hesitated for another few seconds. Finally, she stepped back. 'I—I can't do it.'

Julianus's expression twisted in fury. In the blink of an eye, he was next to Renata. He gripped her wrist in one hand, her hair in the other. 'Do it now, or I'll start cutting your fingers off!'

'I can't!' Renata wailed, trying to twist away. 'I can't kill her!'

'YOU DON'T HAVE A CHOICE!' Julianus shoved Renata towards

Cynthia, his hand guiding her knife. 'I'll do it myself—'

'STOP! STOP!'

Cynthia threw herself downwards. Her shoulders strained and popped, dislocating painfully, but it didn't matter. She was already healing, and then she was free. She snatched at Renata's arm, twisting it until Renata screamed, and the knife dropped to the ground. Julianus and Cynthia both dived to the floor after it and Cynthia grabbed the handle.

'RENATA, RUN!'

'CYNTHIA!'

'JUST RUN!' Cynthia and Julianus were tangled together. After a moment, he gave up on the knife. His eyes glowed an unearthly red as he lurched like a snake and sank his fangs into Cynthia's arm. She yowled, trying to throw him off. His fangs dislodged and he fell backwards; Cynthia jabbed the knife into his arm.

It parted his flesh like butter, and Julianus howled in pain.

Suddenly, Julianus was thrown off her. He landed on the ground in a heap, some distance away. Someone touched Cynthia's shoulders, trying to pull her up. She brushed them away.

'Cynthia, Cynthia, stop.' It was Nathan. 'Come on, let's get you out of here.'

'Nathan—what's going on?'

'I'm sorry it took us so long to get here.' Nathan pulled her to her feet, edging her away from the vampires, who were all watching the spectacle. Julianus had pulled himself to his feet, his expression wrathful. He was facing off against someone; at first, Cynthia didn't recognise the man. Then he turned slightly towards Nathan, and she realised who it was.

Damien von Klichtzner.

Jeremiah's friend, Council employee, and Lily's father. Damien was the oldest—or had been the oldest—vampire Cynthia knew. If he was here, she was safe. They all were. He'd fix this. Cynthia swallowed a sob, letting Nathan lead her away.

'I was so scared—I wasn't sure if you got my message—'

'I did,' Nathan said. 'We were already looking for you, you just went silent mid call… Anton tracked your phone until you went out of his range. We guessed you were here, but I had to wait for Damien. I'm sorry.' Nathan's expression was fraught with sincerity. 'We're going to fix this. I've spoken to Jeremiah.'

'Okay,' Cynthia said shakily. 'Okay.'

'You're making a mistake!' Julianus cried. 'I am not your enemy!'

Cynthia and Nathan turned back. Damien held something in his hands, something long and thin and wooden.

'Wait,' Cynthia started, 'what's—'

She blinked, as the first vampire collapsed to dust. Then another, and another. There had been a half dozen vampires around, at least, and suddenly they were all dead. Nathan squeezed Cynthia's hand hard.

'Cynthia, we need to—'

'It's too late.' She pulled away. 'Leon, NO!'

A brisk wind brushed her face and was gone. Damien and Julianus flew apart, both of them landing in the dirt at the side of the lake. In their place stood Leon, he held a box in his hands, small, metal, and lit with an eerie red glow.

'Julian!' he bellowed. 'Listen to me!'

Cynthia was already descending the slope again. Nathan grabbed her arm, holding her back. 'Wait—'

'You've had your time!' Julianus stumbled to his feet. Blood covered half his face. 'You had centuries!'

'I built this city from nothing!' Leon shouted. 'There was nothing here when I arrived. You think you can take it from me?' He tipped his head back, laughing. 'You're a fool, a fool with a desperate plan. Did you really think I wouldn't guess what you were doing? But all of it was for nothing. I drank Cynthia's blood hours ago. It runs through my veins, and my blood through hers. I can complete the curse without her!'

Cynthia went cold as realisation slammed her—Leon had wanted her blood—he'd tricked her into exchanging blood—had any of it been to help her? Before her eyes, he opened the box, slowly and lovingly, and the air was filled with a sudden, cloying sense of unimaginable evil. It was like nails down a chalkboard, a thousand screams of children dying, the knowledge that there was something in the dark, watching—it was indescribable, and it brought Cynthia to her knees. Nathan fell beside her, both of them fighting against the enormous pressure of a magic that no human, no mortal could command. When Cynthia managed to look up, the only person still standing was

Damien. Shoulders hunched, he weathered the storm. He lurched forwards, slamming against Leon, and both vampires rolled to the ground, fighting too fast for Cynthia's eyes to follow. The box went flying, landing at Julianus's knees. He shut it, and the pressure eased, but Damien and Leon were still fighting.

Surely, surely Damien had to win. He was the strongest person Cynthia knew.

But Leon fought like an enraged animal, always moving, his every swipe and punch deadly, and it was Damien who began to tire, Damien who was slammed against the ground, who coughed up blood.

Amidst it all, Cynthia never saw Julianus coming. He seized her from behind, almost yanking her hair from the roots as he wrenched her head to the side.

'ENOUGH!' he roared, making Cynthia's ears ring.

Everyone froze. It was so silent, Cynthia could hear her own pulse thundering in her ears. She strained her head sideways, trying to ease the pressure on her hair. Across from her, Leon stepped away from Damien, righting himself slowly, staring at them.

'If it's true what you said,' Julianus began in a deadly tone, 'that you don't need her blood anymore, then why did you bring the shifter here?'

'To keep her safe from you,' Leon said staunchly. His hands were opening and closing into fists; his eyes seemed too wide for his face. He stared at Cynthia, something in his gaze that was too deep for her to possibly comprehend.

'Ah-hah,' Julianus whispered triumphantly. 'So that's it. After all this time… she actually means something to you.'

Leon's eyes flickered from side to side. 'Release her,' he demanded.

'Lift the curse.' Julianus wrapped a hand around Cynthia's neck, his thumb over her jugular. 'Lift it, or I kill her.'

'She means nothing to you!' Leon cried.

'And everything to you,' Julianus said. 'What's more important? Revenge… or Cynthia?'

Leon shook his head. 'You deserved that curse.'

'Deserved it?' Julianus laughed bitterly. 'My people have gone a year without blood. Vampires are starving and dying in the street!'

'A year?' Leon's voice was hysterical, half a laugh, half a sob. 'You trapped me in a box underground for a hundred years! You complain about a year? For a hundred years, I was unable to move, unable to feed, always conscious—' For the first time, Cynthia saw the madness in his face, deep and inconsolable. 'I ought to have killed you as soon as I came back, but it was too easy a punishment!'

'Punishment!' Julianus cried. 'You tortured us—'

'You tricked me!'

'We had to do something! You endangered our entire community.'

'Everything I did was to keep us safe!' Leon rushed across the grass, snatching up the box. Julianus's fingers tore into Cynthia's neck, wrenching a scream from her lips, and Leon froze.

'How much can she take?' Julianus asked. 'How long will your blood keep her safe?'

Leon only stared. A stillness came over him; he was as lifeless as a statue made of marble.

'Leon,' Cynthia choked, against the pain of her slowly-healing neck. 'Leon, lift the curse.'

'I can't,' he choked. 'I can't.'

'You can. Revenge isn't worth this.' Cynthia swallowed against a sob, her breath hitching with pain. 'You're better than this. Let it go.'

'Berlin was my home. They took it from me.'

'I know. I know, but home isn't just a place. It's what's in your heart. Please.' Cynthia met his gaze, feeling as though she was looking at him across a chasm a million miles wide. 'Lift it for me.'

'I...' Leon bowed his head, and Julianus released Cynthia. She stumbled down the slope slowly. Leon clutched the box.

'Give it to me,' Cynthia whispered. 'Let me help you.'

Leon held the box out. Cynthia could hardly bare to touch it, but she forced herself to go ahead. 'What do I need to do?'

'Hold it.' She held it steady. It was surprisingly heavy for its size. Leon bit his wrist, holding his arm out. Before he reached the box, he stopped. Hi eyes widened in surprise.

'Cyn—thia,' he burbled, blood spilling from between his lips. He stumbled forwards a step, and his body dissolved into dust.

'NO!' Cynthia shrieked. 'LEON! NO!' She whirled on Julianus. His right hand was covered in blood—Leon's blood—and before her eyes he licked it. His pallor was easing as the curse lifted.

'WHAT DID YOU DO THAT FOR?' Cynthia screamed. 'HE WAS GOING TO LIFT THE CURSE.'

'Sometimes, renewal is necessary,' Julianus said simply.

Incensed, Cynthia tossed the box aside—now weightless. She snatched Renata's knife from her waistband and jammed it into his abdomen. Julianus's eyes widened. He began to laugh, hysterical and cruel.

'You're too late! The curse is lifted; I am immortal once more.'

'Fuck you!' Cynthia snarled. To her surprise, Julianus sagged forwards. He seemed to be in pain. Then he looked at Damien, betrayal in his eyes. Damien strode over and plucked a wooden stake from Julianus's back. He'd thrown it so fast Cynthia hadn't even noticed.

'Jeremiah sends his regards,' Damien said coldly. His hand darted out, and he wrenched Julianus's heart from his chest. It beat for a second, between them. Cynthia watched in horror as Julianus, too, collapsed into dust.

Damien let the dust run through his fingers, before wiping the mixture of blood and dust onto his trousers. He turned to Cynthia. She braced herself, but all he said was, 'I'm sorry.'

He turned away. 'I must call Jeremiah,' he told Nathan.

'Okay,' Nathan said. His face was pale; his eyes seemed too big for his face. He looked at Cynthia, and she had a sudden sense that the chasm between them had narrowed a little. Then he looked away.

'Do you… want a moment?'

'Y—yes,' Cynthia whispered.

'I'll be by the car. I'm going to see who I can call to… clean things up.'

Cynthia nodded numbly and watched him leave. Her cheeks were stinging, and once Nathan was out of sight, she wiped her hands over her face. They came away sticky with blood and tears.

She felt hollowed out. Leon was gone… and yet, she'd hardly known him. So many questions left unanswered. But somehow he'd touched her life so deeply, in such a short time. She knelt, carding her fingers through the mess of dust and blood on the ground. Some unlucky soul was going to clean this up… how sick of a thought was that? This had been a person, two people, actually. Two people who had fought each other and almost taken down an entire city because of it.

The tears started to flow properly, then. Cynthia knelt there, sobbing, for an indeterminate period of time, pouring her feelings out… all of the things she'd never got to say…

'Cynthia?'

She looked up. Nathan had returned. He looked like he'd cleaned up a bit, and his expression was very apologetic.

'We should go,' he said gently.

'Y—yeah,' Cynthia whispered. She shakily pushed herself upwards. As she did, her hand bumped something hard. Pausing, she picked it up. It was Leon's amulet; somehow, it hadn't turned to dust. Cynthia slid it into her pocket and turned to face Nathan. 'Let's go.'

EPILOGUE

DAMIEN SEEMED TO FILL the apartment to the bursting point. Whenever Cynthia left her room, she felt like she was going to bump into him, which made her at once uncomfortable, a little scared, and sad. Every time she saw Damien, she thought of Leon.

They were the same, after all. The remnants of an extinct species, forced to fight for safety every day of their lives.

Not that unlike Cynthia herself.

The thought hurt.

She was due to leave on Thursday evening, but by Tuesday she couldn't bear it any longer. Leaving her packing half finished, Cynthia headed to the hall and put her shoes on.

The front door opened before she could grab the handle. It was Nathan.

'Hey,' he said awkwardly, avoiding her gaze. Things were, if possible, even worse between the two of them than they had been. That hurt, too; the knowledge that external forces could come between them like that. Cynthia's world for the last few years had hinged on being able to trust her friends. She couldn't stand the thought that she might have lost that.

'Hi.'

'Going out?' Nathan asked.

'Yeah… just for a walk. I'm going a bit stir crazy, I think.' Cynthia hesitated. 'Want to come?'

'Sure,' Nathan replied.

They set off together. It was a hot, sticky afternoon. Nathan stripped his jacket off, leaving him in just a T-shirt and his cargo trousers. Cynthia tied her hair back.

'I went to the memorial,' Nathan said at length.

'Yeah?' Cynthia had mentioned it to him the previous day during a lengthy debriefing on the whole debacle. Official hunter record, or whatever.

'I can't see it,' Nathan said. 'Not enough magic, I guess. Makes sense that you'd need a certain amount, or every human with traces of magical blood would be stumbling over it.'

'That's a shame,' Cynthia said.

'I thought maybe if you went with me...' Nathan trailed off awkwardly.

'Sure, we can try now.'

They took the bus to Kreuzberg and climbed through the park. It was chock full of tourists with cameras, not exactly ideal circumstances, but they persevered anyway. They had to wait a few minutes for a group of Americans to clear out, before Cynthia could step up to the memorial. Nathan stared intently at it, but eventually shook his head in defeat.

'I can see where the magic is,' he said, 'but I can't see through it.'

'I didn't know magic could work that way,' Cynthia said.

'Magic does whatever its wielder intends, as far as I know,' Nathan said. 'There aren't really limits on the possibilities, only on the amount of power a spell would take. It's like warding. You can ward any species out—even humans.'

'So this is warded against humans?'

'Spelled, but yeah, that's effectively it.' Nathan sat on the ledge beside her. 'Read it to me?'

'Sure.' Cynthia cleared her throat. 'Uh, sorry about the accent.'

'That's okay.'

'*Denkmal für die in den Hexenkriegen verlorenen Vorfahren. 749 – 1179 AD.*' She glanced at Nathan before continuing, 'Agnesia. Filip. Adalhard. Engelrade Berggren. Gennaio. Tyesca. Helga. Leonhard.' She paused.

'Leon?' Nathan asked.

'I think so,' Cynthia said softly.

'So whoever made this thought he was dead.'

'Unless there was another Leon.' Cynthia shook her head. 'I guess we'll never know. Theobald. Zemislav. Mirołada. Cateline d'Allaire.' There were at least fifty names. Cynthia read each of them, stumbling over the pronunciation of names that had fallen out of use hundreds of years ago. Finally, she read, 'Andriet du Boys. Gerhard von Klichtzner.

Amelina von Klichtzner. Siegfried von Klichtzner. Magdalena von Klichtzner.'

When she finished, she looked at Nathan. His expression was grave.

'An entire species,' he whispered.

'There might be others left over.'

'People like Damien,' Nathan said. 'Survivors.' He shook his head. 'It feels wrong.'

'I know.'

'That this was allowed to happen… That we killed Leon…' He shook his head again. 'I want to do something about it.'

'But what?' Cynthia asked. 'This is what always happens… I mean, look at the shifters. We get hunted. Witches fight vampires, and vice versa…'

'I don't know.' Nathan looked frustrated. 'How do we protect everyone when we can barely protect the people right in front of us?'

Cynthia leant back, her shoulders pressing against the reassuringly firm stone. At times like these, she appreciated monuments that had stood for centuries. They made her feel part of something larger. The world went on, despite periods of instability.

Nathan broke the silence. 'By the way, I looked up the place you said Leon was from. Brandehuse.'

'Yeah?' Cynthia felt a pang in her chest and swallowed against a sudden lump in her throat.

'It's the old German name for a village in Schleswig-Holstein, near the Danish border,' Nathan explained quietly. 'The modern name… is Oldenburg.'

'The Vampire of Oldenburg.' Cynthia laughed dryly. 'At this point, I'm not even surprised.'

'The Vampire of Oldenburg?'

'Just another urban legend.' She shook her head. 'Renata mentioned it to me.'

'Berlin did remember Leon,' Nathan remarked thoughtfully, staring out over the grassy hill. 'Even when his name had been forgotten… people never really forget.'

They would now, though. Humans had short memories. Cynthia's chest ached, an ache she was going to have to learn to live with. Leon was gone, and all she could think of was the unfulfilled potential.

'I don't blame you,' she said. 'For what happened, I mean… I know you didn't want me involved.'

'I should have done more,' Nathan said unhappily.

'I'd have got involved anyway,' Cynthia admitted. 'I didn't realise it at first… but my story and Leon's were always going to overlap.'

'How do you know?'

'Because…' She let out a long sigh. 'Will you come with me to meet someone?'

'Sure,' Nathan said. 'Now?'

'I guess it'll have to be.' Cynthia checked her phone. 'If we go now, we might catch him before he leaves for work.'

Nathan, confused but trusting, accompanied her on the train east. When they arrived at Schulze-Bohsen-Straße, he examined everything with interest. Outside number thirty-seven, Cynthia checked the doorbells with their neat labels and found the sticker reading *Gideon Hüber*.

'This is it,' she said quietly, pushing the bell.

'Gideon Hüber was one of the names I gave you,' Nathan remarked.

'Yeah. He's the bartender at *Verzaubert*, the one I told you about.'

'The one who saved you?'

'Yeah.'

The intercom crackled suddenly. 'Hallo?'

'Hi, this… this is Cynthia.'

There was a long pause, then the door buzzed. 'Come up.'

They took the lift to the ninth floor. Gideon was leaning against the doorway of his apartment, watching them with a serious look on his face.

'Cynthia,' he said. His gaze flickered to Nathan, then back to her face.

Cynthia cleared her throat nervously. 'Hello… Justin.'

Gideon frowned. 'You may as well come in.'

The apartment was a mess. A suitcase sat open on the sofa, a few odds and ends already stacked in it. Gideon moved it to the floor so they could sit.

'Tea? Coffee?'

'You're leaving,' Cynthia said.

'I have to. I reneged on the deal with the vampires; I'm not safe here anymore.'

Cynthia pressed her lips together. She'd thought she had exhausted her capacity for intense emotions, but clearly she had more to give.

'Tea, maybe,' Gideon suggested, watching her carefully. Cynthia nodded.

Once they were all sitting with a cup of tea, Nathan asked, 'You're Justin Gastrell, then?'

'I am,' Gideon—Justin—confirmed. 'When did you figure it out?'

'I…' Cynthia swallowed and blew on her tea, before launching into the story she'd pieced together. 'Julianus said you refused to do the ritual because he wanted to sacrifice me. After that, everything started to make sense. The dates matched with what I knew about when you arrived here. Then, you were the one who saved me. You said you had a daughter.' She shook her head.

'I should have known you'd figure it out.' Justin took a sip of his tea, before sighing and setting the cup aside. He unsnapped a leather cuff from around his left wrist. The moment it left his skin, his appearance warped and twisted, before settling on features that were both familiar and utterly foreign to Cynthia. Blond hair which had grown a little too long, the same brown eyes she often saw in the mirror, suntanned skin, tattoos. Now that she looked, she could see the similarities between Justin and Gideon that she had missed before: the leonine air, the broad shoulders, the barely-contained strength. Justin looked older though. More tired.

'It's nice to finally meet you,' he said, Gideon's voice from Justin's mouth.

'Hi,' Cynthia said weakly. After a pause to collect her thoughts, she added, 'You knew it was me, all along. That I was your daughter, I mean.'

'I did. I got a horrible shock when you walked into the bar.' Justin shook his head. 'I wanted to grab you and hustle you right back out again, put you on a flight back home. But I was so close to earning the right to stay. I thought I could avoid your attention.'

'But then I got involved.'

'I did try and warn you.' Justin sighed. 'At least I know you have a healthy distrust for witches. Too healthy, as it turns out.'

'Yeah, because sometimes the witches are the good guys.' Cynthia shook her head. 'For what it's worth, I'm sorry I caused you trouble.'

'Not at all.' Justin smiled sadly. 'I'm glad we got to talk.'

'Where will you go now?' Nathan asked.

'Anywhere that needs me.' Justin shrugged and picked up his tea again. 'Wherever there are supernatural communities, there are troubles that need sorting out. I can usually buy myself... some level of immunity, let's say, by helping out local councils. Doing their dirty work, so to speak.'

'Hired muscle,' Nathan said.

'I do the same job as you.' Justin's eyes danced with amusement. 'Except I do the illegal parts.'

Nathan laughed. 'I guess that's true. You won't tell us where you're going next?'

'I'm sure we'll cross paths again.' Justin nodded to Nathan. 'But I'd hate to give you a head start. In case Jeremiah decides the witch community could benefit from cleaning house. You understand.'

'I do.'

'Couldn't you come back with us to Oxford?' Cynthia asked. 'Nathan could speak to Jeremiah—'

Nathan was already shaking his head.

'I don't think that's a good idea,' Justin said.

'But *why?*'

'Not all of us get the start in life that we'd like to have had,' he explained. 'I'm glad that your mother did well for you, in spite of the circumstances, but for my part... I've too many sins to reckon with to ever live the life that you're suggesting. I'm sorry.'

'What kind of sins?'

Justin shook his head. 'I'd rather you didn't know. But... this doesn't have to be goodbye. If you'd let me... I can continue to write.'

A maelstrom of emotion was whirling in Cynthia's belly. Disappointed, she said, 'It's a bit hard to read your letters, knowing I can't write back.'

'We might be able to work something out,' Justin said. 'I can give you a phone number. So long as you promise not to pass it on.'

'I'd like that.'

'Good.' Justin dug paper and a pen out of his suitcase, writing the number in his familiar scrawl. Cynthia took the paper, crumpling it against her chest.

'There is one thing I'd appreciate,' Justin said softly.

'What?'

'I'm leaving first thing in the morning, and I still need to pack, otherwise I'd do it myself. On my behalf, it would be good if someone could look in on Renata. Make sure she's… doing okay, I suppose. Let her know that it isn't her fault for getting dragged into things when I broke the deal.'

His eyes bored into Cynthia's, and she felt what it was like to be on the receiving end of fatherly disapproval for the first time. It was as though he could tell that she'd still been harbouring secret resentment towards Renata for attempting to kill her.

'I… suppose… I could do that.'

'Thank you.'

They lingered for another half an hour. Cynthia found herself reluctant to leave. She'd just found her father. But, finally, he said, 'I really must finish packing.'

'I suppose I ought to, too,' Cynthia muttered.

'You're going back to Oxford?'

'Yeah… there's nothing else here for me now.' Cynthia sighed. 'Not that there ever was to begin with, I guess. Seeing as the Deckers were never really my friends.'

'Friendships are complicated amongst supernaturals,' Justin said. 'You never know when someone's going to be forced to make a difficult decision in the name of personal safety. We never know what we'll do, who we'll betray, until we're forced to make those decisions. One day, you're the person who faces the consequences. The next, you might be the person hurting your friends… because maybe that's the only way to save your family. Those are the choices we make, and those are the choices we have to live with.'

'Yeah.' Cynthia glanced at Nathan. He looked pensive. After a second, he caught her eye and stood.

'Let's go. It's almost dinnertime.'

Cynthia nodded. At the door, she hugged Justin goodbye.

'Keep in contact,' she said. 'Or I might have to go looking for you again.'

'Heaven forbid! You find enough trouble as is.'

Cynthia giggled.

As they headed back out to the street, Nathan said, 'It's funny the way things work out, isn't it?'

'All that drama,' Cynthia said, 'and he was right in front of me.'

'Yeah.'

'The stupid thing is that Leon did lead me right to him.' Cynthia swallowed against the pang of grief in her chest. 'We were right here.'

'I wonder how he knew?' Nathan asked.

'Me too,' Cynthia said. 'I wonder so many things. Julianus—' Her voice hitched. 'Julianus said that Leon could sway the city to his will. I don't really believe anything else he said, in the end, but I think that might have been true.'

'Like magic?' Nathan asked.

'Leon didn't call it magic.' Cynthia shrugged. 'I don't think that's how it works. I mean, I don't think it's like witch magic, like Monica's magic, say. I'm not even sure what to call it.'

'Maybe he just understood Berlin.'

'It was his home,' Cynthia said. She paused, considering. 'I suppose, if you had lived in one place for so long… I wonder if I'll ever know anywhere that well?'

'Maybe,' Nathan said. 'I don't think I know Oxford that well. But then, I also don't think I'll be tied to Oxford forever.'

'Me neither,' Cynthia said. 'I'm not sure I want to. We've got complacent. And…'

'There's so much to discover,' Nathan said.

'Yeah, that.' She turned her face towards the sun. 'A thousand years. I don't think he ever even left Germany.'

'He lived in a different world to us,' Nathan said. 'They all do. Jeremiah, Damien. The things they'd do to survive… would kill us.'

Cynthia thought about what her father had said. 'I don't know. I think we might surprise ourselves one day.'

'I hope not,' Nathan said.

'Me too.'

They headed home in silence, but it was more companionable than earlier. Something had shifted between them. Cynthia no longer felt the regret she had before, with Nathan. They'd been too young, in many ways. Too inexperienced.

That evening, over dinner, Cynthia voiced a question that had been on her mind since leaving Justin's apartment.

'How far is it to Oldenburg?'

'Three hundred kilometres, give or take,' Nathan said.

'Too far to go before we leave?'

'We could probably do it if we drove,' Nathan said, 'but we'd have to leave very early in the morning. Why?'

Cynthia pulled Leon's amulet out of her pocket. 'I thought maybe we should bury this, or something.'

Nathan looked thoughtful, but it was Damien who held out one elegant, long-fingered hand. 'May I see it?'

'Okay.' Cynthia passed the amulet over hesitantly. Maybe she shouldn't bury it. Maybe she should keep it. But that didn't seem right, either. It wasn't hers, and Leon's story hadn't really been hers, either. Not considering she'd only known him for a few short weeks.

Damien took the amulet, turning it over in his fingers, studying it.

'Do you know what this is?' he asked finally.

'No. Leon wore it… He said it was a family heirloom,' Cynthia said.

'Have you seen it before?' Nathan asked.

'I've studied them.' Damien set the amulet in the middle of the table. 'It's called a bracteate. They were common amongst Germanic and Norse tribes. This one is for safe passage home.' He indicated the runes around the outside. 'A Norse prayer.'

'I wonder where he got it,' Nathan said.

'Quite possibly, one of his ancestors was a seafarer,' Damien said. 'Or they could have found or stolen it. Viking skirmishes were common along that coastline. There are Germanic and Norse artefacts everywhere.'

'It's that old?' Cynthia asked in surprise.

'At least fifteen hundred years old, at an estimate,' Damien replied. 'See here?' He turned the amulet over carefully, indicating several runes which were carved into the back, clumsily. 'These runes are different to the ones on the front. West Germanic, from the Westphalian area.'

They all looked the same to Cynthia. She nodded along, trying to look like she understood.

'What's the significance?' Nathan asked.

'I'm not sure.' Damien studied the runes. 'This says Leonhard.' He paused, an expression of understanding creeping onto his face. 'This spells Amalric… Emelrich. Another name.'

'A relative?' Nathan asked.

'Indeed.' Damien tapped the last set of runes, a pair set beneath the two names. 'This is the runic combination for twins.'

Cynthia's heart lurched in shock. She looked up at Nathan,

realisation dawning on both of them at the same time.

'Leon had a brother.'

THE END

SEE MORE BY THIS AUTHOR

TRANSLATIONS

Kann ich Ihnen helfen? – Can I help you?
Bitte – please
Danke – thank you
Bitte sehr – you're welcome
Entschuldige – excuse me
Guten Abend – good evening
Nein – no
Kommission für übermenschliche Angelegenheiten – Committee for Supernatural Affairs
Das ist das Gebiet des KUAs – That is the remit of the KUA
Auf Wiedersehen – goodbye (formal)
Du störst mein Gemälde – You're blocking my painting.
Guten Morgen – good morning
Scheiße – shit
Sie müssen mir helfen! Ich muss die Hexen finden – You have to help me! I need to find the witches!
Gestaltwandlerinnen – shapeshifters (female)
Genau so wie Santiago, sie hört uns nicht zu – Just like Santiago, she doesn't listen to us.
Sie ist nur ein Kind – She's just a child
Eine Gestaltwandlerin meldet sich bei uns – A shapeshifter would like to register with us.
Sie bittet um ein Audienz mit Julianus – She is requesting an audience with Julianus.
Kommen Sie näher – Come closer
Wir beißen nicht. – We don't bite
Halt! Lass mich! – Stop! Let go of me!

Enjoyed this book? Catch Nathan's story in WICKED MAGIC.

Hunters are supposed to hate vampires—but everyone will betray their people for a price. Nathan is about to discover his.

Nathan is a vampire hunter on the cusp of graduation. He's been training for this his entire life: the moment he qualifies and joins the rest of his family in their noble calling.

If only it were that simple.

His grades are a mess, his social life is a disaster, and what's worse, his best friend is a witch! Add to that, his vampire uncle is back in town and his crush might just be supernatural too, and you have one big melting pot of potential parental disapproval. Nathan doesn't think he can take much more, and then the dark mages come to town.

As bodies begin piling up in the streets, Nathan finds himself pulled deeper into political intrigue and a deadly plot that will pit him against his own family. When the girl he likes comes under threat, Nathan races against time to solve the mystery... well aware that with every step he takes, he comes closer to his father exposing all his secrets.

I don't like new people. They come into our town and don't know the rules. They get up in our business. They mess things up.

That's why when James Maddock walks into my bar, I'm suspicious. He might act like a nice guy, but for sure he spells trouble.

And that's the last thing I need just when I've got my life on track.

Suddenly, the hounds are baying at the doors. My tentative peace with the local gang, the Iron Fists, is exploding. People I thought I could trust are turning out to be enemies in disguise, and people I was certain were dangerous seem to want me on their team. I don't know where to turn. I don't know who is a friend and who a foe.

What I do know is this: when the dust settles, the only person I can rely on to have my back… is me.

AFTERWORD

I hope you enjoyed reading Cynthia's adventures as much as I enjoyed writing them. If you want to discover more about Cynthia's world, sign up for my newsletter at https://www.margotdeklerk.com/landing-page. Subscribers will get a free prequel to the Vampires of Oxford Universe.

If you have time, please also consider leaving a review on the retailer where you purchased the book and on my Goodreads page. Reviews are the best reward an author can receive.

I hope to see you again when the next book launches.
Sincerely,
Margot de Klerk

ACKNOWLEDGEMENTS

It's that time again: the book is finished, the final edits are done, my formatter is working her magic, and all that's left is to say thanks. The author who works alone is nothing more than a myth. Just like it takes a village to raise a child, so it takes a team to produce a book. I'd like to thank the following people for their contribution:

Kate, who edited the book and caught all my silly mistakes (you think you know English until you work with an editor…).

Pierre, who fitted me into his busy reading schedule. Always a privilege to make the elite list of books he reads in a year.

Josh, who created the illustrations for my website. It's always a delight to see your characters come to life.

Francesca, without whose 3:00 AM WhatsApp messages none of my books would exist.

Debra, whose enthusiasm is my biggest reward upon completing a new manuscript.

To the team at E-book Launch, who created the gorgeous cover.

And last, but certainly not least, Bev: formatter, cheerleader, proofreader, and much more. You kept me sane through sleepless nights and endless rewrites of the end chapters. Thank you, thank you, thank you.

Margot de Klerk is an author of all things paranormal fantasy. She is most often found in her favourite coffee shop typing furiously on her computer with an iced latte at hand. When not writing, she enjoys photography, travelling, sewing, and various sports.

Follow her on social media, subscribe to her mailing list, and get information on new books: